SNARING EMBERLY

GIGI STYX

AUTHOR'S NOTE

This dark romance book romanticizes red-flag behavior for entertainment. If you're offended by gaslighting, forced pregnancy and birth control tampering, do not continue reading.

Imprisonment
Improper use of a meat tenderizer
Male genital mutilation
Mental illness.
Murder
Mutilation
Organized crime
Orgasm denial
Panic attacks
Pet play (mentioned)
Post-traumatic stress disorder
Pregnancy symptoms
Psychological abuse
Rape (mentioned)
Revenge
Sex toys
Sleep paralysis
Spanking
Suicide bombing (threatened)
Urophilia (mentioned)
Voyeurism
Waterboarding
Weaponized incompetence

Reader discretion is advised. If you find any of these topics distressing, please proceed with caution or consider choosing a different book. Your mental health matters.

"When your man stabs you in the back, don't just walk away with your dignity. Strike back with with a meat tenderizer to the balls."

— *Emberly Kay.*

TRIGGER WARNINGS

This is a dark romance that includes dub-con, graphic depictions of torture and violence, and sexually explicit scenes. If any of this content is triggering for you, please do not read this book.

Triggers include:
- Abduction
- Assassination
- Attempted suicide
- Birth control tampering
- Bondage
- Breeding kink
- Compulsive lying
- Coprophilia (mentioned)
- Cremation of living people
- Degradation
- Desecration of a corpse
- Dismemberment
- Domestic violence (mentioned)
- Drugging
- Drug production
- Elder abuse
- Exhibitionism
- Financial abuse
- Forced marriage
- Forced pregnancy
- Fraud
- Gaslighting
- Immolation

To all the bad bitches who own their feminine rage and delight in a damn good grovel.

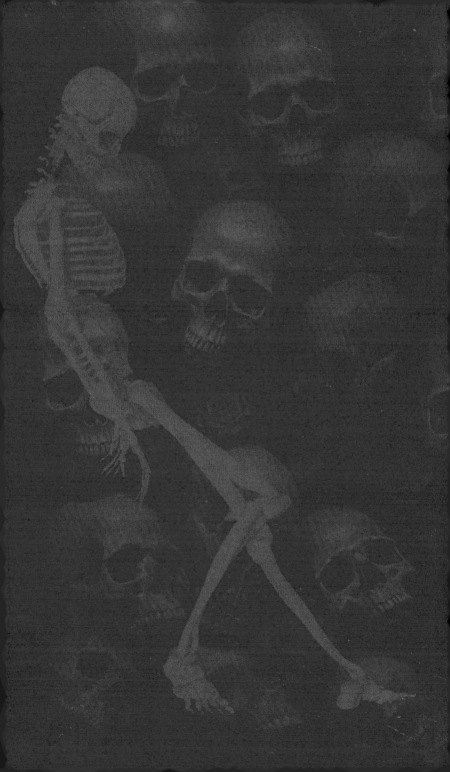

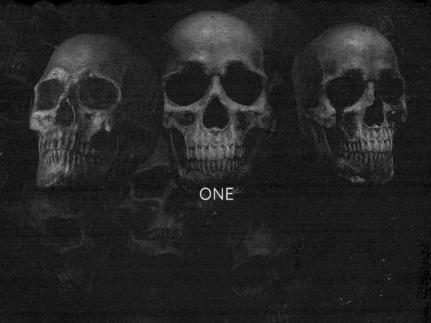

ONE

ROMAN

When a man steps out of death row for a murder he didn't commit, the first thing he wants to do is kill a motherfucker.

The jacket I wore when I was arrested no longer fits my expanded muscles, so I sling it over my shoulder like I'm walking off a yacht instead of leaving the New Alderney State Penitentiary. I didn't expect to be freed so soon after obtaining hard drives crammed full of blackmail material, so my five o'clock shadow looks more like a quarter to midnight.

Fuck it.

I can shave after part one of my revenge.

The afternoon sun has turned the concrete courtyard into a sauna, making sweat bead across my hairline and trickle down my spine. My skin itches and not because of the heat. Now that I'm no longer a prisoner, I'm twitching to lash out at the procession of guards flanking my steps.

Officer McMurphy with the double-Ds leans in close, reeking of jasmine perfume. "Don't be a stranger, Montesano."

Ignoring her, I shift my attention to the sharpshooter aiming a rifle at me from the tall concrete tower. After four years and three hundred and forty-seven days, my sexual options are finally no longer restricted to getting sucked off by a crooked prison guard.

I nod, not because I plan on seeing her again, but because she's a reliable mule. Our arrangement allowed me to run the family business from the joint, letting me save it from falling into ruin.

There's no doubt she'll continue to smuggle merchandise into the prison in my absence, but our personal association has come to an end.

"Roman!"

Vincent waves through the gates, wearing a ten-thousand-dollar tailored suit and a manic grin. Behind him is the silver 1965 Mercedes Cabriolet that Dad and I painstakingly restored after collecting it in lieu of a casino debt. I tear my gaze away from the reminder of what I've lost and focus on Vincent.

Our family lawyer has aged since my incarceration. He's lost at least twenty pounds, looks like he's shrunk three inches, and his once-full hairline has receded into a steel-gray circlet.

I flick my head in acknowledgement, the itch in my skin intensifying to a burn.

The gates open and release me to the desolate highway that surrounds the prison. Vincent's arms wrap around my shoulders before I can inhale my first breath of freedom.

Every instinct in my body screams at me to snap his neck, but I didn't escape one death sentence to blunder into another. Instead, I give him a lackluster pat on the back.

Before Dad's sudden heart attack and the series of events that led to the decline of our family empire, this man was Uncle Vincent—a long-standing trusted advisor.

He pulls back from the embrace, his smile widening. "Welcome back, son. You have no idea how much we've missed you."

I glance over my shoulder to the other side of the gates, where Officer McMurphy and her colleagues still linger.

"Let's take this discussion somewhere else," I mutter.

Vincent nods and heads for the driver's seat, but I clamp a hand on his shoulder. "I'll take the wheel."

His jaw drops, and he gazes up at me, his aged features etched with surprise. It's the first expression he's made that isn't fake.

"You sure, Roman? I don't mind taking you back."

Back into another ambush? I keep that thought to myself. Vincent doesn't need to know I'd rather place my hand in a meat grinder than let him lead me anywhere.

I slide into the driver's side, the seat still warm from the sun. Its leather scent is familiar yet tainted with the thought that this backstabber helped an even bigger bastard to pick apart Dad's possessions.

Vincent settles beside me into the front passenger seat and clasps his hands. His gaze irritates the right side of my face, but I focus on the road ahead. At the first twist of the key in the ignition, the engine roars to life. I pull out from the prison grounds and onto the highway.

Wind rushes through the open windows, whips back my hair and reminds me I'm free. I inhale a deep breath and fill my lungs with the first rush of air that doesn't remind me of that shit hole.

"Roman—"

"Don't speak."

Vincent stiffens.

As he should. While I was locked up, it took my brothers and me years to unravel the mess he and his accomplices made of the business. Then it took a grand-scale massacre to work out how. Thanks to the efforts of my cousin, Leroi, the men responsible for taking everything from our family are dead.

All but one.

Vincent only lives because I need a piece of information to enact the next stages of my revenge.

Scrubland whips past us in a blur, which soon darkens to sparse trees and then dense woodland. I make one stop for gasoline, which I pump into jerry cans that I load into the back seat. When I slide back into the front, he shudders.

"Tell me again which assets we lost to Frederic Capello," I say, the mere mention of the man who destroyed us making me grimace.

"Why are you asking this question again? You already know—"

"Humor me."

He gulps. "Casino Montesano plus the hotel, the shipping company, the loan company, the stock portfolio, the real estate, and whatever was in the safety deposit boxes."

I nod.

"Where are all these assets now that Capello is dead?" I ask.

"It's…" He rubs the back of his neck. "He's only been dead a few days. His estate is still in probate."

"Meaning?"

"The law firm is going through the legal process for distributing belongings to his heirs."

"Who should all be dead."

Vincent clears his throat.

"But then, our belongings should never have ended up in the hands of that double-dealing snake."

"Capello was blackmailing your father," Vincent blurts. "I didn't realize what was happening until it was too late."

"You already said that."

Blackmail was the only explanation for why Dad signed over his assets to a second-rate underboss like Frederic Capello. I never understood what kind of information was worth more than the wealth our family had built up over generations and had thought Dad was weak until Leroi killed the entire Capello family.

Once they were all dead, we obtained a cache of hard drives.

Turned out, Dad wasn't the only person with dirty secrets.

Judges, jurors, journalists—you name them, Capello held enough filth on anyone capable of sending a man to the electric chair with the most circumstantial evidence. That was just one of the many reasons he had to die.

"Send the law firm the paperwork and order them to transfer back those assets to the family," I say. It's not a request.

"Capello still has a surviving heir. A child he's spent decades searching for," Vincent says, his words heavy with the accusation that I ordered the assassinations that secured my freedom.

"I know. An illegitimate daughter named Emberly Kay."

His quiet gasp tells me he didn't expect us to conduct our own research. When the last of my appeals failed, my brothers, Benito and Cesare, hired an out-of-town firm of private investigators to dig up everything they could on the woman whose murder landed me in jail.

They found nothing to connect her to anyone we knew except Frederic Capello. Strangely, the DA never mentioned that the dead woman was a childhood friend of one of his mistresses. Our detective continued digging and found Capello's long-lost daughter, Emberly.

As far as we know, Emberly has lived a life of poverty. She and her deceased mother changed addresses more frequently than most women change their hairstyles, suggesting they were on the run. Her birth certificate says father unknown, and the report also concluded she has no idea her father is a violent mobster who left her millions.

"Are you going to kill her?" Vincent asks.

"Will that get us back what was stolen?"

"No," he rasps. "Capello's lawyers are still searching for the young woman to claim her inheritance. If she isn't found, then the assets will go to his third cousin, Tommy Galliano, in New Jersey."

My jaw clenches, bringing up every ounce of resentment I have toward another double-dealing bastard. Galliano isn't just the friend of our enemy, he's the scumbag who lured away our newly widowed mother and made her his wife.

Five years ago, when Dad was alive and the organization wasn't so fragmented, we might have been able to handle the Galliano family. But not now. Not yet. Emberly Kay is a more accessible target that I'll keep alive until I get back our stolen property.

Vincent's gaze still bores into the side of my face, but I hold my silence and continue toward Beaumont City until we reach the dirt track that leads to an isolated cabin.

That's when I take the turn at speed, scraping branches down the sides of the car and sending dirt flying.

"What's going on, Roman?" Vincent asks, his voice tense.

"We're taking a detour."

He reaches for his inside pocket, presumably to get his gun. My fist connects with his temple, knocking his head into the window. I wince at the damage to my beloved car and continue driving through the woods until we reach the cabin.

Benito is already waiting for us beneath the shade of a

huge tree with his arms crossed over his chest. When I park, he opens the passenger-side door and drags Vincent to where Cesare is adding the last few branches to a waiting pyre.

While my brothers truss Vincent up with ropes and lay him atop the unlit wood, I reach for the cans of gasoline on the back seat. The old man jerks awake at the first splash of liquid.

"What are you doing?" Vincent slurs.

"Capello didn't blackmail Dad into signing over his assets." I empty the can over his spluttering face.

Vincent screams as realization hits his balding head. "No, Roman, please!" He hurls himself off the bonfire, but Cesare throws him back on the pile of branches. "All I've ever been to your family is a friend."

"How did it work?" I ask, not bothering to address his bullshit. "Did Capello blackmail you into forging Dad's signature, or did you trick him into signing?"

"That wasn't me," Vincent screams.

"We have Capello's hard drives," Benito says. "We've seen the footage he shot of you strangling that woman."

Cesare shoves the edge of his shovel into Vincent's gut, making him double over. I place a hand on my youngest brother's shoulder, warning him not to ruin the bonfire.

"What I don't understand is why you allowed Capello to frame me for your sick perversion," I say.

Vincent squeezes his eyes shut. "Capello held my family hostage and threatened to kill them if I didn't do everything he demanded."

Cesare huffs a laugh and pulls out two cigars, but I exchange a glance with Benito. His story is entirely possible. As Dad's second in command, Capello was capable of some heinous shit, but Vincent could have reached out to us for help.

"Why didn't you say something?" I ask. "Dad would have killed Capello for threatening them."

Vincent's mouth opens and closes, but he makes no sound because there was no threat. Capello made Vincent scam Dad out of his assets in exchange for keeping quiet about the murder.

"That's what I thought." I nod.

Cesare lights his cigar and takes a few puffs before handing me the second, along with a box of matches. Keeping my eyes fixed on Vincent's, I place my cigar to my lips and strike a flame. In an instant, my mouth fills with the sweet tang of tobacco, and I blow out a cloud of smoke.

"Any last words before you join Capello in hell?" I take a long drag.

"Please." Vincent's voice breaks. "I'll do anything."

"You've done enough. You stole from our family, strangled a woman to death, framed me for her murder, and stayed on our payroll pretending to get me off death row. I'm going to enjoy watching you burn."

I throw the match on Vincent's bound body and step back, letting the flames race across his suit and into the branches. Vincent's screams ring through the air, mingling with the sound of the crackling fire.

The gasoline accelerates the blaze, creating tall flames that engulf Vincent's flailing limbs. Cesare cackles and tosses a log onto the old man's head, sending out an explosion of sparks. I snort. My baby brother still finds joy in mayhem.

Benito watches on, unimpressed. He's more level-headed than the two of us and prefers cooking books to barbecuing betrayers.

As my nostrils fill with the stench of burning flesh, I pull another long drag from my cigar. The rich taste of tobacco cancels out Vincent's stink, and I inhale the smooth, smoky aroma.

"How's the plan going to ensnare Emberly Kay?" I shout over the melody of Vincent's broken screams.

Benito pulls out his phone and fires up an app. "I've installed surveillance in the apartment she shares with another girl and sent leaflets offering free VIP entrance to the Phoenix. It's only a matter of time before one of them visits the club."

"Good."

The screaming stops when Vincent loses consciousness. My nostrils flare, and I'm tempted to pick up a rake to shake him awake, but I'm distracted by an image of a half-naked woman. She's slender with a head of wild curls and a peachy ass I'd like to fuck.

She walks across her bedroom and out of the range of the camera, robbing me of what looks to be a promising show.

"Do we kill her?" Benito asks.

"Not unless we want the lawyers to give our assets to Tommy Galliano. I'll get a few contracts drawn up for each of the assets Capello stole, and she'll sign them over to me."

"How are you going to get her to do that?"

I smirk, imagining her begging for mercy. "I can be very persuasive."

Vincent's body tumbles out of the bonfire, but I shove it back into the flames with my foot. Burning him alive wasn't nearly as satisfying as I imagined. Five minutes of agony isn't equal to five years on death row.

My gaze drops back to Benito's screen, where the dark-haired woman in black lingerie slips on a dress and a pair of heels.

I'll just have to exact the rest of my wrath on Emberly Kay.

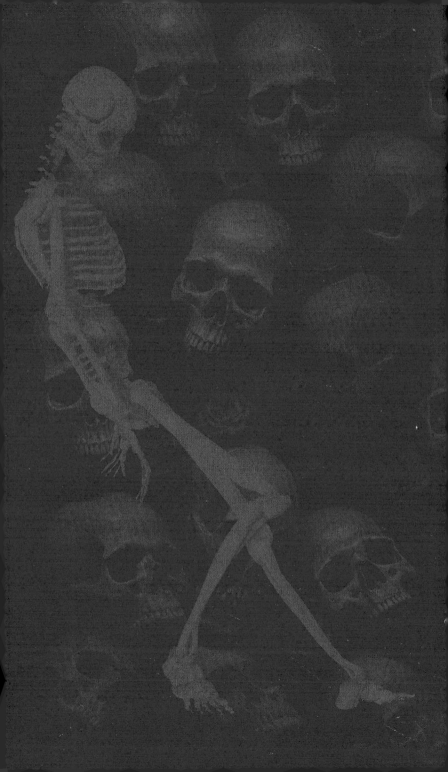

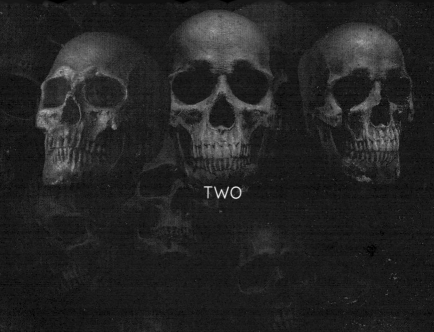

TWO

EMBERLY

I glare down at the man who swore to the gods that my paintings would achieve a five-figure sum at auction. He's a greasy little slug with beady black eyes he conceals beneath pink sunglasses.

Gerard Lafayette sits primly in his gilded chair, pouring himself a cup of tea. Rings adorn each of his fingers, including his thumbs, each of them probably costing the sum he promised me for my art.

"What else can I tell you, Ms. Kay?" he drawls. "I can only auction paintings for what the buyers are prepared to bid, and that's five hundred."

My hands curl into fists. "You promised me a ten-thou-sand-dollar reserve—"

"Did I?" His eyes widen in mock surprise, and he opens a drawer and pulls out some papers. "Where, precisely, does it say on the standard contract that Gallery Lafayette guarantees such a lofty sum?"

I snatch the papers from him and scan the wording, only to find a page at the back with the schedule of commissions.

As discussed, artwork sold for over ten thousand would result in a fifteen percent commission.

Now I see the scam. The contract mentions nothing of the promised reserve price. Without a law degree, it would be impossible to spot this kind of loophole.

"This isn't what we agreed," I say.

He tilts his head and smirks. "It's not my problem if you failed to employ an attorney to dissect the terms of our agreement, Ms. Kay. Consider yourself lucky to have sold anything at all in this declining market."

My blood simmers at his condescension. "But five-hundred dollars isn't even enough to cover the cost of my time and materials."

He takes a sip from a gold-plated cup and raises his pinky finger. "Like I said. New artists seldom reach princely sums."

That's not what he told me last month. In fact, Gerard Lafayette invited me to one of his auctions, where every painting had sold for at least twenty-five thousand. Hell, all the starting bids were five-figure sums.

I'd been looking forward to watching my paintings sell for small fortunes at tonight's auction, only to find that they weren't even on display. When I asked if he'd decided not to include my art, Lafayette told me they'd been sold... for a fraction of what he'd promised.

"Give me back my paintings. I'll sell them online myself."

His brows pull together, and he stares up at me as though I've just asked him to hand over the Mona Lisa and all its preliminary sketches.

"What?" I snap.

"Ms. Kay, you signed a contract with Gallery Lafayette, and the paintings are now sold. You can't just take them back."

The contents of my stomach roil with frustration. I can't believe I fell for his underhanded practices. He never once mentioned selling my work in a second auction.

My gaze darts around his office, finding sculptures and smaller paintings stacked against the wall but no sign of my huge canvases. He's a fucking swindler. I glare down at the gilded tea service with steam still rising from the pot, and understand how this asshole can afford such beautiful antiques.

"I told you," he says. "They've already been delivered to the buyer, and before you ask, Gallery Lafayette is not at liberty to divulge their identity."

Tears burn the backs of my eyes and fury burns my blood. All those months I spent cleaning the police precinct to pay for studio time and materials, all those sleepless nights I sacrificed toiling on my paintings, only for my efforts to be wasted on a scammer.

"I'll sue," I say.

Lafayette snorts as though he hears that threat every day. His beady little eyes glimmer beneath the pink sunglasses, eager for my next move.

"Then just give me my money," I snarl.

He tilts his head. "Did you not read your contract?"

"Fifteen percent commission, right?" I pull out my phone, fire up the calculator app, and talk through the numbers. "You sold five paintings at five hundred each. That's two and a half grand. Minus fifteen percent is—"

"Two thousand one hundred and twenty-five," he drawls, "But your contract states that all artwork sold under ten thousand is also subject to a commission of twenty-five percent."

I gulp. That amount might cover the rent I owe, but I was really counting on the auction to pay off a few more debts.

"Alright then," I rasp. "I'll take cash."

Lafayette wags a finger. "There's also a fixed fee of five hundred."

My jaw drops. "Five... What?"

"Every auction incurs expenses, Ms. Kay. Marketing, staff costs, utilities, refreshments, shipping, etcetera, etcetera. Gallery Lafayette would go broke if we didn't impose a fixed fee for low-level transactions. It's all in the contract."

I glance down at the schedule of payments spread across his desk. The five-hundred-dollar fixed fee didn't concern me at the time I signed the contract because Lafayette promised me a reserve price of ten thousand.

The legalese was so cleverly worded with so much doublespeak. I could have avoided all this if I'd had the money to hire a specialist contract lawyer.

Before I can form another protest, he adds, "That's per item."

Realization kicks me in the gut. I'm beyond screwed.

"You're telling me I owe you?"

He nods, seeming proud of his invisible loophole. "A twenty-five percent commission on five paintings sold for five hundred dollars per piece, plus the fixed fee of five hundred dollars per item comes to three thousand, one hundred and twenty-five dollars. I'll take cash."

The fury simmering in my belly reaches a boiling point. I clench the edges of his desk with so much force that my knuckles turn translucent. How dare this slimy little man smirk at my distress. If he thinks he can make me pay for the dubious privilege of selling my artwork in his gallery, he's as deluded as he is ugly.

"My boyfriend's a police detective," I blurt, my stomach twisting at bringing up my abusive ex. "I can report you for fraud."

"Is he also incapable of reading and understanding contracts?" Lafayette asks.

Bitterness rises to the back of my throat. Jim wouldn't just laugh his ass off and side with the smug bastard. He'd lock me in his spare room, then beat me senseless and hold me captive for another year.

I shove that thought aside and focus on the immediate threat.

"Every artist in New Alderney is about to know how you scam the vulnerable," I say, my voice low. "I'm going to document this on every social media platform until you and your shitty gallery get canceled."

His smirk fades, and he rises from his seat, trying to look intimidating. My lip curls. At five-ten, Gerard Lafayette is exactly my height. With his double chin and the paunch stuffed beneath his tailored suit, he looks pathetic.

"Nobody will believe the word of a bitter artist with such minuscule talent," he snarls.

His words hit like a hot knife to the heart, radiating pain across my chest. My insides twist and churn at him denigrating my abilities, and I force myself not to flinch.

When Lafayette's eyes glimmer at having hit a raw nerve, the backs of my eyes sting with the onset of tears.

Jim used to tell me every day that my paintings were shit. He used to punctuate that point with his fists. According to the great detective, real artists painted recognizable subjects like sunflowers or girls wearing pearl earrings.

"That's right, Ms. Kay," he says, his smile widening. "Your work only reached five hundred dollars because the market doesn't reward mediocrity. I gave you a chance because you looked like the kind of artist who would do anything to succeed. I had an entire business strategy worked out to help you reach your goals, but you've chosen to be an ungrateful cunt."

My fury reaches a boiling point and the edges of my vision turn red. Fingers tightening around his desk, I upend the entire thing with a scream. Pens, papers, teacups and hot tea clatter to the marble floor, making Lafayette jump back.

As I walk out into the gallery, he screeches something about calling the cops. The crap on his desk probably cost more than everything I own, but I don't give a damn. I'm tired of men treating me like I'm nothing more than an object to be used and discarded.

The next asshole who fucks with me will get more than just a scalded dick.

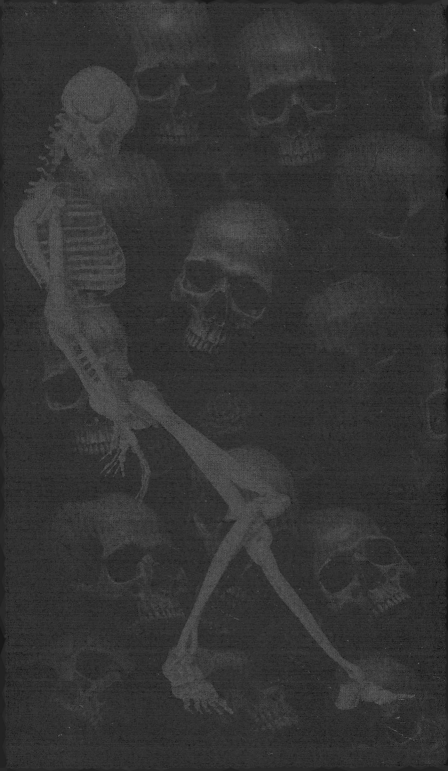

THREE

ROMAN

Some bastard leaked my release to the news. Now, my mugshot is everywhere, along with a list of my illegal businesses. All alleged, of course. The reporters are spinning my release as a failure of the justice system and a threat to the safety of New Alderney.

What they don't understand is that I'm cleaning up my territory and the streets, eliminating anyone who ever dared to conspire with Capello to steal from my family.

I don't give a damn about my reputation, but I was hoping to get the jump on my enemies before word spread that I was free. My scientist disappeared one night with her team, with the formula for an extremely potent form of crystal meth and four-million-dollars' worth of laboratory equipment and supplies.

Which is why I need to multitask.

I shut off the hose, step back, and motion for Cesare to pull the rag off Ricky Ferraro's head.

The weasel-faced informer lies on the tiled floor,

thrashing from side to side within an upturned chair, filling our nightclub's staff bathroom with gurgled screams.

The Phoenix nightclub is the legitimate business we use to launder drug money, but there's only so much income this establishment can claim to earn without looking suspicious. Since the majority of our legal operations are under Capello's portfolio, this is now the unofficial Montesano headquarters.

Cesare yanks off the wet cloth.

"Stop screaming, Ricky," I say. "The sooner you hand over the passwords, the sooner this will all be over."

We already have a hacker searching through Ricky's phones, computers, and tablets, tracking down every scrap of information that could lead us to our missing team of meth cooks.

We once used Ricky to send misinformation to the police. After I got arrested, he switched sides and started funneling details of our operations to Capello.

It's thanks to him we lost shipments of guns, cocaine, our lab, and our brilliant scientists. Since their meth is still out there on the streets, I can only assume they're still alive.

Ricky coughs out a mouthful of water. "I swear to God," he cries. "I don't know nothing."

With a snort, Cesare slaps the cloth back over Ricky's face. "Give me the hose."

"We need to keep him alive." I turn on the water and point the spray at Ricky's mouth and nose.

My little brother steps back and grumbles. I'd ordered both of them to keep their heads down during my incarceration, which is why Cesare is eager to crack heads.

Ricky chokes, convulses, and coughs again, but nothing can keep the fluid from entering his lungs. I shake my head as he bucks in his restraints, trying to break free. Waterboarding isn't my usual style, but I'm still dissatisfied with how quickly it took Vincent to burn.

A heavy fist pounds on the door and Benito steps inside. I turn off the water and wait for my brother to speak.

"We've got the address," he says.

"Now, can I have the hose?" Cesare says, his voice eager.

I hesitate, not wanting to cut short my revenge until Benito adds, "Our new attorney is waiting for you in the office."

Cesare snatches the hose and grins. "Don't worry, brother, I'll take really good care of Ricky."

Yeah, right.

Smirking, I follow Benito out into the hallway, already writing Ricky off as dead. He's a small fry compared to the prospect of ensnaring Emberly Kay.

The new lawyer Benito dredged up is an older man named Nick Terranova, who is well-versed in Vincent's screw up. He's a second cousin, who knows exactly what will happen to him if he's disloyal.

Benito and I sit with him in the office. Even though I've muted the monitors that take up the walls opposite, muffled dance music still filters in through the walls. We need a quieter location for business meetings. A nice legitimate-looking office building with security guards and a receptionist because I can't run our family empire from the back of a club.

I tell Nick about my plan to abduct Emberly Kay and force her to transfer everything she's inherited from Capello.

The older man shakes his head. "That's risky."

"How so?" I ask.

"You're going to abduct the girl, hold her hostage, and make her sign a bunch of contracts to give back the assets her father stole. That's duress."

"So?"

"Not only could you end up back in jail, but any contracts formed under duress aren't even enforceable. She might even run crying to her cousins, Tommy and Matty Galliano."

My lip curls at the reminder of those New Jersey bastards, and I lean back in my seat. "How is she going to claim duress if she's dead?"

Nick gives me a slow nod. "You're going to kill the girl?"

"I'm not a murderer," I reply with a grin, but the answer is yes.

When Capello framed me for murder, I wanted to gut that fat bastard and make him eat his own entrails. Benito talked sense into me and suggested that we let our cousin Leroi shoot him through the skull along with all his descendants to leave no messy traces. Now, I'll have to satisfy myself with his long-lost daughter.

We spend the next few hours discussing the state of our organization, interrupted by employees from across the business stepping in to congratulate me on my release. Even our tailor drops by with a new suit tailored to fit my new measurements.

Nick rises from his seat. "I can draw up the contracts for all the assets you listed, but I suggest buying them from her if you want to make the agreements iron clad. That way, Tommy Galliano, the lawyers handling Capello's estate, or any other interested parties won't be able to dispute them in court."

My jaw tightens at the thought of paying to reclaim items that are rightfully ours. I want to keep the girl in a room and terrorize her until she decides to do what's right.

"I'll think about it," I mutter.

With a nod, Nick picks up his briefcase and walks out.

As soon as the door clicks shut, I turn to Benito. "The

first thing we're getting back is the casino. There's only so much dirty money we can run through the Phoenix."

He rubs his chin. "I thought you'd make her sign over the bank accounts and safety deposit boxes?"

"We have to get hold of her first." I pick up my phone and fire up the surveillance app. The room she rents is empty. "What times is she alone?"

"You planning on picking her up from her home?"

"I'm not waiting for one of your fliers to lure her to the club."

Benito's face twists into a grimace. "You don't want to end up back in jail. If anyone sees you sniffing around her apartment—"

"They won't," I say.

"Because you want an alibi for every move you make. Last time—"

"Last time, we were all thrown off by Dad's sudden heart attack, and we didn't know Frederic Capello was waiting in the wings to steal our assets and frame me for a crime I didn't commit."

Benito shakes his head, exhales a weary breath, and pushes his glasses up the bridge of his nose. My little brother has always been too cautious, and what Capello did to our family has turned him into a compulsive worrier.

Who can blame him? With Dad dead, me in jail, and Cesare running rampant, he's had more responsibility than any man can handle.

I clap him on the shoulder. "Relax. When I pull this off, you'll be in charge of the finances, and I'll handle the rest. Deal?"

The smile he gives me is strained, but that's Benito. He's bookish, mild-mannered, and was always meant to be the family attorney.

"Give me the casino and the attached hotels," he says.

"Deal." I shake his hand.

A knock on the door interrupts our moment. Cesare bounds in, dripping water on the floor, looking like he's swum a mile in Lake Alderney.

"Your girlfriend just stepped in," he says, his eyes dancing.

I turn to Benito and grin. "You finally got a girl?"

With a sniff, he points at the monitors on the wall. "He means yours."

My gaze snaps to the screens. "Where?"

Cesare picks up the remote and points it at the middle monitor. The image zooms in through the entrance of the nightclub, where a sextet of women has gathered around the coat check.

I rise off my seat, round the desk, and stand in front of the screen to examine their faces until I find Emberly. She's the only one with unruly dark curls that tumble down her shoulders and is wearing a dress made of denim patchwork that hugs that round, sweet ass.

My mouth falls open and all the air leaves my lungs. Seeing her on a large monitor is not the same as catching glimpses on the surveillance app on a tiny screen. She's taller than I expected, with olive skin that reminds me of her father's. I take in her delicate features and snarl. No spawn of Frederic Capello has any business being so beautiful.

It would be almost a crime to torture a woman so exquisite or with a body so alluring, but I won't allow lust to cloud my judgment.

Maybe I'll finally deserve the five years I spent on death row. The only thing better than watching those pretty features twist in agony as I force her to sign over her inheritance would be giving Capello a front-row seat from hell.

Cesare wraps an arm around my shoulder. "Fuck her up, bro."

He doesn't need to tell me twice.

By the time I've finished with Emberly Kay, she'll be begging for death.

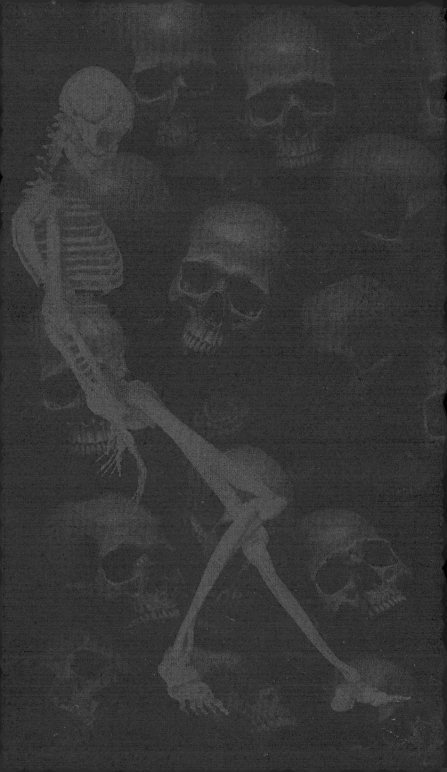

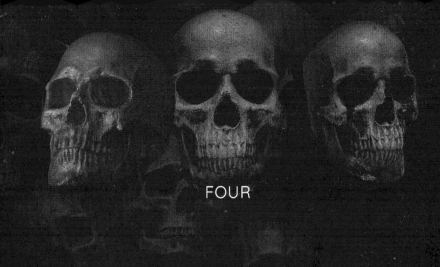

FOUR

EMBERLY

I'm still stinging from being scammed by Lafayette when I walk into the Phoenix with my roommate and her friends. They wouldn't let me spend Friday night moping around the apartment and dragged me out for their girls' night.

Apparently, we're the lucky recipients of a flier granting us free entrance to both the club and its VIP section. Maybe the bar staff will let me drown my sorrows and help me forget I'm swimming in debt.

Music pounds through the overhead speakers as we crowd around the coat check. I glance toward a set of double doors that lead to the club's interior and hope to hell that this ticket isn't a bait and switch to lure us in to buy overpriced cocktails.

"Ember." My roommate, Annalisa, tugs on my arm. "Your turn."

My gaze snaps to the coat check girl and I shoulder off my jacket and offer it to her with a weak smile. Her gaze sweeps up and down my patchwork denim halter neck.

"Nice dress," she says with a broad grin.

"It's made of jeans she bought at a thrift store," Annalisa yells over the music.

Everyone in the foyer, including Annalisa's friends, turns in our direction to scrutinize my outfit. An itchy flush creeps up my neck and blooms across my face, making me squirm.

If I wasn't so broke, I'd find somewhere else to live, but my room at Annalisa's apartment is a steal. She often says things that make me feel uncomfortable, but this is the first time she's embarrassed me in public.

That's how things escalated with my ex. I made excuses for his behavior and brushed off the warning signs until it was too late. I can't repeat this mistake. If I don't fix this situation right now, she'll only get worse.

Avoiding the coat check girl's eyes, I accept the ticket, stuff it into my pocket, and shoot Annalisa a glare. "Did you have to announce it to the entire club?"

She loops her arm through mine and laughs. "What? It's a compliment. While the rest of us are splurging on designer threads, you're saving cash by thrifting."

Her friends burst into peals of giggles, and I cringe at what's beginning to look like the New Alderney version of *Mean Girls*. I'm not usually such a pushover, but I'm still reeling from a slew of misfortunes that make the Lafayette art scam look like a minor inconvenience.

We enter the club's main room just as the music changes to the hot girl summer song that's going viral on social media. Annalisa's friends burst into high-pitched squeals and rush to the dance floor, but I grab my roommate by the arm and hold her in place.

She flashes me a grin. "What?"

"I'm not one to fuck with. Do you understand?"

Her smile falters. "What do you mean?"

"Don't make a mockery of me by announcing things that are none of your business."

She widens her eyes in an exaggerated expression of shock. "Stop being so sensitive. Nobody cares about your oversized paintings or your second-hand clothes. You don't always have to be the center of attention."

My lips thin. If I hadn't recently escaped a violent, gaslighting narcissist, I would back down and apologize, but I'm tired of taking shit. Shit from her, shit from conniving gallery owners, and shit from ex-boyfriends who don't understand the meaning of the word no.

I tighten my fingers around her wrist. "If you can't give me basic respect, you and I are going to have a serious problem."

Annalisa rolls her eyes and snorts. "Fine, whatever. Let's just dance."

She jerks her arm out of my grip and hurries toward her friends, who are already beckoning her over to the dance floor. I follow after her, my jaw tightening. All these little setbacks are a steady drip of acid on the already tight band holding together my self-control. One of these days, someone's going to say the wrong thing, and I'll unleash hell.

By the time I reach Annalisa, her friend, Christina, is handing out bottles of wine coolers.

"Ember!" Annalisa spreads her arms wide and pulls me into a hug as though I didn't just call her out for her disrespect. "Let's dance."

Christina shoves a wine cooler into my hand, and I take a long pull off the bottle, letting the cool, sweet liquid wash away my irritation. The music pounds through my veins and I let my body relax.

By the time I'm halfway through the bottle, I'm moving to the beat, deciding to shelve the bullshit, enjoy the free drinks, and work out how to fix my life in the morning.

The girls fall into a dance routine of well-practiced repeated steps and turns that look choreographed. I watch them for a few moments before joining in, and Annalisa slips her fingers into mine.

"I'm so glad you came out with us tonight," she says with a boozy grin. "You don't know how much I love being friends with an up-and-coming artist."

"Right." I pull my hand away and force a smile.

Guilt twangs at my heartstrings, and I swallow another gulp of my wine cooler. Did I overreact about her comment about my dress? Maybe I allowed my encounter with Lafayette to cloud my judgment.

Sometimes it feels like there's a guillotine at my neck. Other times, I picture myself at the center of a conspiracy, but it's mostly my imagination. My peculiar upbringing doesn't help. I grew up without a father to balance Mom's extreme persecution complex, and it's fucked with my sanity.

I can't get consumed by paranoia. I can't let myself become like Mom.

"Hey." Annalisa elbows me in the ribs.

My gaze snaps to hers, only to find her looking at a spot on the other side of the club. "What?"

"That's the guy who just got released from prison."

"Where?"

I follow her gaze through the dance floor and past a cordoned-off area where there's a bar and well-dressed people sitting on leather seats. Three dark-haired men stand together, their gazes focused in our direction.

They have to be related, not just because they all share the same olive skin, sharp features, and even sharper suits, but they're all similarly imposing. The one in the center is the tallest, with a superhero's physique, looking like he pumps iron.

He raises his chin as though acknowledging my presence, but I dismiss the gesture as a figment of my overactive suspicion. There's no way in hell a man that good looking would be checking out a woman in a thrift store dress.

"Who are they?" I ask, without skipping a dance step.

"The Montesanos." She leans into me and adds, "The one in the middle is Roman, who's all over social media. He's the boss who ran the mafia from jail."

I snatch my gaze away. There was a news story a few days ago, where someone had broken into a mansion and murdered the entire family of the man who owned the Capello Casino. Maybe those murders and his release are connected.

Shit.

After a disastrous relationship with a cop, I hate anything related to the law and lawlessness. If I'd known the girls were taking me to a club patronized by the mafia, I would have stayed at home.

Annalisa tosses her hair. "Roman Montesano was supposed to be on death row, but he's here, looking at me."

"For fuck's sake, don't look back," I mutter. "Every day women fall prey to traffickers. What if he's some kind of pimp?"

She huffs a laugh, as though she hasn't read all those articles about young women going to clubs and ending up sold into brothels. Sex trafficking is rife in New Alderney, and I won't let her become the next statistic.

Over the next few songs, Christina and Annalisa use the flier to get beer, shots, and even champagne. The alcohol soothes my nerves, and my worries fade into the background.

Later, even more booze appears, and more girls join the edges of our little dance troupe, including one in a gold dress and pretty sandals who introduces herself as Sera. I introduce her to Christina, Annalisa, and her friends as though I'm the party's hostess.

Men gather around us like vultures, acting like they've never seen a bunch of women follow the same dance steps. When the music turns sultry, they swoop in for slow dances.

A vice-grip clamps around my wrist. I whirl around and lock eyes with the face that haunts my nightmares.

It's Jim, my abusive ex.

Adrenaline races through my veins, jump-starts my heart, and pushes out a strangled scream. I left town, abandoned my friend group, quit my job, and changed my number so I could leave no traces when I escaped.

How the hell did Jim track me down to this club?

He looms over me, his face so flushed that it overpowers his red hair. Every vein on his temples protrudes with the force of his fury, and his pale eyes burn with incandescent rage.

Like most police detectives, he doesn't wear a uniform, but I swear there's a gun protruding through his jacket. Flinching, I try not to think about the last time he slammed its butt into my head.

"Thought you could just disappear and forget about me?" he snarls, as though I owe him something.

My pulse quickens. My breath shallows. My eyes dart around for an escape. He won't try anything on a busy dance floor in front of witnesses. Will he? He was always careful not to hit me in front of civilians.

Swallowing back a bout of nausea, I tap into every coping mechanism I learned from my therapist at the women's shelter and force myself to meet his bloodshot eyes.

"Let go of me." My voice trembles.

"What the hell are you doing in this shithole?" he sneers, letting out a cloud of alcohol-scented breath.

"How did you find me?"

"When the gallery owner filed a complaint into the system with your new address, I rushed over to your apartment." He nods in Annalisa's direction. "Your roommate said to check in tomorrow because you would be at the Phoenix."

Shit.

"Now, answer my question," he growls. "What made you think I would ever let you leave?"

Sweat breaks out across my brow. How about keeping me prisoner? Forcing me to have sex? The degradation, the violence, the financial abuse? I want to spit all this in Jim's face, but I don't want things to escalate.

Instead, I yank back my arm, but his grip only tightens.

"There's a warrant out for your arrest," he says.

The implication of his words kicks me in the gut. He's going to use his authority to drag me out of the club. If anyone intervenes, he'll just explain his heavy handedness as police business.

I need to get out of here.

Now.

I turn my body toward the last few stragglers looking to grab a girl for a slow dance. Maybe if he thinks I've moved on with someone else, he'll leave. It's wishful thinking, but I don't know what else to do.

Jim yanks me into his chest. "The owner of the art gallery says you stole a diamond-encrusted antique teaspoon that's been in his family for centuries."

My heart skips a beat. Lafayette trumped up a charge of theft? Shivers run up and down my spine at the prospect of going to jail.

"H-He's just making it up out of revenge because I threatened to report his shady business practices," I say.

"We have video evidence of you at the scene of the crime."

"What?"

"Look at me, bitch." He grabs my chin and forces a glare into my eyes, his pale blue irises narrowing as his pupils dilate. "You're facing jail time for assault, vandalism, destruction of property, and the theft of a valuable object."

My stomach lurches. Technically, I'm guilty of the first two, maybe even three. The camera must have caught me upending his desk covered in knickknacks and a fancy tea set containing hot liquid. Depending on the angle the footage was shot, it wouldn't be a stretch to frame me for the theft of an imaginary spoon.

Cold sweat breaks out across my skin and trickles down the back of my neck. Anything is better than returning to the house where he kept me prisoner.

"There's a patrol car waiting outside to take you in, but I can make it go away," Jim says, his gaze dropping to my lips. "Just say the word."

Revulsion ripples through my gut. The thought of what this monster will demand in return for a favor makes me gag. I can't face him or his abuse. Not now. Not ever.

Death would be better than being beaten, violated, and held captive.

Stepping backward, I gather up enough courage to say, "I'd rather rot in jail than go back to being your punching bag."

He bares his teeth, a sign that I've pushed him too far. "You're talking a lot of shit for someone who's soon about to be alone in a cell with a broken camera." Lowering his voice, he adds, "Do you know how many overdosed whores we find in the morning choked to death on their vomit?"

Every fine hair on the back of my neck stands on end. Jim has done a lot of heinous shit in the past, but he's never threatened to inject me with drugs. The venom in his stare tells me he's enjoying my terror, and he can't wait to have me arrested and at his mercy.

I need to get the fuck away.

Or think of a way to make me less of a target.

"It's too late, Jim," I say, gathering every ounce of my imagined strength. "I already have a new man. And he's powerful."

He flinches, his fingers loosening. Maybe he didn't think I would survive without him, but I take advantage of his momentary surprise to twist out of Jim's grasp and stumble back toward the edge of the dance floor. His face goes cold, and I swear the whites of his eyes turn redder.

How could I have been so blind not to see this maniac's red flags?

"You don't have a new man." He curls his lip, his features a rictus of contempt.

"He's here in the VIP section, watching me dance," I reply, trying to keep my voice from trembling.

Jim flicks his head toward the cordoned-off space. "Prove it."

My insides churn with a sickening sense of dread. Things are only going to get worse for me when Jim catches me in a lie. He's already detailed my impending cause of death. If I don't produce this mystery boyfriend, Jim might carry out his threat.

I can't let that happen. Jim needs to believe I'm no longer vulnerable and alone.

One of the vultures hanging around us will have to play the part of my new lover. Out of the corner of my eye, I see a large figure approach. Perfect.

Turning on my heel, I grab the nearest male body and lunge at his lips. The man stiffens at first but gives in to the kiss. His lips are inviting and soft, tasting of cigars and expensive whiskey.

He wraps his arms around my waist, pulls me tight against his muscular chest, and deepens the kiss. My eyes flutter shut, my core floods with heat, and my clit throbs in sync with the rapid beat of my heart.

I melt into his much larger body, already forgetting that my ex is about to arrest me for a crime I only half committed.

It's only when the man's huge erection presses into my belly that I come to my senses and pull away. I turn to Jim, the pulse between my thighs still hammering, and check that he's convinced I have a new boyfriend.

Jim backs away, his mouth falling slack, his skin paling to the shade of diluted milk. "I-I'm sorry," he yells over the music. "I didn't know."

My brows pull together. What's gotten that bastard so spooked? Jim loves to dominate other men because he thinks he's all-powerful and above the law. I whirl around to look the man in the face and meet a set of piercing brown eyes belonging to the biggest Montesano brother.

Not just any Montesano brother, Roman, the mafia boss who just got released from death row. Up close, he's even more chiseled with sharp cheekbones and an aura of danger that sets my nerves alight. And he stares down at me like I'm his last meal.

Fuck!

I don't want to spend the night in jail terrorized by Jim, but I sure as hell don't want the attention of a mafia boss who should be in prison, either. With a nervous cough, I step away, but Roman's arm whips out, and he grabs me by the waist.

"Where do you think you're going?" he says in a deep voice that sends shivers zipping up and down my spine.

"Home?" I rasp.

His eyes darken. "You're going to stay here and finish what you started."

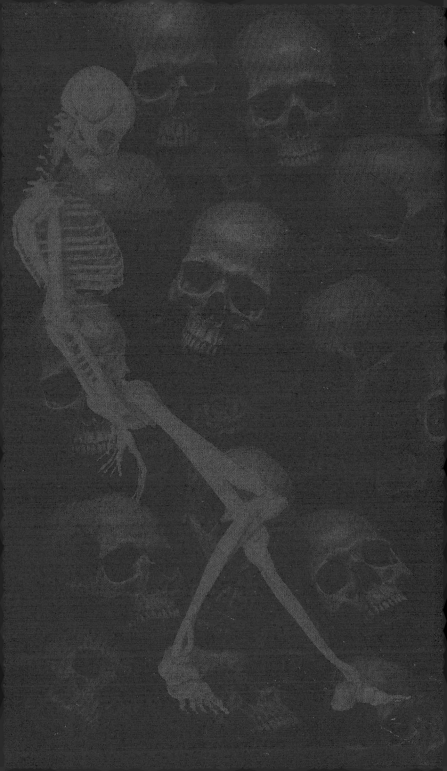

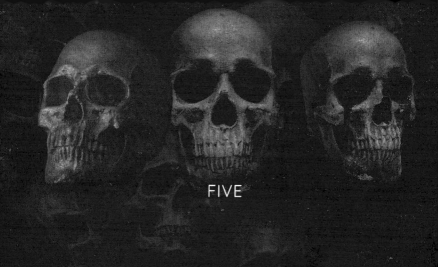

FIVE

ROMAN

If my lips are tingling, then it's because no one has kissed me since before my arrest. If my heart is pounding hard enough to break through its cage, then it's because I'm moments away from restoring the family's stolen assets.

My current state of excitement is in no way connected to the woman squirming in my grasp, but I have to admit my first encounter with Emberly Kay has been a surprise.

The man who was harassing her has the look of an incompetent cop. I eyeball the red-haired bastard until he turns around and vanishes into the crowd on the dance floor. He's the type of power-mad asshole who would call for reinforcements because the girl who rejected him had the audacity to kiss a felon.

I escort Emberly through the VIP area and gesture to two of my men to guard the back door. They nod back and move in position toward the exit.

She tries to drag her feet, but I keep her moving until there's nowhere for her to escape.

"Hey." She places a palm on my chest, her eyes widening with alarm. "Where are we going? Let me go."

"You owe me an explanation."

I walk her through the door that leads to a private hallway. As soon as it swings shut, the music dims enough for me to hear her rapid breaths.

I release my hold around her waist and glare down into her wide eyes. "What the hell was that back there?"

"Sorry." She takes a step backward, trying to create a little distance. "My ex was trying to throw me in jail."

"Since when was rejecting a man a criminal offense?" I smile to lighten the mood. "You'll have to give me a better explanation than that, sweetheart."

She dips her head and rubs the back of her neck. "He says there's a warrant out for my arrest and he offered to make it go away."

"Let me guess, with a roll in his back seat?"

A shudder shakes her slender frame. "Most likely in a cell."

"That's why you assaulted my lips?"

Her head snaps up, and her eyes flare. "Don't act like you're defenseless. You kissed me back!"

"I'm not even a day out of prison and you've dragged me into your domestic dispute with a cop."

She flinches, her gaze turning to the side. The sag of her shoulders tells me she feels bad about her rashness, or at least that's what she wants me to think. After all, she's the daughter of Frederic Capello, who was a duplicitous snake.

Stepping back, I wait for her next move because there has to be a catch. I can't believe Emberly Kay has fallen so easily into my lap.

Experience has taught me to look a gift horse in the mouth and slice open its belly to check for Trojan soldiers. At the very least, I need to exercise caution. Abducting her kicking and screaming with her policeman ex-boyfriend nearby is begging for a trip back to prison.

So, I'll play it cool and let the spawn of my enemy walk into my trap.

"Sorry," she says with a sigh. "I just grabbed the nearest guy. If I'd known who it was, I wouldn't have risked your parole."

I don't bother explaining to her I was exonerated. Instead, I lean against the wall and fold my arms. "He can't have you arrested for rejecting his advances."

She pauses, as though needing time to construct a reasonable lie. "I had a fight with a gallery owner who scammed me out of my paintings." She glances over her shoulder toward the door. "Look, I'd better go."

"And run straight into that cop and his reinforcements at the entrance?"

"What?" she asks, her voice shrill.

I flick my head toward the fire exit. "Use the back door. That way, you can avoid an ambush."

She shuffles on her feet, her gaze darting from me to either side of the hallway. I can see traces of Capello mostly around the nose and cheekbones, and of course, the green eyes. The difference is that Emberly Kay pulls off those features better than Frederic or his psychopathic twin sons ever did.

"Alright." She steps toward the exit. "Thanks for your help and sorry again for the kiss."

"Sure." I stroll after her at a distance, keeping my gaze off her slender waist, curvaceous ass, and long legs.

In a few seconds, Emberly Kay will step out into the alley running along the side of the club, and spot the patrol car containing the two officers on my payroll who texted earlier to give the heads up that a detective had just entered our club.

She won't know they're permanently stationed close to the building to make sure we have our own people on site to deal with problems off the record. Anticipation throbs between my ears in time with my excited pulse. I hold my breath as she opens the fire door and pokes her head out into the dark.

As predicted, Emberly doesn't step out. I'm rewarded with the stiffening of her delicate shoulders before she darts back into the hallway and stares at me with wide eyes.

"Problems?" I ask.

"They're outside," she says, her voice breathy with alarm.

"What do you mean?" I close the distance between us and reach for the door.

"Don't!" She grabs my bicep.

I glare down at her hand until she releases her grip.

"Sorry!" She steps back with her palms raised. "There's a police car out there. Jim said they'd come to arrest me."

"Jim?" I ask.

"My ex," she says. "Is there another exit?"

"Only the front, where I expect Jim will be waiting with some officers."

"Maybe I can wait them out."

I laugh. "That strategy never worked for any criminal."

She gulps, her chest rising and falling with rapid breaths. "Then I'm screwed."

Rubbing my chin, I make a show of frowning, giving the impression I'm wrestling with a decision.

"Maybe there's somewhere I can hide?" she asks.

I draw back, cross my arms, and hold my features into a neutral mask. "Hey, lady. I'm not looking for trouble. I just got out of prison. Hell, I don't even know your name."

"Please." Her voice breaks. "I can't afford to get arrested either. And it's Emberly. Emberly Kay."

Emberly stares up at me, her eyes pleading. She'd look even better on her knees, begging me for mercy. I want to draw out this moment, enjoy her desperation, but that might be pushing my luck too far.

"Okay." I make sure to sound gruff. "There is a way to get you out of this club and away from the police, but it won't be free."

She hesitates, all traces of desperation vanishing like smoke, her eyes narrowing. Caution etches her pretty features, and her lips turn downward.

"What's the catch?" her voice trembles. "What do you want in return?"

Stepping forward, I look her full in the face. "Another kiss."

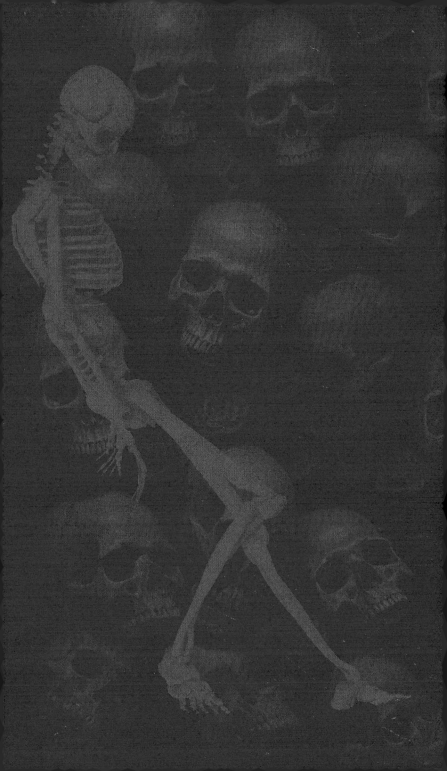

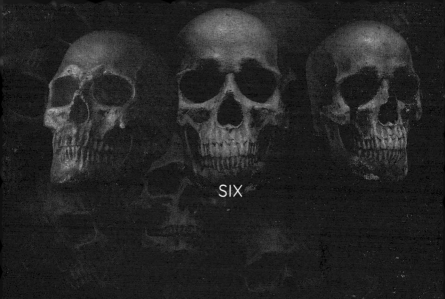

SIX

EMBERLY

Roman Montesano stands so close to me that I wither under his body heat. My gaze bounces from his full lips to eyes that bear down on me with an intensity that makes my heart stutter.

Mafia men are dangerous, especially those who've spent time in prison for murder. The New Alderney Times once wrote an exposé about a trafficking ring that stole women in clubs to sell into sexual slavery. If I'm not careful, I might end up the next victim.

I should make my excuses and leave. Walk out of the club and deal with the police. Isn't that what they say? It's better the devil you know?

Except I know exactly what will happen if I accept Jim's offer of help. He'll be the perfect boyfriend until he slips up and gets belligerent. Then the next time, I'll wake up with more than a black eye and a cracked rib. Worse, Jim's promise to help me evade arrest is bullshit. Without a second thought, he'd murder me in a cell as punishment for leaving.

Roman tilts his head and raises his brow for an answer.

My heart thumps against my ribs like a trapped animal desperate to break free. I can't go back to a relationship I already know will be abusive.

Could I make a deal with a mafia boss? People don't get shoved on death row for no reason. He's either a killer who bribed his way out or an innocent man with enemies powerful enough to get him executed. Either way, getting involved with him is dangerous.

But it's not like he's recruiting me to transport drugs. He only wants a kiss.

"Why?" I rasp, my throat suddenly dry.

"Why would I risk my freedom for a stranger on the run from the cops?" he asks.

I shake off the loaded question. "Why do you want another kiss?"

"Because..." He leans closer, his lips looking so soft and inviting that I have to force my gaze up to meet his eyes. "When you kissed me, I froze. I never wanted my first kiss with a woman in five years to be because I was caught off guard."

And with someone not of his own choosing.

Roman leaves out that part, but I hear it all the same. My guilty conscience asks why I had to molest a man with worse legal troubles than my own who held such value in kisses?

"Oh." My gaze lowers, and I shuffle on my feet to shake off a rush of prickly heat. "Sorry. I didn't mean to ruin your first—"

"It was memorable," he says with a soft chuckle. "Just not what I expected."

My teeth worry at my bottom lip. He just wants a do-over to make up for the experience I ruined. He's not asking me to join the Cosa Nostra.

It's just one kiss.

One kiss and he'll smuggle me out of the club, so I won't get arrested. After that, I'll never have to see Roman Montesano again.

"Just one?" I ask.

The corners of his lips lift into a smile. "If you want more, I won't object."

His deep voice curls around my libido and gives it a gentle squeeze, and my skin surges with heat. I don't even want to focus on the second part of that sentence because I can't remember the last time I was in the presence of a man I found so physically attractive.

My heart pounds so hard that its vibrations reach that sensitive spot between my legs. I'm overthinking something that should be simple. It's just a kiss.

An ache forms deep in my core. If it's just a kiss, then why does it feel like the start of a scorching hot adventure?

Roman's gaze flickers down to my lips, and I swear I can see his eyes smolder with desire.

I shake off that thought. This is ridiculous. It's been an eternity since I had a good orgasm and I'm overheating. Projecting my sexual frustration. Getting myself hot and bothered over one simple kiss.

I slide my hands up the lapels of Roman's jacket, feeling the hard contours of his pecs. His heartbeat echoes beneath my palms like a bass drum, infusing my own with a rhythmic thump.

I'm surrounded by the masculine scents of leather, cedarwood, and musk. I inhale deeply, my pulse quickening, and get swept up in a rush of anticipation. This promises to be the most exciting thing I've done since moving to New Alderney.

As I rock forward on the tips of my toes to reach Roman's lips, his large hands encase my wrists, and he pulls away.

My chest deflates. What did I do wrong?

"Not here," he says, his voice husky and low.

"Where then?" I ask, already sounding breathy.

"We need to use the kiss to smuggle you out."

My heart lifts. "Oh."

"Let's go." He wraps an arm around my waist and pulls me to his side.

Roman is so tall I have to lean against his chest and tilt my head to meet his gaze. An unusual experience for me, considering I'm five-ten and look most men in the eye. His stare is dark, intense, and heavy enough to make my knees buckle.

The strong arm around my back is the only thing keeping me upright when he opens the fire door and lets in a gust of cool air. Outside is a dim alleyway on the side of the club, illuminated by the patrol car's brake lights.

My heart rate cranks up several notches and teeters on the edge of paranoia. What if Roman thinks I'm not worth the trouble of saving and delivers me to the police? If I'd just been released from prison, the last thing I'd want was to help a female fugitive escape the law.

The police car's passenger side door opens, and an officer steps out. My fight-or-flight kicks in and I prepare myself to bolt, but Roman sweeps his forearm beneath my knees and cradles me to his chest.

My eyes widen. "What are you—"

His lips capture mine, silencing my protests and burning my suspicions into ash. This is his plan to sneak me past the police. Unless Jim had the foresight to send a message to all nearby units that a fugitive is on the run, the officer approaching us won't think I'm the woman connected to the incident at Gallery Lafayette. Instead, he'll dismiss me as Roman's celebratory hook-up.

I wrap my arms around his neck and let him take

control. His full lips devour mine with a hunger that makes my head spin. When his tongue pushes its way into my mouth, I moan for more. My fingers find his hair, and I tug at the strands, desperate to deepen our connection.

Somewhere on the border of my consciousness, footsteps retreat down the alleyway, then a car door opens and closes.

My chest inflates with triumph.

He did it. Roman saved me from the police, but now he needs to keep moving. I thread my fingers through his hair and moan, encouraging him to continue. This kiss can't stop until I'm halfway down the street, away from Jim and his colleagues.

Roman carries me in the opposite direction, toward another source of light, where I hear movement. I crack open an eye and spot a chauffeur holding open the door of what looks like a limousine.

Right. My alcohol-ridden brain tries to make sense of what's happening. It's because he's driving me to safety.

He doesn't seem like a sex trafficker.

I melt into the kiss, my grip around his neck tightening as he lays me on a leather seat. The door closes behind us with a soft thud as he settles over me, his hand tracing circles over my thigh. Now that his full attention is on mine, the air between us crackles.

"You're doing so well, sweetheart," he murmurs into the kiss. "Keep playing your part."

As the limo reverses out of the alley, one of its tires bounces over a pothole and jostles Roman's hard length exactly where I need it the most. I tilt my hips, desperate for more friction.

"Fuck," he groans. "You feel so good."

He grinds against my needy clit and breaks our kiss to press kisses on the sensitive column of my neck. Heat floods my core, and all sensation concentrates on my sensitive bundle of nerves.

This is the first time I've ever been pleasured by a man in such luxurious surroundings. Determined to enjoy this moment while it lasts, I cling onto his shoulders and move against him as the limo rounds the corner and drives away.

Alarm bells orbit my awareness, reminding me that our bargain is complete. Roman has transported me out of the club, and I've given him a kiss, but when his lips travel down to my breasts, my mind short-circuits.

He unties the strap of my halter, pulls down the patch-work fabric, and closes his lips around my nipple.

My back arches and I whimper.

The hand on my thigh trails a slow path toward my panties, and he moans, "I want to eat your pussy."

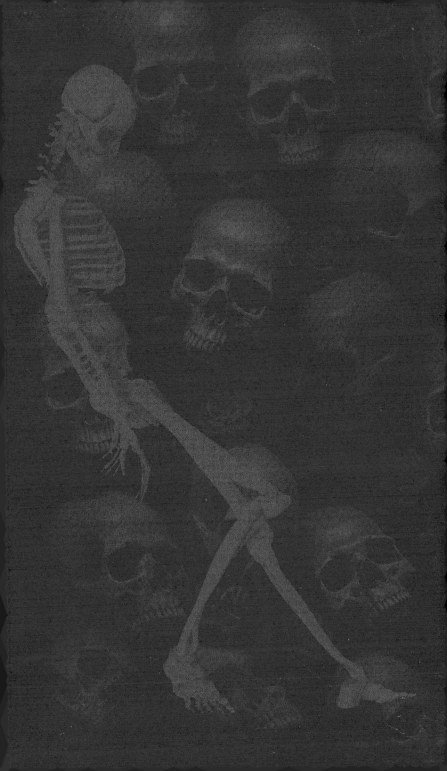

SEVEN

ROMAN

When a predator has a single chance to trap his prey, he will say or do anything for success, even if it means going down on the daughter of his enemy. I'm so excited at the prospect of clawing back my family legacy that my cock grows hard.

My arousal has nothing to do with the woman writhing beneath me and filling my ears with needy moans. Nothing to do with her soft curves or vanilla scent, or how she's grinding against my dick.

I suck her thick nipple and roll the other between my fingers. This is about keeping her distracted until the limo passes through the mansion's gates.

A police car's blue and red lights shine through the tinted windows, reminding me what's at stake. There's no telling if the squad car behind us is tailing us because I'm a person of interest or because the cops have already worked out her location.

Either way, I'm not taking any chances.

At some point tonight, she'll realize she's been abducted.

I'd prefer that to happen when we're far away from anyone who might come to her rescue.

"Oh, Roman," she groans. "That feels so good."

"That's right, baby," I murmur around her nipple. "I want the entire city to hear you scream my name."

I run a hand up her inner thigh and push her legs further apart. She arches into my touch, wanting more. Needing it.

Her breathy moan makes my cock push painfully against my zipper, but I ignore the traitorous bastard. It wants to slip inside her tight heat, already forgetting that the little heiress squirming against it owns hundreds of millions of dollars' worth of our family's stolen property.

I rub slow circles over her skin, trying to slow down the pace. She can't climax too soon because the moment her head clears, she'll revert to overthinking and become skittish at the thought of being trapped alone with a former jailbird.

As my fingers skim the lace of her panties, she gasps and bucks her hips.

"You wet for me, baby?" I ask.

She grips my shoulders, trying to push me down to her pussy. "There's only one way to find out."

My fingers close in around her nipple and I squeeze hard, making her arch and moan. As the limo slows at a stoplight, the air fills with a blast of sirens.

Emberly rises up on her elbows, her green eyes widening. All traces of horniness give way to suspicion.

"What's happening?" she asks, her voice tightening with confusion.

Shit. If I don't think fast, all my hard work will go to waste.

"Ignore it." I push her back against the seat. "They're not coming for us."

"Are you sure?"

"Someone will knock if either of us is under arrest." I

pull her dress down her hips and toss it to the other side of the limo. "There. Now, you're unrecognizable."

She glances out of the window and gulps, the gears in her mind spinning. Her fog of lust is wavering, as is her trust.

"Emberly, is it?" I ask, my voice soft.

She nods, her chest rising and falling with rapid breaths, her eyes still on the traffic.

"Even if the cops wanted to get you, they'd need a warrant to check my vehicle."

She bites down on her bottom lip.

"The doors are locked. They couldn't get in if they tried."

Still no reaction.

"I will protect you, baby. You're safe with me." To punctuate my point, I swipe my thumb over her clothed clit.

When her eyes finally snap back to meet mine, I hold back a triumphant smirk.

"Let me take care of you." I shuffle backward to position myself between her spread legs, but she grabs my lapel.

"You're wearing too many clothes," she says.

"Tell me what you want, sweetheart," I say, unable to hold back a grin.

"Take it off." She rises, slides her hands beneath my jacket, and slips it down my shoulders. Then she loosens the buttons of my shirt, and her eyes widen at the sight of all my ink.

I smirk. "See something you like, baby?"

"Maybe." She drags her fingertips over my chest, leaving trails of liquid fire.

My jaw clenches with the effort it takes to hold back the force of my desire. I suppress a sharp inhale and grab her wrist. "Stay down," I force back the growl in my voice. "If one of those officers comes over and knocks on the window, you need to stay hidden."

"Oh, shit." She flops down on her back and flings a forearm over her face. "I didn't think."

"Relax," I say with a smirk and rub the pad of my thumb over her swollen clit again. "I'll take care of the cops."

"A-Alright," she whispers.

I lower my head between her legs and press kisses on her inner thighs. Her skin is inviting and soft beneath my lips, and when my nostrils fill with the sweet scent of her arousal, it takes every ounce of effort not to tear off that scrap of fabric and claim what I'm owed.

The limo drives ahead, and the patrol car's flashing lights fade into the evening traffic.

Emberly lifts her hips and moans. I take that as an invitation.

The fabric of her panties is soaked and straining so tightly against her pussy that I can make out every delicious detail. Frederic Capello would be rolling over in his grave to know his daughter is such a horny little slut. If she wasn't, then luring her to her new prison wouldn't be so easy.

My cock chooses this moment to swell bigger than it has in living memory. That's because she's the first woman I've gotten close to in five years who wasn't a crooked prison guard. I bite back a moan and glance up at the window. We haven't even joined the highway.

This is moving too quickly. I've got to make this last. Keep Emberly on the edge until I can get her home.

"Fuck," she moans.

"Do you always give men you've never met erections, or is it just my lucky day?" I ask.

"P-Please," she whispers.

"Please what, sweetheart?" I run the flat of my tongue close to the lace of her panties.

"You said you would eat my pussy."

My lips curl into a smirk, and I run the tip of my nose

over the fabric straining across her clit. "I said I wanted to, not that I would."

She groans. "What's the difference?"

Four miles.

Twenty minutes if the traffic is good, which it seldom isn't. Most likely, I'll have to keep her in a constant state of neediness for at least thirty-five.

I suck hard on her inner thigh, making her gasp.

"The difference is consent," I murmur. "You won't get a lick of pleasure unless you beg."

She moves to sit up. This time, her eyes flash with frustration. "Seriously?"

My eyes narrow. "Do you know what I promised myself every night I spent on death row? If I ever managed to prove my innocence, I would only get involved with women who knew exactly what they wanted. So, Emberly, if you want me to make you scream tonight, you're going to beg for it."

She shoots me a glare from between her legs, her chest rising and falling with rapid breaths. Her lips are parted, swollen, and utterly delicious. She paints a beautiful picture of debauchery with her curls framing her pretty face like a wild mane, and her eyes burning with green fire.

I'm going to enjoy extinguishing that flame.

"Fine, alright, whatever," she snaps. When I don't respond to her little tirade, she adds, "Please."

"I'm waiting." My tongue ghosts over her clothed slit.

"I want you to lick my pussy until I come," she grits out.

"Say it again," I ask, "And use my name."

She exhales a trembling breath. "Please, Roman," she whispers. "Please lick my pussy until I come all over your face."

My cock leaps in anticipation. If she continues with that dirty mouth, I won't last twenty minutes, let alone thirty-five.

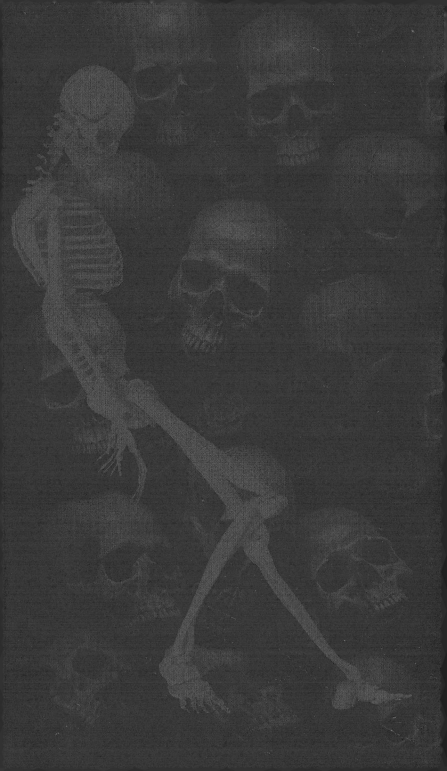

EIGHT

EMBERLY

In twenty-four years, I've done a lot of reckless shit. Smashed a window at the age of four, cut the brakes of my art teacher's car when I was fifteen, and moved in with a creepy cop at twenty-three.

Each of them felt necessary at the time and each had negative consequences.

But none of these compare with lying on my back naked in a locked limousine, begging the mafia boss between my open legs to eat my pussy. Roman Montesano isn't just dangerous. He probably hasn't had a woman since his arrest, and I'll take the brunt of all that pent-up sexual frustration.

Our bargain is complete. He's already helped me escape the police, and I've already given him the kiss he wanted in exchange. It's time to sit up, find my dress, and make an excuse to leave. But when he pulls aside my panties and blows on my clit, the little voice in the back of my head that's waving red flags disappears under an onslaught of pleasure.

The last memory I had of sex was unpleasant. I know that letting this gorgeous man give me an orgasm will get me into trouble, but my need for release overpowers my common sense.

"I knew you'd have a pretty little pussy," he murmurs, his breath hot and wet against my folds. "But I'm going to make it squirt."

The muscles of my core clench. I can't tell if it's in response to the compliment or to the promise.

"Y-You think?" I ask.

"I guarantee it, baby."

He circles my clit with his wet tongue. I'm so sensitive that I swear I can feel every taste bud. The pleasure is slippery and hot and velvet, and before I can even process all the sensations, he positions a thick finger at my entrance.

Whatever reservations I have about hooking up with a mafia boss dissolves under the promise of that orgasm. That's all right. I can leave as soon as he's made me climax.

"You taste even better than I imagined," he says.

My nipples tighten, and every nerve ending of my body thrums with anticipation. All thoughts of leaving the limousine fade with the engine's gentle rumble. As Roman circles my entrance with his finger, I make a mental note to ask him if he knows an affordable attorney.

"Relax, baby," he says, his tongue moving with up-and-down motions that make every nerve ending sing. "I'm going to take really good care of you."

He says those words with such conviction that my muscles relax into the leather seat. No other man has ever made such assurances and been able to back them up, but every instinct tells me that Roman wants to give me as much pleasure as I can stand.

His lips close around my clit as he pushes a finger into my opening. White-hot sensations shoot through my core. They're so intense that my thighs clamp around his head as if to hold it in place.

"That's it, sweetheart," he says as he licks and sucks and fingers me to the brink of ecstasy. "Let go."

I do.

For several marvelous minutes, my mind melts. The tight ball of tension that houses my problems also uncoils. My inhibitions evaporate, and I surrender to Roman's touch. Every nerve ending thrums with pleasure, and I can't help but moan.

"Just like that," he murmurs. "You're even more beautiful when you're grinding against my face."

Even if I wanted to, I couldn't stop my hips from jerking. My body quivers and shakes at his command, and all I can do is grab handfuls of his hair as I ride out the sensations.

Lust clouds my senses, and the pleasure sharpens into a razor-thin edge. I'm so close to orgasming that my skin breaks out in sweat and my eyes roll toward the back of my head.

Just as I'm about to tumble, Roman pulls back, leaving me aching.

My eyes snap open, and I release a desperate cry of frustration. I raise myself up on my elbows to glare down at the man between my legs.

"Why did you stop?" I ask through panting breaths, trying to hold back a surge of frustration.

His irises are so dark that they're almost black. "You don't get to come without permission."

My eyes widen, though I shouldn't be surprised. It makes sense that Roman would be dominant. Those types of men get turned on by making women jump through flaming hoops to get the simplest of favors and even then, they fail to deliver.

Heat rises to my cheeks, adding to the ache escalating between my legs. I hold back my usual snappy response.

Roman has me so worked up that I'll play along with his mind games. Then I'll switch back once I get my orgasm.

"You want me to beg again?" I ask.

When his gaze drops to my exposed pussy, I can't help but bite down on my lip to keep from moaning. He swipes his tongue over full lips that glisten with my arousal, reminding me of a predator about to devour his prey. My thighs tremble, the muscles of my core clench, and every part of me wants to volunteer to be his next meal.

"Do I want you to beg?" He repeats my question as though its answer is obvious. "What do you think?"

Light me a fire because I'd jump through any kind of obstacle if it meant getting Roman to finish what he started.

The limousine makes a right turn onto a highway in the opposite direction of my apartment. Somewhere in my sex-addled brain, I remember not telling him where I lived or even having agreed to being taken home.

Why the hell would I want to go home when the cops know my address? It's not like I have a second hideout, and I'm too fixated on Roman's mouth and too invested in getting an orgasm to care.

"Yes, please," I whisper.

"What's that, beautiful?" he asks, his full lips quirking. "Tell me what you want?"

I take a deep breath, releasing the last of my inhibitions. "Please suck my clit and make me come so hard I forget my name."

He makes a low growl that causes all the fine hairs on my body to tremble with anticipation. "How about I fuck that hungry pussy with my tongue? Would you like that?"

My heart races at the suggestion, and I whimper. "More than anything. Give it to me, Roman. Please."

His eyes rise to meet mine, and I see a need so intense, I

can't comprehend it through all the lust fogging my common sense.

"Then that's what you're going to get," he says, sounding almost cold.

My mind freezes in the hunger of his gaze. As I shift backward on the seat, Roman dives between my thighs again and lavishes my pussy with an open-mouthed kiss.

The pleasure is so overwhelming and sudden that I collapse back onto the leather seat. All my reservations unfurl and evaporate into the ether. Roman eats me like a starving beast, each swipe of his tongue infusing me with molten fire.

I'm panting, shaking, surrendering to his desire, but just as my pleasure peaks, he withdraws his tongue. My breath hitches. Does this man want to give me a stroke?

His tongue traces a slow, meandering path down my slit, pausing for him to suck each labia. I cry out, overwhelmed with frustration. Why is he switching up the rhythm whenever I get too close?

"Roman." My voice is a high-pitched whine. "Please, stop teasing."

He hums against my folds, making me shiver with pleasant vibrations. "But you moan so prettily."

"You should hear how prettily I moan when I come."

His deep chuckle sounds almost cruel. All I can say is that this man knows the effect he has on women and loves making me suffer.

"I'm going to enjoy breaking you." He grabs my ankles, slides his tongue into my pussy, making me cry out.

What does that even mean? I'm already a panting, broken mass of desire.

Roman slides in and out of me with rapid, shallow thrusts. Pleasure builds with each stroke, and my hips rise and shudder in counterpoint to his movements.

I squeeze my eyes shut, press my head back into the leather seat, and gasp. He positions my feet on his shoulders to deepen the angle and pushes in and out of me until I'm crying out his name.

"Oh, god... your mouth," I moan.

"God has nothing to do with this mouth, but if you carry on being a filthy girl, it will take you to heaven," he growls.

My clit swells, becoming so sensitive that it twitches with the tiniest gust of cool air from the vents. I raise a hand to touch it, but Roman grabs my wrist.

"I'm the only one who makes you come," he says, and his tongue thrusts even further.

"But I can't come like this," I say between panting breaths.

I feel Roman's facial muscles forming a smile as though I've stated the obvious, and he plans on keeping me on the edge until I either beg or break. He continues those delicious strokes, occasionally bumping my sensitive bundle of nerves with the tip of his nose.

"Please, Roman," I rasp. "Let me come."

His satisfied rumble confirms my suspicions. He's getting off on my desperation just as much as I'm getting off on his skillful tongue.

The limo veers off the highway and ascends an incline, but it may as well be driving me to heaven. Each time his nose grazes my sensitive bundle of nerves, he brings me closer and closer to nirvana.

Pleasure coils within my core, and my walls constrict. I curl my fingers even tighter into his hair and groan.

I have never been with a man with so much self-control. Even when Jim was being nice, he only ever went down on me long enough to warm me up for sex. The few lackluster pumps that followed always left me unsatisfied. Roman is a refreshing upgrade. He's the kind of man who thinks beyond his own pleasure and doesn't need to rush.

"That's it, baby," he says, his voice wicked and rich and deep. "Let me take you apart."

"Wh-What?"

His answer is a rumbling laugh that vibrates through my core. Roman keeps me teetering on a delicious precipice, seeming so attuned to my body that he knows exactly when to ease off the pressure.

My throat releases a keening cry.

I love it. I hate it. I can't get enough of it.

Minutes roll by, maybe even an hour, but I lose track of all my senses, including the passage of time. All I can focus on is holding onto the exquisite pleasure before he lets it slip away.

Roman lavishes my clit with gentle suction before pulling back. In the absence of pleasure, my eyes snap open. I blink away the haze on the edges of my vision and focus on his face.

The limousine's dim interior accentuates his strong brow and the shadows beneath his cheekbones, making his beautiful features almost sinister.

A shiver runs down my spine and settles between my legs. "Why have you stopped this time?" I ask.

"Do you still want to come?" he asks in a voice as smooth as velvet.

"Of course," I reply with a frown. "Why do you even need to ask?"

"Then you'll have to do it around my cock."

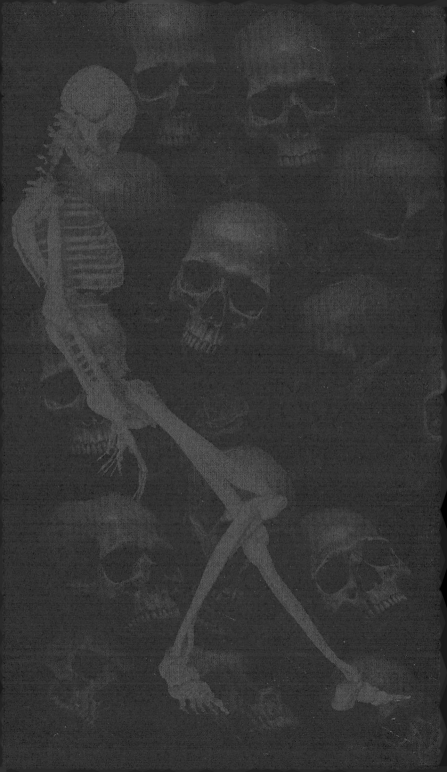

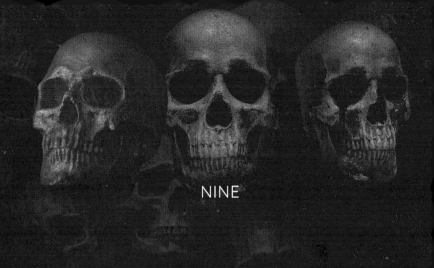

NINE

ROMAN

No sacrifice is too great for my family.

When I discovered Dad died while fucking another woman, I buried the details to preserve his reputation as a family man. When our mother left us to marry Tommy Galliano, I refrained from ordering a hit on him, even though he was Dad's longest-standing rival.

I stayed on death row for eighteen months longer than necessary to wait for the perfect moment to arrange the murder of Frederic Capello, along with anyone powerful enough to retaliate against my brothers.

Nothing is too onerous for the people I love, but I'll be damned if I lick Capello's daughter to completion.

The car stops outside the mansion's front steps, but there's no sense of nostalgia. I haven't seen my home since I was arrested without bail, but I can't take my eyes off her face.

She stares up at me with a flush that spreads down her neck and across her chest, which rises and falls with rapid breaths. Her curls tumble around her face in a wild halo that cascades down to thick, wine-colored nipples.

She's slender and wiry, with a tight belly that curves down to a thatch of dark curls. The exposed lips of her pussy glisten in the dim light, and her arousal soaks the leather seat.

I have to admit she's beautiful and would have made the perfect little mafia princess.

If her mother hadn't escaped New Alderney while pregnant, Capello would have married Emberly off to a powerful family to form an alliance. She would have birthed strong, handsome sons and lived a life of luxury and style. But I plan on ending her life the moment she's signed over my property.

"Is this what you want, baby?" I thrust my hips, showcasing the erection pushing against my pants. "You want me to fuck you hard and fast until you scream?"

"Yes." She reaches out a trembling hand to run her fingers over my clothed shaft.

Her touch fills me with tiny bolts of electricity. If only Capello could see his precious daughter naked on the back seat of my limo, begging for my dick.

"Yes, what?" My fingers close around her wrist.

"Yes, please."

"If you want my cock, you'll call me Mr. Montesano or sir."

She gulps, her gaze flickering up to my eyes before dropping down to my erection. "Yes, sir." She exhales the word like a prayer. "May I touch it?"

My chest inflates with pride. Emberly Kay is not a natural submissive. From what I've seen so far, she's feisty, scrappy, and unafraid, but I'm taming her with the promise of sex.

I place my jacket over her shoulders. "Put this on."

She slides her arms into the sleeves, and I wait for her to fasten the buttons before pressing the intercom. Even though I don't plan on letting her live a second after I've gotten what I want, she's mine, and I won't share.

"We're ready," I say.

"Yes, sir," Gil replies through the speakers.

Gil is a former boxer who once took a bullet for Dad and is one of our organization's meanest and most loyal enforcers. He exits from the front and walks around to open the door.

I step out into the night, inhaling my first lungful of fresh air scented with the juniper trees that surround the mansion and the hill it sits on. Then it strikes me, I never have to return to Alderney State Penitentiary. I'm free.

"Welcome home, boss." Gil grins so widely that his eyes turn into slits.

My jaw clenches, and I force back a rush of emotion. I can't even enjoy this moment of freedom because I've got to fuck Capello's daughter into submission. Instead, I meet Gil's smile with a nod.

"It's been too long," I say, my words gruff. In a much lower voice, I add, "Get everyone together tomorrow morning. We need to talk about the future."

He nods. "Yes, sir."

I reach into the limo to scoop Emberly out of the back seat and into my arms. My nostrils fill with her vanilla and cinnamon scent mingled with the sweet musk of her arousal. The prospect of pounding into her until she screams my name makes my cock surge so powerfully that I become lightheaded.

"Hold tight," I say, my voice a low growl, and she places her hands on my shoulders.

By the time I turn toward the mansion, it's to find the entire staff gathering on its stone steps. Sofia, our housekeeper, stands in the middle, her smile faltering. It looks like Benito already briefed her on the identity of our special guest.

Emberly raises her head, shrieks, and buries her face in my shoulder. I chuckle, understanding her reaction.

My great-grandfather had the mansion built in the style of a Roman villa he'd grown up around in Salerno, Italy, only grander. It's a two-story limestone building covered in ivy and a grand porch with carved wolves snarling at each pillar. Decades later, my grandfather added a four-story tower with a balcony, allowing for sweeping views across Alderney Hill and beyond.

I moved out after my first job and used to hate coming back here because it was so pretentious. Now, all I see is a family home filled with memories.

Emberly clings to my neck as I take her up the stairs, past the applauding staff members, and through the double doors. I spare a moment to kiss Sofia on both cheeks and thank her for the daily food packages that kept me sane during my imprisonment.

The thought of carrying Capello's offspring through the threshold like a bride fills my veins with a twisted sense of triumph. Emberly Kay isn't here to be my wife, she's here to be my toy. My pretty little plaything.

I take her across the marble hall, up the stairs, and through the tall white door that leads to the tower.

She raises her head, takes in the winding staircase, and asks, "Where are we going?"

"Somewhere the staff won't disturb us while I fuck you into submission."

Her full lips part with a question, but I silence her with a kiss. She moans, seeming to enjoy the taste of her arousal on my tongue, and relaxes against my chest.

Several moments later, we reach the room at the top of

the tower and step into a chamber decorated in silver and varying shades of ivory. Moonlight shines in from the twin patio doors that lead to the balcony, illuminating a large bed. I drop her down on the mattress and glare down at my prey.

She looks so vulnerable and small wearing my jacket, even though she's taller than the average woman. I draw back, my cock trying to push its way out of my pants.

"Strip."

Emberly rises onto her knees and unbuttons the jacket, revealing that phenomenal body.

"Come here." When she moves to shuffle to the edge of the bed, I raise a finger. "On your hands and knees."

Her features show none of the usual indecision or resistance. She gets into position and crawls across the mattress. Her pert breasts sway with the movement, and her lean muscles ripple with each step.

I would move to the other side of the room and make her continue toward me so I can enjoy more of her submission, but my cock is tired of waiting. Instead, I cup her chin and force her gaze to meet mine.

"You should know I won't be gentle," I say.

She nods, her pupils so dilated that I can barely see any traces of green.

"I'm going to fuck you hard, make you scream, and you're going to love it."

"Yes," she whispers, her desperation turning my blood to liquid fire.

I release her chin. "Now, take out my cock."

She reaches for my fly, her fingers trembling so much that it takes her a few tries to undo the zipper. My cock springs free, making me groan with relief.

Emberly makes a strangled sound. "Oh fuck. It's so big."

I smirk. "You're going to take every inch and cry for more. Now, say hello to it with those pretty lips."

With a soft whimper, she licks her lips and draws forward. I'm no stranger to women being intimidated at the sight of my cock, but knowing she's the daughter of that bastard has me hotter and harder than ever.

Her breath warms my overheated skin. When she presses a kiss on my crown, my arousal surges until I'm reeling on my feet.

She gazes up at me through long lashes, her eyes full of awe. A twinge of longing strikes my heart. I could get used to seeing that face. I could get used to seeing her on her knees every day, begging for my cock, but I'll have to savor her while she lasts.

Emberly Kay is nothing more than a tool. She's the key to reclaiming what's ours.

She parts her lips, and her tongue flickers over my tip to lap up a bead of precum. Electricity sparks through every nerve, making my knees buckle. I tighten my grip on her hair, and she winces.

I'm in control of how she sucks my cock. Not her.

"Open your mouth," I command.

She parts her lips.

"Now, stick out your tongue."

Her obedience is like a shot of the most potent aphrodisiac, and the sight of that pink little tongue goes straight to my balls.

"Good girl."

I slide my cock all the way into her mouth and hit the back of her throat. She gags, and the sound is enough to drag me to the edge. Fuck. At this rate, I'm going to come too soon.

My fingers in her hair twist with enough pressure to make her squeeze her eyes shut and whimper.

"Eyes on me," I snarl.

Her gaze snaps up to meet mine.

"Just like that. I'm going to take your throat hard and fast. If you please me, I'll fuck your pussy. Would you like that?" I ask with a hard thrust.

Tears gather in the corners of her eyes, and she nods. I draw back and reenter her with a snap of my hips. The muscles of her throat close in around my crown, making me see fireworks.

I don't give her a moment to catch her breath and keep pounding into her with full force. Watching her gag and choke on my cock is too much. I'm in danger of exploding. Releasing my grip on her hair with a shove that has her blinking, I grip the base of my shaft and hold back my climax.

"Turn around and hold on to the headboard," I growl.

Her lips part, and she gazes up at me with a mixture of desire and fear. "Condom?"

"Of course." I reach into my pocket, extract a foil wrapper, and tear it off with my teeth. "Get into place."

"Yes, sir."

I step back, letting her crawl to the headboard. It's silver-framed and upholstered in ivory silk, but I wish it had posts so I could bind her wrists.

She grips the headboard with both hands, her knuckles turning white. Despite her wiry frame, her ass is the perfect peach. After slipping on the rubber sheath, I kneel behind her and run a hand down the length of her back, making her shiver.

"Push your thighs farther apart," I say.

She obeys, her breaths ragged. I slide my fingers over her ass cheek and squeeze, drawing out a desperate whimper.

"You should see how good you look on your knees with your legs spread, showing me that sweet, wet pussy."

The needy sound that slips from her mouth makes my

cock throb. I run it up and down her slit and revel in the obscene sound of her wetness.

"Please," she whispers. "I need it."

Who am I to turn down the request of a lady? I line up my crown with her entrance and drive in hard and deep. I nearly lose it at the sound of her pleasured howl, but I force back the sensation with a sobering thought.

Emberly Kay should enjoy her final moments of pleasure because I'll make sure she goes out with a bang.

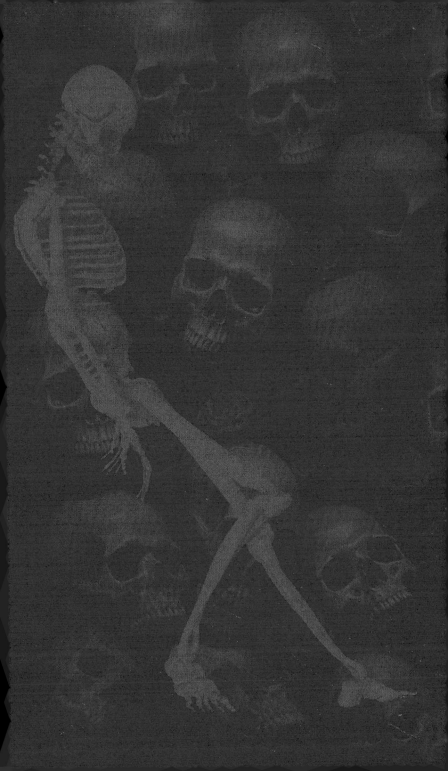

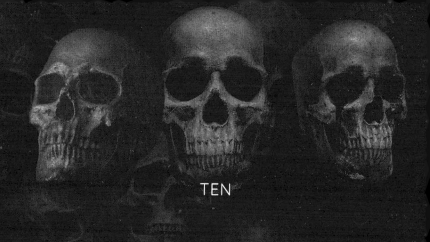

TEN

EMBERLY

Roman enters me with a hard thrust that lights up every nerve like fuses of dynamite. My eyes snap open and I cry loudly enough to echo off the walls. I knew he was big, but nothing prepared me for this incredible stretch.

My fingers tighten around the headboard as he draws back his hips, and the walls of my pussy quiver with anticipation. I'm so slippery and wet from all that foreplay when Roman slams back into me, all I can feel is raw pleasure.

This is fast becoming my favorite position.

I grind my hips back against Roman with his next thrust, making him groan. He leans closer, his chest pressing against my back, and his hot breath tickling my ear.

"Fuck, baby, you're so tight," he growls.

"Maybe it's because you're so big," I say, my voice choked.

Roman pumps into me faster with shallower strokes. The hands that were holding my hips steady roam up my rib cage toward my breasts. His fingers find my nipples, teasing and pinching them until I'm clenching and moaning.

"Oh, God," I cry.

"Guess again, sweetheart," he says. "Get my name wrong and I won't let you come."

"Roman," I rasp.

His large palm hits my ass with a sting that travels straight to my clit. I scream, my pussy tightening around his thick shaft.

"What did I tell you to call me?"

"Sir." I gasp.

"Say it again, only louder." He threads the fingers of his other hand through my hair and yanks my head back.

I squeeze my eyes shut and moan, "Yes, sir."

Roman rewards me with an extra hard thrust that hits my g-spot. "You like that? You want more?"

Golden stars fill my vision and launch my mind into orbit. "Fuck," I cry out as he slams into me again. "Yes."

I've never been fucked so hard and so thoroughly. It's a pity that the man giving me the best sex of my life is a mafia boss I never plan on seeing again after tonight.

He pounds into me without mercy or restraint, pushing me further and further into a space of pure euphoria. I never knew until this moment that this is exactly how I like sex—rough and hard enough to make me forget my name, let alone my worries.

Roman fucks me so hard that his balls slap against my clit with every stroke. Each thrust brings forth a burst of rapture that grabs me by the throat. My climax is so close I can barely breathe. If he edges me again, I think I'm going to die.

"You want more, baby? Tell me what you need."

"Harder," I say through a gasp. "Fuck me harder."

He gives me exactly what I need, his thrusts growing more forceful. The sound of our bodies colliding fills the room, blending with my desperate moans.

Through all this pleasure, I can't help but regret that the man I'd least want to get involved with would be the one to have the level of self-control to give me the best sex of my life. But I won't complain. Instead, I'll enjoy every second of this pleasure before it's gone.

"You feel so good," I say, the words breathless. "I never want this to end."

Roman's teeth clamp down on my earlobe, sending a jolt of pain that acts like lighter fluid on my already sparking nerves.

Molten heat floods my veins and surges straight to my swollen clit. Pleasure builds within my core with an intensity that's almost unbearable. My pussy clenches so tightly around his hard shaft that his thrusts become even more shallow.

"Come for me, baby," he snarls. "Let me feel that sweet little cunt tremble around my cock."

His words detonate an explosive orgasm that sends out shockwaves of ecstasy. My back arches, and my muscles go taut. It's as though my body's conserving all my life-force to get through this climax. The walls of my pussy tighten around his shaft, each spasm so powerful and deep I feel them up my spine and down my inner thighs.

I can't see, I can't breathe. I can't do anything else but ride out these insane sensations until my body can wrestle back control.

Finally, my lungs release and I scream my orgasm in a voice I barely recognize.

"Good girl," I hear him say through the haze of pleasure. "You're doing so well."

Warmth rushes through my chest, and I can't help but bask in his praise.

Roman releases his grip on my hair and strokes my shoulders throughout the orgasm, while his other arm wraps around my waist, keeping my back connected to his chest. His heart pounds through my body as I ride out the sensations, and my ears fill with his ragged breath.

"You're so beautiful when you come," he says, his words hoarse.

Heat blooms across my cheeks, and I savor both the compliments and his embrace. I've never felt so physically attuned to another person, which is silly because we didn't even fuck face to face. I rest my brow against the headboard, making sense of the tangle of ecstasy and emotions.

"So perfect," he adds, his words soft.

I exhale a ragged sigh. Even though I plan on ghosting him in the morning, fucking Roman Montesano has been unforgettable.

"Thank you." I turn my head toward him and smile, wondering if he'll send me back in a limousine or an Uber. Either way, it's probably not a good idea to return to my apartment. By now, Jim would have gotten over the shock of seeing me kiss Roman and arranged reinforcements or started staking out my home himself.

My heart sinks, and all my euphoria drains away with a sigh. Why do I have to be thinking of that asshole at a time like this when I should be luxuriating in the afterglow? I try to shove the thought of Jim away, but I can't forget his threat to assault and murder me in the cells.

Roman's deep chuckle breaks me out of my thoughts. "You're thanking me?"

"Yeah," I say with a giddy laugh. "That was pretty incredible."

"I haven't finished with you, sweetheart." He rolls his hips, showing me that he's still hard.

A moan slips from my lips. "More?"

"Did you think we were done?" he asks.

"We're not?"

"What do you think?" He pulls us backward, so he's sitting on his heels and I'm still straddling his hips and facing the headboard. "You're going to give me one more."

My throat dries. This has to be some form of variant on reverse cowgirl. I'm so relaxed and loose from that orgasm that I'm not sure I can even hold myself up, let alone ride.

Roman delivers a hard slap on my thigh that makes me flinch.

"You want to come again?" he growls.

"Um... Yes?"

"Then you'd better earn it," he says, his voice harsh. "Get up and ride my cock."

A shiver runs down my spine. All traces of the man who whispered sweet words of encouragement and held me as I climaxed are gone, replaced by something colder. Something more... demanding. Crueler.

Ignoring the fine hairs on the back of my head standing on end, I cling to the headboard for leverage, raise my hips and slide up his length. As the crown of his cock stretches my opening, Roman grabs my hips and pulls me down, burying himself deep.

I gasp at the sudden sensation of fullness, and Roman groans.

"That's it, little slut," he says. "Ride me like you mean it. Take what you need."

"Yes, sir," I moan.

His hands guide my movements as I roll my hips and grind against his length. "Show me how much you want this cock. Let me see what you got."

His words are both a command and a challenge I can't resist. As I rise, pleasure builds with each thrust and I'm soon moaning and panting. My mind tries to dredge up a reason for Roman's earlier shift in demeanor, but it's impossible to focus when I'm so lost in pleasure.

When we build up a rhythm, Roman's hand leaves my hips and travels back to my breasts. This time, he squeezes my nipple hard, delivering a burst of pleasure that feels like an electric shock.

"Aaah," I moan.

"You look so good like this." He rolls the nipple between his fingers as though trying to prolong the pain. "So beautiful when you're taking my cock like your life depends on it, but you can do better."

"W-What?"

"I want to see you lose control," he growls, his voice thick with desire. "I want to hear you scream my name like it's your last night on earth."

"Yes!" My hips jerk uncontrollably, making Roman's chest rumble with a satisfied groan. Moments after the sensations subside, he gives my nipple an even more vicious pinch. My brain is so scrambled the intense pain registers as pleasure.

I throw my head back and cry. "Fuck, please don't stop."

"That's it, baby," he says, his voice husky and low. "But now you're going to strangle my cock."

Roman's other hand travels down to my clit, which he rubs with up and down strokes. The muscles of my core contract around his erection, making me quiver, straddling the edge of release.

"Good girl," he says with a groan. "So tight. So sweet."

My mind spins as I cling to the headboard, my hips jerking faster and faster at his unspoken command. Just as I think the pleasure can't get any more intense, his finger and thumb close in around my clit.

"Now, scream for me," he snarls and squeezes hard.

The sensation of being struck by lightning hits me in the core, forcing out a shriek that makes my ears ring. My second orgasm is so powerful that I convulse against his chest.

Roman's powerful arm holds me in place, and his hips drive into me with deep, forceful thrusts. "That's it, slut" he rumbles. "Squeeze that cock. Make me fill your tight little cunt with my cum."

As he continues filling my ears with filthy words of encouragement, I turn my head to make eye contact, but he grips my neck and forces my gaze back to the headboard.

He slams into me one last time before my ears fill with his guttural roar as his cock pulses once, twice, three times before hot fluid fills my core. I spasm around his shaft, my inner muscles pumping him dry.

We both tumble to the mattress, landing on its soft surface with a bounce. Roman is still inside me as we spoon, his arm draped around my waist, keeping me cuddled to his chest.

"You were so hot, baby," he murmurs in my ear. "Exactly what I needed."

"Mmmmm." My eyelids flutter shut.

"I could fuck you every moment until you expire."

There's nothing I can say to a statement like that because I don't plan on sticking around for any kind of long-term, or even short-term, relationship. As soon as I catch my breath and get some feeling back into my muscles, I'm going to ask him for my clothes and for a ride back into Beaumont City.

Roman nuzzles his face into the crook of my neck and doesn't say anything else. The warmth of his body and the rhythm of his breaths lull me into a deep state of relaxation that makes me melt.

Right now, I'm safe from my legal troubles and Jim. After snoozing, I'll come up with a solution to keep me out of his clutches.

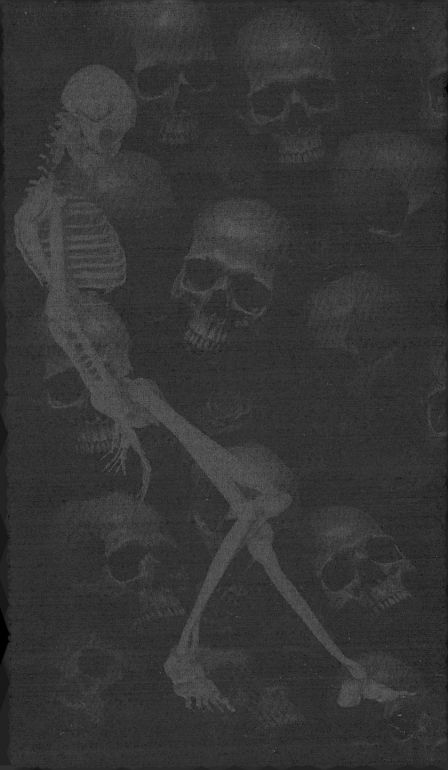

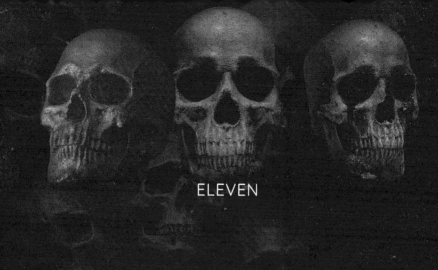

ELEVEN

ROMAN

Moonlight streams through the window, casting the room in silver light. I lie on my side with my face buried in a mane of unruly curls, inhaling the mingled scents of caramel, vanilla, and cinnamon. I want to bury my cock in that tight heat once more and never come up for air.

Her peachy ass nestles against my groin, eliciting renewed stirrings of arousal. Now that I've tasted Emberly Kay, I want more.

But I can't.

Her delicate breaths fill my ears, and the warmth of her body seeps into my skin. The triumph I felt earlier at having lured her into the tower fades, tempered by something bitter.

My first taste of freedom was with Capello's daughter. I could have taken up Officer McMurphy's offer. She clearly wanted to see me in an environment outside the prison. I could have bent one of the female bar staff over the table to bust my first out-of-jail nut.

Hell, any of the women I used to bang would have been a better choice.

Now, the memory of this woman will be ingrained in my psyche until the day I die.

Fucking Emberly was like inhaling clean air after spending half a decade breathing the stench of confinement. I need to get the hell out and replace her with someone else before I become addicted.

When I was encased in that sweet cunt, I forgot she was the daughter of the man I didn't get the chance to eviscerate. I was powerful, happy, free. And she was a beautiful woman who took everything I gave her and demanded more.

It took everything I had to remember my goal, but nothing has ever felt so damn good.

Even spooning her and inhaling her sweet cinnamon scent feels like getting decades of birthday and Christmas gifts I never knew I needed.

I need to leave. Now.

Once her breathing evens, I slide out from behind her and ease off the mattress. She mumbles something and I still, waiting to see if she'll open her eyes. I shake off that thought. It doesn't matter. I have her exactly where I want.

Emberly Kay will never leave this room alive.

After tucking myself back into my pants and slipping on my shirt, I pick up my jacket off the marble tiles and walk to the door.

Benito stands at the top of the stairwell with his gaze fixed on the screen of his phone. His head snaps up to give me a disapproving glare.

"Did you have to fuck her?" he asks.

"Shhh!" I ease the door shut and turn the key. "She's sleeping."

With a scowl, my brother slips the phone into his pocket. "What are you doing?"

I walk past him down the stairs. "You should be happy I didn't abduct her as planned."

"But the sex?"

"What difference does it make?"

"She's the same age as Cesare," he says.

"What's wrong with a ten-year age difference?" I ask. "Women mature faster than men."

He sighs. "And they're unpredictable enough without them getting emotionally involved. When she realizes you used sex to lure her into her new prison, she'll become less terrified and more belligerent."

I open the door and walk down the hallway, passing Great-grandfather Paolo's portrait. He's grinning in a white fedora with a lit cigar between his teeth. Back in the twenties, he was the coolest, meanest motherfucker who owned the entire state of New Alderney.

"Roman?" Benito prods, bringing my attention back to his complaint.

"Then we'll forge her signature." I turn toward my old bedroom.

"That won't work."

"Why not?"

"Without her fingerprints all over the document, no one will believe she signed over hundreds of millions of dollars' worth of assets."

I want to tell him to relax, but he adds, "Tommy Galliano is next in line for Capello's estate. In his place, I'd contest those documents and prove to a judge that she'd been tortured. I'd even have the papers checked for minute traces of blood."

My jaw clenches. Benito is a pain in the ass, but I can't fault his logic. It's one thing to abduct a woman and intimidate her into compliance. Quite another to fuck two orgasms into her and stab her in the back. Emberly Kay might refuse to sign those contracts out of spite.

Sofia emerges from the top of the stairs and gestures toward the master suite. "I freshened up your room."

My steps pause. "But it's Dad's."

Not anymore. Dad died with a mystery woman who wasn't my mother. The same week I was framed for a crime I didn't commit, she abandoned my little brothers to shack up with Tommy Galliano.

"You've been the head of the family for years," Benito says.

I turn to meet my brother's eyes. He nods and smiles for me to continue.

Sofia opens the door and steps aside. "It's time you took your rightful place."

The heavy burden that's been crushing my chest for half a decade finally lifts, leaving my heart swelling with a mix of gratitude, relief, and joy.

Exhaling all my tension in an outward breath, I let all thoughts of Emberly Kay fade into insignificance. What's more important now is that I'm no longer running the Montesano empire from a prison cell.

I'm home and on the cusp of restoring everything that was taken from us.

"Yeah," I say, my voice choked. "It's time."

"Is there anything you'd like for breakfast?" Sofia asks.

I nod. "Crostata, but instead of the usual filling, I want apples, vanilla, and cinnamon."

Sofia hesitates for a moment before saying, "Of course, sir. Good night."

"And it's Roman."

She finally cracks a smile and leaves with Benito.

They've decorated Mom and Dad's room with similar neutral colors to Emberly's new prison. It's four times the size, with a bed fit for a king. The iron headboard curls and fans in the pattern of peacock feathers ending with oval swirls dipped in gold.

I chuckle. This has to have been Cesare's idea. He and I both know the importance of having somewhere to tether a woman. I try not to imagine Emberly cuffed to the metal posts, helpless and whimpering as I pound her into submission, but my cock lengthens, wanting us to run back upstairs for another round of fucking.

Shit.

I run my fingers through my hair. That thing I had with her upstairs was a one-off. It was a distraction to get her through the gates without alerting the police. That's all.

After tonight, I never need to lay eyes on the woman. Benito can deal with her since he's the most level-headed. Cesare and I can handle the bastards who defected to Capello, as well as the assholes he installed into Dad's legitimate businesses.

I undress, shower off her sweet scent, and slide into bed, thinking about all the work I need to do to restore the family empire. All traces of the band of tension residing around my heart are gone, replaced with something new.

Hope.

Hope for the future. Hope for the Montesano legacy. Hope to finally put things right.

After Emberly signs those contracts and I've regained control of our stolen assets, I'll find a suitable woman. One with bright eyes, dark curls, and a body that drives me wild. I'll reach out to another prominent family, see if they have any daughters, and make a strong alliance.

I breathe easy for once and fall into the best sleep of my life. The only thing that's missing is a woman.

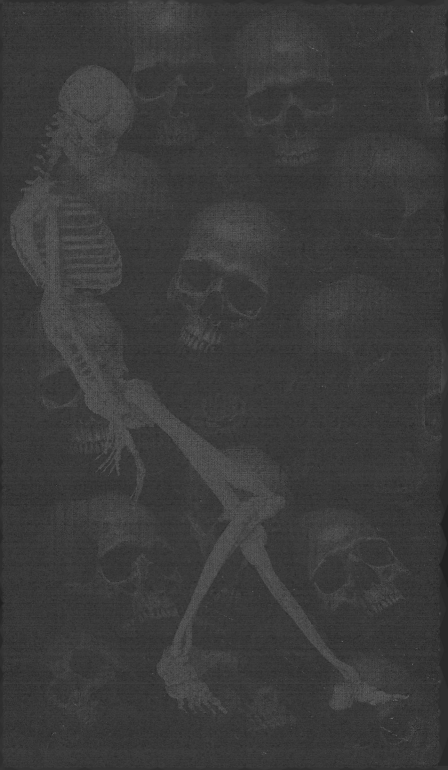

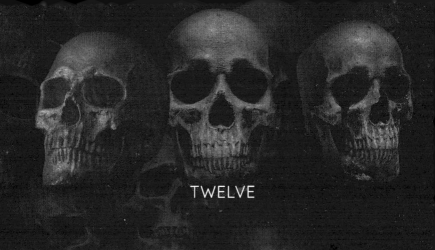

TWELVE

EMBERLY

Jim's fingers close around my neck as he thrusts into me over and over, repeating the same string of words. I deserve this punishment. I'm talentless. Worthless. Ungrateful. Nobody will ever love me but him.

I can't move, can't breathe, can't do anything but stare at my reflection in his cold blue eyes.

It's just a dream. It's just a dream. I need to wake the fuck up.

Jim isn't really here trying to choke me to death. I'm just in sleep paralysis.

My brain left REM sleep before my body, leaving me trapped in a nightmarish hallucination. This vision of Jim is only my bogeyman, and the person reflected in his eyes is the part of me I resent for not leaving sooner.

Slowing my breathing, I focus every ounce of concentration on moving my pinky finger. It's futile.

Jim squeezes harder, trying to cut off my air.

My heart accelerates.

This. Is. Not. Real.

I repeat those words over and over, trying to remain calm, even though a part of me believes I've found my way back into his clutches. When the woman reflected in his pupils shrieks, my body jerks awake.

My head pounds, and sunlight streams through my closed eyelids. The membranes of my throat scratch and burn, as though I've spent the entire night trying to scream through being choked.

I must have been sleeping for hours, because the warmth of Roman's chest against my back is gone. Shudders run down my spine, and I exhale a shaky breath.

No matter what Jim said last night, I won't let him drag me back to his house.

No man will ever make me their captive.

I open an eye and wince against the bright light. Through blurry vision, I glance across the white bedroom to an empty balcony and then to an open door that leads to an unoccupied bathroom. At some point last night, he must have retired to his bedroom.

I tell myself this is probably for the best as I heave my legs out of bed. If Roman gave me another round of sex, I might never want to leave, and that would be disastrous.

I shuffle over to a door that leads to a walk-in closet lined with empty rails devoid of clothes. Vague recollections from last night filter through my brain fog. I was so drunk that I left my dress in the back of Roman's limousine.

Shit. How much did I fucking drink?

Turning a full circle, I survey the room. I'm still partially drunk and in a stupor, but there's no sign of his jacket. Maybe I can fashion a toga out of the bedsheets and wander around until I can find someone to help.

When I try the door that leads to the staircase, it's locked.

No.

Fucking.

Way.

I can't be locked in the bedroom of a man who just slithered out of prison, off death row, no less. My fingers tighten around the doorknob. I rest my head against its wooden surface and force my breaths to slow.

Now is not the time to panic.

Maybe there's a trick to opening this door. Some handles need to be pulled counterclockwise, and others require a little jiggling. I need to try every single door-opening technique before jumping to conclusions.

I turn it to the left, and it doesn't budge, then to the right and still nothing. I try pulling it, shaking it, and even pressing down. But. It. Won't. Budge.

My jaw clenches, and the pulse between my ears pounds hard enough to drown out the desperate roar of blood. This can't be happening. I can't have walked into another man's snare.

I'm naked.

Trapped.

In a mafia mansion.

By a man tried and convicted for murder.

"Roman?" I rasp.

There's no answer.

Of course, there isn't. He's probably on the other side of the building, doing something illegal.

"ROMAN!" I yell, my heart already pounding against my ribcage.

I wait for a cruel voice to tell me I'm a prisoner, the way captors do when they taunt their victims in psychological thrillers, but the only sound in the room is my own heavy breathing.

"Somebody help me," I scream, already knowing it will be futile.

Everyone in this mansion is either an employee of Roman Montesano or one of his equally dangerous brothers. Over a dozen people saw him carrying me out of the limousine like a hunting trophy, and none of them said a word.

They even fucking applauded, congratulating him for getting away with being a scoundrel. These people have probably covered up hundreds of murders.

Dread plummets in the pit of my stomach like an anchor, trying to drag me into the depths of panic. I pound on the door to the beat of my frantic heart, forcing in breath after breath after breath.

I can't afford to lose my shit.

A year of living as Jim's captive has shredded my nerves. I'm left with PTSD, paranoia, and the mere thought of being confined again makes me heave.

My therapist at the women's shelter says I'm suffering from cleithrophobia. I'm not scared of tight spaces, only terrified of being trapped.

"HELP!"

Sweat breaks out across my brow, and my gaze darts from side to side. What am I doing? No one's coming to my rescue. I'm a fucking prisoner. This is exactly what happened with Jim, but accelerated.

No amount of crying and screaming will set me free. The last time, I swore to myself never to end up in another abusive situation. I'm no longer that deluded young woman who gives men the benefit of the doubt. I can think clearly, strategize, and act.

Backing away from the door, I glance around the room for items to help me escape. There's a huge bed, a matching dresser, a pair of bedside tables, each holding a heavy-looking lamp. Directly opposite the door is a floor-to-ceiling set of glass doors that lead to a balcony.

My heart skips a beat. I dash across the room to the

French doors, but they're locked. One quick search around its frame says that there's no other way of opening it without a key.

Fuck these mafia bastards. What do they want from me, anyway? I'm a nobody. My debts aren't even substantial enough to attract the attention of a bailiff, let alone a big player like Roman Montesano.

Unless he's a sex trafficker.

My stomach, along with the anchor lodged inside it, drops to the marble floor and yanks down my heart. How could I have been so stupid as to ignore my intuition?

Shit.

If I don't find a way out, my future could be a hundred times worse than death.

I spin around, wondering how the fuck I got myself into such a terrible mess. I've lost my clothes, my phone, my purse, my keys. My hope.

Shallow breaths ghost over the tops of my lungs, and the room tilts at an awkward angle. Fuck. What is this, vertigo?

If I ever get out of this, I will never again drink wine coolers, shots, or champagne. Those free drinks clouded my judgment. They made me think that running off with a mafia boss was a better option than the devil I knew.

Shivers run down my spine, and every inch of my skin erupts into goosebumps.

Jim all but said he was going to kill me for leaving, and I know he meant every word. God knows what would have happened to me in that cell. He gave me no choice but to run off with a man powerful enough to stand up to him. But now I could be facing months if not years of forced prostitution.

I didn't escape an abusive boyfriend to end up enslaved by a crime lord.

I can't let this happen.

My gaze falls to the dresser. I yank open each drawer, but they're empty. I rush into a white-tiled bathroom, only to find nothing more useful than the toilet brush.

I turn back toward the bedside table and hone in on the heavy-looking lamp. Its base is a curved marble but could also be ceramic. When I pick it up, it's cold and solid and heavy.

Perfect.

I unplug it, grab the sheet off the bed, and tie it around the lamp to create a makeshift weapon. There's a tree within jumping distance of the balcony. If I can get close enough, I can use it to climb down to the ground.

My chest loosens, and I take a deep breath. I will not allow the mafia to turn me into a sex slave.

I will break free or die trying.

Adrenaline courses through my veins and powers my steps. I rush to the balcony doors with the lamp hanging from the sheet that I've fashioned into a sling. I glare at the fourth pane of glass on the bottom right.

I swing, and the heavy marble strikes the windowpane, forming a spider-web of cracks. I swing again and again and again until the glass shatters.

Shards fall away, letting in a gust of juniper-scented air. I loosen the sheet, and the lamp drops to the floor with a heavy thud. After laying the large swathe of cotton over the glass, I get on my hands and knees and crawl out onto the balcony.

My heart pounds so hard its reverberations reach my fingertips. Now that I'm outside, the tree doesn't look as close, but the balcony's ledge is thick enough for me to balance on to attempt a running leap.

I take a deep breath and force myself up to stand, but all the blood rushes south, making me light-headed, and I'm forced to brace my arms on my knees.

What am I more afraid of, getting trapped, getting trafficked, or breaking my neck? My brain comes up with another alternative: breaking all my bones and getting trafficked anyway.

Fucking hell.

My mind's eye fills with a younger version of myself running around Jim's house, checking doors, windows, and screaming in a choking panic. I shake my head to dislodge the memory, but it only becomes more visceral, more vivid.

I double over and hyperventilate, trying to expel the terror.

"Stop this," I say through clenched teeth. "I'm no longer trapped. I'm free."

I huff out a furious breath and straighten, powered by a surge of resentment. Resentment at Jim for being an abusive narcissist, resentment at Mom for not paying for daycare and locking a four-year-old in a studio and for sowing the seeds of my phobia, and resentment at myself for letting myself get lured into this mess.

I snatch up the sheet and a large shard of glass, then slice and tear the cotton into multiple strips. One to create a bra top and another to make a loincloth.

The last thing I want while escaping a mafia stronghold is to be naked.

Male laughter rises from the gardens. I peer over the edge of the balcony to find a trio of men staring up at me with broad grins.

One of them waves, while the other cups his hands under his chest to mimic boobs, and the third whistles.

I stagger back, slicing my foot on a pane of glass. So much for my plan to sneak out.

"Damn it!"

Ignoring the pain and the catcalling from below, I wrap the strips of fabric around my crotch and then my chest.

Even if these assholes have spotted me, I have to keep moving.

Just as I'm about to cut another piece to wrap around my injured foot, the bedroom door flies open with a loud bang.

I whirl around to find a large man standing in the doorway. He's muscular but not as jacked as Roman, dressed in a tailored suit, and wearing a pair of glasses.

He looks so similar to Roman that this must be one of his brothers. I'm pretty sure he was at the club last night, but I wasn't exactly looking at him.

The man strides in, his features hardening. "What do you think you're doing?"

I back toward the balcony's edge, my heart hurtling itself against my ribs. In a minute, he'll knock me out and I'll wake up in a grimy brothel, already addicted to a cocktail of drugs.

Escape or die trying.

I scramble up the balcony's stone railing and balance on its ledge, clutching the glass so tightly that my fingers become slick with blood.

"Come any closer," I scream, "And I'll fucking jump!"

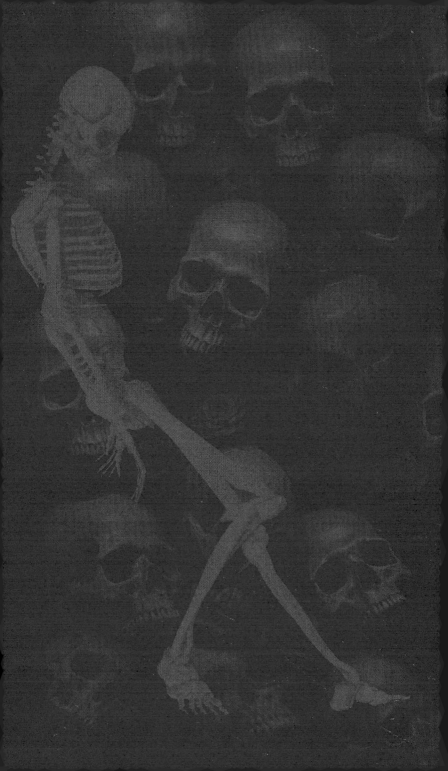

THIRTEEN

ROMAN

Hours later, I drift back into awareness. My mind is mostly alert before the wake-up call, but it never sounds. My body floats on a bed of clouds more comfortable than the mattress Officer McMurphy snuck into my cell. It takes me a moment to remember that I'm no longer in prison, and I fall back into a light sleep.

Instead of dreams, my mind dredges up the recent memory of pounding into Emberly Kay. Only we're not on a bed, we're fucking through the night sky. I'm riding her through golden stars toward the moon in a spray of peacock feathers. She bucks against me, her sweet pussy squeezing the life out of my cock.

A trio of heavy knocks jerk me awake.

I sit bolt upright, my heart pounding. "Who's there?"

The door swings open and Benito steps in, his face flushed.

"What is it?" I ask.

"There's three squad cars outside the gates and a detective with a warrant out for the arrest of Emberly Kay."

I run my fingers through my hair. "Tell them she isn't here."

His nostrils flare. "That's going to be difficult, seeing as she's just smashed her way through the balcony door and is standing on the rail."

My jaw drops. "What?"

It takes me a heartbeat to remember that the tower is around the back and out of sight from the gates.

"She's screaming at the top of her lungs, bleeding DNA everywhere, and threatening to jump."

In the blink of an eye, my mind goes from half asleep to fully alert. The thought of hundreds of millions of dollars jumping off the balcony is the punch in the balls I need to launch myself across the room and grab my little brother by the lapels.

"What do you mean, she's threatening to jump?" I growl.

Benito grips my fists and scowls. "Exactly what I said. You left her naked and unshackled. Now, she's made a shank out of a pane of glass and has wrapped herself up like a mummy."

"Where is she?"

"Still on the ledge where I left her." Benito shoves me back with a surprising amount of strength.

There's no time to be impressed by his newfound fighting prowess. I need to get to Emberly before she does something stupid, like kill herself before signing over her inheritance.

I race down the hallway, passing a shrieking Sofia, who presses herself against the wall. As I round the corner to enter the tower door, I catch a glimpse of Benito jogging after me, holding a doctor's bag.

It takes mere seconds to reach the top of the stairs, yet I'm already sweating by the time I turn the key in the door.

I burst through the room to find Emberly balancing on the ledge, wearing a pair of torn sheets like a bikini. Blood pours from the hand holding a knife-sized shard of glass. Her curls stand up at all angles, reminding me of a modern-day Medusa. When she glares at me over her shoulder and snarls, my hopes of reasoning with her turn to stone.

"Stay the fuck back or I'll jump!" she shrieks.

I raise both palms in surrender, trying to appear non-threatening.

Her wild eyes rove over the tattoos on my chest, and she gulps.

"Emberly, what's this about?"

"What's this about?" She asks with a hysterical giggle. "You're the one who locked me in a room. You tell me."

My jaw clenches. "I didn't—"

"Don't deny it," she yells.

"Hear me out," I growl. "The door must have locked itself when I went downstairs to make us breakfast."

"Liar!" she screeches, her voice shrill.

What's wrong with this chick? A line like that would have worked before I got locked up, or at least earned me the benefit of the doubt.

I soften my voice and pull my brows into a confused frown. "Emberly, why would I lock you in a room when you gave me the best night of my life?"

"Bullshit."

The second part of what I said was the truth, even though she's right that I have a valid reason to keep her confined. Holding back a growl of frustration, I step forward.

"S-Stay away." She brandishes her shank like a short sword.

"I know you're upset, but I'm not bullshitting. I have no

reason to imprison you in my family home in front of witnesses."

She stares at me, her chest rising and falling with rapid breaths, accentuating her hardened nipples straining against the sheet.

My cock twitches. Emberly Kay might be batshit crazy, but she's fucking hot.

"Take a look into the garden," I say. "By now, my men will be standing below the balcony, ready to catch you before you fall. Someone has already called for a tarp. Jumping won't solve a thing, but if you step off that ledge, I'll take you out for a nice brunch."

Her eyes narrow and she gives me a side-long stare. Maybe she's considering my offer.

I take another step toward her, but she screams, "Get back!"

The door behind me creaks open, and Benito steps in. My hackles rise. My little brother says nothing, but last night's warning rings in my ears about sex making Emberly uncooperative.

What do they say about the fury of a scorned woman? They're a pain in the fucking ass. If platitudes don't work on this insane bitch, then maybe she'll listen to a threat. I know just how to make myself look like the better option than escaping, and it's all thanks to her ex-boyfriend, the cop.

"Benito, tell her what you said when you interrupted me in the kitchen while I was making Emberly's coffee."

My brother clears his throat. "That the police are at the gates."

"What do they want?" she asks, her voice trembling.

"Is your name Emberly Kay?" Benito drawls. "If so, there's four squad cars and a warrant for your arrest."

She lets out a strangled cry. I'm compelled to wrap my hands around her delicate neck and squeeze until she spits out my stolen wealth. I shelve that thought for after I've talked her off the ledge.

"You're lying," she says.

Still keeping my eyes fixed on Emberly, I turn my head to where Benito stands at the door. "There's only one way to find out. Benito, you have my permission to let the police through the gates. Let one of them deal with her."

"No!" she shrieks.

I turn back to her with my brow raised. "Who do you think will get blamed if you jump? Those bastards are itching to shove me back into death row."

She swallows, her eyes wide.

The morning sun shines through her dark curls, coloring their ends a beautiful shade of amber. I don't think I fully appreciated the extent of her beauty until now. It's almost tragic that it's wasted on someone I'll have to kill, but I can't stop staring.

"Put down the shank," I say in the tone of voice I'd use to coax a frightened kitten.

The glass drops from her fingers and lands on the balcony floor in several bloody pieces.

My chest swells with triumph, and I already imagine my brothers and myself shooting down the casino lights and replacing them with the Montesano name.

"Good girl." I take several steps forward and meet her huge green eyes with a nod and a smile. "Now, step off the ledge so I can take care of you."

She shakes her head, her lips trembling.

"What's wrong, sweetheart?" I ask, my voice softening.

"I don't want to be trafficked."

My gaze snaps to Benito, who offers another shrug. Of all the reasons I imagined for her little stunt, this was the last. I still can't muster up an explanation for this freak out apart from women's intuition or Capello insanity.

"Who told you I was a trafficker?"

Her shoulders rise into her curls. "When I woke up, and the door was locked…"

I wait for her to complete her thought, but she lowers her head.

"Baby, that's not how it works, and the Montesano family doesn't deal in that kind of filth."

Especially since we lost all the strip clubs when Vincent tricked Dad into signing over the real estate to Capello, but I digress.

My palm lands on my chest, and I take another step forward. "I'm not a monster. I'm just a man who wanted to show his appreciation for the best night of his life. The reason I took so long was because I wanted to make breakfast myself to prove that you were more than just a one-night stand."

She looks down at me from the ledge, her eyes flickering with hope. "I don't believe you."

"You don't have to." I take another step toward the balcony door.

Benito tosses a pair of flip-flops at my feet.

I give him a nod of thanks and slip them on while sliding the key into the lock. "Come down off the balcony railing."

The balcony door swings open, and I step over the broken glass.

Emberly skitters backward down the balcony ledge, leaving bloody footprints before pausing at the corner with her arms outstretched like a tightrope walker.

My heart sinks. Obviously, my sweet talking only worked from a distance.

The men below laugh and shout and whistle. I make a mental note to deal with those assholes later. Right now, I need to focus on the key to securing our legacy.

"Emberly," I growl.

"Roman," Benito whispers a warning.

I shake my head. Coaxing her won't work. Neither will appealing to her reason, because I must have fucked her senseless. This madwoman has made up her mind that I've brought her here to be trafficked.

"I'll give you a count of five," I say, my voice threatening and low. "If you don't get off that ledge, I will spank your pussy until it cries for mercy. After that, I'll bend you over this railing and fuck you into submission."

Her cheeks turn red, and her breathing quickens. "Then you'll hand me over to one of your pimps?"

"I already told you that the Montesano family doesn't sell women. One."

She shoots out her arms. "Stay back."

I take another step toward her. "Two. At the rate you're bleeding, you'll get light-headed, slip on that blood, and break your neck. Three."

Emberly's eyes widen. "Wait!"

This has gone far enough. I refuse to fall for her bullshit. "You need first aid. Four."

"Do you swear you won't let anyone else touch me?"

"On my life," I say, meaning every word because I plan to keep her perfectly safe... At least until she's signed over the assets.

When the time comes, it will be me who puts the bullet through her pretty head.

"Alright." Emberly glances down at the glass strewn across the concrete floor.

I scoop her into my arms, my knees wanting to buckle with relief. Burying my head in her wild curls, I inhale her cinnamon and vanilla scent. "You're safe with me," I murmur. "Now, let me heal those cuts."

As I carry her into the bedroom, Benito appears at my

side and injects her with a needle. Emberly doesn't flinch, but her eyes are already heavy-lidded.

"What did you do?" I growl.

With a shrug, Benito tosses the syringe back into his doctor's bag. "It's the thinnest gauge needle. She won't have felt a thing."

"What did you give her?"

"Ketamine." He glances up at me, his glasses catching the light. "It will keep her out of trouble while you deal with the army of angry cops."

Fuck.

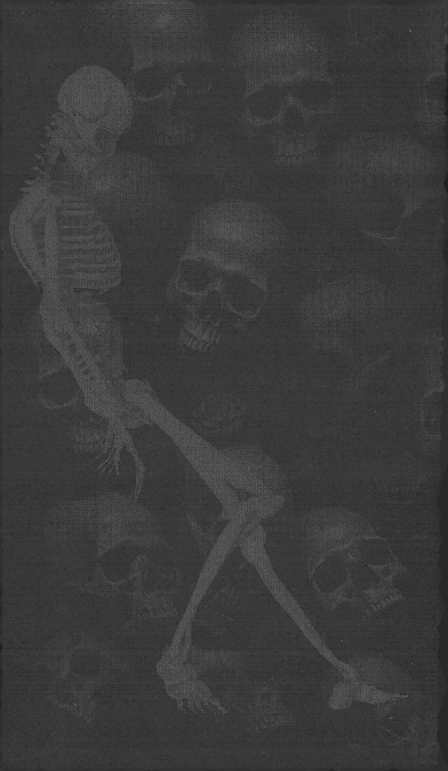

FOURTEEN

ROMAN

I'm already beginning to miss the simplicity of prison, when all my surprises would arrive after Officer McMurphy served breakfast on her knees with a blow job. Back then, I would eat Sofia's morning meal delivery at my leisure before reading through documents and listening to voicemails.

Emberly's head lolls back, her body limp from the effects of the drug. Warm blood seeps from the cut on her hand to my chest, eliciting a wave of possessiveness.

She doesn't have the right to slice open her palm. If anyone is going to make her bleed, it will be me.

"Ready?" Benito asks.

With a grunt, I adjust my grip on the unconscious woman. "Get me a robe while I put her downstairs, where she can't do anything stupid."

Benito disappears out of the door with his doctor's bag, leaving me wondering what part of law school made him so adept with drug dosages. Maybe he learned about it from Cesare?

Cradling Emberly to my chest, I descend the stairs after

him at a more leisurely pace and study her features. She's exquisite when she's not accusing me of being a trafficker, but I'm not fooled. Running through those veins is the blood of a Capello. It wouldn't surprise me if she'd stolen a fortune's worth of artwork from that gallery.

When I reach the ground floor, Sofia is already waiting by the door of a guest room with a stack of towels. Instead of her usual black dress and white collar, she wears a fitted tunic and a pair of pants.

So much has changed since I was gone.

Sofia takes one look at Emberly's sleeping face and meets my gaze. "How long will she be out?"

"Long enough for me to deal with the cops at the gate," I reply, my voice gruff.

"Will she be needing meals for the week?" There's a note in the housekeeper's voice that suggests she's asking how long I plan on keeping Emberly alive.

"Yeah." I open the door and step into a guest suite decorated in the same pale colors as the tower bedroom and lay her on the bed.

With the same efficiency she used to deal with our messes when we were young, Sofia shoves towels beneath Emberly's bleeding hand and foot.

My jaw tightens at the sight of her wounds when I remember what my brother said about leaving traces of blood on the contracts. Emberly won't be an easy prisoner.

Benito arrives moments later, still carrying that leather bag along with a purple velour bathrobe with black silk lapels.

I snort. "What am I, Hugh Hefner?"

He bristles. "While I'm coordinating a team of armed men to rescue your meth lab, you and Cesare are wasting time with unsuitable women."

My brows rise. Once again, Benito has a point.

"The cops want to search the house for her. If you walk out there with blood smeared over your chest, you'll give them probable cause."

I shrug on the robe and fasten it around the waist, while Sofia wipes my exposed skin with a cloth.

"See what you can do about those cuts," I mutter and pat Sofia on the shoulder. "We're going to need a week's worth of clothes for our guest."

Benito whirls around. "You're keeping her alive that long?"

"Maybe. Nothing about this woman is predictable."

After checking my pajama bottoms and feet for any tell-tale signs of blood, I leave Benito and Sofia tending to Emberly.

Walking through the mansion's hallways is like a trip through the past. Very little about the decor has changed since before my arrest, yet the person I am is drastically different.

What I once thought was a grandiose museum is steeped in our family history. Each Montesano patriarch has made his mark. For example, Dad was the one who reduced the fortune his forefathers built up over generations and I'll be the one who gets it back.

Staff members greet me as I pass, including the guards at the door. They've worked for the family for decades, but the comfort and ease from the old days is gone.

Capello was once Dad's most trusted friend. We used to call him Uncle Freddy. Benito was even best friends with his twin sons. If Emberly had known her father, she might have been a companion for Cesare, since they're both twenty-four.

That Capello motherfucker sat at our table, ate our food, and drank our wine. He was one of the family, yet he and several others drove knives through all our backs.

How many of the people are also waiting for their moment to strike?

I take my time walking down the outdoor steps, inhaling the familiar scents of juniper and freshly cut grass. Danillo, the head gardener, straightens from pruning one of the many shrubs that border the front entrance and welcomes me back home.

With a nod, I move past him and toward the black sedan parked in the courtyard. Gil leans across the driver's seat and opens the passenger side door.

I slide into the seat beside him. "Where's Cesare?"

"With some woman he brought back from the Phoenix," he replies, his voice flat.

"Who?"

"Rosalind. Your cousin Leroi's crazy ex. He took her to his playroom."

My shoulders stiffen. Playroom? I have enough to handle with the cops on my back.

It would take a good ten minutes to reach the front gates on foot, or half as long if I cut through the trees, so Gil drives me through the grounds, passing the gardens. The morning sun glints off the surface of the pond, giving me a stark contrast from prison. As we round a bend, I catch the first glimpses of the cops beyond a barricade of our vehicles at the front gates.

"There's too many men out front," I say. "Move some of them around the estate's perimeter. I don't want any of those bastards sneaking in through the fences."

Gil grunts. "Are you coming today?"

"Where?"

"To the address you waterboarded out of Ricky Ferraro."

My lip curls at the memory of our former informant who sold out the location of our meth lab. "Let Benito get started without me."

Gil nods, then pauses to give me a wary glance.

"What?" I ask.

"What's so special about that broad?" Gil asks.

"Apparently, she's a petty art thief," I mutter.

Emberly Kay's connection to the Capello estate is on a need-to-know basis. The woman is unpredictable enough without someone revealing the truth that she's an heiress to a fortune and the spawn of my sworn enemy.

I blow out a breath. Most women in her situation would give up or try to wheedle their way out of being imprisoned, but Emberly perched on the balcony like she was walking a tightrope.

She's nothing like I expected, and a grudging part of me even admires her spunk.

"Get out your phone and record our conversation." I say, my adrenaline surging in anticipation of a challenge.

Gil parks behind the other cars, and we step out. As I walk past the procession, the men around the barricade offer more greetings. I take a deep breath and shove down my excitement. The cops don't know for certain that I'm imprisoning Emberly.

Hell, even Emberly is confused about my intentions. I meant every word when I said she wasn't being trafficked. It's not her body I want. It's her fortune.

That pasty asshole from the nightclub stands beyond the iron gates, holding a bullhorn. He's run his fingers through his red hair so many times that it lies on his head like a filthy mop. The black suit he wears does nothing to hide that he's a sore loser who can't stand the thought that his ex-girlfriend chose me instead of him.

There's three cop cars and a black sedan parked behind him with their occupants marching toward the gates like they're ready to storm a castle.

"Good morning, officer," I drawl, my voice laced with sarcasm. "To what do I owe the displeasure?"

The man's face tightens. "We have a warrant for the arrest of Emberly Kay. We need to search the premises."

"And you are?"

"Detective Jim Callahan from the Beaumont City PD," he says. "We know you have Emberly Kay."

I cock my head to the side. "Emberly who?"

"Don't play games with me, Mr. Montesano. I saw you with Emberly last night at the Phoenix."

"Which one was she?" I ask. "I entertained a lot of young ladies last night and lost track of all their names."

My men snicker. A few more of them pull out their phones to record Emberly's ex, whose face has turned a sickly shade of red.

Callahan clenches his teeth. "Witnesses saw you take her through the club's back exit. Shortly after, your limousine left the premises and drove here."

I glance at Gil and then toward the others who are still recording. "Are you following my staff? Because that's harassment. The state of New Alderney already owes me millions in compensation for my false imprisonment."

He's about to retort, when I add, "Do you even have a search warrant?"

He pales, his gaze darting from side to side.

"That's what I thought," I reply with a sneer. "I'll forward this footage to my lawyer and add it, along with your confession, to the growing pile of evidence against your department."

A muscle in his jaw flexes, and he looks like he wants to say something, but he's smart enough to keep his mouth shut. The officers surrounding him shift uncomfortably, most likely wondering why the fuck they followed this clown to my gates.

"Kindly leave before I call 9 1 1," I say.

Callahan shoots me a glare before turning on his heel and walking back to his vehicle with a stick up his ass. I curl my lip. This bastard wanted to molest Emberly in a cell.

I turn to Gil. "Find out everything you can about this guy."

"Sure thing, boss," Gil says.

I wait for the cops to reverse down the hill before letting Gil drive me back to the mansion, where I find Benito leaving the room I left Emberly in, carrying vials of blood.

"What's this?" I raise my brows.

"The woman at the Di Marco Law Group wants a DNA test," he replies.

"You couldn't take a swab from her mouth?"

He smirks. "It's probably filled with Montesano DNA."

A laugh bursts from my chest. "You're an asshole."

"Am I wrong?"

Shaking my head, I enter the guest room, not wanting to confirm or deny Benito's statement. Emberly lies on the bed wearing a fluffy white robe with bandages on her hand and foot.

I sit on the edge of the mattress and twine my fingers through her curls. "Are you awake, sweetheart?"

Her eyelids flutter open, and she groans. "What happened?"

"You fainted. I brought you downstairs and tended to your wounds."

She squeezes her eyes shut. "My head hurts."

"A hangover," I reply with a fond smile. "The alcohol must have finally worn off."

"But I was mostly sober this morning when I woke up."

"Jim Callahan was at the gates with a warrant for your arrest," I say as a distraction. "I drove him back, but it looks like he wants to return with a court order to search the house."

She flinches, her eyes flying open. "Oh shit. I've got to get out of here."

I place a hand on her shoulder. "And go where? He's probably staking out your home."

She flops back on the mattress, defeated, exactly where I want her. With the blackmail material we found on Capello's hard drive, no judge would ever approve a search warrant for my house. As long as she stays here, she's completely safe. From Callahan, at least.

"What did you do to earn four cop cars and a small army of officers?" I ask.

She makes a strangled noise. "Nothing."

"Emberly," I say. "Don't forget, you're putting my freedom at risk."

"I upturned a table. That's it." She pauses for so long, I wonder if she's fallen asleep. "But the gallery owner says I stole an antique spoon."

"That's it?" I ask.

"I swear," she rasps.

I stroke her cheek, feeling skin smoother than velvet. "It looks like your ex is desperate to get you under his control."

She nods.

"And he won't stop coming after you until he's got you handcuffed and kneeling at his feet."

She shivers.

My fingers slide down to her jaw, and I study her delicate features. Beneath this veneer is a personality more complicated than I expected. She's passionate, impulsive, and jumps to astute conclusions.

There's a part of her that understands my intentions are nefarious, but she could never guess what I really want. The detectives we hired told us she spent her childhood with a single mother and has no clue about the identity of her real father.

Keeping Emberly will require more than sweet words or locked rooms. She'll do anything to secure her freedom, which I can use as leverage. The best way to handle her is to give her what she wants while emphasizing what she doesn't.

The cop seems to frighten her more than the prospect of staying here, so why not use that to my advantage?

"I know a guy who makes fake IDs so convincing they'll pass any background check," I say. "They'll take a few days to complete, but after that, you could disappear."

She finally raises her head and gazes up at me through tear-streaked eyes. My heart twists with a sick sense of envy. The only man who should make her shudder and cry is me.

"With a new name and credentials, you can finally escape Jim Callahan," I say to press my point.

"I can't afford to pay for forgeries," she whispers.

The corner of my lips lift into a smile. "You're an artist, right?"

She nods, her eyes brimming with hope.

"Make me a portrait for my office, and I'll cover the cost of the ID and even give you twenty-five grand so you can get a new start."

Her lips part. "Are you serious?"

I nod, my chest inflating with triumph. "But you have to stay here until I get the ID."

"Thank you."

Her eyes flutter closed, and she releases a happy sigh. She falls back onto her pillows and drifts back to sleep.

I rise, trying to stop my lips from quirking.

Sleep well, Emberly Kay. The next time you awaken, you won't even realize you're still my prisoner.

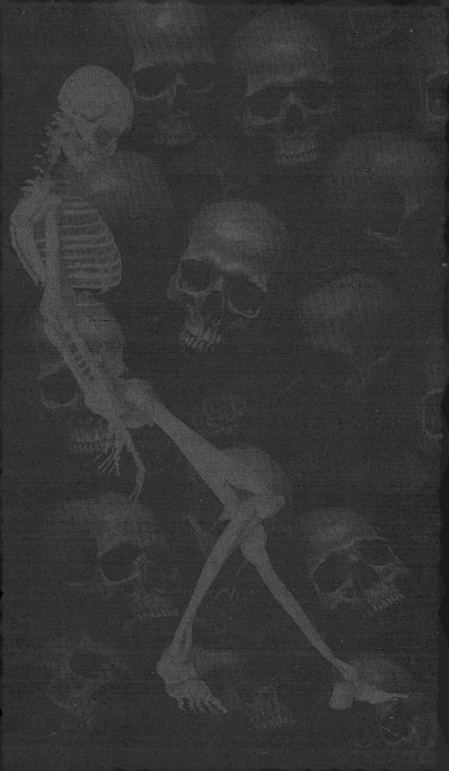

FIFTEEN

EMBERLY

My mind feels like it's been wrapped in cotton wool and my stomach churns like a washing machine. I lie on my back, watching a blurry version of Roman Montesano stroll to the other side of the room and disappear through the door.

When I raise my arm, it's twice as heavy as usual, so I let it flop to the mattress. What the hell was in those drinks? Last night, I was buzzed. Now, I'm completely numb.

I make a mental note never to mix my booze again, even if they're free. My eyes close, and I drift back to sleep.

A sharp knock on the door jolts me awake. I crack open an eye to find a curvaceous woman in the black-and-white uniform of a housekeeper striding toward me with a tray.

"Hi," I rasp.

"You're awake," she says, her features unsmiling. "Mr. Montesano wanted to make sure you had something to eat."

I push myself up on my elbows and glance at the covered plates she's left on the bedside table. "What time is it?"

"Two fifteen," she says from halfway across the room.

"Wait."

She pauses and glances at me over my shoulder.

"I left my dress and shoes in Roman's limo. My purse and phone are back at the Phoenix."

Even saying this makes me cringe. Sometimes, I act first and think later, but what I did last night, and this morning, was ridiculous.

Roman Montesano trafficking women through one-night stands? What was I thinking? I don't even want to remember tying strips of cloth around my tits and crotch so I could jump off the balcony like Tarzan. If I continue acting up like this, I'll end up crazy like Mom.

The housekeeper stares down at me like she's waiting for me to make a point. I shift on the mattress, my gaze hardening. "Could you please ask Roman to give me back my stuff?"

She inclines her head and retreats toward the door. "I will speak to Mr. Montesano when he returns."

"When will that be?"

"He's a very busy man," she says. "I expect he has much to do today."

In other words, the master is too important to run my stupid errands. Fair point. He is a mafia boss who just got released from prison, but I can't wait around for my fake ID in a dressing gown.

"Do you have a phone?"

She turns around, her lips tightening. "Mr. Montesano doesn't want you using the landlines in case they're tapped."

"What about a cell phone?"

"You'll have to ask Mr. Montesano."

I bite back my sarcasm. "How about some clothes?"

Her gaze softens, and her lips quirk. "Mr. Montesano asked me to provide you with whatever you need. I'll have something sent over."

Gasping, I hide my surprise. I was seriously expecting her to drop a hint that Roman wanted me to stay naked.

She slips out of the room, letting the door click shut. I wait for the sound of a key turning in the lock, but there's nothing more than the soft sound of retreating footsteps.

What the hell made me think Roman would hook up with a complete stranger and then keep her hostage? He probably only brought me upstairs to have some privacy while we fucked.

The answer is simple. No matter how much my therapist tried to help me overcome my trauma, my history of being held captive, combined with my captivity phobia, keeps making me assume the worst.

I slide off the mattress, pad across the room on bare feet, and test the doorknob. When it opens, I glance out into the hallway to find Sofia speaking to a man the size of a gorilla. He gazes at me over her shoulder and winks.

My heart skips a beat, and I jerk back into the room, recognizing him as one of the men who'd leered up at me while I was freaking out on the balcony.

Shit. I'll never live that down.

I shut the door, walk back to the bed, and pick at an afternoon breakfast of croissants, yogurt, and a fruit salad. After downing the orange juice and coffee, I poke at the waterproof bandages and wonder why the cuts don't sting.

Maybe whoever tended to my wounds used a local anesthetic?

Bizarre.

I enter a marble-tiled bathroom similar to the one upstairs, and treat myself to the longest, most luxurious shower, using Acqua di Parma toiletries that feel and smell like an entire month's living expenses, including groceries. It feels so good that I even enjoy a soak in the tub.

The bath oils combined with the warm water relax my

muscles and dissolve my intrusive thoughts. I lie back and exhale a long sigh. A girl could get used to this level of pampering, but that would mean being attached to the mafia.

I shake my head. Sex with Roman was mind-blowing, but I'm not crazy enough to get involved with a man whose full-time job is organized crime.

Once I've painted Roman's portrait and gotten my hands on that fake ID, I'll leave New Alderney and go somewhere Jim won't ever think of looking.

A knock sounds on the bedroom door. I sit up in the bath and shout, "Hello?"

"It's Sofia," says a female voice, "With clothes and a phone."

By the time I climb out of the bath, slide on a robe, and enter the bedroom, the housekeeper has already gone. Four shopping bags sit on a dresser, along with a smartphone.

My jaw drops. When I asked for clothes, I was expecting her to gather something lying around the mansion, not purchases from a boutique. Roman must have requested these items this morning after I agreed to paint his portrait.

I rifle through the bags, finding lingerie, a leather jacket, fitted pants, pencil skirts, mini dresses, and a selection of either silk or low-cut tops.

There's even three pairs of Prada shoes in my size.

My stomach drops.

Everything has a designer label I recognize from the fashion district. There's Armani, Gucci, Versace, and Valentino. Is this going to be another situation like Gallery Lafayette where he deducts the costs from the price of my paintings and I end up in debt?

I walk to the door and look out into the hallway, only to lock gazes with a pair of men chatting against the walls, who turn their attention to me and straighten.

A shiver runs down my spine, and I retreat.

Roman said I wasn't a prisoner, but why do I feel trapped? I pick up the phone and dial Annalisa's number, but a mechanical voice tells me I need credit to complete the call.

My jaw clenches. What's the point of having a phone that can't make any calls? I try accessing the internet, but the Wi-Fi is password protected.

Paranoia rises to the surface, making my heart pound. Everything so far is adding up to me being held captive, from the men stationed not-quite outside my door, the expensive clothes, to the phone that's as good as a fucking brick.

I shove the device into my pocket, adjust my bathrobe, and walk outside.

Sure enough, the two men stop talking and step closer as though they've been ordered to keep me from escaping.

"What can I do for you, Miss?" asks a giant of a man with cropped black hair and a nose broken in two places.

"Did Roman tell you to keep an eye on me?" I ask.

The man's face morphs into a neutral mask. "Mr. Montesano just wants to make sure you're safe."

I flinch. "Safe from what?"

They exchange glances before the smaller of the pair speaks. He's a wiry man with a pencil mustache. "The boss was worried you might hurt yourself again."

"What do you—"

Realization hits me like a slap and my jaw drops. Do they think I'm suicidal? "Roman can't believe I'm going to do something stupid, can he?"

The large one's shoulders rise to his ears. "I saw you this morning on the balcony. Mr. Montesano just wants to make sure nothing like that happens again."

Heat flares across my cheeks and races down to my chest. "I'm not about to jump from the ground floor."

GIGI STYX

The men's eyes meet again. One of them even rubs the back of his neck before turning vaguely in my direction.

"We're just following orders, Miss," he says, avoiding eye contact.

I grind my teeth, not quite believing this bullshit. There are a dozen ways I could off myself if I was really trying. The housekeeper left me with cutlery and breakable china, I could have swallowed any of the chemicals in the bathroom or fashioned the items in the bedroom into a noose.

Explaining this will only further convince them I'm a danger to myself, so I bite my tongue.

"Can I at least have the Wi-Fi password?" I ask.

The large one narrows his eyes, and it takes every effort not to explode into a temper and punch another dent in his nose.

"Am I a prisoner?" I ask.

He rears back. "No, Miss."

"Then why can't I have the internet?"

He doesn't answer, and I know why. Roman doesn't want me emailing anyone for help. The man has more red flags than a communist parade, starting with the fact that he's a mafia boss.

Alarm bells ring through my ears, warning me to take drastic action. I suck in a deep breath and force down a rise of panic. These men are only doing their job. If I'm going to scream at anyone, it should be Roman.

"Could you call him, please?" I ask from between clenched teeth. They both give me blank looks before I clarify. "Roman Montesano?"

The smaller of the pair pulls out his phone, takes a few steps away and starts dialing, while his larger colleague steps in front of me to block my path.

My lips tighten, and I refrain from rolling my eyes.

Whatever.

Bowing my head, I strain my ears trying to listen to the conversation, but he's mumbling too quietly to make out the words. I can't even tell if he's speaking English.

When eavesdropping doesn't work, I fold my arms across my chest and stare at the ceiling. Am I turning into Mom and thinking someone's out to get me?

Maybe?

My throat tightens.

No.

Jim all but told me he wanted me dead and had the means to cover up my murder. He's never once made an empty threat. Staying here is my only way of avoiding Jim, but who's going to keep me safe from Roman? I wrack my brain, trying to work out what Roman could possibly want, but my mind still returns to the ridiculous idea that I'm being trafficked.

The shorter man clears his throat, interrupting my thoughts. "Miss? Mr. Montesano wants to have a word."

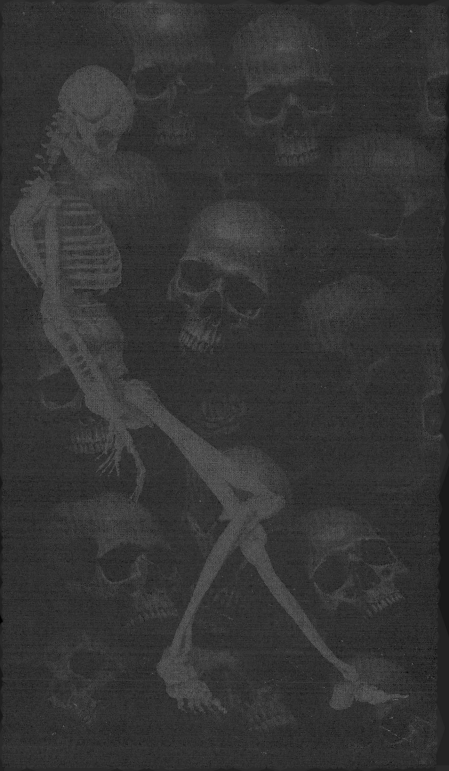

SIXTEEN

ROMAN

By the time Gil and I arrive at the shootout, it's already over. Smoke rises from the center of a complex of abandoned storage units tucked behind a dilapidated warehouse. Two of my men stand guard close to the building's entrance, where a body lies in a pool of blood.

Gil whistles. "Nice place to hide a meth lab."

Thank fuck Cesare dragged that intel from Ricky Ferraro before drowning him with the hose.

Benito steps out of the building, wearing a bullet-proof vest and a scowl. "What took you so long? Someone saw us coming and started shooting."

I haven't been late for anything in five years, yet Emberly Kay is already throwing off my focus. That bullshit needs to stop. Shaking off thoughts of that chaotic woman, I turn to my brother.

"I was making our houseguest more comfortable in her new room."

He leans close to me and whispers, "Same way you made her comfortable last night?"

Snorting, I sling an arm around his shoulder. "Everything is under control. Some women just need a little tender loving gaslighting."

We continue through the building, passing more of my men, and descend a stairwell leading to the underground lab. The first hints of chemicals fill my nose as we descend, and my heart skips several beats.

Our college-level chemists produced the best quality meth on the market with minimal waste, making it our most lucrative business. One night, they disappeared along with all their equipment, leaving behind bloodstains and broken glass, suggesting a violent struggle and a potential abduction.

This is the first of many assets we're clawing back from our enemies.

The lab equipment is still intact, save for a few broken glass beakers. Our scientists huddle in the corner of the room, wearing protective suits with their gloved hands raised to the ceiling.

I lock gazes with our lead chemist, Dr. Isabella Cortese. These five years of captivity have aged her prematurely. Her black hair is streaked with gray, but her eyes still shine with the same keen intelligence.

"Isabella, it's me." I close the distance between us. "You're safe, now."

Recognition flickers in her eyes. "Roman?" her voice breaks. "What are you doing out of jail?"

I pull her into a hug and let her cry on my shoulder, my chest tightening with a pang of guilt for not being able to rescue her sooner.

"We're taking you all out of here," I rub her back. "My men will get you and your team out of here and back to your families."

"These years have been torture," she rasps, and gives my arm a pinch so hard that it takes every effort not to flinch.

"Is there a problem?" I whisper into her hair.

"Headcount," she whispers back.

Isabella's team was younger and was made up of her son and a few others around the same age. Yet there's an older man in protective gear who looks nothing like a nerd.

Releasing the hug, I draw back and say to Benito, "Please escort Dr. Cortese and her team outside."

As each of them trudges past, I reach into my holster and pull out a gun, keeping it hidden at my side. The suspicious man moves in the middle of the procession with his head down and his breathing labored. As soon as he passes, I grab him by the neck and shove him against a vat.

"Who the fuck are you?" I hiss and press my gun to his temple.

"I'm Dr. Cortese's colleague," he replies.

"He's our jailer," Isabella says, her voice rising.

I tighten my grip on the man's neck. "Search him."

Gil and a few others move in and frisk the man, finding a gun hidden beneath his protective suit.

My phone rings, and I clench my teeth, knowing I should probably answer whoever's calling. The only pressing situation I have right now is Emberly Kay, who should be appeased with her new phone and designer clothes. I've instructed the men to give her anything she wants within reason.

If her asshole ex has miraculously found a search warrant, my people have orders to take her to the basement beneath the wine cellar.

I let the call go to voicemail and the last of Isabella's team leaves the lab, then order Gil to lay the man on a table. My phone sounds once more, and I switch off the ringer.

Turning my attention to the stranger, I say, "You're going to tell me who you work for."

The man gulps. "I was sent here to keep an eye on things."

"By who?"

"He'll kill me," he says through panting breaths.

Nodding, I put the gun back into its holster and reach into my inside pocket for a knife. "And I'll carve you up slowly if you don't."

He rears up, his face twisted with anguish, but Gil and the others pin him down. I grab hold of his ear and ease the tip of the knife between the scalp and the cartilage, using the technique Dad taught me for carving a roasted chicken.

"Stop," he screams.

I continue slicing until his ear comes free, and the wound gushes with blood. "Who sent you?"

He breathes hard through clenched teeth, his skin so sweaty and pale I wonder if he'll faint.

"Please," he rasps. "He said he'd kill my family."

My nostrils flare. I grab hold of the tip of his nose and position the knife at the edge of the nasal bone. Whoever Capello worked with to steal my meth lab is still in our organization or they've defected. Either way, they're going to die.

"I can keep going all day. Now, give me a name."

He squeezes his eyes shut. "G-Galliano."

The word hits like a punch to the gut, and my heart sinks. Tommy Galliano isn't just Capello's cousin, he's the leader of a powerful mafia family in New Jersey. Galliano probably helped Capello stab our family in the back.

If he's involved in this, then we may have to prepare for war.

"Roman?" Benito's voice breaks me out of my musings.

"What?" I turn to find my brother standing in the doorway with a phone.

"There's a call for you from home. It's urgent."

I wipe my knife on the man's shirt before slipping it back

into my pocket. As I take the phone, I lean into the man and murmur. "When I come back, I expect you to have more information. Any more delays and I'll slice off the body parts you actually need."

He shudders and makes a strangled noise that tells me we're on the same wavelength.

I take the phone from Benito. "What?"

"It's Dominic. Sorry to trouble you, boss," whispers a male voice, "But your house guest is going nuts. She's wandering the halls half naked and wet."

The image flashing through my mind sears my veins with fiery rage. It's bad enough that some of the men saw Emberly before she covered her body with the sheets, and now she's giving them another show.

I take a deep breath and stride through the hallway and up the stairs. "What has she done now? Put her on the phone."

By the time I exit through the storage unit and enter the courtyard, all the scientists are gone, along with many of the cars.

"Roman?" Emberly's voice echoes through the speaker.

"It's me."

"Am I a prisoner?"

"Of course not," I lie, my voice smooth. "What's wrong? The last time we spoke, you were content."

"It's the clothes. Everything you bought costs more than what you'd pay for the portrait."

"So?"

"Then I'd be in your debt."

I run my fingers through my hair and swallow back a groan of frustration. Why can't this woman be like the rest of them? Easy to please and quick to forget.

"Emberly," I say with a sigh. "Those items were a gift to make up for this morning's misunderstanding."

"Oh." She falls silent for several heartbeats, making me wonder how else she plans to bust my balls. "How soon will I get my new ID? Will it be counterfeit?"

My jaw clenches. "My guy isn't a forger. He's already reaching out to people at the Department of State and the DMV. These things take time."

"Alright, but how long?"

I chuckle, the sound bitter. "Don't forget, you need to paint me that portrait first."

She hesitates. "When will you sit for it?"

"If I say tomorrow, will you go back to your room and put on some clothes?"

Her response is rapid breathing. I glare up at the sky, wondering if it would be easier to force her to sign over our assets at gunpoint before putting a bullet through her head. Coercion might be worth the risk because Emberly Kay refuses to be a normal hostage.

"Can someone take me to my studio?" she asks, her voice still breathy. "I need to pick up—"

"I will provide you with everything you need." When she makes a strangled sound, I realize my mistake and wince. "Do you still think you're a prisoner?"

She swallows before saying, "Yes."

"Ask yourself why I would want to keep you against your will." I pause to give her time to think. "Are you rich and famous?"

"No."

"Are you connected to a powerful family that can pay your ransom?" I ask, already knowing about her impoverished upbringing.

Emberly's mother escaped Capello while she was pregnant, leaving her daughter ignorant of her true identity. No matter how much he tried, the woman eluded his attempts to track down his only daughter. With every Capello bastard dead except Emberly, she has no idea she's the wealthiest woman in New Alderney.

"Of course not," she whispers. "But why are you helping me?"

"You came to me, remember?" I reply with a soft chuckle. "For as long as I live, I won't forget the way you ambushed me with that kiss. Then when I found out why you did it, I wanted to protect you from that crooked cop."

"Really?"

"Really. Last night was the most memorable I've had since forever."

She huffs a laugh. "Now I know you're bullshitting."

"You didn't enjoy yourself?" I lower my voice. "Because I swear, I made you come all over my cock."

Her breath catches, and my dick stirs at the memory of that sweet pussy and how I fucked her throat. Movement from the corner of my eye throws a metaphorical bucket of water over my libido, and I glance down at what's left of the pool of blood.

"Ask Dominic to show you footage of that cop at the gates, trying to force his way in to get to you," I say. "Then you'll see the real bad guy."

"Alright." She pauses. "Will I really see you tomorrow?"

"We'll eat breakfast together on the patio and then I'll let you take some sketches. How does that sound?"

"Perfect," she says, sounding more relaxed. "And please tell Dominic to connect your phone to the Wi-Fi."

"Alright, baby. Pass the phone back to him."

I wait for Dominic to speak before reminding him to give Emberly anything she wants, as long as she stays within the grounds. I also ask him to show her clips of this morning's encounter with the cops.

When I hang up, Gil is at my side, his shirt spattered with blood. "Everything okay, boss?"

"How quickly can we convert the pool house into an art studio?"

He frowns. "That's where Cesare keeps his kinky furniture. Last I heard, he's still entertaining a woman."

I grind my teeth. "Order all the art supplies someone needs to paint and tell my brother to move his dungeon to the basement like every self-respecting pervert."

Gil hooks his thumb toward the door. "You sure about this, boss? I thought you'd want to relocate the lab—"

"The lab can wait. I want the art studio ready by tomorrow morning."

As Gil lumbers toward the car, I walk back through the doors. There's no point in having a meth lab if I can't launder the cash it produces through a casino.

To get it back, I need to do whatever it takes to keep Emberly Kay from becoming suspicious.

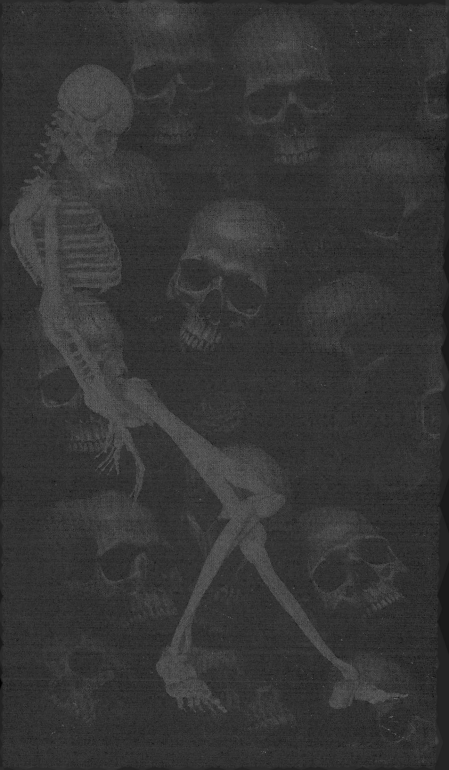

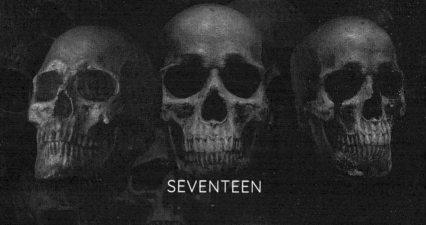

SEVENTEEN

EMBERLY

I hand back the phone and slink toward the guest bedroom, my insides squirming. After the stunt I pulled this morning, it makes sense that Roman would want me watched. I still don't know what to think of his generosity.

Ugh.

I'm becoming just like Mom.

"Miss?" Dominic asks.

I turn around to meet his gaze. "Yes?"

"The boss says I should connect your phone to the Wi-Fi and give you anything else you need."

I walk back to him with my eyes fixed on my bare feet and cringe at the droplets of water I've left on the marble floors. Maybe seeing Jim after all this time has thrown me off-balance. The man always had a way of making me doubt my sanity.

Dominic hands my phone to his taller colleague, then scrolls through his own handset to show me his photos app. "He also said you should see this."

"What?"

As the other man sets up my connection to the internet, I watch footage of Roman confronting Jim and a group of police officers at the gates of his mansion.

The way Roman handled them was skillful, as though he's spent a lifetime outwitting law enforcement—probably because he has. My breathing shallows as he makes a mockery of Jim, eliciting eruptions of laughter from the onlookers. He's so confident, so fearless.

If I could have a fraction of Roman's raw power, I wouldn't feel so exposed.

But I'm not a mafia boss, surrounded by armed men. I'm a broke artist still reeling from Jim's abuse. I want to trust Roman, but not even he is immune to the corrupt arm of the law.

Sweat breaks out across my brow, or maybe it's my wet hair that keeps dripping into my face. Jim didn't just bring a warrant for my arrest. He came with armed backup.

I'm beyond screwed.

After taking back my phone, I return to my room where I dry off and change into the La Perla lingerie, a pair of luxurious capri pants, and a silk blouse from Valentino. Everything is exactly my size, down to the Prada flats.

Either someone measured my body when I was unconscious, or Roman's observation skills are exceptional. I shake off the thought of him watching me while I slept and leave the room to take a walk.

If I'm going to stay here, I may as well know about potential escape routes, right? Not because I plan on leaving, but no one sits in a restaurant without looking for all the exits. It's the same principle.

The two men from outside my room direct me to the front doors and follow me at a distance.

The grounds are just as spectacular as the mansion, which isn't surprising, considering I count at least five gardeners. A warm breeze mingles the smells of fresh-cut grass, pollen, and evergreens, reminding me I'm far away from Beaumont City.

Vibrant flowers adorn the landscape, their blooms glowing in the afternoon sun. I stroll down a stone pathway that runs along the lawn and leads to a large pond.

Standing at its edge, I watch schools of multicolored koi. They're so mesmerizing that I kneel down to brush my fingers through the water.

"Miss?" Dominic rushes to my side, his voice tense. "Please stay back."

Straightening, I give him a skeptical look. "Why? Are they piranhas?"

He clears his throat and glances at his companion for inspiration, who gives him a you're-on-your-own shrug.

Whatever.

I walk around the edge of the pond and continue to the evergreen forest at the garden's perimeter. As I step into the dense foliage, I'm hit with the overwhelming smells of juniper and damp earth.

"Where are you going?" Dominic asks from a few feet away.

My teeth snap. Does he think I'll impale myself on a branch? Without sparing a glance in his direction, I answer, "Exploring. Is that allowed?"

He hesitates. "Sure, but wouldn't you prefer the flower beds?"

"No." I stride through the greenery. The ground is spongy underfoot with the occasional snap of twigs. "This is Alderney Hills, right?"

"Yeah," he says, almost grudgingly. "You planning on reaching the highway?"

I ignore him and continue walking until the trees thin and I meet a brick wall that's over a story high and topped with barbed wire and cables that look electric. Beyond the barrier is a line of conifers so tall I have to bend my neck backward to see their tops.

Alderney Hill is the most exclusive district in the state, with houses that date from the start of the twentieth century. Roman might be a mafia boss, but he's also what my roommate Annalisa would call old money.

The men trail after me as I follow the wall around to a set of iron gates manned by a quartet of armored guards, complete with machine guns and jeeps. They all stop what they're doing to stare.

My stomach plummets. Even if I wanted to escape, there's no way I could scale that wall or get past those guards. Who knew mafia bosses warrant this level of security?

"Where are you going now?" Dominic asks, sounding like he's already sick of being my babysitter.

"Over there." I point into the woods on the other side of the driveway and quicken my pace.

An hour of aimless wandering confirms my suspicions. This isn't a family home, it's a fortress. I should feel reassured that Jim can't get in, but there's also no way to overlook that I can't get out.

As we reach a stretch of lawn that leads to a pool house, my mind conjures up an idea to test Roman's intentions. I turn around to look at the two men, who stiffen.

"Hey, can I go back to my apartment to pick up a few things?" I ask.

Dominic's eyes narrow. "Like what?"

"My sketchbook, art supplies, cosmetics, and clothes."

"Let me speak to Mr. Montesano when he returns."

"Can't you call him?"

"You have a roommate?"

"Yes, why?"

"Then she can keep your shit safe while you wait," he says in a tone that suggests he won't continue the conversation.

I roll my eyes and head toward an olympic-sized swimming pool backed by a limestone structure with columns that mirror those of the mansion.

My brows rise. Whoever said that crime didn't pay was a liar, because Roman has to be making tens of millions if not more.

I hurry around the pool to the building, passing through the columns to a set of floor-to-ceiling windows. Strangely, the men following me wait at the other side of the pool. Maybe this place is out of bounds to the employees.

Inside is a gorgeous lounge with a wooden dining table and cream sofas, along with a huge fireplace. I continue to the doorway because I'm a nosey bitch.

As I push the door open, I lock eyes with a naked woman strapped to a chair that I can only describe as a contraption. Her arms are stretched on both sides and attached with straps to a crosspiece around its back. Its seat is split, making it impossible to close her legs.

I notice several things at once:

She wears a gag that forces her mouth open.

She's covered in fresh bruises.

She's bleeding on one side of her breast.

She doesn't have a scrap of body hair.

She's pissed.

My legs turn to lead, as does my breakfast. The room is filled with more torture and bondage equipment than a sex shop. Is this where Roman went this morning when I woke up? Is this what he's planning for me?

"A-Are you alright?" I ask her.

The woman widens her eyes and flicks her head toward the door. Strangled noises emerge from her throat because she can't form words through the gag. I can't decipher if she's warning me to run for my life or telling me to fuck off.

Shudders run down my spine. No wonder those men refused to come any further. Roman wouldn't want them leering at his adventurous playmate. I examine her features for signs of distress, but she just looks irritated.

What kind of person leaves a woman tied up, unattended, and unable to use a safe word?

The door behind me opens, and a dark-haired man steps out, wearing only a pair of black jeans. He's almost as tall as Roman, with a muscular physique, his chest covered in skull tattoos.

My breath catches, and my heart leaps to the back of my throat. It's the third Montesano brother.

He turns to me, his grin maniacal. "Have you come to play?"

I step backward on legs threatening to collapse. "I-I was looking for Roman. I didn't realize anyone was here."

His gaze skims up and down my body, making me feel just as naked as the woman tied to the chair. "My brother isn't here right now. If you ask nicely, I can keep you entertained until he returns."

If Roman has red flags, then the predator prowling toward me is a flashing neon sign. There's no appropriate response to a suggestion like that, so I turn on my heel and run.

His laughter echoes behind me, but I don't stop moving until I'm on the other side of the pool where Dominic and his colleague wait for me with matching grins.

"See anything you like?" the taller one asks, his eyes sparkling with amusement.

"There's a woman in there, tied to some sort of bondage chair. I-Is she okay? Does she need help?"

I cringe the moment I say those words. I don't know the

ins and outs of BDSM, but I got horrible vibes from that guy. What if she's there against her will?

The men double over as though I'm a one-woman comedy special. My cheeks flush, and I suppress a shudder. "Who was that man?"

"Cesare Montesano," Dominic replies. "The youngest."

"So? What was going on there didn't seem safe, sane, or consensual. Someone needs to step in and make sure she's okay. She was bleeding and wearing a gag."

More laughter. Dominic's face contorts with so much mirth that he looks like he's in pain. Tears roll down his cheeks, making me wonder if I misread the scene. Maybe I'm projecting. In that woman's position, I would be in a full-blown panic.

I head toward the mansion, making a mental note never to return to the pool house under any circumstances.

Everything is piling up, and I've had enough. In the space of twenty-four hours, I've been scammed, threatened with murder and assault, had a one-night stand with a mafia don fresh off death row, woken up in a locked room, cut myself while trying to leap off a balcony, seen footage of Jim and his backup wanting to drag me to jail, and now, I've been propositioned for kinky sex.

I'm no prude, but a girl's got limits.

"Where are you going?" Dominic asks.

"Back to my room."

Tomorrow morning, I'll paint Roman's portrait and as soon as I get my new ID, I'm getting far away from this madhouse.

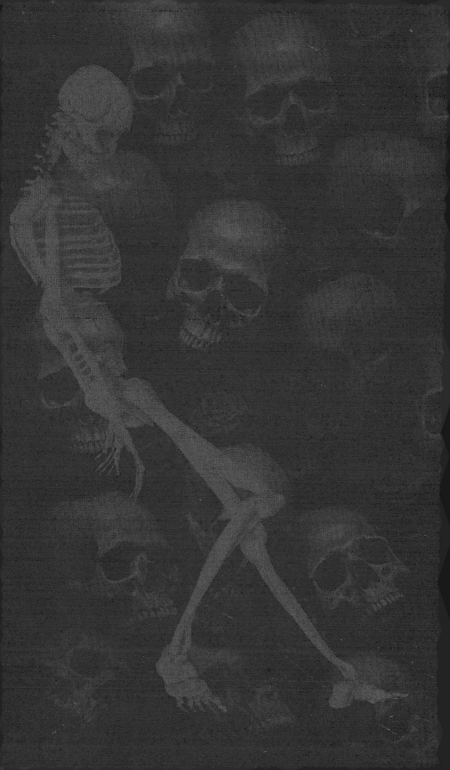

EIGHTEEN

EMBERLY

I spend the rest of the afternoon and evening reliving the events of the crazy day and pacing my room like a caged tiger. Switching from looking out into the gardens to trying on every item of clothing Roman bought me, including the lingerie.

Everyone in the house thinks I'm a nutcase, except perhaps Cesare Montesano, who may or may not be a psychopath. I shouldn't judge, considering this morning's antics.

Roman is being incredibly patient with me, but it's hard to trust his intentions. Mafia bosses aren't white knights who help damsels in distress unless there's some kind of angle. They're not even morally gray. What I can't work out is what exactly he wants from me.

Sofia delivers delicious home-cooked lasagna for dinner, which I pick at, along with two bottles of wine. In between sips, I surf the internet, trying to find anything that can help me figure out Roman's game.

Recent news says an anonymous source submitted new

video evidence to exonerate him from the murder of Ingrid Asher, a forty-five-year-old schoolteacher from Beaumont City. An article in the New Alderney Times said that his previous trial was fraught with corruption, evidence mishandling, witness tampering, and jury intimidation, which led to the false verdict.

I continue reading down to the comments section, where someone mentions the strange coincidence of Roman's release from prison just days after the Capello massacre. Over fifty replies come from different people speculating on whether Frederic Capello died because he framed Roman, murdered his father, and stole his casino.

My mind races and my head spins. I don't know what's the truth and what's speculation, but everyone seems to agree that Roman was framed. Anger burns through my chest, heating my blood. If the new evidence hadn't come to light, Roman would have been executed in the electric chair.

"Shit," I whisper. "How has he remained so sane?"

In his position, I would want to lash out at everyone, starting with anyone connected to the man who framed me for murder. None of the official articles will speculate on who wanted Roman behind bars, but I can't help thinking about the mafia family that was massacred last week.

I spend the rest of the night sipping wine and watching a true crime documentary on YouTube about the conspiracy that confirms the speculation in the comments. Days after Roman's father died of a heart attack while at the Phoenix nightclub, Roman was arrested for murder and held without bail. Then Casino Montesano was renamed the Capello Casino before undergoing huge-scale renovations and the building of a second hotel.

It doesn't take a genius to work out that the Capello family took advantage of Enzo Montesano's death so they could steal the casino. My only disappointment is that Roman wasn't able to execute the revenge himself.

As the evening wears on and the wine runs dry, I gain a new understanding of Roman. He's a man who has suffered injustice and wants to save me from the same. Maybe that's all there is to his kindness.

My eyes fall shut and I drift into a dreamless sleep, determined not to allow myself to give into paranoia.

———

A loud bang jerks me awake. I sit up, my heart pounding, and I glance from side to side. The room is dark, even though traces of sunlight peek in through tiny chinks in the curtains.

It takes several frantic seconds for me to sort out my thoughts and realize I'm in Roman Montesano's downstairs guest room.

Was that a gunshot or a backfiring car? I close my eyes, clutch at my pounding head, and groan.

There's no way in hell I drank two bottles of wine. I try to tell myself they were only half-bottles, but the throbbing hangover says otherwise. So much for self-restraint.

"What time is it?" I grope around for my phone and find it underneath the other pillow.

The display says 11:55 AM, which has to be bullshit. I couldn't have slept away the entire morning. Sofia would have woken me for breakfast.

I swing my legs off the bed, stumble toward the door, and poke my head into the hallway. Dominic and the same huge guy from yesterday lean against the walls, deep in conversation.

"Hey," I croak.

Their gazes swing in my direction.

"What time is it?"

"Nearly noon," Dominic says with a grin, his gaze traveling up to what's probably a bird's nest of curls.

Shit.

Roman and I were supposed to meet up this morning for the portrait.

"Where's Roman?" I ask.

They exchange glances before the taller one says, "He knocked on your door at six. When you didn't answer, he came in and tried to wake you, then he left."

"What?" I shriek.

"He said you were dead to the world."

"Where is he now?"

He shrugs. "I ain't the boss's secretary."

"Can you call him to say I'm ready?" When the man hesitates, I turn to Dominic and say, "Please?"

Dominic sighs, pulls out his phone, and taps on its screen. He presses it to his ear and waits several seconds before saying, "It's gone to voicemail."

"So, I'm stuck here another day?"

Now it's Dominic's turn to shrug.

"Shit!" I retreat into my room, storm across the room, and yank the curtains open.

Bright light assaults my eyes, making me wince. When I turn around, all signs of last night's drinking are gone, replaced with a bottle of water and a glass.

I clutch at my throbbing temples, trying to sort out my jumbled thoughts. This isn't a setup. Nobody but me drank all that wine. Maybe the super-rich get a selection of bottles with their meals and I just have zero willpower.

This is my fault. Nobody can reasonably expect Roman to wait all morning for a portrait when I'm the one who missed our appointment by drinking myself stupid.

Stupid. That's what I am.

Jim is desperate to drag me into a cell and punish me for

leaving his abusive ass, Lafayette wants to frame me for a crime I didn't commit, and the only man willing to help me probably thinks I'm a flaky drunk.

Opportunities like Roman Montesano don't come every day. I need to sober up and stop wasting time second-guessing his motives.

I walk to the bathroom, splash cold water over my face, and run my wet fingers through my curls so they're no longer a frizzy mess. Once I look half human, I slip on a silk kimono and walk out to face the two men.

"Could you please call or text Roman and ask him to reschedule? I'm ready to see him now."

The larger man swaggers over. "Look, Miss. The boss ain't some lackey you can stand up whenever you feel like it. He's a busy man who has better things to do than wait around for a lush."

I flinch, my eyes widening.

Dominic slaps a hand on the man's chest. "Easy, Tony. The boss says she's his guest." He turns to me, his face softening. "Why don't you go back to your room. The boss said he would try you again tomorrow morning."

Just as I'm about to object, Sofia appears from down the hallway, pushing a trolley containing several dishes. I inhale the aromas of freshly baked bread and garlic, making my stomach grumble.

Both men pick up plates and start eating, while Sofia pushes open my door and sets the table.

I stand back, watching her lay out garlic bread, gnocchi, and a huge salad along with two full bottles of wine.

"No alcohol for me," I rasp.

She turns to me and smiles. "I left you one of each so you could make your choice."

"I said no wine."

She retreats toward the door. "You don't have to drink it."

"Sofia."

As the older woman slips out into the hallway, I rush to the table, grab both bottles, and follow her. Tony and Dominic move into position with their plates and block my passage.

"What are you doing?" I ask.

"The boss says you should eat lunch, seeing as you missed breakfast," Dominic says.

"When did he tell you that? This morning?"

The corner of Dominic's mouth lifts into a smirk. When I turn to Tony, he glances to the side, unable to meet my gaze.

Every paranoid thought surges to the surface. Does Roman want to keep me in his mansion? Everything I've seen so far indicates he wants me drunk and unable to complete this portrait.

I'm not going to freak.

I'm not going to freak.

I'm not. Going. To. Freak.

"Where's all that stuff I asked for from my apartment?" I ask.

They exchange glances.

"Did you even go to pick up my drawing materials?"

Tony shovels a forkful of gnocchi into his mouth and chews. Dominic does the same. I take that lack of answer to all my questions as a no.

"Where's Roman?" I snarl.

"Out," Tony says, spattering me with sauce.

My jaw tightens. Talking to these lackeys is a waste of time. And for reasons I don't want to consider, Sofia has doubled the serving of wine to full-sized bottles. I'm not being paranoid. Not when I'm being slapped in the face by so many warning signs.

I clutch at my temples. Am I being unreasonable?

Maybe, but if Roman really wanted to sit for a portrait today, then why don't I have my art supplies? Why didn't he shake me awake? I've never blacked out on two half-bottles.

They let me sleep on purpose because I'm a prisoner.

"You're lying," I say.

Tony gives me a blank stare. "Huh?"

"You two are covering up for him, using the wine as an excuse."

Dominic smirks.

That's all the confirmation I need. Roman plans on avoiding me so I can't paint that portrait and earn the money and fake ID I need to leave. Maybe this pseudo confinement is stage one in a schedule of manipulations to lure me in that bondage chair.

Fuck that.

I try to push past them, but they're a solid wall of muscle. A wall that's impossible to scale.

"You're keeping me here against my will," I say, my voice breathy.

Dominic winks.

My stomach drops. That's a fucking confession.

"Am I or am I not a prisoner?"

Neither man responds.

"Answer me!"

Palpitations squeeze my heart, bringing up a fresh wave of terror. I swore to myself that I would never fall under the control of another man, and now I can't fight my way out. I can't talk my way out. I can't even make a move. I'm trapped. There's only one option left: Roman needs to be so sick of my presence that he casts me out through the gates.

I turn on my heel, storm into my room, and hurl the first

bottle. Glass shatters against the wall, creating an explosion of red. I throw the second over the pattern and watch it create a shower of splinters and white wine.

My door slams open, and both men stand at the threshold with their mouths agape.

"What are you doing?" Dominic asks.

"What does it look like?" I snap. "Fucking things up."

Tony steps forward, but Dominic elbows him back. It looks like Roman ordered them to keep their distance. Good. Then the only way I'll stop trashing this room is if Roman comes down here himself.

"Do either of you have a blade?" I ask.

They both give me blank looks.

"I'm not going to hurt myself." I hold out a palm.

Dominic smirks, reaches into his pocket, and produces a flick knife. I step back, wondering if it's a trap, but he places a forkful of food in his mouth as though wanting to watch the show.

"Put it on the floor," I say and slip my feet into a pair of flats. There's no way I want to slice open my toes.

He tosses it at my feet.

I pick it up, upend the table, and let the plates crash to the floor.

"Woah!" Tony says.

"One of you two had better call your boss because I won't stop smashing up his fancy mansion until you put him on the phone."

When neither of them makes a move, I stab through the TV screen, expecting one of them to yell or even pick up the phone. They continue watching, so I slash at the curtains. I pick up a vase and throw it at the two men, making them duck out of the doorway.

My heart pounds, and voices filter through the sounds of

carnage. Maybe one of them called Roman at the first sign of smashing glass?

A little voice in the back of my head tells me I'm acting crazy. This behavior is whiny, childish, ungrateful. I ask that voice what it would do if it were held captive by a mafia boss, and it falls silent.

The last time I gave a man the benefit of the doubt, I became his hostage. I was assaulted, beaten, debased. I would rather die than let myself become a victim again.

So, I tell that little voice to go fuck itself. It's the same critical bitch that asked me why I didn't notice Jim was a violent abuser. If it wants me to be polite in the face of potential danger, it needs to haunt a doormat.

I step out into the hallway to find Roman walking toward me, his features tense. On his right is an equally athletic-looking man with sharp features, closely cropped hair, and coloring so similar to Roman's that they could be brothers.

Next to the stranger is a petite woman I recognize from the nightclub. She danced beside us, wearing that beautiful gold dress. What was her name, Sera? I even introduced her to Annalisa and the others.

Our gazes lock, and we exchange frowns. What's she doing here?

Roman looks through me as though I don't exist, and my mouth falls open.

What the hell?

I smash a vase, and he doesn't even flinch. When I scream, it only elicits the barest of smirks.

"Fuck you," I snap.

He sweeps past with his guests as though I have panic attacks every day. The only one that pays me a scrap of attention is Sera, who spares me a confused glance.

"Roman," I howl, but a hand grabs my arm.

Tony bundles me back into my room and shuts the door.

I don't know what the fuck is happening, but I don't like it. Even if I could leave, Jim is still prowling about, waiting to hurl me into that cell.

For the next several minutes, my tirade continues. I slash the paintings, and force myself to ignore the guilt that squeezes my chest at destroying art. If it's valuable, Roman can afford to get it restored. Even the bed doesn't miss my attention. I slash at the mattress, slice open the pillows, and make it rain feathers.

I don't care if they think I'm crazy. Something isn't right. It's not paranoia if everyone surrounding me acts like a jailer.

The door slams open, and I whirl around. Roman storms in, his features a mask of fury.

My stomach lurches. The rage in his eyes burns through what's left of my courage, leaving me wondering why the hell I chose to antagonize a man so dangerous. Without meaning to, I step back toward the wall.

"What do you want?" He stands so close that I feel the heat of his wrath.

Raising my chin, I force myself to meet his glower. "You're going to answer my questions. This time, without any bull—"

He wraps a hand around my neck, cutting off my words.

Alarm explodes through my chest. I part my lips to scream, but he silences me with a kiss.

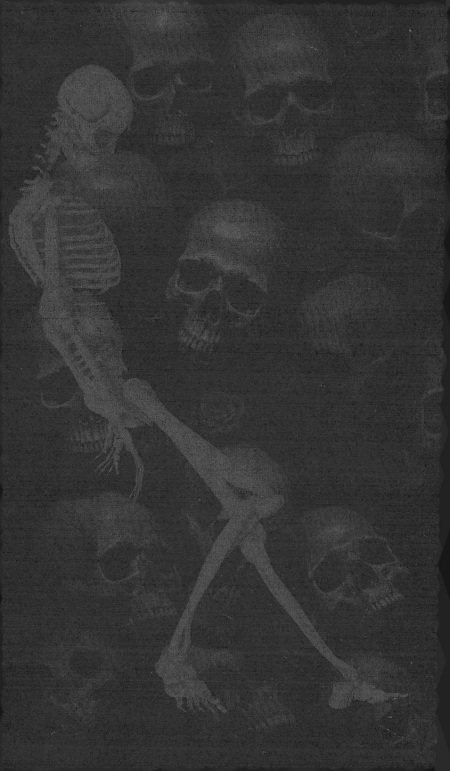

NINETEEN

ROMAN

Everything is going to shit.

A member of the family my cousin Leroi was supposed to have killed has risen from the dead. It's Samson, Frederic Capello's legitimate son, and he has a clear claim to my stolen assets, rendering Emberly Kay not just penniless but also useless.

Useless until we track Samson down and eliminate him from the line of inheritance.

The woman Cesare picked up from the nightclub is an assassin sent to murder us in our beds, and she's too much of a kinky masochist to submit to interrogation.

And Emberly Kay is getting suspicious.

Leroi promised he'd find Capello's last surviving son and deliver his head to the Di Marco law firm, so Emberly can claim her inheritance. In the meantime, I need to keep her busy.

The wine trick worked only once. Judging by her tantrum of mass destruction, nothing's going to satisfy her except her new ID and the twenty-five grand I promised to pay for my portrait.

I glare down into her huge green eyes, my grip around her neck tightening. Her chest rises and falls with rasping breaths, pushing her nipples through the silk of her robe.

There's no point in sweet-talking a woman who can see through my bullshit, so I take a leaf out of the Gianni Bossanova playbook and slam my lips onto her mouth.

Gianni Bossanova was a guy in the joint imprisoned for first-degree murder and grand larceny. He was what women would call a silver fox and so charming he made the female guards blush.

He had some crazy-as-fuck theories, particularly about the more troublesome sex. According to Gianni, the quickest way to shut off a woman's brain is through her pussy. The most surefire way to make her addicted is to give her the best orgasm of her life.

It's something to do with a hormone called oxytocin that makes people feel attached. I only listened with half an ear, but it explained why many of my casual fucks always wanted to upgrade to full relationships.

At first, Emberly stiffens and hits her head against the wall. Then she slams her fists on my chest.

Whatever she says next fades to nothing when I slip my tongue in her mouth and wrap my arm around her waist. She tastes of anger, frustration, and spearmint, but beneath the bitterness lies a hint of desire.

Her tongue thrashes against mine as though trying to win a silent battle, but I explore her mouth until she melts.

Gianni said that male saliva contained enough testosterone to get even the most frigid women hot and horny. From the way Emberly's punches are turning into pushes, I'm still not entirely convinced.

She jerks her head to the side. "Get off."

I tighten my grip around her neck. "What more do you want from me, Emberly?" I snarl into her ear. "I protected you from that cop, provided you with a secure place to stay, healed your self-inflicted wounds, and you smash up my guest room?"

"Don't turn this around," she hisses. "You're imprisoning me, and I want to know why."

"This is crazy."

"This is gaslighting."

I laugh but feel zero mirth. Who the fuck has been getting into her head? She should be clinging to me, grateful that I'm protecting her from that dirty cop. Instead, she's looking past my generosity and seeing my true intentions.

"You're the one who grabbed me, or is your brain so addled you've already forgotten?" I say through clenched teeth. "You begged me for help and now that I'm giving it, you have the nerve to accuse me of being a trafficker?"

Her face flushes.

"Are you normally so paranoid, or are you just naturally ungrateful?" I ask.

When she flinches, I know I've found a vulnerability, so I press forward with my attack using every technique I overheard in the Gianni Bossanova playbook.

"You're the kind of pampered little princess who likes to throw tantrums when she doesn't get whatever she wants."

"Fuck you," she snarls. "You don't know anything about my life."

"I've seen enough to know that when a man gives you help in your time of need, you tear up his home and make wild accusations."

She raises a hand to deliver a slap, but I grab her wrist and slam it into the wall.

Leaning in, I lower my voice several octaves. "Tell me

something, Emberly Kay. Are you pissed that I offered you twenty-five grand instead of fifty?"

"Of course not," she rasps. "You're just—"

"Then what's made you so frustrated? It can't be the quality of your room because it's fit for a princess. It can't be the clothes because they're more than an artist could afford. I can only guess that your frustration comes from not getting enough cock."

Her mouth drops open, and her face reddens. "What?"

"I fucked you good and hard that first night and you're pissed that I haven't given you more."

Her eyes widen. "You're insane."

"But you're not denying it."

She splutters. "I don't want to fuck you."

I bring my mouth so close to hers that I can almost taste her lips. "You sure about that?"

"How did this conversation turn from me being a prisoner to me being sexually frustrated?" she replies, her voice breathy.

"Because it's true."

"You're wrong," she says.

"If I slipped my fingers into your panties, would I find you wet?"

"Don't you dare," she snaps.

I raise a brow. "Is that a no?"

She squeezes her eyes shut. "You're messing with my head."

I lean even closer and bite down on her exposed neck. She cries out and slaps at my shoulder, but doesn't tell me to stop.

My hand slides between her legs and slips beneath her silk robe to find she's wearing no panties. When my fingers meet her folds, they're already slick.

"You're soaked," I growl.

"What are you doing?" her voice rises.

"You wanted my attention. Now you have it," I snarl. "And you're going to keep getting it until you beg me to stop."

"I wanted answers, asshole." She slaps my chest. "I also want to leave."

"Here's what you need." I circle her swollen clit, and her hips jerk.

"Roman," she snarls.

"Do you want me to stop, baby?"

She answers with a roll of her hips. Turns out that Gianni Bossanova wasn't bullshitting. Women *are* too easily distracted with sex.

"That's what I thought." I push two fingers into her tight, wet heat and rub her clit with my thumb. Her pussy clenches around my digits, and she shivers.

"Fuck, baby, you're so tight."

She whimpers.

My cock chooses this moment to press against her thigh, wanting to join in on the action. I ignore its pleading to get free and focus on the woman in my arms.

"Is this what you want, little Emberly?"

"Oh, fuck."

Her breath comes in ragged pants and her hips move against my fingers. She grabs at my shirt with one hand, not knowing if she wants to bring me closer or push me away, while the other digs nails into my shoulder.

I quicken my pace, making her features contort with ecstasy. The flush on her cheeks darkens, making her even more of a beautiful tableau. I could look at that face come apart every day and never get bored. There's more than a small part of me that will miss her when she's dead.

"Roman," she cries.

Smirking at the way my name rolls off her tongue, I

resolve to make her death painless. Maybe even a little pleasurable. It's the least I can do for how she keeps me entertained.

"That's it, baby," I growl into her ear. "This is exactly what you wanted. Now, come for me."

Her pussy clenches around my fingers. She shudders and wails, "You bastard—"

I cut off her potential tirade with a crushing kiss. Her body quakes with the climax and I thrust harder, deeper, until her muscles trap my fingers in their grip.

My cock throbs, desperate to be encased in her tight heat. I'm about to unzip my pants and give into its demands when her nails scratch across my cheek.

Fuck.

I yank my fingers out of her pussy, grab her arm, and march her toward the door. She cries out, punches my arm, and tries to pull away, but I'm no longer playing.

Gianni Bossanova didn't know a fucking thing about taming a feral little gorgon. Emberly is just as uncontrollable as ever and needs something more than sex to keep her subdued. It's time to move onto Plan B.

"Where are you taking me?" she shrieks.

"Pool house," I snarl.

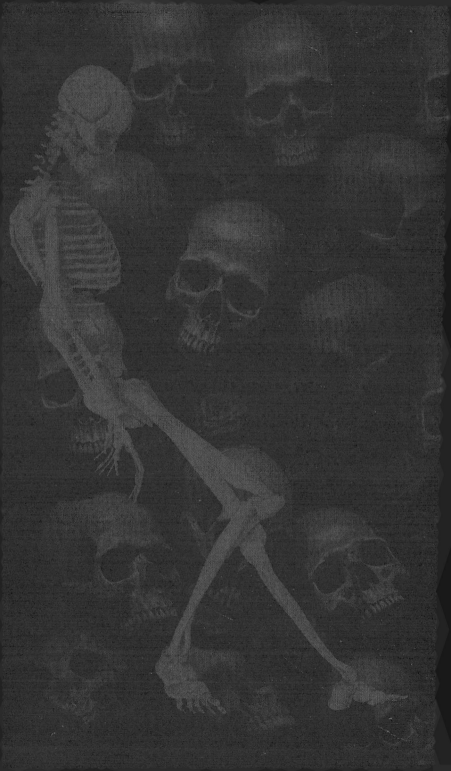

TWENTY

EMBERLY

Wait.

What?

I'm still trembling from the aftershocks of that orgasm when Roman marches me across the debris strewn all over the room and into the hallway. There's no sign of Tony or Dominic and I can only assume he told them to get lost after they failed to stop me from trashing his guest room.

But that's the least of my worries.

I'm not going anywhere with Roman when he's in this mood, let alone the place he and his brothers torture women sexually.

"Roman." I slap at the hand encasing my bicep. "I'm sorry."

He continues down the hall with the determination of the terminator.

"Don't do this." I dig my heels into the floor, but that only results in being dragged across the marble.

Shit.

He's going to tear off my clothes, strap me to that

GIGI STYX

contraption and then... My mind goes blank. I can't wear that gag or endure chains and whips and confinement.

Sweat breaks out across my brow, under my arms, and down my back. I shouldn't have scratched his face. Now, he's going to put welts across my back or somewhere much worse.

"Roman, please." My voice breaks.

Ignoring my pleas, he continues dragging me like luggage.

My knees buckle and my legs collapse. I throw my weight back, making him pause to stare down at me with eyes so cold that I shiver.

"What are you going to do?" I ask.

He bares his teeth, already sick of dealing with my shit, scoops me off the floor, and slings me onto his shoulder like a sack of rice.

"Roman." I slam my fists onto his back. "Let me go."

He delivers a hard spank to my ass.

My legs stiffen. "Ouch! Stop."

"That's what you get for being a brat," he says.

I wait for him to give me the option of walking to the pool house like an adult or being carried, but he strides into a gentleman's study lined with mahogany bookshelves and continues toward a set of French doors.

He crosses a huge patio and walks down the garden path toward the pool and the stone building where Cesare had that naked woman tied up.

Shudders run down my spine. It looks like I'm about to find out exactly why he brought me to his home. Roman probably interpreted my forwardness at the club as a request to play in his dungeon, and now he's going to give me exactly what he thinks I want.

Sunlight lashes my back, and birds chirp from distant trees, adding to my sense of dis-coordination. My stomach heaves at the mingled scents of juniper and chlorine as we reach the pool. If I don't do something right now, I might not survive the bondage and torture.

"Safe word," I say, my mind dredging through everything I know about BDSM. "This isn't safe. This isn't sane. And I don't consent."

When that doesn't work, I wriggle in his grasp, but that only earns me another hard spank.

He steps through the pool house doors and into the shade, casting my mind into despair. Tears gather at the corners of my eyes and slide up my forehead into my hairline. I didn't escape the clutches of one violent psychopath to end up tied to the bondage chair of another.

"Stop." My screams echo off the walls. "This is serious. Stop!"

Roman sets me down on a rug, and I scramble to my feet, ignoring the sudden head rush that fills my vision with stars.

When I blink them away, there's no sign of the sofas and dining table I saw the day before. Instead, there are wooden tables laden with art supplies I can barely afford, along with different sized easels, studio lights, and two chairs.

My jaw drops. Roman has created an artist studio. All those worries about bondage were just in my head.

No.

I know what I saw.

And I remember those guards laughing as I ran to the other side of the pool. They even told me that the man inside was the youngest Montesano brother, Cesare, who was into kinky shit.

I turn to meet Roman's unsmiling face.

"Isn't this a playroom?" I ask, my voice wavering.

His lips tighten. "The space in the back was another guest room when I lived here. I didn't know my little brother used it for BDSM."

"Where's all his equipment and toys?"

"Gone."

"And the dark-haired woman?"

"Home," Roman says in a tone that warns me to mind my own business.

I walk to the door and push it open, finding a bedroom along with one of the cream sofas I saw the day before. Everything is decorated in warm shades of white, like a blank canvas waiting for love.

"Is all this for me?" I ask, my voice breathy.

"There aren't any other artists living under my roof," he replies. "But if you're not happy here, you can leave."

I whirl around, my head spinning. "Roman...This is so generous. Thank you."

He only taps his unmarked cheek with his index finger, and I walk to him on trembling legs. Why is he so calm after I destroyed his property and damaged his beautiful skin?

Guilt and gratitude war within my heart as I place my hands on his chest and raise myself to my tiptoes. Inhaling his masculine scent, I press a kiss on his cheek.

Who could blame him for being pissed that I jumped to all the wrong conclusions? Roman isn't a bad guy. He's just not used to communicating his every thought.

"I'm sorry for scratching you," I murmur. "Thank you for my studio."

He nods, which only makes my chest ache with remorse. Roman has so much self-control. If I were him, I'd be shaking me until my teeth rattled, screaming that I told you so.

"Stay here if you want or leave," he says, his words gruff. "The supplies are for your portrait and to give you an... outlet."

My pussy throbs. Does he think I'm some kind of horny bitch that either needs to fuck or paint? I ignore the jab and rest my head on his shoulder. "What about the guards?"

He shakes his head. "I called them off since they make you uncomfortable."

I draw back. "And the stuff from my apartment?"

"My contact at the police department looked up your address. There's a squad car circling your neighborhood. It looks like your ex is having you watched. We're working on getting your things out without him discovering for sure that you're staying with me."

"Oh."

"Go on." He gestures at the table full of supplies. "Let me know if there's something I've missed, and I'll send someone to the store."

"But you've gotten me so much already," I whisper.

His eyes soften. "I insist."

My heart flutters. Every time I think Roman Montesano is a cold-hearted kidnapper, he surprises me by being nice.

"Alright." I walk around, surveying the wooden tables and finding everything I could have ever wished for as an artist. Oil paints, white spirit, varnish, boar bristle brushes, painting knives, charcoal, pencils, and color wheels. There are even watercolor paints and paper.

Canvases of varying sizes lean against the far wall, ranging from the seventy-two-inch ones I use to those as small as letter-sized paper.

My breath catches, and my eyes sting with tears. This is incredible. It's even more meaningful than the designer clothes because these supplies are all premium brands I'd always wanted to use but could never afford.

"I don't know how else to thank you, Roman." I shake my head, my throat thickening. "This is perfect."

He raises his brows. "Is there something else you want to tell me?"

His gaze intensifies to the point where I can't even look at him. Thank you can never be enough and sorry is too weak an apology for all my craziness.

When I remember that he was imprisoned for a crime he didn't commit, something inside me breaks. I'm no better than the judge who convicted him on flimsy evidence and nearly had him executed.

"I was wrong for ever doubting you," I say, still not meeting his eye. "The worst part was that the gallery owner accused me of stealing when I was innocent. Then I did the same thing to the only person who's ever offered me help. Roman, I'm so sorry."

Roman places his fingers beneath my jaw, lifts my chin, and makes me look him full in the face. He gazes down at me, his features softening with a compassion that makes the backs of my eyes sting.

"You were scared," he says. "I brought you here and then left you alone with your thoughts when I should have been offering you comfort. I'm sorry, too."

I blink, loosening tears, which roll down my cheeks. I don't deserve a man like Roman Montesano.

He brings his head close to mine, and my heart skips a beat. Is he going to give me a kiss?

"We have so much in common," he says, pressing his forehead to mine. "Neither of us can stand to be imprisoned. My first few weeks on death row were torture, and I want your time here to be pleasurable."

"But you set up this art studio for the portrait, right?" I ask, ignoring my instinct to ask why he just compared his home to death row. "In exchange, I'll get my new ID and the money I need to start a new life."

His expression flickers before morphing into a broad smile that makes the corners of his eyes crinkle.

"Of course, baby," he says. "I'll come here and meet you tomorrow."

Roman cups the base of my skull and kisses my forehead as if I'm precious.

Or maybe he's savoring the moment because in a few days, I'll be gone?

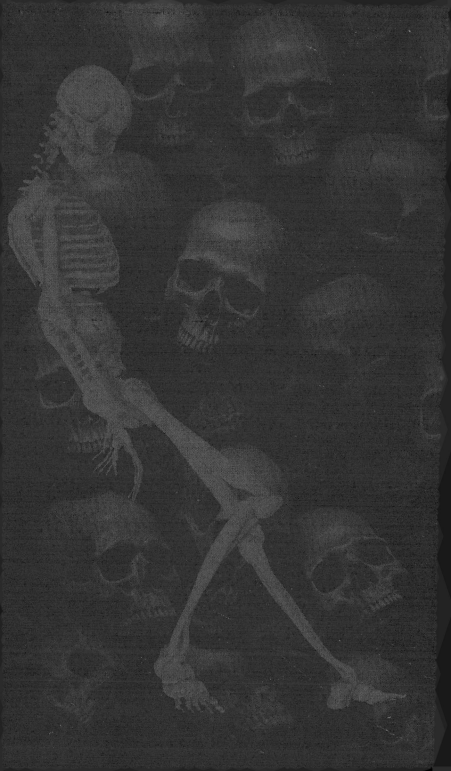

TWENTY-ONE

ROMAN

Whenever I used to run track around prison, I would close my eyes and picture trees blurring as I rushed past with the snap and crack of twigs underfoot.

For thirty sweet minutes, I would imagine that I was free, but it turns out that nothing beats being at home.

Home is full of sounds and smells and sensations I can't replicate. Birds chirp, leaves rustles, and the first vestiges of sunlight filter in through the trees. The air is thinner at the top of Alderney Hill than it is downstate. It's like being in my own fucking Disney movie.

Something else I failed to factor in were the constant interruptions. Even at the crack of dawn, a man can't get any peace. I've already had to tell two assholes not to disturb my run and now I'm headed to the pool house to see the biggest pain in my ass.

I can't let Emberly finish that portrait because Leroi still needs to track down Samson Capello. It doesn't matter that Emberly is Capello's daughter when his eldest son exists and can take control of the estate. My entire plan to get back my assets will collapse if her half-brother is alive, so it's up to me to keep Emberly under control while we manage this little setback.

My cock aches at the thought of her tight, wet pussy gripping my fingers as she submitted to my dominance. The scratches on my cheek sting. A reminder of her pathetic show of resistance. I snort. There's only one way to tame that little wildcat, and that's on her hands and knees. But who's got time to fuck her into obedience?

As I pass the rose garden, the phone tucked in my waistband buzzes. I answer without looking.

"What?"

"Blood test results came back," says the gravelly voice of Nick Terranova, the lawyer helping us claw back Emberly's inheritance. "There's a 99.999% chance of the girl being Frederic Capello's kid."

"You hear that from the Di Marco Group?"

"No, I took a separate test using DNA from my contact at the funeral home."

I chuckle. "Nice."

"It's only a matter of time before they send over the paperwork that gives her full ownership of all her father's assets."

I grunt.

"Your rightful assets," he adds.

Terranova's poor phrasing isn't what's making me pissed. The reminder that Samson Capello is still an obstacle that needs to die before we can get the law firm to transfer everything to Emberly has me mad as hell.

"Keep me updated," I mutter before ending the call.

I jog along the edge of the pool and make two soft raps on the French door, hoping she'll still be asleep.

"Come in," she yells from inside.

My jaw tightens. Of course, she's awake. The alcohol trick only worked on her once.

I step inside to find her hidden behind an easel concealing all but her bare feet and legs. She steps out from the canvas, wearing a full-body apron that conceals her curves and exposes the peaks of her slender shoulders.

My breath hitches at the sight of her untamed beauty and her curls disheveled from sleep. They coil in all directions like a nest of snakes, framing her pert nose, swollen lips and sleepy, jade eyes.

Her gaze roves over my body, and I can tell by the way her eyes darken that she's not thinking about painting. I pull back my shoulders and preen, knowing she likes what she sees.

"You naked under that?" I ask.

A flush spreads across her cheeks, runs down her neck, and disappears into the apron. My brows rise, and I wonder if it's reached her breasts.

"I can't get those designer clothes you bought me splattered with paint. It will never come out."

"Turn around." I make a circling motion with my finger.

"Why?" she asks, her eyes flashing.

The corners of my lips lift into a smirk. How quickly can I distract her from starting that portrait? "I want to see if you're wearing panties."

She shifts her weight from side to side and fidgets with her hands. Her throat bobs, and her nipples poke through the heavy fabric. "What the hell is your problem?"

My smile broadens. Emberly is adorable when she's flustered.

"Are you thinking about that orgasm I gave you yesterday, because I didn't wash my hands last night." I bring my fingers to my nose and groan.

Her jaw drops, and she breathes hard through parted

lips. She takes several moments to regain her composure before gesturing to my clothes. "You're supposed to be wearing a suit. How can I paint a business portrait when you're all hot and sweaty from a run?"

"Want me to go back and change?" I hook a thumb over my shoulder.

All traces of her discomfort morph into a scowl that rivals the goddess of wrath. "So you can find some pressing business issue and disappear?" she snaps. "No way. I'll just have to sketch you nude."

My brows rise. "You want me to strip?"

"Yes," she says. "Take it all off."

"Can you handle me naked, baby?" I lower my voice, watching her shiver.

Her gaze leaves mine, and she waves me to a chair. "Artists see nude men all the time. It's called life drawing."

Annoyance flares across my skin at the thought of her sketching other men. I consider asking her what else these models do for her when she picks up a stick of charcoal and disappears behind her huge canvas.

I set my gun and phone on the floor, toe off my sneakers, and kick them aside. As I peel off my clothes, my cock decides now is the time to compete with those naked men.

Emberly pokes her head out from the other side of the canvas and stares at my dick.

"What are you doing?" she whispers.

"Making myself comfortable." I lower myself into the seat and cup my erection.

She walks out from behind her canvas, clutching her stick of charcoal so tightly that it looks on the verge of snapping. Her breaths quicken as she continues to glare at my cock.

It lengthens and hardens under her attention and produces a bead of precum. Maybe it's still mad at me for not fucking Emberly against the wall when I had the chance. Maybe the horny bastard knows her days are numbered and wants to make the most of the time she has left.

Whatever its reason for saluting, I do nothing to stop its progress. If I can't distract Emberly with innuendo, maybe she'll appreciate a show.

"If you're not careful, that will end up in the painting," she says, her voice distant.

"Then why don't you get closer and take a better look?"

She disappears behind her canvas without another word and scribbles, but the thought of her studying any part of my anatomy makes my blood heat.

I stare at Emberly's feet. They're pretty, with beautifully shaped toes unadorned with polish. My cock surges at the thought of them running up and down its shaft. I let my gaze wander up her delicate ankles and lean calves, which move around while she sketches.

It's almost like a dance.

Does she need to relieve some of that pressure on her pussy?

Her feet pirouette as she peeps out for a glance at my body, and I ache for the chance to see what she looks like as she creates her art.

Without thinking, I rise off my seat and walk around the canvas to examine her work. Her charcoal strokes are delicate, capturing my body's silhouette.

"Nice work," I say.

She spins around. "The subject isn't supposed to move."

"I was curious." My hands encircle her waist, and I pull her into my chest, inhaling her sweet cinnamon and vanilla scent.

"Sit down and I'll show you what I've done afterward," she says, her voice sharp.

"But I'm curious about what you're not wearing under that apron."

My hands slide down to her curvaceous ass. The fabric there is light and thin enough to let me feel the heat of her skin, but I need more.

"Behave," Emberly murmurs. "I'll never finish the portrait if you keep being so distracting."

"Show me what you're wearing underneath and I'll sit down."

"Promise?" she whispers.

"I swear on my life."

"Fine," she says with a sigh. "Let go."

I release my hands, but I don't step back, my gaze raking up and down her slender form.

Emberly pulls the thick strap of her apron over her head, letting one side fall loose, and all sensation rushes south. Underneath it, she wears the burgundy silk bra and thong I bought for her two days ago.

The last time I saw that perfect little ass, she was bent over while I fucked her from behind. Now, I want to repeat the experience with her covered in paint.

"There," she says. "Now it's your turn to keep your end of the bargain."

"All of it," I say.

She huffs and pulls off the apron's other strap, and the fabric falls to the floor. My cock aches with the need to slide beneath her thong and encase itself in her wet heat.

"Turn around."

Her shoulders stiffen, and her fingers tighten around the stick of charcoal. My breath quickens at the prospect of calming her from another meltdown, but she turns around to fix me with a glower.

I sweep my gaze down to the nipples pebbling through the silk, along her flat belly, and to her slender thighs. Those long legs are wasted keeping her standing when they could be wrapped around my waist.

"Now, will you please sit down?"

There's an edge to her voice that's no longer playful, so I back toward the chair with my eyes still glued on her body. How the hell did Capello sire two worthless sons and then manage to produce such a stunning daughter?

"If you want me to stay in my seat, you should stop disappearing behind the canvas. I need to watch you do your art," I say.

With an annoyed breath, she arranges her easel to the side, so I get her full profile. As she bends to pick up her apron, I add, "Leave it."

Emberly turns to me with her eyes narrowed. Her scowl plus the color on her cheeks tell me she's thoroughly sick of my bullshit. Hiding my smirk, I lower myself into my seat and arrange myself into a new position.

"Roman, you were sitting angled to the right with your elbow on the arm."

I slouch to the right and rest my cheekbone on my fist. "Like this?"

Her lips tighten. "More upright."

Straightening, I balance my chin on my fist, my gaze never leaving her face. "Better?"

"No," she snaps, her nostrils flaring.

"Come here and show me."

Eyes flashing, she storms over, grabs my wrist and moves it to the chair's arm and jostles me back into my original pose. Heat radiates from her body as she moves me back into position.

"Like this," she says, her voice tight with frustration. "And sit up straight."

As she pivots to return to the canvas, I grab her by the waist. "Where are you going?"

"To finish the sketch," she says.

"Are you intimidated by the sight of my cock?" I ask.

She glares down, her green eyes darkening, her cheeks an even deeper shade of red. "What are you talking about?"

"You're jumpy." I lower my right hand to my erection and grip it at the base.

Emberly's gaze follows my movements, and her lips part as I squeeze tightly enough to release another bead of pre cum. Her eyes track the fluid traveling down my shaft with rapt fascination.

"Are you trying to distract me from continuing the portrait?" she asks.

I frown. "I thought you said you were an expert at painting naked men."

She purses her lips. "There's more to life drawing than huge erections."

"So, you think I'm huge?"

I lavish my shaft with long, languid strokes.

She shoots me a venomous glare. "Stop playing with that thing and focus on looking professional."

"My cock has been aching since I made you come yesterday," I say, my voice deepening. "It can't stop thinking about how your tight little pussy clenched around my fingers like you were trying to milk them dry."

"Are you thinking it or is your penis?" she asks, her gaze dropping to my cock.

"Same thing." My strokes quicken.

"Roman—"

"Say that again," I groan. "My cock loves the sound of my name on your lips. Correction. It loves being encircled by your lips."

"No." She gulps. "And if you don't stop stroking yourself, I'll turn this portrait into a giant cock."

I raise a brow. "Get on your knees, and I'll show you its best side."

"You're so full of shit."

My fist makes a slow, sensual slide up my shaft. "I'm full of something, but it isn't shit."

As she retreats, her blush blooms across her chest and into the lacy cups of her bra. I continue caressing my cock with slow, controlled strokes.

When she returns to the canvas, her movements are less graceful, more stilted. I continue jerking off, imagining her so aroused that she can't draw. The charcoal snaps between her fingers and falls to the floor with a dull thud, but she doesn't reach down to pick it up. Instead, she's too busy staring at my erection.

I slide forward and part my legs, so she can get a better view of my balls. Her breath shallows, moving in and out of her parted lips.

"Roman, you need to stop," she says, her thighs squeezing.

My chest fills with a deep groan. "Keep talking like that and I'll come all over your canvas."

"You're an asshole."

"Says the woman who's undressing me with her eyes." My hips jerk in time with the movements of my fist. "I feel objectified."

"You can't undress someone who's already naked," she says, her words quickening.

"So, you admit to objectifying my cock?"

Her scowl deepens. "You're objectifying yourself."

My strokes quicken. My balls tighten, and the pressure builds. The only thing more beautiful than seeing Emberly when she's pissed is watching her lose control. It should be her grabbing at my cock with her delicate fingers, begging me to paint the canvas of her face with my cum.

"No wonder they locked you up," she mutters. "That thing should be illegal." Despite her protests, she edges closer, her eyes never leaving my shaft.

The sight of her desperate for a front-row view ignites a fuse that makes my balls explode. I climax so hard that my body seizes with shudders. Spurt after spurt of warm cum splatters over my abs and reaches my chest. Some of the droplets even hit my chin.

Emberly clenches her legs so tightly that it looks like she's trying to stem her arousal. Maybe I could have convinced her to let me take her on the floor or against the wall, but I can't give her everything she wants.

There's no telling how long it will take Leroi to kill her half-brother and move her up to becoming her father's sole heir. I need to keep her distracted and off-balance until then.

As long as she's frustrated, confused, and aching for my touch, she won't think about portraits, fake ID, or leaving.

I rise off my seat and walk toward her, my ego thrumming at how she shrinks into her canvas.

"What are you doing?" she shrieks.

"Getting cleaned up. Feel free to join me in the shower if you need a helping hand." I throw a smirk over my shoulder. "Or if you want something longer and thicker."

She stares after me through wide eyes, her chest rising and falling as though deciding whether to jump on my back or tackle me to the floor.

Bring it on, Emberly Kay.

I will fuck you against the bathroom wall until you pass out.

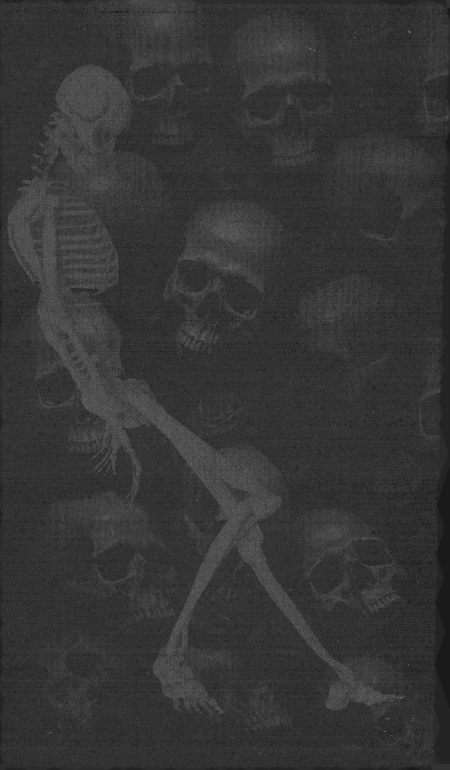

TWENTY-TWO

EMBERLY

I can't move, I can't think, I can't do anything but stare after Roman's broad back. My mouth hangs open, and I've stopped breathing. The pulse between my legs pounds so hard that its vibrations travel down to my toes. What the hell just happened and how on earth did I lose control of the situation so quickly?

He was supposed to sit for a portrait. I even woke up extra early in case he arrived while I was asleep. I thought I'd prepared myself for anything that could go wrong, but nothing prepared me for this. Now, all I can think about is how his muscles tightened as that huge cock erupted fountains of creamy, pearlescent cum.

This is the first time I've seen him truly naked, and he's glorious. He makes Michelangelo's David look emaciated. That first night we fucked, it was from behind with him mostly clothed. I got to see his chest during the second round, but I'd been drunk and unable to appreciate his perfect physique.

His invitation to join him in the shower echoes through my ears, picking up volume with each frantic breath.

I'm so tempted.

Yesterday, when he made me climax on his fingers, there was a part of me that wanted more. I wanted him to throw me down on the destroyed mattress and take out his fury by pounding into me so hard that I would see heaven.

Instead, he swept me off my feet and brought me to an art studio beyond my wildest dreams. He's made up for every dismal birthday and underwhelming Christmas in a ridiculously sexy package.

Roman Montesano isn't anything like I expected. I thought he would be a ruthless gangster who treated women like objects or cattle to be sold in the skin trade, but I couldn't be more wrong. In between his playfulness, there's a softer side that only wants me to be safe and content.

I walk over to the chair, gather his phone, shoes, clothes, and gun, and carry them into the bedroom in case he wants to get dressed after getting clean. Each step sends friction against my aching clit that makes my skin tingle with need.

Maybe I should surprise him in the shower and order him to get on his knees. A giggle bursts through my chest. Roman is extremely talented with his tongue.

Or maybe not.

He'd only distract me with orgasms, then lay me on the bed and we'd fuck until he runs out of time for the portrait or I'm too satiated to care. I shake off thoughts of sex and focus on my goal.

All I need now are a few sketches of Roman's face before I even consider putting paint on the canvas, so it's best for me to wait for him in the studio.

As I push open the door and step back into the other room, my clit makes a painful throb and rubs against the fabric of my panties. Roman got me so hot and wet that moisture has seeped through the silk. At this rate of sexual frustration, all I can think about is him and his wretchedly tempting body.

My head won't clear until I get an orgasm.

I continue to the chair and hike my foot up on Roman's seat. It's still warm from his body heat, and I close my eyes.

Shivers skitter down my spine and settle into my pussy. What would he have done if I'd climbed on his lap and rode that juicy cock?

I slip my fingers beneath the silk and rub tight little circles over my swollen clit. Roman would probably have liked it if I grabbed his shaft and took what I needed. My throat resounds with a groan. That's what I should have done—fucked him so hard that he collapsed against the chair and stayed still for the portrait.

There's always next time.

"Is this a private party or can anybody join?" asks a deep voice.

My heart leaps to the back of my throat. I turn around to find Dominic standing in the middle of the room. The guard smiles so widely his pencil mustache disappears into his top lip.

I snatch my hands away from my pussy and skitter back toward the canvas, where I left my apron. How the hell did I not hear him entering?

"What are you doing?" I yell.

He places a hand on his chest. "Easy, Miss. I ain't here to hurt you."

"Get out of here." I pick up my apron with trembling hands and slide one strap over my head, followed by the other.

Dominic continues staring at me like I haven't just told him to leave.

"Roman's in the other room," I add, trying to keep my voice from trembling.

He grins as though he thinks I'm lying. Of course he would. He thinks Roman's still being evasive. He obviously didn't see Roman posing for me in the studio.

"Now that Tony isn't around to eavesdrop, we can finally talk," he says.

"What do you want?" I snap.

Dominic raises his palms in the universal gesture for surrender. "Hey, I'm a friend." He glances from side to side, taking in all the canvases and the supplies. "So... You're an artist?"

"Roman?" I yell and back toward the door.

"Easy," he says, his smile fading. "What I have to say is for your ears only, and it's about why the boss doesn't want you to leave his estate. Ever."

My ears prick at his ominous tone, which makes my mind spiral toward suspicion. He's just hinted that I won't pass through those gates alive. Or at all.

"What are you talking about?" I ask, my voice lowering.

"Your Mom was Lena Kay, am I correct?"

I don't answer because he could have dredged up that information online.

He nods as though taking my lack of reply as a yes and continues, "Did you ever meet your old man before he died?"

My jaw tightens. Nobody but Mom ever knew the identity of my dad. I even checked hospital records and my birth certificate, which said 'father unknown'. She remained tight-lipped about him until she died.

When I sent a DNA sample to one of those ancestry companies hoping to track down my blood relatives, they didn't even bother to reply. There's more information on what's going on in the Bermuda Triangle than on the identity of my father.

"What do you know about my dad?" I ask.

"Only that he never stopped looking for you and your mom. My uncle kept you both hidden."

My jaw drops. This could be a crock of bullshit. I never told anyone that Mom was always paranoid that we were being hunted.

"What do you mean?" I ask, my voice guarded.

Dominic steps closer. "Your old man never had another daughter. Not one of his own blood, and he would have been so happy to see you turned out so nice."

My heart pounds so hard that my rib cage rattles, and its reverberations fill my ears with hollow thuds. "You don't know my dad. Nobody does."

"Lena did. So did my uncle."

"Who's your uncle?" I whisper.

"I doubt that you would even know him. Once Lena left New Alderney, she made sure to change addresses so she couldn't be found."

My breath catches and a chill runs down my spine. How could he know this?

"Then who is my father?" I ask, trying to buy time and calm my rising panic.

He closes the distance between us and smiles, revealing gold molars. "Do you think I'll give you that information for free?"

As his gaze travels down my apron, realization slaps me in the face. All this talk was an angle to get me naked. Lots of women have daddy issues, especially those with blank spaces on their birth certificates. Dominic probably pieced together a few facts he gathered about me and conceived this story as a way to get a free fuck.

I roll my eyes, attempting to gain a semblance of control. "Whatever you're selling, I'm not interested."

His shit-eating grin morphs into a snarl. He lunges forward, grabbing me by the throat in a grip that cuts off my air.

I part my lips to scream, but he clamps a hand over my mouth before I can make a sound.

"Pity," he snarls. "I'd hoped to get some pussy before doing this, but you've left me no choice."

Alarm punches me in the chest, infusing my veins with cold adrenaline. Terror floods every corner of my soul as I struggle to breathe. I thrash against him, desperate to escape, but he's too strong. Sound catches in my throat, but it's so strangled that it won't reach Roman through two sets of walls and a shower.

"You were marked for death the moment your old man died," he hisses. "If the boss didn't kill you, then someone else would have put a bullet through your skull."

I curl my fingers into claws and swipe at his eyes, but he grabs my right wrist and pins it above my head. His grip around my neck tightens, delivering an explosion of pain as I try to force out a strangled breath. My left hand continues to fight, but he easily avoids it.

"Some girls like to be choked while they're fucked. It makes them see stars." He carries me over to the wall and kicks open my legs. "It'll be the last thing you'll see before you die."

Flames sear my lungs and my chest collapses. I struggle to suck in air, but his grip around my throat is too tight. My eyes bulge with each failed attempt to inhale, hurling my psyche over the knife's edge of panic.

"Stop," I rasp, the word barely audible. "Roman—"

Dominic slams me so hard against the wall that my spine

explodes in agony. My eyes squeeze shut, and tears roll down my cheeks.

He licks a path up the side of my face and growls, "Sam sends his regards."

My head spins, and my consciousness sinks toward oblivion. Dominic's face morphs into Jim's, and my mind replays another episode of abuse.

Jim returning home from a long day of work, furious to find his father still at the house. The old man working Jim into a frenzy that I was giving him sass. Palpitations race through my heart as the memories flood, blurring the lines between present and past.

Dominic's sneer dissolves into Jim's snarl. That time his father goaded him into violence, Jim pinned me against the wall like this and fucked me in front of the old man.

I tremble and thrash, the same as I did when he degraded me in front of his dad. Back then, I knew it would end. Now, I can only pray that it will.

Black clouds my vision as Dominic, or maybe Jim, squeezes my neck tighter, and I run out of air.

My heart stutters.

This is it.

I'm going to die.

Then I'm jolted back to awareness by a heavy thud, and his grip loosens.

I fall to my hands and knees, inhaling noisy breaths that verge on screams. Oxygen fills my lungs, but does nothing to ease my panic. Darkness fills my vision, but a tunnel of light expands with each frantic heartbeat. Everything is blurred. All I can make out is one huge figure striking another.

It's Roman.

He stands over Dominic's crouched form, hitting him over and over with the butt of his pistol.

The shock of the assault still punches me in the chest. I

skitter against the wall, trying to catch my breath. No matter how much I continue to inhale, the oxygen fails to register. It's as though my lungs still think I'm being choked.

"You piece of shit," Roman punches Dominic so hard that he crumples like a broken marionette.

The towel around Roman's waist lies in a wet heap on the floor while he continues raining blows down on Dominic with the kind of savagery that makes my hair stand on end.

Blood spatters across Roman's tanned skin, and his handsome features twist into a mask of rage that makes him look monstrous.

I've never seen such raw savagery, not even from Jim at his cruelest. Roman fights like he's powered by a legion of demons, each battling for their chance to draw blood. He's vicious, savage, relentless, and attacking with wild abandon —just like a berserker warrior in the throes of a frenzy.

My heart stutters, and I clutch at my chest. Will I be next? Will Roman's violent rampage be directed at me?

The thump of fists meeting flesh turns wet, and my spine stiffens at the sound of Roman's brutality drawing blood. I clap both hands over my mouth to muffle a scream, making his head jerk in my direction.

When our eyes meet, his expression softens. He drops the gun and wipes a bloody hand over his face.

My gaze bounces from Roman to the man lying on the floor. Dominic's head and face is a mess of blood and broken flesh. The only sign he's still alive is the slow rise and fall of his chest.

Roman stands, his face a deceptive mask of calm. His gaze never leaves mine as he crosses the room, stops at my side, and holds out a hand.

All traces of the enraged beast are gone, but my limbs refuse to cooperate. Experience says that people don't switch from monster to man. Roman is either that monster in a mask or a man fighting to protect what's precious. I'm not naïve enough to think I've become that important to him after just a one-night stand.

When I don't take his hand, he reaches down, gathers me into his arms, and pulls me to his chest. Blood soaks my apron and fills my senses with the scent of copper.

"It's alright now, baby," he murmurs. "You're safe."

I can't fight. I can't flee, so I freeze.

He buries his head in my hair, inhales deeply, and groans. I can't stop feeling like I'm trapped in the maw of a beast.

Who the fuck is Sam?

Why does he want me dead?

And was he telling the truth about Roman's nefarious motives?

I might be safe from Dominic, but who's going to keep me safe from Roman?

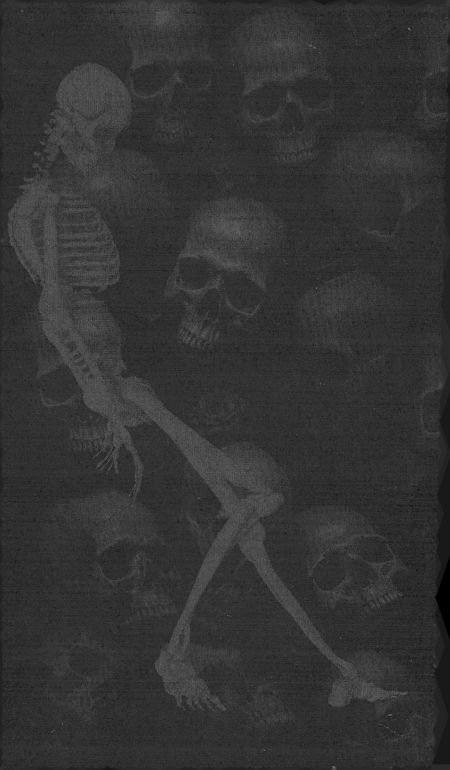

TWENTY-THREE

ROMAN

Fuck. I almost lost Emberly. If I had spent a minute longer in the shower, she could have died.

The only reason I left Dominic alive is because I need answers, starting with why a long-trusted employee was choking the life out of the woman standing between me and my family fortune.

Emberly trembles in my arms but refuses to lean against my chest, no matter how much I try to pull her close. Her trauma response goes beyond the shock of being choked.

I draw back and cup her face with both hands. "Are you hurt, baby?"

She shakes her head but won't meet my eyes.

"Tell me what you need."

"Who am I to you?" she rasps.

"What? Do you still think I'm trafficking—"

"No." She finally meets my gaze with bloodshot eyes.

I want to return to Dominic and beat him until his skull shatters, releasing a spray of blood, eyeballs, and brains. Emberly is my prey. Mine. Nobody gets to hurt her but me.

"Tell me the truth." Her voice trembles. "Why am I here?"

"Because you need my help," I say.

Her face remains unchanged. Unconvinced.

"Because letting you go will put you in the clutches of that dirty cop."

"All this for a one-night stand?"

I close my eyes and exhale. "You're more to me than just a fling. You can trust me, Emberly. I will slice through every motherfucker's hands before they even get close to touching you."

When I open my eyes again, she's staring at me as though what she hears is bullshit.

Because it is.

I won't let her die... yet.

"Dominic acted like he knew about my mom," she says.

A knot forms in my gut. I keep my features even. "Where is she?" I ask, already knowing the answer. "Does she need protection, too?"

"She's dead."

My brows draw together. I part my lips with what I hope looks like confusion. "I don't understand. What's the significance?"

"He said he knew about my dad."

I stop breathing for the second it takes to realize he might have told Emberly about her inheritance. My mind spins for something to make me sound ignorant. "Maybe he read your birth certificate? What did he want?"

"Who is Sam?"

"Sam?" I ask, my brain unable to muster up a plausible lie.

"The last thing Dominic said as he choked me was that Sam sends his regards."

My heart plummets into my stomach at the prospect of her discovering my plans. Samson Capello, her unknown older half-brother, and the last legitimate heir to my stolen assets, hasn't just found out about Emberly's existence. He knows I'm keeping her under guard.

That slimy bastard sent an assassin after Cesare. Now, he's trying to have Emberly killed.

"Is Sam connected to that cop?" I ask.

Her face twists. "Don't play ignorant. Stop lying!"

I grind my teeth, fill my lungs with air, and exhale my frustration in an outward sigh. "Can't you see what's happening?" I meet her watery gaze. "Dominic must be an undercover cop. He's either trying to get me back to prison or working with your ex."

Her face pales, and her pupils dilate until her irises become tiny rings of green. Even her breath becomes faster, shallower, and more erratic, as though she's on the verge of panic.

"What?" she whispers, her eyes widening.

The tension in my gut relaxes. I've found a sore spot I can manipulate over and over to distract her from the truth. Emberly Kay is so terrified of falling into the clutches of her former boyfriend that she'd rather accept the hospitality of an ex-con.

I nod, as though adding weight to my claim. "Every organization has a mole, but I never knew it would be Dominic."

"Do you think he could be a detective?"

I run the pad of my thumb over her cheekbone. "Or working for the cops. Whichever is true, he won't get away with hurting you."

Emberly deflates, her lashes lowering. "Why are there so many people out to get us?"

When I pull her into my chest, she finally relaxes into

my embrace. "I made a mockery of the justice system by proving them all to be a bunch of corrupt idiots. That's why they'll stop at nothing to get me back behind bars."

"And me?"

I press a kiss on the top of her head. "Some cops are psychopaths. Jim Callahan thinks if he can't have you, then nobody will."

She makes a strangled noise and trembles. "Oh, god."

Anyone watching this would call me a heartless bastard, but I never wanted her to suffer... Much. Maybe a little at first, but I want her death to be painless.

I hug her tighter. "Don't worry. We'll stay one step ahead of that bastard. He won't get away with hurting you. Not while I still draw breath."

Emberly's quiet sobs pull at my chest, igniting an inferno of rage toward those dirty dealing assholes. How typical of a Capello to send out a hit on his own sister.

Scooping Emberly into my arms, I carry her across her studio and into the bedroom, where she left my clothes and phone.

Laying her on the mattress, I murmur, "You need to be checked out by a doctor."

"Stay with me." She grabs my arm.

"I swear it," I say, and mean every word. "Let me take off your apron."

She lets me undress her down to her underwear and tuck her under the covers. I press another kiss to her forehead before wiping the blood off my hands. Then I grab my phone and curl up at her side.

"Thank you," she murmurs.

I slide my fingers through her curls. "For what?"

"For always saving me."

My throat tightens. Sex with Emberly is clouding my

senses. It's understandable, since hers is the only pussy I've had in five years. Now she's stirring up unwanted thoughts. Thoughts like how I'm a dick for comforting her from her brush with death when I plan on being her executioner.

"I'm no hero. I'm a beast."

She exhales a broken laugh. "Yeah. I saw that from the way you smashed Dominic's head like a pumpkin, but you're *my* beast."

"You're not scared of me?" I ask.

"Because you beat up the man trying to strangle me to death?" she asks, her voice trembling. "Fuck no."

She's lying. That or the man she's running from is far worse than what she witnessed. Either way, she's brave. Anyone else would be halfway to the gates.

I hug her close, my heart warming. "That's my girl."

For the next several minutes, I rock Emberly from side to side, all the while exchanging rapid texts with Cesare and Benito. Right now, they're the only two fuckers I can completely trust.

What I said about there being a mole in my organization was no lie. Dominic was working with Samson Capello, and I need details, starting with where that sister-slaughtering bastard is hiding so I can pump him full of bullets.

Emberly's body relaxes against mine and her breathing evens. I check my phone, seeing a message from Cesare letting me know he's already dragged Dominic out of the studio with a promise to keep him alive.

Good.

A knock sounds on the door. I'm about to tell my brother to fuck off, when a female voice says, "It's me."

"Sofia."

She peeks inside. "You weren't in your room, so I brought breakfast for two."

"Do you have your gun?" I ask.

She frowns. "Of course."

"Stay here. If anyone but me, my brothers, or Dr. Brunelli steps through the door to the pool house, you have my permission to put a bullet through their skull."

After getting dressed, I walk through the mansion and into the wine cellar, pull on the door disguised as a pair of stacked barrels, and descend the darkened steps.

Great-grandfather Paolo had the basement excavated during the prohibition era to store the family's distillery and private reserves of alcohol. Grandfather Giovanni divided the space into separate chambers, and Dad converted a few of them for interrogations and long-term confinement.

I follow a trail of blood to the first interrogation room, where Dominic sits naked in the windowless space on a metal chair bolted to the floor. Thick straps attach his arms, legs, and neck to the furniture, making sure he can't so much as flinch.

Cesare leans against the wall, which is soundproofed with gray insulation. The only source of illumination comes from a flickering lightbulb, which he installed to make the place look sinister.

"Is he awake yet?" I ask.

"Pretending to sleep." Cesare nods toward his bruised face and whistles. "I'm impressed he's still alive."

"I only hit him once on the head, then focused on breaking his bones."

My brother snickers. "Makes them last longer."

"Long enough to talk."

"I ain't saying shit." Dominic's words are garbled. I'm surprised he can even form sentences through a mouthful of broken teeth. His face is a mass of swelling and open wounds that leak blood over his chest.

I fold my arms. "We don't have time, so I'll keep this brief. Benito is with your daughter as we speak."

"Bullshit." He spits a spray of blood.

"Verona Marino, freshman student at Tourgis Academy?" I ask.

He stiffens. "You wouldn't."

I lean over him, my teeth clenched. "Five years ago, I would never have stooped so low, but our family was betrayed by its most trusted friend. I've had years to guarantee that the next insider who fucks with us will become a cautionary tale."

He shivers. "Boss, you can't—"

"Call Benito."

Cesare walks to the landline and dials the academy. My other brother wouldn't have reached it so quickly, but he called its principal in advance, informing them to pull out Verona for an urgent call.

"Hello?" a soft voice sounds through the speakers.

"Baby," Dominic says.

There's a pause before she replies. "Papa?"

"Yeah, it's me," Dominic replies, his voice heavy with grief.

"Are you okay?"

"I'm fine, baby. But you need to listen to me carefully. I need you to leave the academy right now and go to your aunt's place. Don't ask questions, just go."

"Sorry," Cesare says. "Benito hung up."

The corner of my mouth lifts into a smirk. Benito would never hurt an innocent schoolgirl, even under orders. Young Verona is perfectly safe. I only need to frighten Dominic enough to loosen his tongue.

"I'll kill you," he snarls and jerks against his restraints.

"Why did you strangle Emberly?" I ask.

"Fuck you."

I turn to Cesare. "Call Benito. This time, I want to hear Verona scream."

"Wait," Dominic says, his voice rising with panic. "A man representing Sam Capello came to my house two nights ago and dropped a hundred grand in cash, offering me a million for the hit."

"Did he explain why?"

He shakes his head. "Only that I needed to get her alone by saying I knew her parents."

"And who are they?" I ask.

"Some woman called Lena Kay who ran from New Alderney while she was pregnant with Emberly and kept moving around. He didn't tell me about her father, only that he was very important and dead."

I nod. Samson wouldn't be stupid enough to divulge that my houseguest would become an heiress upon his untimely demise, otherwise anyone who thought they had a chance with Emberly would be after his head.

"How long have you been working for the Capello family?" I ask.

"I haven't," he blurts. "It was one job that would set my daughter up for life. I've never worked for them before."

"Roman?" Cesare asks.

I run a hand through my hair. The most important thing is that Emberly doesn't know about her inheritance.

"See if you can get the truth. I want names of anyone who's even remotely compromised, as well as information on Samson's location."

Dominic groans a protest, but I'm no longer interested.

"Do I keep him alive?" Cesare asks.

"Yes," I reply through clenched teeth. "Every mother-fucker living under my roof or working in my inner circle needs to know the consequences of betrayal. And for touching what's mine."

I stride out of the interrogation room with Dominic's screams ringing through my ears. Emberly will be awake soon, and I don't want her feeling abandoned.

If she gets enough time alone, she might start unraveling the lies.

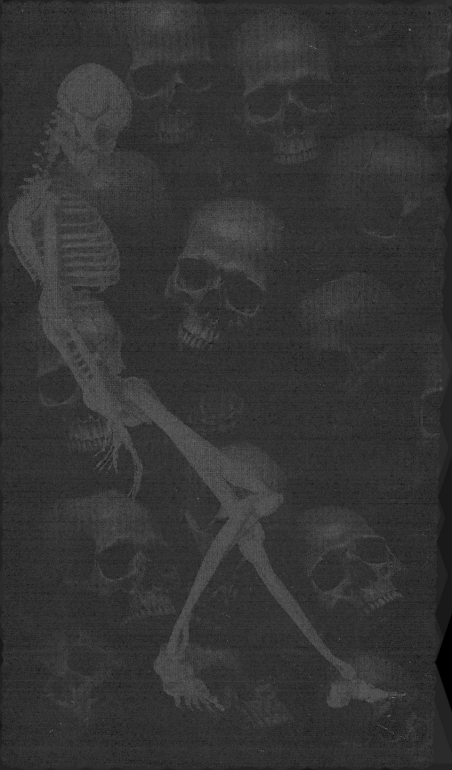

TWENTY-FOUR

EMBERLY

My throat burns, my chest pulls tighter than a corset, and every muscle in my body aches from struggling against Dominic's overwhelming strength.

Everything hurts, including my head, which pounds in time to the beat of my pulse. I can't process anything other than his final words.

Sam sends his regards.

The memory of his hands around my neck, his hot breath on my face, and his malicious grin burns into my vision, as does a kaleidoscope of memories related to Jim. I jerk, but a pair of strong arms hold me in place.

It's Roman.

If he hadn't arrived in time...

I push that thought away, only for it to be replaced by Dominic's brutal assault and that sinister sentence. Whoever he is, Sam is still out there, and he still wants me dead.

Roman was animalistic when he beat Dominic to the brink of death. The attack loops through my mind, building in intensity with each viewing. Dominic immobilized me, choked me, tried to rape me. He made me feel so terrified and helpless I thought my heart would burst.

Could Jim really be connected to Sam? Jim was a violent, abusive prick, but I left before his rages became deadly. I hate him with every fiber of my being, but he never made me fear so much for my survival.

Roman's explanation doesn't make sense.

"Are you awake, baby?" The familiar deep voice is a balm on my frazzled nerves.

"Roman?" I whisper.

"You're safe with me."

"Where's Dominic?"

"Being questioned by Cesare."

His psycho dungeon master brother? "Good."

"Are you ready for some cooling gel?" he asks.

"Do you have something for my head?"

"I brought the entire medicine cabinet. Anything you want." He helps me sit up and rests my back against the headboard.

Roman slides out of bed and takes a moment to stretch. Dappled sunlight streams through the window and caresses his back, accentuating the way his muscles ripple as he walks across the room. He pauses at a dresser covered with various medications and chooses a bottle and a tube. Then he walks to an ice bucket and retrieves a pack.

I stare down at my lap and sigh. This isn't the first time I've been choked. Jim used to grab me by the neck whenever he was angry and cut off my air. It was terrifying, but he always threw me down and allowed me to breathe when he was satisfied. Dominic had no intention of letting me live.

Shit. Not only is my mind replaying nearly getting strangled, but it keeps dredging up my worthless ex.

A shudder runs down my back. I thought I was a survivor. Is this the attack that finally breaks my spirit?

"Tylenol?" Roman's voice cuts through my thoughts.

"Please."

He hands me two pills and a glass of water. As I swallow them, he lifts my chin and rubs a menthol gel over my neck. The cool sensation sinks into my skin, soothing the burn on the outside. He pushes my head down, applies a thick layer around the back, which helps to dull the pain.

"Thanks," I rasp.

He rubs a gentle circle on my back. "Sofia made honey and marshmallow tea for your throat. Do you want to try it?"

Tears burn the backs of my eyes. I bow my head and swallow through the agony. "Why are you being so nice to me?"

"Emberly," he says. "Look at me."

I lift my head and meet his stern features and eyes so dark they penetrate my soul. What does Roman see? A perpetual victim or a damsel in distress? Will he end up like Mom and see a burden too heavy to shelter?

"When I brought you here, I wanted you to be safe from that bastard cop. I made the mistake of trusting my men to either protect you or stay out of your way, and for that, I'm sorry."

A lump forms in my throat, and I swallow.

"I swear to god, Dominic will not go unpunished. He will regret ever causing you pain."

His dark eyes shine with a sincerity that makes my heart ache. Roman means every single word. My chest tightens with the thought that no man apart from him has ever rushed to my defense.

"Can I try that tea?" I whisper.

Roman's gaze softens, and he strokes my hair until my eyes flutter shut. "Of course, baby. Anything for you."

The mattress dips with his movement. I melt against the pillows and sigh, only for him to bring the cup to my mouth.

"Drink," he says.

I part my lips and sip the warm liquid, letting it coat my tongue. It's spicy and sweet, and exactly what I need to soothe my throat. Peeking through my lashes, I meet his intense stare. No one could ever fake this level of concern.

"Thank you," I murmur, my eyes heavy.

He makes me drink the entire cup before setting it aside. "There's plenty more if you want it."

I nod, but questions bubble up the moment the sweetness leaves my tongue. "Why did he do it?"

With a sigh, Roman slides back under the covers. "I don't want you upset."

"Nothing can be worse than the way I feel."

"You really want to know?"

I turn to stare at his perfect profile. "Just tell me."

He closes his eyes. "Dominic finally admitted that a crooked cop paid him ten grand to take you out."

"What?" I place a hand over my mouth. "But he said Sam sent his regards. Who is Sam?"

"Have you heard of Samuel Johnson?"

"No."

"He's Jim Callahan's superior." A muscle in Roman's jaw flexes. "They were trying to get to me through you."

"What do you mean?" I ask.

"The woman I was accused of murdering died of strangulation," he says, the words bitter. "If Dominic killed you, I would be the most obvious suspect. And this time, there'd be no video evidence to prove my innocence."

I blink over and over, trying to process this new information. My mind spins, and I can hardly find my voice. "Jim's boss wants to frame you for my murder?"

"Yes," he growls through clenched teeth. "And I can't believe one of my trusted men would have gone to such lengths as to hurt me through you."

Somewhere in that sentence is the suggestion that I mean something to Roman, but this new revelation makes me tremble. "Oh, my god. What are we going to do?"

He turns to me, his features grave, his brows furrowing into a deep V. "You're going to get better, while I'll figure something out. While you were sleeping, I had motion sensors installed around the perimeter of your pool house. If anyone so much as thinks of coming here to fuck with you, we will both know."

I gulp. "Do you think it will happen again?"

He laughs, the sound so low and hostile that the fine hairs on the back of my neck stand on end. "I'm going to set an example of Dominic, so anyone considering crossing me will think twice before doing it through you."

"Alright." I nod, my mind zipping in all directions. I don't know how to feel. Safe because Roman can crush my enemies or terrified because I'm in the presence of someone capable of such violence?

When he presses a kiss on my temple and pulls me into his muscular chest, my body melts against his warmth. Everything I've seen of Roman indicates he means me no physical harm. What if there's comfort in knowing that the man I'm with will do anything to make sure I'm protected?

I hate ping-ponging from one extreme thought to another. I hate falling back to my ingrained paranoia.

"Rest, Emberly. You're safe with me."

As my eyelids flutter closed, I ask, "What was in that tea apart from the honey and marshmallows?"

"Sofia said she added some calming herbs. Do you want some more, baby?"

"Maybe later," I murmur against his bare chest.

Roman scoots down the bed until he's lying flat against the mattress with me sprawled on top of him like a rag doll.

His fingers thread through my curls, infusing my scalp with pleasant tingles.

His heart beats a steady rhythm beneath my ear, lulling me into a deep state of relaxation. I could lie here forever in his arms. He's quite calming when he's not beating a man half to death or carrying me to uncertain fates like a sack of rice.

Roman Montesano is an enigma. Sometimes it feels like he's my guardian angel, other times it feels like he's my captor. Maybe my mind is so frazzled by suspicion and intrusive thoughts that I can't tell the difference.

As I drift into slumber, his phone buzzes and he shifts to pick it up.

"What?" he whispers.

"Everyone is gathered on the front steps, ready for your announcement," says the voice on the other end.

Pausing, he shifts and murmurs, "Emberly?"

I pretend to sleep.

"Give me five minutes," he whispers.

He calls my name again, and I continue acting like I'm too far gone to hear his voice. Roman places a soft kiss on my forehead before slipping out of bed and pulling on a pair of pants.

My heart pounds as I crack open an eye and watch him leave the room, then I count to twenty before sliding out of bed and slipping on a robe and a pair of flip-flops.

The front door clicks shut, and I walk to the bedroom door and poke my head out into the studio. Through the floor-to-ceiling windows, I watch Roman stride along the edge of the pool and up the path that leads to the mansion. Clutching the wooden frame, I stay in place until he disappears through a set of patio doors.

That's when I make my move.

The gardens are cast in shadow, and clouds cover the

sky, letting out the barest peeks of sunlight. Shuddering at the ominous atmosphere, I wrap my arms around my chest and continue toward the mansion.

My flip-flops slap against the stone tiles, but nobody's around to hear me approach. Instead of entering through the patio doors, I walk around the building's perimeter toward the sound of chatter.

"Gentlemen," Roman says, his voice so cold that my steps falter. "I don't need to remind you how this family was broken apart five years ago by betrayal."

I quicken my steps, passing rose gardens and keeping close to walls covered in climbing plants and the occasional group of fragrant shrubs.

"Every traitor who left with Frederic Capello will pay for stabbing us in the back. I want you all to prepare for a war. We're going to take back what's ours and restore this family to its former greatness."

The men applaud and cheer.

Based on what I read online, none of this is surprising, but it turns out that I was right. The Capello family was either behind his imprisonment or took advantage of the Montesanos' downfall. Roman must have been the one who ordered their massacre.

His speech continues along the same lines, and I inch closer, trying to work out how I feel. No one can be a mafia boss without murdering, but what if all the people he kills are crooks? After today, it looks like the police are also criminals.

I reach the corner and peer in the direction of the mansion's grand entrance. Roman stands on the steps, flanked by Cesare and the brother with the glasses who ordered me to step off the balcony. Behind them are Tony and a bald man about the same size.

Roman turns to the huge men. "Bring him out."

They lumber up the stairs, through the double doors, and return, dragging out a naked man covered in bruises and cuts. He's barely conscious, and his face is hidden within a mass of blood and swelling. It has to be Dominic.

"This morning, Dominic crept into the pool house and nearly killed a woman under my protection," Roman bellows. "After everything that's happened to this family, one of you dares to betray us for money."

Chatter fills the air, but it's muffled by the pounding of the pulse between my ears. Every paranoid thought I ever had about Roman vanishes into the ether.

Roman was telling the truth. Jim's superior, Samuel Johnson, paid Dominic to strangle me to death.

"The next motherfucker who messes with my house guest won't die so easy." His sharp voice cuts through my thoughts. "Anyone who so much as looks at her funny will lose their eyes. Anyone who smirks in her direction will lose their teeth. Anyone who touches her loses their hands. You understand?"

The entire courtyard falls silent.

"Put him on the ground," Roman orders with a sneer.

He steps aside to let the two men toss Dominic down the stairs.

"This is what happens to those who cross this family." Roman points his gun at Dominic and turns his gaze across the crowd of men, looking each of them in the eye.

The first gunshot makes me clap both hands over my mouth to stifle a yelp. Roman fires more shots, joined by his brothers, making the body on the steps twitch and jerk with each bullet.

Cheers ring through the air, and I freeze. The only part of my body able to move are my lungs, which inhale air tinged with the scent of gunpowder.

Roman turns his head to the left, and our eyes meet.

Adrenaline shoots through my system like an electric shock. I duck back behind the corner and take off running.

I just got caught witnessing Roman and his brothers murdering Dominic.

How the hell will he react to my snooping?

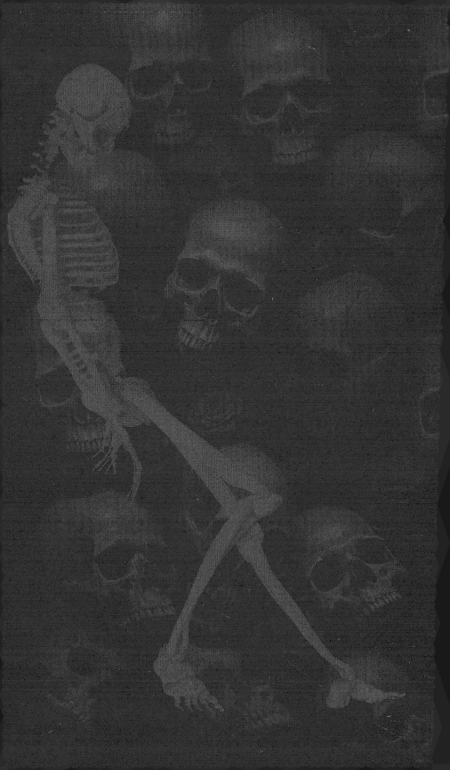

TWENTY-FIVE

ROMAN

Emberly now stays in the pool house, not daring to leave after seeing me make a public example of Dominic. According to Sofia, she's eating all her meals and filling her canvases with paint.

Since there's been no more meltdowns or demands for my presence, she's either terrified of what she witnessed or finally satisfied that I'm not her captor. Regardless, she's exactly where I need her—quiet and contained.

I walk around the new meth lab, surveying stainless steel tanks and vats and tubes. The engineers have moved the equipment from the Galliano hideout to this new location and restored the machinery to its former glory.

According to Isabella Cortese, Galliano wouldn't let production stop for maintenance, which led to more waste and a substandard product. They also cut the meth with copper salts to turn it green.

"Everything's all tested and ready for production, boss," says the engineer. "When are you expecting the cooks?"

I grin down at the gray-haired man who installed the lab

at our original hideout. "Monday. Make sure there's enough supplies to last the team a month."

"You got it." He gives me a salute and disappears behind a row of tanks.

Gil sidles up to me and snickers. "You're in an unusually good mood."

I smirk. The past few days have been stressful, but have pushed me further toward my goals. The Di Marco Law group received a delivery of Samson Capello's head, thanks to my cousin Leroi and his new girlfriend.

Our lawyer texted earlier to say the executors of the old bastard's estate are ready to transfer funds from Capello's personal bank accounts to one of our choosing. Now, they need Emberly's signatures to transfer ownership of the stocks, the casino, the loan company, the property portfolio, and the vaults containing Dad's stolen gold.

"After so much shit luck, things are starting to go my way," I say.

Gil nods his agreement. "But what are you going to do about Tommy Galliano moving in on our turf?"

My stomach sours along with my good mood. I turn to my trusted companion and weigh up solutions.

"Word would have spread to New Jersey by now that I've taken back the meth lab. Galliano will send someone down to check out the situation, and we'll be ready."

Gil rubs his chin. "With guns?"

"Whatever it takes. Anyone who enters our territory without permission will be sent back to New Jersey in pieces."

We walk out of the lab, ascend the stairs, and continue through the parking lot of Beaumont City's busiest shopping mall. Grandfather Giovanni was involved in its construction in the sixties and made sure the builders created an additional underground level. It was his secret hideaway, and now it's mine.

At this time of the afternoon, the parking lot is filled with shoppers and cars. Gil and I make our way to a black BMW with a small procession of our men.

"What do you know about art?" I ask Gil.

"Fuck all," he replies. "Why?"

"I need a list of everyone connected with us that might have links to the art industry. Can you do that?"

"Sure. You looking to buy your house guest a gift?"

"You could say that." Grinning, I make a mental note to ask the same question to Benito. Now that Emberly is ready to gain her inheritance, it's time to put the next phase of our plan into action.

———

Hours later, I put aside my plans to drop by the pool house because a representative of the Galliano brothers called the house, asking permission to cross our territory for a meeting.

The casino would have been the perfect place to stage such a meeting, but it's currently occupied by Capello loyalists who would sooner side with the Gallianos than face the family they betrayed.

I give Galliano's man permission to enter the Phoenix on the condition that he come alone. Any backup will be hunted down and killed on sight.

Gil and I sit in the club's VIP section, watching the dance floor. Cesare is in the back office, surveilling the security cameras, and Benito is in an office building opposite the club with a rifle trained on the entrance.

We've stationed men around the building and across the block, with our pet cops in their patrol car in the alleyway.

A tenth of the men on the dance floor are connected to

me in some way and they're ready for a shootout. When it comes to Galliano, nobody wants to take chances.

Despite the precautions and the potential for shit to go awry, I sit back in the armchair, sipping a glass of whiskey and looking the picture of not giving a damn.

A waitress approaches and presses her fake tits on my shoulder. "Can I get you anything, sir?" she asks.

"No." I wave her away.

Gil straightens. "You can get on my lap, sweetheart."

I'm too focused on the entrance to pay attention to the waitress's reaction, but she does not sit on Gil's lap. When a group of girls enters instead of Galliano's envoy, I turn my gaze to the dance floor.

My fingers twitch with the urge to pull out my phone and watch Emberly on the surveillance app, but I resist. Tonight's going to require balls of steel. Any acts of violence against Galliano's man could start a war we're not prepared to win.

Gil leans into me and mutters, "If I was in your position, I'd be balls deep in pussy."

"You could be if you weren't so crass."

He snorts. "Nah. If you told her to sit on your lap like I did, she'd be all over you like gonorrhea."

I turn to him and grin. "Quality, not quantity."

"You've got an admirer." Gil raises a glass toward the dancefloor.

"Not interested."

"You haven't even looked. She's hot."

I shoot him a warning glare and he raises a palm in mock surrender. "Just looking out for your best interests, boss."

If he knew anything about Emberly, he wouldn't bother me with other women. She's special, and I'm not just talking about the assets she inherited. Emberly is one of the few women I've encountered who keeps me second-guessing.

Out of morbid curiosity to see what Gil deems attractive, I glance at the dance floor and find a short blonde with a generous hourglass figure with her head turned toward us like an owl. She and her procession of female companions all perform the same dance steps, looking like they've practiced for the occasion in advance.

The woman raises a hand, and I glance away.

"You could at least say hello," Gil mutters.

"You have her," I reply.

Gil was one of the first people to visit me in prison and pledge his loyalty outside of the immediate family, even though Capello had declared himself the Don of New Alderney. He's been a loyal supporter over the five years of my incarceration. I even consider him a friend.

"She's coming over," Gil says with a snicker.

I roll my eyes. Nothing about this woman stands out apart from her boldness. Compared to Emberly, she's a clone of every other overdressed girl on the dance floor.

"Deal with it."

Gil rises from his seat and raises his palm, most likely telling her that this section is for VIPs only. She waves a flier in his face that I can only assume was the one Benito shoved through Emberly's mailbox.

I sit up in my seat. Is she the roommate?

Gil wraps an arm around the blonde's shoulder and hands her a card, which she slips in her pocket, just in time for a gray-haired bastard wearing too much fake tan to approach our table.

He's built like a lightweight boxer, wearing a black turtleneck that stretches to his chin. It's Tommy fucking Galliano himself.

Strangely, I thought he would send his less aggravating brother, Matty.

I bring my glass to my lips, keeping my expression

neutral. Coming here instead of sending a representative was an insane move. It wouldn't surprise me if he's brought backup in case I punch him in the throat.

He flashes me a smile of teeth so white they turn blue in the strobe lights. "Is this seat taken?"

I gesture for him to sit.

The man lowers himself into the armchair beside mine, and I swear I hear the creak of his leather pants over the loud music.

"You've got a lot of fucking nerve showing your face in New Alderney," I growl.

"Is that any way to speak to your stepfather?" he deadpans.

Hot fury surges through my veins, making every muscle tense. That fucker will die for luring our mother to New Jersey, but not before the time is right.

Galliano raises his brow in a silent request for me to lash out, which only confirms my suspicions that he's trying to provoke a war.

"She stopped being your wife when she died," I say.

He rubs his chin with a gloved hand and smirks.

My jaw clenches. I refuse to let this scaly bastard slither under my skin.

"You're right," I say, my voice even. "I forgot my manners. Let me be the first to offer my condolences on the loss of the entire Capello branch of your family."

His features darken. I would bet my left nut that the reptile sitting beside me helped Capello ruin us. I'm going to look forward to filling him with bullets.

"What are your intentions toward Emberly Kay?" he asks.

I tilt my head. "Emberly who?"

His eyes narrow. "Don't fuck with me, boy. Everyone knows you have Cousin Freddy's girl."

Leaning back in the chair, I hold my features in a cold mask. With Samson dead, Emberly is next in line for the inheritance. If she dies, Capello's wealth goes straight to Galliano.

I need to choose my words carefully. Emberly is the only thing standing between Galliano and the Capello millions. If a runt like Samson can bribe one of my men to kill Emberly, there's no telling how Galliano would stop us from reclaiming our property.

"I served five years on death row because your cousin framed me for murdering a woman," I say through clenched teeth. "Now, it's time for me to earn that sentence."

The corners of Galliano's lips twitch. He doesn't give a fuck that Emberly is his blood relative. All he cares about is what he stands to inherit once she's dead.

"Revenge had better be all that you want from her, or you and I will have a problem."

"That's rich, coming from the man who stole my meth lab," I snarl.

The veneer of civility cracks. He flashes his teeth and hisses, "It's mine."

"So, you admit to stealing our scientists and equipment?"

"They were a gift from my cousin Freddy."

"Who stole them from us the moment he framed me for murder," I snarl. "You owe us for five years' worth of product that our lab produced, and we never received."

Galliano's jaw hardens. "We don't owe you shit. If you have a problem, you can take it up with Cousin Freddy."

My eyes narrow. "Is that a threat?"

"Take it however you want, but if I don't get back my cook, there will be consequences."

"Cook?"

"Isabella Cortese," he snarls. "That woman belongs to me."

My lip curls, but I don't dignify the comment with a response. There's not a chance in hell that a classy, intelligent woman like Dr. Cortese would want to associate with the man who kept her and her team hostage for nearly five years.

"You have an hour to leave New Alderney," I say. "Any Galliano sympathizer found within the state limits will have to take up their complaints directly with Frederic Capello in hell."

Scowling, Galliano stands without another word and walks away.

As Gil follows him through the club and out through the exit, I knock back the contents of my glass. This isn't how I planned our first meeting, but the confrontation was inevitable.

Frederic Capello respected Tommy Galliano enough to include him in his will, which makes him a danger to Emberly. Galliano is also trying to move in on my territory, which is something I won't allow, even if it means war.

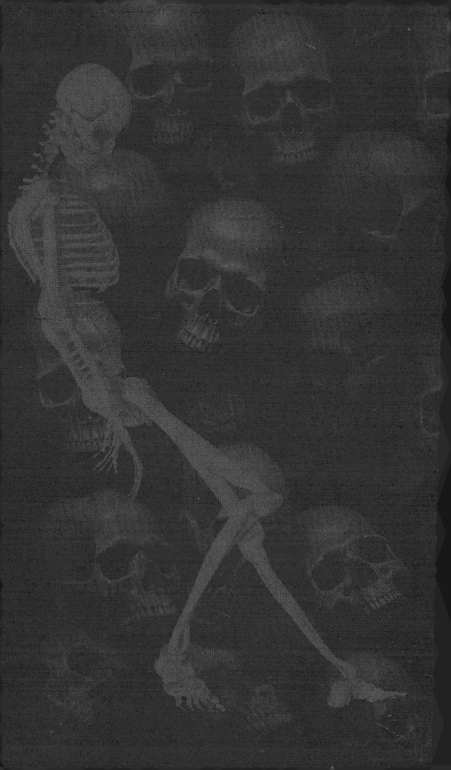

TWENTY-SIX

EMBERLEY

Three days pass after the incident on the front steps and there's no sign of Roman, which is probably for the best. I'm not looking forward to his reaction to what I witnessed. My mind can't stop replaying Dominic's broken body being riddled with bullets, Roman's brutal attack, and the horror of being so viciously choked.

The swift justice almost makes up for being strangled, but I would prefer that it didn't happen at all. If Roman killed to protect me, does that make me an accessory to murder?

I stay mostly within the confines of the pool area, occasionally taking the watercolors to the manicured gardens for inspiration. Every so often, I catch glimpses of Cesare Montesano across the grounds, who blows kissy faces or wags his tongue.

On the fourth day without Roman, I open the front door to find a four-feet tall trunk covered in Gucci canvas on a trolley. I glance around, looking for signs of whoever brought it, but the pool area is empty.

There's a blank envelope on top, and I pull out a card that says:

The items from your apartment, as promised.

Love,

Roman

My lips part with a gasp. Roman arranged for my thrifted clothes to be put in a designer trunk? This thing probably costs more than a car.

Butterflies rise in my chest as I wheel the trolley inside. If he's trying to buy my silence with expensive luggage, then he's overpaid. At least this means he isn't mad that I saw him murder Dominic.

Wow, that was callous.

I wait for a wave of guilt to arrive, but feel nothing. Dominic deserved that brutal beating. He tried to end one life and ruin another.

A knock sounds on the door. I whirl around, my heart soaring. "Come in?"

It swings open, and Annalisa steps in, her gaze shifting from side to side before landing on the trunk.

"So, this is where you've been?" she says, her voice tight.

"What are you doing here?" I ask.

She places her hands on her hips. "You were late with your rent, so I walked up to your boyfriend and demanded cash."

My jaw drops. "You didn't."

"Not really." She grins. "I couldn't get close to him, so I spoke to his second in command and told him everything."

Second in what? I picture the brother with the glasses and frown. She sure as hell can't be talking about Cesare.

"Okay, and how did you get here?" I ask.

She raises a shoulder. "We hooked up last night and he saw the bruises."

"Wait." I roll the trolley into the bedroom so it's out of

the way and I can have a moment to think. "Start from the beginning."

I sit Annalisa on the chair and walk to the other end of the studio, where there's a kitchenette with a fully stocked refrigerator. For the first time since moving into the pool house, I open a bottle of white wine.

"Here you go." I hand her a full glass.

She takes several large gulps and sighs. "That night you threw yourself at Roman and left me to walk home alone, there were police outside our apartment with a warrant for your arrest. What the hell did you do?"

My mind races. "Did they hurt you?"

"Answer my question."

I pour myself a glass of wine and take a sip. "Some gallery owner wanted to strike back before I reported him on social media for being a scammer."

"But what was the warrant for?"

"Vandalism, assault, and theft of a silver spoon?" I shake my head, not quite believing that one slimy bastard would set off such an unusual chain of events.

"Are you sure about that?" At my blank look, she adds, "They don't usually send so many police officers for petty crimes."

"One of them was my ex," I mutter.

Her eyes widen. "So, he was trying to get revenge for being dumped?"

"Something like that." My brows pinch. I really don't want to talk to her about Jim. "But how did you get here?"

Annalisa launches into an account of how the police have harassed her every day that I've gone, urging her to use every method at her disposal to lure me back to Beaumont City.

My stomach churns. I lean against the counter with my arm around my middle, trying to hold in my nausea. Jim didn't make such bold efforts to find me when I first escaped. Why is he doing so now?

The only thing I did differently was approach galleries to sell my work, which was something I wasn't confident enough to do under his constant gaslighting.

"I'm so sorry." I murmur. "None of this makes sense."

"I actually thought you were a murderer." She polishes off her wine, sets the glass on the floor, and rolls up her sleeve to expose a livid bruise. "The red-haired detective cornered me on the street, accusing me of knowing your location."

I gasp. "Jim did that?"

"That was his name. Detective Jim Callahan."

"Oh god," I say with a sigh. "Someone needs to stop that man."

"That's what Gil said." She wiggles her shoulders and smirks.

"Right." I rub the back of my neck. "The one you called Roman's second in command."

She nods. "We were at the Phoenix last night, taking advantage of the VIP flier when I saw your bae."

"Bae?" I shake off the word and focus on the rest of her story.

"Gil swaggered over and chatted me up. He couldn't get enough of me."

"I thought you said you approached them about the rent?"

Ignoring me, she continues. "He bought all of us champagne and took me back to his apartment for the hottest night of my life. When he saw my bruises, he growled."

"What did he say?"

Annalisa's features pinch into a scowl, and she lowers her voice. "Who did this to you?"

"Oh."

"I told him everything about the harassing cops, and he got on the phone, called a few numbers, and asked me if I wanted to stay in his penthouse until the heat died down."

"And you said yes."

She pouts. "What choice did I have?"

Fuck. I can't believe my shitty luck with men is now getting Annalisa hurt. I walk across the room and flop down on a seat. "You're right. I'm so sorry for dragging you into my chaos."

She waves away the apology. "Emberly, I knew sharing an apartment with an artist would bring me clout, but this is the most exciting thing that's ever happened to me."

I blow out a long breath, trying to make sense of the mess I've created of Annalisa's life. If I had known causing a fuss at Gallery Lafayette would summon a lowlife like Jim, I would have cut my losses and walked out.

Because of Gerard Lafayette, I'm now living in a mafia stronghold and Annalisa is staying with a henchman who is definitely not Roman's deputy.

"Gil drove me back to the apartment in the middle of the night, where a few others brought the trunk. He asked me to pack a bag for myself and help you move all your things."

I nod, still numb from the shock that Jim assaulted Annalisa.

Two sharp knocks sound on the door, which opens to reveal Sofia. "Would you like lunch inside or by the pool?"

"Pool." Annalisa shoots out of her seat. "Oh my gosh, I didn't know you had a maid!"

I cringe at my roommate's lack of tact. "Sofia isn't—"

"It's alright, Miss Emberly," Sofia replies, her voice sharp.

Annalisa follows Sofia out, where she sits at an outdoor table like royalty. My shoulders sag. I'm glad Gil rescued her from being assaulted and harassed and I want her to be safe, but I hope Roman won't allow her to stay with me.

I walk out of the pool house to find Annalisa holding up an empty glass. "Do you have Château Lafite Rothschild?"

"The family only drinks Italian wine." Sofia sets a bottle on the table beside a gift box large enough to hold a beach ball. "Mr. Montesano wanted you to have this."

I stare down at the label on its white surface, expecting it to reveal another brief message.

"Oooh, the Dolce Vita Boutique!" Annalisa says with a squeal. "It's one of the most exclusive in Alderney Hills. Let me see."

"Let's eat first." I grab the box and take it into the pool house, and set it on the bed in the back room.

When I return to the outdoor table, Sofia is halfway down the path that leads to the mansion and Annalisa turns to me with a half-finished glass and a scowl.

"How is it fair that you stole the man I saw first, got a free art studio, and a trunk worth over fifty grand?"

The person I was before my life turned to shit would clap back, but I still have flashbacks from Dominic's attack and subsequent execution. I don't know where I stand with Roman, and the appearance of my roommate feels ominous. My shoulders sag. I hope to god that Roman didn't bring Annalisa to keep me company for the duration of my stay.

Not only am I sick of her backhanded comments, but I can't stand the thought of leaving here without seeing him again.

The devil on my shoulder suggests doing something to get his attention, but I'm afraid of Roman. I'm afraid of what that might provoke.

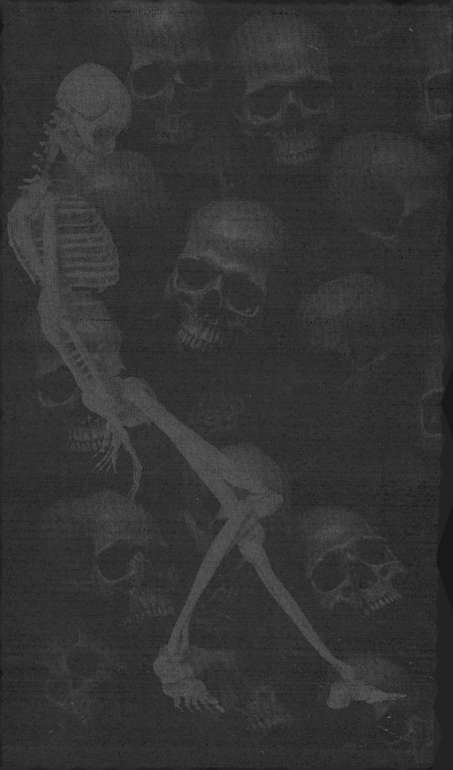

TWENTY-SEVEN

ROMAN

War looms on the horizon, and the only way to avoid destruction is to strengthen our ranks. The casino was Dad's base of operations, yet we're confined to the Phoenix. Galliano's allies might be stationed there, but we can't weed them out until after wrestling back control.

The next morning, I sit back in my office chair with my fists clenched on the desk. That New Jersey bastard has gotten me so riled up that I can barely focus on our new lawyer's instructions. Even Benito leans against the wall, engrossed in his phone.

Nick Terranova pushes over a document. "This Art Sales Agreement is a hundred percent legit, but with one unfair term."

"Why?" I ask.

"If Miss Kay is as intelligent as you say, then she'll scour the contract looking for a catch."

Benito pushes off the wall. "What catch?"

"I've inserted a clause that transfers her intellectual

property to the buyer, which is highly unusual in the sale of art."

"What if she refuses to sign?" I ask.

"Then you allow her to make amendments." Nick raises his palms and grins. "It's win-win since you don't actually give a fuck about the painting."

I nod, glad that someone's in peak form to focus on the tiny details. One glance at Benito tells me he's back to staring at his phone. I make a mental note to ask what's gotten him so preoccupied.

Nick pushes over a stack of papers. "These are what we do give a fuck about. Each contract represents different assets, namely the stock certificate transfers for the casino and the loan company, the transfer request documents for the stock portfolio. This is the bulk transfer deed for the real estate portfolio, and legal documentation to grant access to the safety deposit boxes and their contents.

I nod. "What's the status of the bank accounts?"

He leans back in his seat and grins. "Thirty million, eight hundred thousand, seven hundred fifty-three dollars, and forty-seven cents. Cash."

"Is it in the account we control?" Benito slips his phone in his pocket.

"Every penny arrived this morning."

Benito and I exchange grins. I send cousin Leroi a silent word of thanks for handing me Samson Capello's head. Now, it's only a matter of time before I relieve Emberly of the rest of her inheritance.

Benito picks up the contract on the top of the stack and flicks through each page. "Let me get this straight. The first few sheets of each are the art agreement. All Roman has to do is get her to sign the transfer portions without noticing the unfavorable clauses."

"I set up each last page to be just a signature sheet." Nick turns to me and says, "It shouldn't be too difficult."

I rub my chin. "She's a cautious one. I'll give her time to study the first contract, so she thinks everything's above board, then I'll work on ways to divide her attention."

Nick waggles his brows and smirks. "I'll bet you know exactly how."

A muscle in my jaw ticks at the thought of him thinking about Emberly in a sexual way, but I let it slide. As far as I know, he hasn't laid eyes on her.

Rising off my leather seat, I smooth down the lapels of my suit. "Let's get started. The quicker she finishes my portrait, the quicker I can get her to sign over the casino."

"Don't forget to keep her here long enough to produce at least five extra pieces of art," Nick says.

I hesitate, and he continues. "This first contract doesn't count. The next five will."

"Right." I walk around the desk and make eye contact with Benito, and gesture with a flick of my head for him to take my place.

I step out of the patio doors, where Gil waits for me by the wall, and we walk side-by-side to the long path that leads to the pool house.

"You sure you're okay with housing that woman?" I ask.

Gil snickers. "I have no complaints. Annalisa's an eager fuck."

"And if she tries to communicate with that cop?"

"You think I'm too much of a simp to put a bullet through her skull?"

My eyes narrow. "Find a way to silence her that doesn't put you on death row."

"Won't be a problem," he says with a shrug.

Up ahead, Emberly and her roommate sit around the dining table beneath the pool house's broad porch. A knot forms in my gut. This is the first time I've laid eyes on her since she spied on us filling Dominic with bullets.

Bringing her little friend here is a test to see if Emberly will talk about what she witnessed or remain silent. As we reach the edge of the pool, the shorter of the pair shoots out of her seat. Judging by the blonde's overexuberance, it looks like Emberly kept her mouth shut.

Clever girl.

"Gil!" she squeals and takes off toward us on a run.

Emberly sets down her fork and rises. I ignore how my insides tighten and offer her a broad smile.

Gil laughs, grabs the roommate, and swings her around before gathering her up in his arms. She grabs his face with both hands and slams her lips onto his mouth.

I look away. Women like that are easy prey. No challenge whatsoever. They see a semi-handsome face in an expensive suit, and all their survival instincts vanish into their pussy. That blonde is a lamb sprinting to the slaughter.

Emberly, on the other hand, remains behind the table and doesn't return my smile. Instead, she casts me a wary gaze.

She's always keeping me on my toes. No matter how many times I reassure her of my intentions, a part of her always slices through the bullshit. I admire her instincts. It makes her more of a challenge.

"Hey, boss," Gil says. "Mind if I clock off early today?"

I wave him off. "See you later."

Gil walks toward the mansion, presumably to take the roommate to his penthouse. He showed me pictures of the joint when I was in prison. It's the kind of apartment I used to love when I was too young to appreciate the comforts of home.

"What's going on between them?" Emberly asks.

"Gil is rehousing her because she was harassed by your cop."

She gulps. "Right."

"And before you ask, they're fucking."

Emberly bows her head. No doubt, the roommate already gave her the blow by blow. I'm guessing she wants to ask about Dominic, but can't muster up the words, considering she snooped after letting me believe she was asleep.

"How's the throat?" I ask.

Her hand rises to her neck. "Better."

"You been drinking Sofia's tea?"

She raises her head and smiles. "Only at night. It makes me drowsy."

I smile back. "You still shaken?"

"A little, but I'll live." Her features fall. "Why are you here?"

"Are you ready to paint my portrait?"

She sweeps her gaze down the length of my three-piece Armani suit, nods, and heads to the door. I take that as an unenthusiastic yes. She's had time to think about what happened and she's wary about being alone with a killer. I don't care as long as she gives me her signature.

Following her, I step into the pool house, which smells of linseed oil, turpentine, and wine. Canvases hang on the wall, filled with vivid colors. Some of the paintings are abstract, others are as realistic as photos, but all of them have a common brilliance that makes my jaw drop.

"Are these flowers from around the grounds?"

"Yeah." She shrugs. "I paint what I see."

"That gallery owner who framed you for stealing was a fool. If he had treated you right, your paintings could have earned you both a fortune."

"His loss," she mutters, her words tinged with bitterness.

I look her full in the face. "What's wrong?"

She runs her fingers through her curls. "You just brought up the asshole who got me into this mess."

My brow rises, and I wait for her to accuse me of being a murderer, but she picks up a large canvas and sets it on an easel.

Nodding, I take my seat and resume the relaxed pose she asked for the last time. Emberly is wrong. The gallery owner might have set off a sequence of events that drove her running into my arms, but she was in my sights the moment I discovered Capello had written her into his will.

"Is this how you want me?" I ask.

"Perfect." She fills the canvas with basic shapes. "Every time you sit for this portrait, you need to wear this outfit."

I frown. "Can't you take a picture?"

"Sure, but it'll be difficult to capture your essence from a digital image."

"My essence?" I raise a brow.

"You're the most complex and multi-layered personality I've ever met." She turns to me and frowns, her gaze assessing.

"Is that good or bad?"

"I haven't decided yet."

I chuckle. This is exactly what I meant about her being a challenge. Most women would be swayed by my power, physique, sexual prowess, or wealth, but not Emberly. She's too invested in uncovering my motives to relax and enjoy the luxuries.

"Take the photo," I say. "My business is unpredictable. There's no telling where I'll be one day or the next."

She hums. "I heard a lot of commotion a few nights ago. It sounded like World War Three."

"There was some trouble in one of the houses down the hill," I mutter, not wanting to get into how we helped Leroi capture Emberly's Capello half-brother.

"You're right." She draws back from the canvas and walks toward the kitchenette. "I will take that photo."

"Do you want me to smile or look pensive?" I ask.

She returns with her phone. "Which do you want?"

"How do you like me?"

She licks her lips, her gaze wandering down my form, and my breath hitches. It's hard to ignore that Emberly Kay is one of the most alluring women I've ever fucked.

Her beauty is raw, unadorned, and without pretense. Every emotion is readable in her vibrant green eyes, on her lush, pink lips, and in the tilt of her head. Her body language is my mother tongue.

Right now, she's thinking that she would like me naked.

"Brooding," she says.

My brows pull together. "That's not what I expected."

"Where do you want to hang your portrait?"

"My office."

"Then it makes sense for you to look powerful and in control." She raises her phone and snaps a picture. "Go on, brood."

"Like this?" My gaze lingers on the swell of her breasts.

She takes another picture, glances at the screen of her device and expands it with her fingers. "Concentrate. Those are bedroom eyes."

I bow my head, close my eyes, and remind myself that the woman standing in front of me is the daughter of my enemy. Her father didn't just steal from us, but I'm sure he was responsible for Dad's death. I only got framed for murder when I started talking about an autopsy.

But does Emberly deserve to die? I can't have her running to a judge accusing me of fraud, and I also can't have her crying foul to her distant cousins, the Galliano brothers.

The cleanest way to deal with her is through a bullet to the head.

"Okay," she says, "Open your eyes."

I stare into green eyes I should despise and see a woman who is nothing like Capello. But it doesn't matter how much I like her. Emberly Kay must die.

She snaps a picture. "That's perfect."

I give her a sharp nod. "We're holding a party tonight, and I want you to come as my date."

"I thought you'd have women lined up from the club," she says, her voice laden with accusation.

It takes half a second to realize that her little roommate might have poured poison in Emberly's ear about where I was last night. The blonde had walked over, intending to speak to me until I sent Gil to intercept her. Gil's a great guy. Any woman would be lucky to attract him, but it has to stick in the blonde's craw that her less conventional friend got this luxurious set up with the mafia boss.

I shake my head. "I was at the club to meet a male business associate."

When she disappears behind the canvas with a huff, I smile. "Nobody compares to you, baby. Are you going to be my date tonight, or do I need to pluck some random bimbo from the club?"

"Fine," she replies, sounding like she's under duress. "I'll be there."

I lean back, my pulse thrumming with satisfaction. Getting the first signature will be easy, considering I've commissioned a portrait, but I already have a plan to get Emberly to sign the bogus contracts.

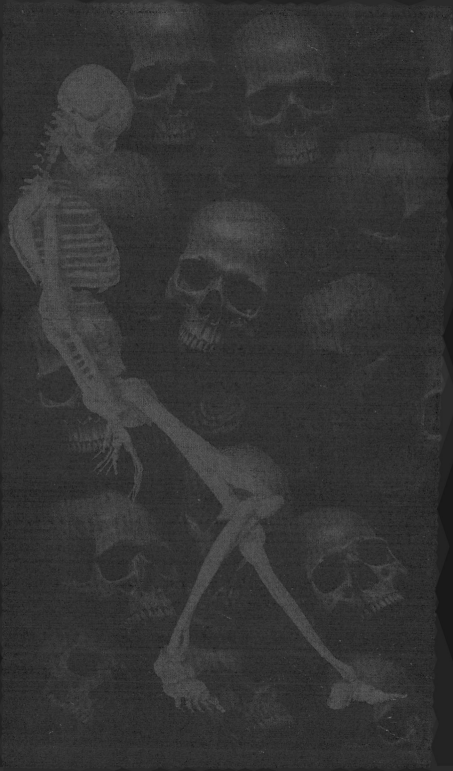

TWENTY-EIGHT

EMBERLY

I spend the rest of the afternoon sketching Roman's portrait, making sure to capture the powerful lines of his posture and the intensity of his stare. The more time I spend with him, the more I'm entranced by his personality.

He's an enigma. I wasn't joking when I called him multi-layered. Sometimes, he's playful, other times, he takes control. Then there's the gentle side of him that tended to my neck wounds and held me while I cried. Roman is a man with compassion, but he's also ruthlessly cruel.

Watching him pistol whip Dominic had been satisfying. My adrenaline had been high, and I was relieved to have such a powerful protector. But seeing him fill his unmoving body with bullets leaves me undecided.

The first thing I paint are his eyes. Up close, they're not just ebony but a deep brown with tiny flecks of gold encircled with black. They're shadowed by a masculine brow that makes them appear much darker.

I'm so engrossed in the portrait that I don't even notice when a pair of large hands wrap around my waist.

"You're progressing nicely," he murmurs, his voice breathy with awe. "I didn't realize you were so multi-talented."

Heat flares across my cheeks, and I squirm within his embrace. I can't remember the last time a man told me I was talented and meant every word. Hearing this from Roman makes me preen, even though there's a part of me that wonders if the compliment has a double meaning.

"Did you ever think I wasn't?" I ask.

"I imagined your art to be more abstract, like what you did with the flowers." He pulls me into his broad chest, the warmth of his body melting away my doubts.

"Oh," I say with a chuckle. "That was me trying to paint like Roger Thango."

"Never heard of him."

"He's one of the African artists whose work inspired the cubist movement." I glance at his profile.

"Like Picasso?"

I nod. "My fine art professor told us it was important to understand the fundamentals before we develop our own style, otherwise anyone can splash anything on a canvas and call it art."

He chuckles. "Smart professor. I've seen all kinds of bullshit sell for millions."

"You're interested in the arts?"

"I only ever viewed paintings as investment pieces until I saw your works," he says. "It's like everything you do carries a piece of your beautiful soul."

My heart flutters. Warmth fills my chest, making my cheeks bloom with heat.

"You buy art?" I ask.

"That was something Benito did with our dad, but you've awoken a new interest."

"Be serious," I say with a chuckle.

"An associate of mine is so talented at forging paintings that fool the experts. I know the gallery owner that sells his work and nothing there is even close to touching your talent."

I spin around in his arms. "Do you have contacts in the art world?"

"The Montesanos have fingers in all pies around New Alderney," he says with a smile. "Why?"

Every instinct screams at me to beg for an introduction. No gallery owner would try to scam me if they knew I was connected to Roman. They could sell my work and I'd be able to leave the state with more than twenty-five thousand dollars to start a new life under a new identity.

I shake off that thought. Roman has done enough for me. Any more favors might keep me here longer than I want to stay.

"No reason," I reply. "I was just curious."

He glances at the wall clock. "It's seven thirty. The party starts at nine. I'll pick you up in two hours."

"Sure." My gaze darts toward the bedroom. "What's the dress code?"

"It's in the box."

He walks around the canvas, leaving me staring at his retreating back. I wait until he's out of the door before returning to the bedroom, where I left the box from the Dolce Vita boutique.

Annalisa had begged me to open it, but I'd grown so sick of her comments, and I didn't want her to belittle Roman's gift. Based on what he's given me so far, it would be something lavish with a hefty price tag, but Annalisa would have found a way to twist it into something bitter.

Who can blame her, considering I brought police harassment to her door, as well as my psychotic ex?

I lift the lid, revealing a stack of smaller boxes. The one

at the top contains a pair of open-toed wine-colored heels with gold embellishments. In the middle one lies a silver strapless bra and matching panties.

My pulse quickens as I open the last box, which is wide and flat and can only contain a dress. After pushing apart the tissue paper, I lift out a floor-length gown the same shade of wine as the shoes but with a diamanté bodice and a thigh-length slit that reveals peeks of sparkling fabric.

"Wow," I whisper. "This is too much."

I hold the gown at arm's length, my breath turning shallow. Something like this has to be a one-of-a-kind design. I don't understand why Roman is being so generous when we both know I'm only staying until I've finished the portrait. If he wants sex, he only needs to ask.

Later, after rubbing paint off my fingers, I finally open the huge Gucci chest, which splits vertically into two sections. The left is a tiny closet with my jackets and coats on wooden hangers and the right consists of five leather drawers.

Annalisa packed all my things carefully, with accessories in the top drawer and my toiletries at the bottom. I shake my head, marveling at her attention to detail, wishing I wasn't always so cynical about people. Sometimes, all I ever see are their faults.

After a long soak in the bath, I tame my unruly curls with a deep conditioning treatment, blow dry it with a diffuser, and apply a light layer of makeup.

The lingerie is a perfect fit, as is the dress, which accentuates my curves and makes my skin pop. How did Roman know I suit autumn and winter shades?

I barely recognize myself in the mirror. The bodice cinches my waist and flares out a little at the hips, creating a more exaggerated hourglass. That thick strip of diamanté-encrusted fabric I saw earlier sweeps behind my right hip, exposing my thigh, while silk fabric swoops from my waist around the front of my hips so I'm not flashing my panties.

The gown is so dramatic that my face looks under-dressed. I approach the mirror and apply darker colors to match the outfit, as well as a bronzer that stretches down to my neck.

When I step out of the bedroom, Roman is already waiting in the studio wearing a wine-colored suit so dark it borders on black, and a plum-colored shirt that accentuates his olive skin.

My breath catches.

We're matching.

His eyes move up and down my form, and a slow smile spreads across his face. Heat rises to my cheeks. He looks like he wants to devour me until I'm a quivering, moaning heap.

"You look beautiful," he says, his voice low. "I can't wait to show you off to all my guests."

I shuffle on my feet. No one has ever looked at me with such intensity before, at least no one who ever wanted to take me out on a date.

"Thanks," I murmur. "You look good, too."

He raises his brows. "Only good?"

"Fishing for compliments?"

"Maybe I am." He puffs out his chest. "What do you think?"

I resist the urge to roll my eyes. No man this handsome could ever be insecure about the way he looks. With one smile, he can make a woman forget he's a killer. Roman could stroll into a nightclub empty handed and walk out with a harem.

"Alright, you're as handsome as the devil," I say.

Roman flashes me a panty-melting smile of straight white teeth. "The devil, you say?" He reaches into the inside pocket of his jacket and produces a black velvet box. "Interesting choice of words, because I fuck like a demon."

Heat floods my pussy. The worst part about that statement is that it's accurate. Not wanting to start anything sexual, I drop my gaze to his hands.

"What's that?" I ask.

"Go to the mirror, he says.

Returning to the bedroom, I try not to quiver as Roman stands at my back, opens the box, and extracts a necklace made up of small diamonds set within tiny silver circles.

It's the most exquisite thing I've ever seen. Most diamond necklaces are arranged in regular patterns, but this one has random groupings of jewels that appear organic. In some places, the links are only one-diamond thick, then they increase to two clumps, then six and any number in between.

"This is so beautiful," I whisper.

"I saw it and immediately thought of you." He drapes it around my throat and fastens it at the back of my neck.

"What do you mean?"

"Unusual. Unpredictable. Unexpectedly unique."

He leans in close and inhales my hair with a deep sniff that makes my skin tingle. Shivers run down my spine and settle in my core.

How the hell can a man seduce me so completely with just a single breath? I turn around and step back, trying to create some distance. Roman is dangerously alluring, and I'm slipping under his spell.

This can't be real.

Men like him don't lavish gifts on women they've only known for a week... or do they? It's not like I've ever met a multi-millionaire. What the hell do I know about the spending habits of the powerful and rich?

"Are you ready, baby?" He offers me his hand.

When I take it, he brings my knuckles to his lips. His dark eyes bore into mine as he leans in and bestows each one with a kiss.

His warm breath heats my skin, and I swallow hard, picturing myself spread out on the bed while he covers my naked body with kisses.

"Yes," I rasp, wanting more.

The corners of his eyes crinkle into a smile that oscillates between warmth to smug satisfaction. Taking my hand, he leads me out of the bedroom, through the studio, and into the night.

Floodlights illuminate the Montesano mansion, making its limestone exterior glow like the moon. They brighten the ivy covering half its walls, making it appear like we're walking toward the setting of a fairytale.

As we approach the patio, I hear the strains of an orchestra playing one of the concertos from Vivaldi's Four Seasons.

"Is this your kind of music?" I ask.

"My tastes are varied. The orchestra will play modern pieces later, so everyone can dance."

We walk through the hallway, where I glimpse a few strangers milling about, all dressed in the same black-and-white outfit with burgundy accents. Roman must have hired a catering company.

"Isn't this the same uniform as Chez Aquitani?"

He turns to me and smiles. "Have you dined there?"

"I wish," I say with a chuckle. "Those snobs rejected me for a cleaning job."

We round a corner to find Gil and Tony standing beside a set of double doors. As soon as they spot us, Gil brings a phone to his ear and holds up his huge palm.

"One second, boss," he says. "I'll open the door as soon as the orchestra switches."

Roman nods.

I turn to Roman and whisper, "What's happening?"

He leans into me and murmurs, "We're making our grand entrance."

I gulp.

We?

Why me? I'm just a nobody who grabbed him by the lapels a week ago and stole a kiss. Now, he's dressed me up to parade me as his plus-one? Roman might be an underworld prince of darkness, but I'm no mafia Cinderella. Beneath the designer clothing is someone who doesn't belong.

My heart pounds and unworthy thoughts race through my mind, picking up speed and paranoia until my brow breaks out in a sweat. Everyone inside will wonder what he's doing with me when he could have a movie star or a mafia princess.

Maybe I'm overthinking things. Maybe Roman sees me as a trophy because he stole me from a policeman desperate enough to storm the gates with backup. Men like him are competitive, and Roman's grudge against the authorities is valid.

Would that be so bad?

Revenge against the police is the only thing that makes sense because there are more beautiful and more connected women than me. This isn't self-denigration, it's me being realistic. Drop dead gorgeous mafia dons might fuck a starving artist once or twice, but would he show her off to all his friends?

I don't think so.

The music quiets, and there's a smattering of applause. A smooth voice announces through the closed door, "Ladies and gentlemen, please welcome your host, Roman Montesano!"

Roman offers me his arm. I take it, my heartbeat cranking up several notches.

Violins play the first notes of *For He's a Jolly Good Fellow*, and Tony and Gil open the double doors.

The ballroom beyond is aglow with chandeliers and overflowing with elegant guests in evening gowns and tuxedos. Everyone launches into thunderous applause, filling the space with a buzz.

The crowd parts, and Roman leads me through the throng. My gaze darts from side to side, taking in the people. I recognize Sofia, Roman's brothers, city officials, and a few faces from the New Alderney Times society pages.

Up ahead, the orchestra continues playing the second verse of the song, which I can barely hear through the pulse pounding through my eardrums.

As we reach the stage, Roman unclasps my arm and brings my hand to his lips for another kiss.

"Stay here," he murmurs into my ear.

I nod, relieved that he doesn't want me to join him onstage, and I watch him mount the steps and head toward the microphone.

"Thank you, thank you," Roman says into the fading applause. "I'm so pleased to see so many familiar faces here tonight to celebrate my homecoming."

The crowd breaks into cheers and whistles. I turn around to see their happy faces when I lock gazes with a gray-haired man whose photo often graces the culture pages.

It's Ernest Lubelli, the owner of the MoCa art gallery.

My heart skips several beats. Should I approach him about my paintings?

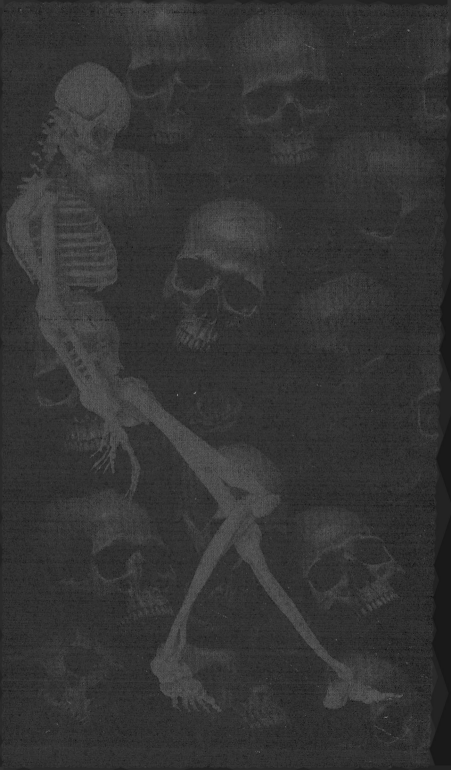

TWENTY-NINE

EMBERLY

I should be listening to Roman's speech, but all I can focus on is that gallery owner. Is he the one Roman mentioned earlier? Since he's invited to this party, he must be a friend, or at least an associate.

Roman thanks his brother, Benito, and asks him to come onstage. As Benito says a few words to welcome all the well-wishers, I move through the crowd toward Mr. Lubelli.

The older man straightens, his gaze fixed on mine. If it's intrigue I see on his features, then it's probably because I walked in on Roman's arm.

"Hi," I murmur beneath the sound of Benito's speech. "Are you Ernest Lubelli?"

"Well, hello," he says with a smile. "Yes, I am. And you are?"

"Emberly. Emberly Kay. I'm an artist."

His brows rise. "Roman mentioned commissioning an up-and-coming painter for a portrait, but he neglected to reveal it was someone so charming."

My cheeks heat. "He didn't mention my name?"

"You know Roman. He's a very private man. Perhaps he wanted to keep you all to himself."

It makes sense that Roman didn't give Mr. Lubelli my name. I'm supposed to be in hiding. I turn toward the stage, where Cesare walks up and says a few words.

The older man places a hand on my shoulder. "Do you have any photos of your artwork?"

Damn it. The one time I get to meet an art dealer and I don't even have my phone. I clear my throat. "Could I send you an email?"

"Of course." He reaches into his jacket pocket and extracts a business card. "When you finish Roman's portrait, I'll be honored to see that too."

The blonde woman standing beside him loops her arm through his as though marking her territory. She's in her late thirties, wearing a red gown the exact shade of her lipstick.

I take the card and shoot her an apologetic smile. "It was nice to meet you, Mr. Lubelli. I'll be in touch."

"Wait a second," the blonde woman says. "Did I hear you say you paint portraits?"

"Um... yes?"

She reaches into her purse and hands me her card.

I glance down at to read:

Di Marco Law Group

Martina Mancini

Associate

When I glance down into her smiling blue eyes, she says, "I've always wanted my picture painted. If Roman's working with you, then it means you're the best."

I suck in a sharp breath. This could be a great opportunity, but could I get away with charging her twenty-five grand?

"Thanks." I return her smile. "I'll be in touch when I finish Roman's portrait."

Without wanting to overstay my welcome, I slip the cards into the bodice of my gown and continue to the front of the crowd, where a waiter hands me a glass of champagne.

Roman is back in the microphone, outlining his plans for expanding his waste management and construction companies beyond New Alderney. I stand back and focus on the rest of his speech, not realizing that Roman's empire encompassed so many legitimate businesses. From the way he talks, I would never even know he was a mafia don, but the number of armed men walking around his grounds suggests otherwise.

Not to mention what I saw happen on the steps of his mansion. There's no doubt. Roman Montesano is a murderer. Though somehow, seeing him kill someone so deserving makes him less terrifying.

"My freedom era will bring about a lot of changes across New Alderney," he says to a smattering of laughter.

"The first thing I plan to tackle is the corruption within the justice system that led to me being incarcerated for half a decade. How many innocent people sit in prisons for crimes they didn't commit? How many have been executed protesting their innocence to their dying breaths? Now that I—"

Gunshots ring through the air, each one hitting Roman's chest with brutal precision. My blood turns to sludge, and my stomach drops to the ballroom floor like a dead weight. I suck in a breath, too shocked to scream.

Roman stumbles back and drops the microphone. Benito rushes to his side, while Cesare covers his brothers and points his gun into the crowd.

Chaos breaks out as everyone screams and runs in all directions, knocking over tables and chairs. Terror seizes my heart in a paralyzing grip, and I stand frozen in place.

How could this happen? How can someone as powerful

and as protected as Roman get shot down in his own home? Which of his enemies would dare move against him? I look around for the shooter, but all I see is a blur of panicked faces.

Eyes swimming with tears, I glance toward where Roman lies unmoving on the stage. Any doubts I had about him evaporate, replaced with a sense of profound grief.

What if he's dead?

The young waiter who handed me the champagne grabs my wrist. "What are you doing?" he hisses. "Run."

As the ballroom fills with more gunshots, he tugs me toward an exit by the stage that goes unnoticed in the mad scramble to escape.

My heart thunders, pumping blood to my extremities. I run along his side, my heels clicking on the marble floor. We burst through the door and into a hallway that leads past a busy kitchen toward an exit.

"Are you alright?" the waiter yells over the sound of more gunfire.

"Y-Yes," I stutter. "Who's shooting?"

"Don't know, but my boss warned us that something like this might happen."

My steps falter. "What?"

He turns to me and grimaces. "Three times out of ten, one of the mafia events he caters for ends in a shooting. I just never knew it would be so bad."

Shit. Roman is lying on that stage, probably bleeding out. What if his brothers also got shot? Who's going to call for an ambulance? I glance over my shoulder, my insides twisting with unease.

He pushes open the fire exit and pulls us out into a paved courtyard occupied by catering vehicles. Some of them are already reversing out of their parking spots and moving down the driveway toward the main gates. The door behind us closes with a thud, reminding me I just left Roman for dead.

"We should go back," I say.

"What for?"

"Roman is hurt. He's going to need medical attention."

"The Montesano don can look after himself." He pulls us toward a van.

Guilt yanks at my heart and squeezes my lungs until I can't breathe. I grab the waiter's collar with so much force that his shirt rips open, revealing his shoulder. "Wait."

"What?"

"Let go of me. I need to know that he's okay."

"Are you insane? Do you want to get killed, too?" He opens the back of his van with one hand.

My gaze drops to a tattoo poking out beneath his shirt. I yank down the fabric, revealing a familiar-looking design. It's a grinning skull atop a symmetrical cross outlined in black. Beneath it in gothic script are the letters NAD.

A breath catches in the back of my throat. It's identical to the tattoo I saw on my psychopathic ex. This waiter is working with Jim. I study his features, trying to work out how someone so young could be an undercover cop. He can't be more than eighteen or nineteen.

"You're one of them?" I yank my arm out of his grip.

He frowns. "One of what?"

I back toward the door. "The police."

His confused expression morphs into something sinister and dark. He advances on me, his teeth bared, his arm outstretched. "I don't know what you're talking about."

My breath quickens and I sidestep out of his reach. With as much stealth as I can manage, I slip off my heels and ready myself for an attack. I'm not mistaken. This isn't my usual paranoia. This guy is connected to my ex.

I grope around behind my back for a handle, but the

door feels like one of those exits that only opens from the inside.

"Come with me," he says, sounding desperate.

"No," I reply, trying to keep my voice from trembling. "Leave without me."

His features twist with anger, and he lunges, but I'm already turning on my heel and sprinting.

"Bitch!"

Heart pounding hard enough to burst, I race around the mansion toward the front steps. My bare feet slap against the cold stone tiles as I pick up speed, desperate to lose him in the crowd. I need to get help from one of Roman's men.

The man's heavy footsteps draw closer and closer with each frantic beat of my pulse. I need to run harder, faster, but my dress gets in the way.

As I round the corner, a large hand grabs me by the arm and yanks me into his chest. I scream.

"You're not getting away," he growls. "Now, stop trying to run and come with me."

"Let go." I elbow him hard in the ribs, making him grunt. "Help!"

He claps a hand over my mouth and drags me back around the corner. "Dumb cunt. Jim said he wanted you alive, but he didn't say not to knock out your teeth."

Adrenaline floods my system, filling my veins with liquid terror. Fight-or-flight kicks me in the gut and takes over my limbs.

I throw my weight backward, making us both fall to the ground. The cop lands first, cushioning the impact, and the base of my skull lands smack into his face. I'm dazed for a heartbeat before my mind snaps back to the present danger.

"Fuck," he roars into my ringing ears.

I scramble off him and onto my knees, but he grabs my

hair and pulls tight. Pain explodes through my skull, filling my eyes with tears.

"If you won't get into the van, then I'll drag you."

He rises, keeping tight hold of my hair, dragging me flailing on my back.

"Help," I scream. "Somebody help me!"

He kicks me in the ribs. "Shut up."

I grab his ankle, trying to throw him off balance, but he breaks free from my grasp and continues dragging me across the paving stones.

"When I bring you to Jim, I'm going to ask him to let me have my turn with you first."

My scalp burns, bringing with it a fresh bout of panic. I grab onto the hand encasing my hair by the root and try to yank him to the ground.

He looms over me and snarls, his features a rictus of rage. "Stupid bitch. You're going to get us both kill—"

A gunshot rings out, sending out an explosion of blood and gore. Warm rain, sticky and coppery and thick, spatters across my face. I gasp for air, my heart lurching, but my lungs refuse to breathe.

The cop stares sightlessly ahead before collapsing on his knees and falling on his face, revealing a dark figure striding toward me with a gun.

It's Roman, looking murderous.

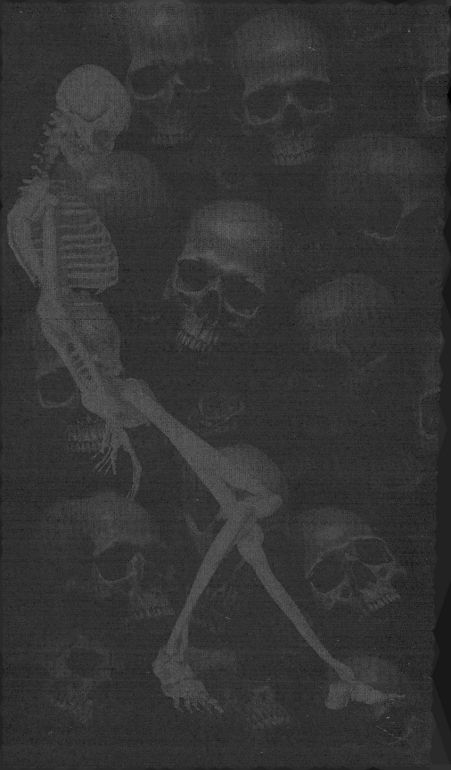

THIRTY

ROMAN

The ballroom and the orchestra behind me explode into screams, and I hit the ground with a thud. The shooter continues firing, and I hope to hell my surveillance people hunt down that motherfucker before he or she escapes.

"Roman." Benito's voice is tense. "You okay?"

I squeeze my eyes shut and check in on where the bullets hit. The pain is dull, like tiny punches, although I may have cracked a rib.

"Yeah. Nice call on the bullet-proof undershirts."

When I crack open an eye, I find Cesare crouched low, pointing his gun into the panicking crowd.

I clutch Benito's lapel. "Make sure he doesn't hit anyone who doesn't deserve it."

He gives me a crooked smile. "Sure thing." His face goes blank the way it does whenever he concentrates, and he presses a finger into his earpiece. "They've already identified the shooter. He's running toward the back wall."

I grunt. "Lock down the exits. Make sure nobody leaves the grounds unless they're legit."

Benito nods.

"And get the observation people to track his accomplices."

We wait until Gil approaches the stage to let us know the ballroom is clear. I ease myself up and clutch at my sore rib. Lightweight bulletproof armor doesn't absorb much of the impact, though it sure as hell protects my insides from getting shredded.

My brothers and Gil surround me, their features creased with concern. Since the bulletproof undershirts were a last-minute decision, no one had the chance to test their effectiveness.

"Where's Emberly? Did she reach the pool house?" I ask.

Gil murmurs something into his earpiece and waits a few seconds before saying, "No one has activated the motion sensors. She's probably still out there, stuck in the crowds."

"Shit." I hurry along the edge of the stage and descend the stairs. My bruised rib throbs with each step. "You three, make sure she doesn't escape the grounds in anyone's car."

Gil and my brothers explode into action, each heading for the ballroom's different exits. I jog toward the one closest to the stage that runs past the events kitchen and into the courtyard where the caterers have parked their vans.

I push the door open and break into a run, trying not to think of Emberly getting crushed in the melee or getting trampled underfoot. She's an intelligent woman, resourceful, too, and knows how to survive. But she's also unpredictable.

Pain lances through my rib, making my chest tighten with every breath. There's no doubt about it. It's either broken or fractured. None of that matters if the key to our fortune escapes and finds her way to the Di Marco law firm or worse, Tommy Galliano.

I reach the exit, shove the door open, inhale a lungful of

fresh air, and groan at the sting. Chatter fills the air from the guests that have spilled out to the front of the house. I scan the courtyard, finding six cars and four vans. One of them has its back doors open, but it's empty.

Emberly could be anywhere.

The air fills with a high-pitch scream. I glance from side to side, looking for its source. Further down the courtyard lies a pair of discarded high-heeled shoes.

At the second scream, I burst into action and run in the direction of the shoes. It could be Emberly. My gut tightens. If anyone is hurting her...

I round the corner to find a skinny waiter dragging a woman by her hair. She thrashes, hiding her face beneath a curtain of dark curls, but the silver sparkles on her dress are unmistakable.

It's Emberly.

My eyes widen, and her screams drown the fury roaring through my ears. Rage sears through my veins at the sight of yet another man hurting what's mine. I reach into my inside pocket and extract my pistol.

She jerks on his arm, making him stumble forward. When the man rights himself and adjusts his grip, I raise my gun and pull the trigger.

The bullet tears through his head, sending out a spray of blood and skull and brains. His grip on her hair loosens, and he collapses to his knees. I break into a run and reach Emberly.

She stares up at me, her lips trembling, but she makes no sound. I scan her face and body for wounds, but can't see anything since she's covered in that bastard's gore. My stomach drops. What the fuck happened to her?

"Emberly," I rasp. "Are you hurt?"

Her breath comes in heavy pants, her eyes never leaving mine. She's either in shock or in too much pain to speak.

"Don't move." I scoop her up off the ground and gather her into my arms. Every limb in her body is rigid, as though she's been injected with a muscle paralyzer.

"It's alright, baby. I've got you," I murmur into her hair.

It's only when those words sink in that her limbs finally tremble.

"Are you hurt?" I ask.

"I-I don't know," she whispers.

"Let me get you inside." I carry her back around the corner and toward the service entrance.

By now, all the catering staff have left the building and are gathered in the courtyard, surrounded by a quartet of my armed guards. I walk past them to find the door wedged open, so I press my palm on a security pad that opens into a stairwell.

When Great-grandfather Paolo built the mansion, he installed multiple staircases so that servants could get around to each member of his extended family. When Dad inherited the property, he closed most of them because they were a security risk.

I hurry up the dark stairs, filling Emberly's ears with whispered reassurances. She trembles, releasing a harsh sob.

"Jim sent him," she says, her voice thick with tears. "He was from the police."

My jaw tightens. I never thought a cop would go to such lengths to get back at an ex, but I make a mental note to handle Jim Callahan.

"He's gone now," I say. "No one can hurt you here."

I carry her through a disused corridor and into the upstairs hallway that leads to the master suite. After laying her on the sofa, I walk into the bathroom, soak a washcloth in warm water, and pull out a first-aid kit.

The first thing I need to do is wipe the mess off her face to see if there's any damage under all that blood.

When I step out, Emberly's eyes are already closed, and her breaths are even but shallow. I crouch beside her and take her hand, only to find her skin cold and clammy.

"Open your eyes, baby," I murmur. "Stay with me."

Her eyes flutter open, loosening tears. "Why does Jim want to hurt me so badly?"

My chest tightens. She still thinks Dominic strangled her on the orders of her ex. Telling her it was her half-brother, Samson Capello, would only make things worse for both of us.

"Don't worry about Jim," I growl, wiping gore off her cheek. "His days are numbered."

She gazes up at me, her eyes shining with hope. "Do you promise?"

"The next time you'll see that motherfucker will be at his funeral. He hurt you, and he must die. It's that simple."

Emberly closes her eyes and sighs. I swipe the cloth over her eyelids and murmur, "Please stay awake. I need to know where you're injured."

"Only a few scrapes and my scalp," she says.

"How did you find out he was a cop?" I ask.

"He helped me escape the gunfire, but I wanted to go back and check on you. When he wouldn't let go of my arm, I grabbed his shirt and saw a tattoo on his chest. It's identical to Jim's."

"A police fraternity?" I gently wipe the rest of the blood off her face.

"Maybe." Her eyes snap open and she cranes her neck, seeming to scan my body for injuries. "How are you still standing? I saw you get shot."

"Bulletproof undershirt," I say with a smile. "If I hadn't worn it, that bastard would have taken you away from me."

She shudders. "Who shot you?"

"Let me worry about that. Focus on getting some rest."

"Alright."

Her broken voice makes my heart crack. Emberly's ex-boyfriend is proving to be unexpectedly more resourceful than anticipated, and that makes him dangerous.

I don't understand why Jim Callahan is pursuing her so relentlessly, but this shit needs to stop. My contacts at the police department will send me everything they can dredge up on that asshole, and then I'll have him followed.

Keeping her talking, I ease off the blood-spattered gown and expose her silver lingerie. This situation has gotten me so riled up that I don't even pause to appreciate her beauty.

After cleaning up the blood, I lay her in my bed and pull the covers up to her neck.

"Thank you," she murmurs. "You're always coming to my rescue."

No, I'm not.

As I gaze down at her, my throat constricts, and I am unable to utter a response. Dark curls radiate across the pillow, framing her beautiful face like a halo. The ache in my chest intensifies into a crushing weight.

If Emberly knew I was more dangerous to her than Jim Callahan, she would never stop screaming. Tonight, I almost lost her, and the thought of that is too much to bear.

I can't catch feelings for her, but this evening's attack has left me reeling. I know, from the depths of my blackened soul, that at some point, I will lose Emberly forever.

Fuck, I can't believe I once thought of putting a bullet through her skull. Watching her create art was mesmerizing, and having her on my arm tonight filled me with so much pride.

She's the most unique person I've ever met and a perfect combination of down-to-earth humility and class. Spirits like Emberly are exceedingly rare and too precious to waste.

I lean down for a kiss, my nose filling with her sweet

scent. Cinnamon, vanilla, and the most intoxicating musk. Every instinct inside me rears up, wanting to devour her, desperate to mark her as mine.

As my mouth reaches her cheekbone, she turns to meet me halfway with parted lips.

When I pull away, her features fall, and her hopeful, beautiful green eyes lose their sparkle. My heart twists at the sight of her disappointment, but I can't stay. Lord knows I don't deserve Emberly.

If I kiss her, I will never leave.

What the fuck is this woman doing to me?

"The shooter's still out there," I rasp. "I need to make sure he doesn't leave."

Turning on my heel, I leave Emberly in my bed, resolving to either stay up all night or sleep somewhere else.

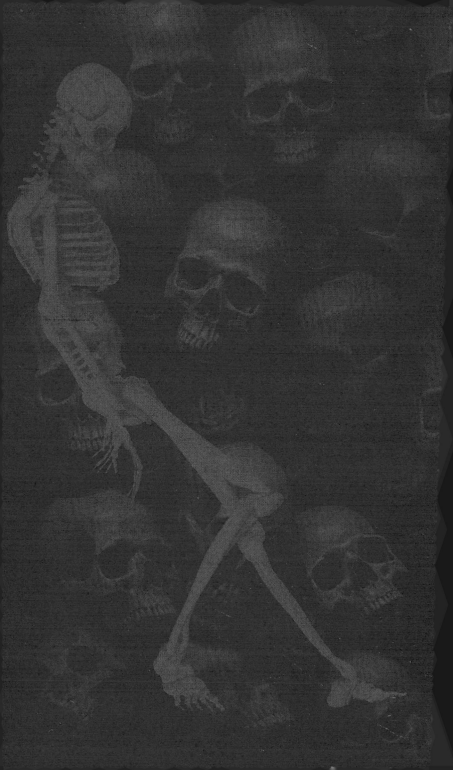

THIRTY-ONE

EMBERLY

The next morning, I wake up with a gasp, my heart pounding so hard that it could break free from my chest. Sweat coats my brow, and every limb trembles as though I'm still under attack.

Gruesome images of the young police officer's head exploding replays through my mind in a relentless assault. The stench of gunpowder and copper invades my sinuses and fills my lungs until I choke. It's harrowing, but nothing compares to the gut-wrenching sensation of being splattered by a rain of brain fragments and warm blood.

Jim won't stop coming after me until he's gotten revenge, and he has the full backing of the police. The only thing standing between my painful, humiliating death is Roman.

I roll to the other side of the mattress, expecting him to be there like he was when Dominic tried to strangle me to death, but it's empty. The sheets are still tucked in, looking like he's stayed up all night.

My gaze wanders around a bedroom twice the size of the

one I have in the pool house. The morning sun colors its pale walls a gentle shade of orange that glints on the iron footboard's gold embellishments.

On my right are floor-to-ceiling patio doors that lead to a balcony tiled in limestone, complete with slimline columns and a matching railing. The cream furniture looks antique and too opulent for guests. This bedroom must belong to Roman.

My fingers grip the pillow, and I inhale the familiar scents of leather, cedar, and something so masculine it slows my pulse. Calmness washes over my frayed nerves at the reminder of how Roman always has my back, offering comfort and protection whenever I'm in danger.

Roman told me that I'm safe, and I believe him. He won't stop defending me until Jim is six feet under and I can finally be free.

A phone rings, snapping me out of my musings. I glance around to find the sound coming from a landline on Roman's bedside table. When it doesn't switch to voicemail, I roll to the other side of the bed and pick up the receiver.

"Hello?" I rasp.

"May I speak with Roman, please?" asks a deep, cultured voice.

"He's not here at the moment," I reply. "Can I take a message?"

The man on the other end of the line sighs. "Please tell him it's Ernest Lubelli, from the MoCa gallery. That's L-U-B-E-L-L-I. We didn't get a chance to speak last night, but I'd like to invite him to the auction we're holding in a few days."

My heart skips several beats. My breath quickens. My throat dries, and my heart beats twice as fast. All the afterimages from last night fade at the prospect of getting closer to my dream.

"Mr. Lubelli?" I try to level my voice to mask my excitement, but my adrenaline is still high and I'm still on edge.

"Yes?" he replies.

"It's Emberly Kay. We met last night."

"Roman's charming date," he says, his voice filled with warmth.

"That's right," I reply, my pulse ratcheting up to a hundred. "Were you serious when you asked to see my paintings?"

"Of course. Roman and his family have such exquisite taste. I'm always looking for the chance to discover a new artist. Do you only specialize in portraits?"

"I-I also paint abstracts, but my art teacher in New Jersey wanted us to have a rounded education. I'm still experimenting, but I like to be inspired by people and nature."

"Well, I'm more than interested in perusing your portfolio," he says. "Do you still have my card?"

My fingers tremble as I slide them deep into my bra and finding the thick paper. "Yes. I'll email what I have today."

"Please be sure to include Roman's portrait," Mr. Lubelli says. "I'm interested to see how you would interpret his classically handsome features."

My stomach drops. Roman sat for me for hours, but the painting still isn't complete. "Sure," I say, my mind racing. "It might take a little time. There's a lot going on in the house right now, and Roman wants me to stay where it's safe."

"That's understandable," he replies with a nervous chuckle. "I hope you didn't get hurt in the chaos."

Swinging my legs off the bed, I stretch and consider Mr. Lubelli's words. Chaos is an understatement compared to nearly getting abducted and being sprayed with gore. But the chance of realizing my dreams might be exactly what I need to cope.

"It was awful," I murmur, "But I always work through trauma with my art. I'll tell Roman you called and email you the pictures in a few hours."

"My date and I barely escaped with our lives. She's even more eager to immortalize herself on canvas." Mr. Lubelli hangs up.

My heart thumps with excitement, both at the prospect of getting a commission from the blonde lawyer and this fabulous opportunity.

If I can get the most prominent art dealer in New Alderney to even look at my work, that would be more than a breakthrough. It will make up for all the bullshit I endured at Gallery Lafayette.

I walk around the room, looking for my gown, only to find it folded on a chair, caked with blood and a pale substance I don't care to identify.

A shudder runs down my spine, making my insides twist with disgust. I can't wear the remains of a corpse. Turning on my heel, I head toward the nearest door, which hides a luxurious bathroom that belongs in a spa. The next door is a walk-in closet that resembles a men's boutique, and I step inside.

It takes a few minutes of rifling through drawers to find a T-shirt, a pair of jogging bottoms, and a pair of thick socks. There's no way in hell I'll find shoes that fit, so I don't bother to look.

When I step into the corridor, I collide with Benito, making him drop his phone.

My reflexes kick in and I reach down to grab it, only to see it open to a video of a sleeping woman. My heart races as I realize it's a surveillance app.

"Don't touch that," he barks.

"Sorry!" I skitter against the wall.

Wasn't he supposed to be the more subdued Montesano brother, who always wore suits and glasses? I thought Cesare was frightening, but Benito wears his refined exterior like a mask.

He snatches the phone off the floor with a ferocity that makes me flinch. Then he gazes down at the woman he's watching, as though checking her for injuries. After shooting me a murderous glare, he disappears into one of the bedrooms, leaving my mind reeling.

What the fuck was that, and who was the woman?

More importantly, why am I being so curious? Delving into any of the Montesano brothers' proclivities could only lead to more trauma. I've barely recovered from being throttled by Dominic and my mind is still filled with repeats of that exploding head.

The only thing I need to concern myself with now is Roman's portrait. Painting is my therapy, the perfect distraction from my mental chaos.

I continue toward the grand staircase, where the downstairs is a flurry of activity. All the waiters are gone, replaced by the domestic staff I usually see milling around the grounds. Roman's men walk the hallways, making the atmosphere tense.

As I reach the door, a deep voice asks, "Are you okay, Miss?"

I turn to find Tony lumbering toward me with his brows creased.

"Yeah." I back toward the front entrance. "Just returning to the pool house."

He nods. "Let me escort you."

"It's alright." I hurry out through the double doors and down the stone steps, where the gardeners are removing trampled plants.

Tony continues after me at a distance, and I hurry around the perimeter of the building, not wanting a conversation about what happened with his colleague. I'm sure Roman must have interrogated him after discovering Dominic was on the police payroll, but too much has happened since then for me to feel safe in his presence.

As I round the corner, I pass the paved courtyard where that cop tried to abduct me in a catering van. It's empty now, but I can't help my shiver.

If I had grabbed any man but Roman Montesano in that nightclub, Jim would have gotten his hands on me already, and I would be dead.

My eyes sting with tears of gratitude, and a lump forms in the back of my throat. I wasted so much time second-guessing Roman's motives. His methods are heavy-handed, but he's genuine about wanting to keep me safe.

He's already taken two lives to save mine, and he made it clear he wouldn't hesitate to kill Jim. What more could I ask for in a protector?

I wait for a pang of guilt, a wave of moral outrage for wanting to see another man dead, but all I feel is relief.

Jim was violent, controlling, and made me doubt my own sanity. He caught me at a time when I was lonely, vulnerable, and short on cash. The only time he was bearable was when he was high. If I'd been thinking clearly, perhaps I would have seen through his mask.

One glance over my shoulder tells me Tony is still following. I round another corner, cut across the lawn, and jog down the paved pathway that leads toward the pool. It's about that time I realize I could have cut through the house like Roman did last night, but I shake off that thought. My nerves are still frazzled.

When I'm halfway across the pool, I turn around to find Tony standing at the edge of the patio, not venturing any closer. That's what he and Dominic did when Cesare used the pool house as his playroom.

I push open the door, stride through my studio, and into the bedroom, where I change into my apron and make two important decisions.

One, I will finish Roman's portrait.

Two, I will give Roman my complete trust.

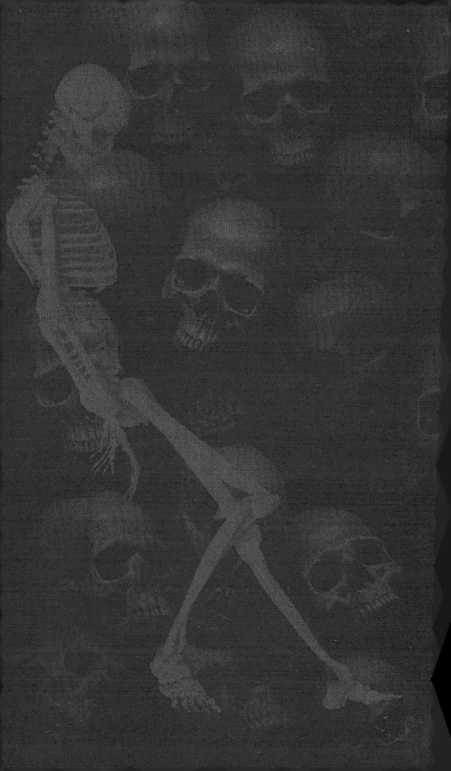

THIRTY-TWO

ROMAN

I glare down at the dead cop's corpse. Sunlight streams through the window, illuminating his pale features. He was too young to get mixed up in whatever corrupt bullshit Jim Callahan was peddling, and now he's paid the price.

Two officers on my payroll stand at either side, staring down at their fallen colleague.

"You recognize him?" I ask.

"I don't know his name," Barzelli says, "But he's definitely a new recruit I used to see around the precinct. Always trying to kiss Callahan's ass."

"And the tattoo?" I gesture toward the skull and cross-bones on his chest.

"Callahan has this way of attracting weak-minded sycophants. Maybe it's a hero-worship thing."

I nod. "Was he sent to murder my special guest?"

Rizzo, Barzelli's partner, shakes his head. "From what I overheard, they wanted her alive."

"Yeah," Barzelli says, sounding bitter. "Also, nobody's noticed an increasing number of whores dying of convenient overdoses. If I were to guess, I'd say Callahan also got to the coroner."

"Thanks." I flick my head toward the door, gesturing for them to leave, where Gil hands each of them a thick roll of notes.

"Anytime, boss," they chorus.

Someone else escorts them out through a side door, and I pick up the computer tablet I'll need for my next interrogation. As Gil and I walk in lockstep down to the basement, my jaw clenches, and my veins fill with fire at the prospect of losing Emberly.

If I hadn't worn the bulletproof undershirt, I would have lain on that stage bleeding to death, while that scrawny bastard transported her through the gates and into the sadistic arms of Jim Callahan.

I shake off the thought, remembering already having locked down the estate. My men were searching all the vehicles. We would have found Emberly in the back of the van, but in what state?

Downstairs, in the first of a series of soundproofed rooms, I find Oscar Lotti, the proprietor of the catering company I hired. He's on his knees with an iron collar around his neck connected to the wall.

Lotti gazes up at me through bloodshot eyes. He's a heavy-set man in his sixties with closely cropped hair who used to be close acquaintances with Dad. That counts for nothing, since his dearest friend stabbed the entire family in the back.

"R-Roman, please," he rasps. "You've got to believe me. I had nothing to do with the shooting."

"I believe you."

The tension in his features morphs into shock. "You do? Then why am I here?"

"One of the staff you brought in was an undercover cop."

His jaw drops. "No."

"How long was he working with your firm?"

Lotti's brow pinches. "The event was too short notice for my regular workers. I had to hire temp staff—"

"So you jeopardized my security?" I snarl.

"I swear to god, if I had known..." He bows his head. "Roman, I'm so sorry."

"So am I." I shoot him in the temple.

Lotti falls to the floor with a thud.

"Really?" Gil asks.

"He knew better than to bring unvetted employees through my doors."

"Good point," he mutters.

"Take him out. Give the corpse a few hours to cool and have him sent to his family. Tell them he got caught up in last night's shooting."

"Sure thing, boss." Gil hesitates.

My eyes narrow. "What?"

"This morning, I was in the bathroom, checking on my bedroom camera..." He rubs the back of his neck and grimaces.

"Spit it out."

"Annalisa was on the phone with someone."

My brows pull together. "The blonde roommate?"

He nods.

"Don't tell me she's also an assassin."

"She was discussing money for delivering your special guest to the cop."

The muscles in my jaw tense at the thought that nobody close to Emberly is a genuine friend—not even me. "Does she know she's being recorded?"

"No," Gil rumbles. "She doesn't suspect a thing."

"Keep it that way." I rub my chin. "And keep her close. If she's in contact with the cop, we can use that to our advantage."

Gil's features relax as though he thought I might have blamed him for the little blonde rat. "Sure."

"And good work."

I continue alone through the hallway and through a door that leads to another protected by biometric security. After placing my palm on the reader, it clicks open, letting out the stench of burned flesh.

A man lies strapped to a table, his chest a mass of broken flesh. Cesare stands over him in a leather apron, holding a scalpel and one of those little blowtorches that chefs use for crème brûlée.

I've got to hand it to my baby brother. He's a creative motherfucker.

The man groans through a metal contraption resembling a ring gag. My gaze drops to the tongue nailed to his shoulder, and I scowl.

"How do you expect him to talk?"

"He's from the Moirai Group," Cesare says. "I didn't know where he kept his tracker. It could have been under a false tooth."

"That's why you took his tongue?"

He shrugs. "Yeah, now I've got him communicating through blinks. One means yes, two means no."

"Did you learn about trackers from your girlfriend?" I ask, remembering the assassin he picked up from the nightclub and 'interrogated.'

He waggles his brows. "You'll never guess where she kept hers."

Sometimes, I wonder if Cesare needs a therapist. Maybe losing Dad, then me and then our mother in such quick succession fucked with his sanity. Maybe he needs to lash out before anyone comes for us again. Or maybe he was broken all along. It's hard to tell, but his loyalty to the family is absolute.

There's nobody on this earth I trust more to watch my back. I wish I'd paid more attention to him when he was little because there are times I don't understand what's going on in his mind.

"Alright then." I tilt my head, feeling the satisfying crack of my neck joints, followed by a wave of relief. The tension in my shoulders lifts, and I focus on the assassin.

He stares up at me like I'm the voice of reason, even though I'm the one he shot. I meet his pale blue eyes and say, "We both know you're not leaving here alive, so I'm giving you two choices. I can put a bullet through your skull and put you out of your misery, or my brother can continue slicing you up and cauterizing your wounds."

His pained groan tells me which option he prefers, but I continue. "Help me identify who you were working with, and I will end you."

The man squeezes his eyes shut.

"Is that a no?" I ask.

Cesare jabs him with the blade. "My brother asked you a question. Are you going to ID your accomplices?"

He opens his eyes and blinks once.

"That's a yes," Cesare says.

"Raise him," I say to my brother. "I want him sitting upright for a digital identity parade."

Cesare moves to the table's center and cranks up a lever that moves the back rest up to form an L-shape. The assassin's pained moans echo across the walls, filling my senses with the sweet cries of his agony.

This is nothing personal. He's only doing his job, but the Moirai Group is New Alderney's largest and most ruthless firm of contract killers. Cousin Leroi once mentioned that it takes a lot to crack their employees. Apparently, the cost of betraying their overlords is worse than death.

I open my computer tablet and the photos app. Last night, my men searched the cars and removed any plus ones who weren't legit. Anyone whose ID matched government records was allowed to leave. The rest were brought back to the house for further verification.

We were left with a series of high-class escorts and people who didn't seem to exist.

"Look carefully," I say to the assassin. "Every time you see one of your colleagues, I want you to blink. Is that understood?"

He bobs his head, making sure to close his eyes and open them once.

Scrolling through the photos is time consuming, and I note each person he identifies as an accomplice. I made sure to include a few red herrings in the selection to test his truthfulness.

At the end, we run through the pictures again, and I ask, "Have we missed anyone?"

He blinks twice for no.

My lips pinch, and I hand the tablet to Cesare, who scoffs. None of the people he pointed out includes Rosalind, who we know for a fact works for the Moirai Group.

"You're lying," I say, my voice flat.

His eyes widen, and he recoils.

"Take off his boxers," I snap.

The assassin struggles in his restraints, making choked noises I can only interpret as begging.

Cesare slices through the fabric with his scalpel, making sure to nick the man's flesh. Blood pools in his upper thighs but soon coagulates and turns black.

The man turns to me, his eyes streaming with tears, his unmarked face contorted with pain.

I lean in close and bare my teeth. "You had your chance to cooperate, but some of the people you chose are trusted associates. Now, it's time for you to spend the next weeks of your existence as my brother's toy."

"Hey, Roman. Look at this." Cesare taps a mark on his hip.

"So what?"

He walks to the side table, sets down his torture instruments, and returns with his camera, then takes a picture of the man's hip. My brow furrows as he expands the image with his fingertips and holds out the screen.

"A wheel?" I ask.

"The spinning wheel of fate," Cesare says. "Rosalind has the same one in the same place."

I shake my head. What is it about secret organizations and tattoos? Admittedly, this one is subtle, but they may as well broadcast their members to the masses.

"Good work." I clap my brother on the shoulder. "There's no point continuing this interrogation when we can find the Moirai Group without his help."

Cesare nods. "What should I do with him?"

I turn toward the door. "He's your toy. As long as he never leaves this room alive, you can do whatever you want."

The blowtorch hisses and seconds later, the air fills with the muffled screams and the stench of seared flesh.

"One more chance to save yourself," I say as I reach the door. "Who is your client?"

He grunts several syllables.

"Samson Capello?" I ask.

He blinks twice.

Of course it isn't. Samson is dead. I immediately think of Jim Callahan. "Then who? Someone in New Alderney?"

Two blinks.

"Someone outside the state?"

One blink.

My jaw tightens. "New Jersey?"

One blink.

My nostrils flare. "Tommy Galliano?"

One blink.

Fuck it.

"How many targets?"

He blinks three times. I don't need to ask. I already know he was sent after Benito, Cesare, and me. That slimy motherfucker. First, he takes our mother. Then my meth lab. Now, he's coming for our lives. And maybe even for Emberly's.

I raise my gun and shoot him in the chest.

"Hey!" Cesare snaps.

"If he hadn't tried to bullshit us earlier by identifying his colleagues, then he would have gotten a bullet through the head. Now you get to play with him until he bleeds out."

I step out into a room where I can get a signal and send Gil a text to check everyone we've held for a birthmark or tattoo on their hip.

My lips tighten, and I grind my teeth. Tonight has been non-stop. I've only had two chances to check on Emberly. She's probably awake by now, wondering where the fuck I've disappeared.

In the time it takes for me to walk upstairs, down the hallway, and into the room where we're holding all the unknowns, Gil has already separated them into two groups. The smaller of them consists of two men and three women in their early to mid-twenties. I recognize one of them as Rosalind, who Cesare picked up at the Phoenix.

I turn to the men holding the larger group at gunpoint. "Let them go."

"What should we do with this lot?" Gil asks.

Good question. It would be a shame to waste all those

lives or let them escape via cyanide pills. I wait for the others to leave before turning to meet the assassin's tense faces.

"I'm going to use you as leverage to cancel the hit on my brothers and me. When your firm agrees to my request, I'll send you back unharmed."

One of them jerks in his restraints as though what I've said is impossible, but I raise a palm. "Whatever your client is paying, I'm prepared to double it. Can you share his name?"

The assassins exchange glances.

"Is it Tommy Galliano?"

Rosalind's eyes rotate to meet mine, and she gives me the barest of nods. I don't acknowledge her answer, though I wonder what Cesare did to her in that playroom. It almost looks like she's on our side. That, or she has an impeccable sense of self-preservation.

I turn to Gil. "Keep an eye on them. If one of them so much as grimaces, I want you to knock them out."

Gil advances on the group of assassins, and I walk out of the room and down the hallway, passing Benito. He's on the phone, trying to smooth out last night's disaster.

Benito is our diplomat. The ivy league-educated one with impeccable manners who can fit into any society event. If I had an official consigliere, it would be Benito. Right now, he deals with the outside world in a way that I can't as a recently released convict.

I continue up the stairs and into my bedroom to find it empty. My breath catches, and my mind conjures up scenarios of men abducting or harming Emberly. Blood roars in my ears, and I clench my jaw, ready to tear the grounds apart until I remember the surveillance app. Fingers trembling, I pull out my phone and to find her working on my portrait.

Thank fuck.

Some of the tension eases at the sight of her so preoccu-pied with her art. Painted eyes, the exact replica of mine, stare out from the canvas, sharpening with every stroke of her brush, and I'm struck by her talent. Her movements are so beautiful and fluid. The way she brings the paint to life is breathtaking.

She disappears out of range, breaking the spell. I'm about to switch to another camera when a text appears from Ernest Lubelli, saying that Emberly recently made contact, and he's ready to purchase her paintings on my behalf.

Good. Everything's in place. I make a mental note to forward him the bogus contracts.

I send a text to Leroi, requesting the best way to contact the Moirai. He responds within ten seconds with a number and an offer of assistance, but I let it slide. Leroi has done enough. The poor bastard is still recovering from a stab wound he got the day he helped us capture Samson Capello.

When I call the number, a male voice answers in two rings.

"Moirai?"

"This is Roman Montesano. Last night's attempt on my life failed, and I have five of your operatives. One of them died in a gunfight and the others are unharmed. Let's negotiate."

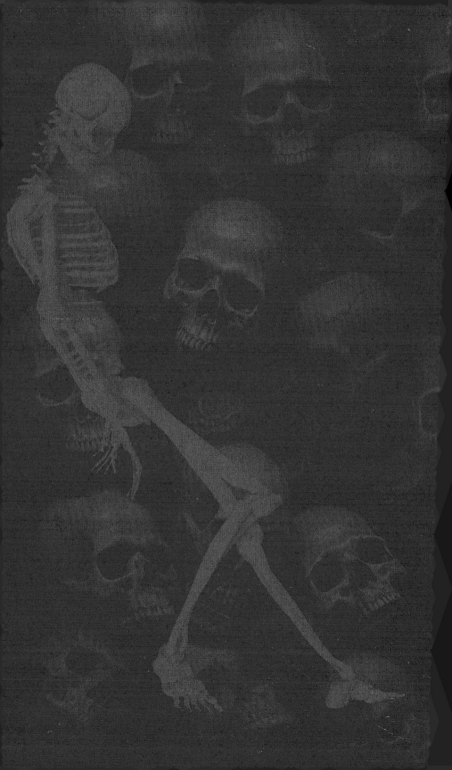

THIRTY-THREE

EMBERLY

Thank goodness my studio's kitchen has a full-sized sink because it's covered in art materials that need cleaning.

I've never worked so hard or intensely on a portrait and by the time I've finished, the ache in my fingers spreads up to my arms, past my shoulders, and embeds itself in my neck. Even the muscles in my upper back are cramping.

None of that matters when every vessel is flooded with euphoria. I barely needed to look at the reference photo I took of Roman because his murderous protective glare is burned in my mind.

Last night was both my most disturbing experience and my most reassuring. When Roman got shot, I went into survival mode and let myself get swept up in the panic. Once the fight-or-flight faded, all I wanted was to be at his side. I couldn't imagine a future without him somewhere in my life.

Jim's obsession with me is relentless. There's nothing worse than knowing the man who wants you dead has a small army of men willing to do his bidding.

My only question is why? Toward the end, Jim had nothing for me but contempt. I was too fat, too skinny, too sassy, too fake in my obedience. I couldn't cook, clean, cater to his needs, or take a beating without creating a mess.

Jim wanted me tiptoeing on eggshells, trying to predict his moods. Even when spaced out on the opiates he would inject, he was never satisfied. I couldn't do anything right.

"Why am I even dredging him up?" I mutter. "Next time, I'll be prepared."

I dip my brushes in turpentine, wash off the paint, and set them on the wooden stand. Rolling my shoulders, I clean the rest of my materials and leave them out to dry before walking back to the completed portrait.

The eyes I've painted for Roman are sharp, and the expression etched on his features is the same one seared into my mind from when he shot that cop. Light and shadow accentuate the contours of his features, bringing out his masculine beauty.

I can't wait for him to see it.

A knock sounds on the window, making me jump. I whirl around to find Roman waiting outside the French doors with a smile. It's the same version of him that sat for his portrait in running clothes and then stroked himself until he climaxed all over his abs and chest.

Ignoring the fluttering of my heart and the heat pooling between my thighs, I beckon him in. Roman steps through the door, his posture sagging.

"Did you even sleep last night?" I ask.

"An hour or two," he replies with a yawn. "How are you feeling?"

I've had an entire kaleidoscope of emotions, ranging from terror to despair to hope. Right now, butterflies are taking flight at the sight of my savior. Crossing the room, I wrap my arms around his waist.

"Better. I can't thank you enough for rescuing me last night. And I'm sorry."

His brows pinch, and he gazes down at me with eyes so intense that my breath shallows. "Sorry for what?"

"Doubting you." I bow my head, unable to withstand his stare.

"Emberly?"

"You wanted to fight the corrupt justice system," I say. "When you saw I was being harassed by a police detective, you did everything you could to help me."

He hesitates, his chest rising and falling with rapid breaths. I imagine he's tired of my perpetual paranoia and from all the fallout from getting shot. The last thing he needs now is my baggage.

I clear my throat. "What I want to say is that I trust you. Completely."

He swallows as though overcome with emotion.

"Roman, I'll never doubt you again."

He cups the back of my head, his fingers infusing me with warmth and comfort. "It's alright, baby. You were scared, but you need to know I'll protect you until my dying breath."

His words are a balm on my frayed nerves. I close my eyes, melt into his embrace, and inhale his familiar scent. "Thank you, Roman. You don't know what it means to have you watching my back."

Roman rocks me from side to side. "I know, baby. I know."

For the first time since I can remember, my heart lifts, and I finally feel safe.

We stand in the middle of the studio for several heartbeats, basking in each other's presence. I wonder what a man like Roman sees in me that's so precious. Maybe fate conspired to bring us together that night because I understand what it's like to feel injustice.

Either way, I've never felt closer to another human than I do at this moment. Roman has seen me so many times at my worst and hasn't rejected me, mocked me, or locked me away. All he's ever given me is understanding.

I want to stay like this forever, but he still hasn't seen his portrait.

"Ernest Lubelli called this morning while you were away," I murmur into his chest.

"Who?"

"The owner of the MoCa art gallery," I say.

"What did he want?"

"He's having an auction in a few days and wants you to come."

Roman huffs. "Are you interested?"

"Of course, but I can't go alone with that maniac on the loose."

He pulls back and looks down into my eyes, his gaze softening. "Let me take you. I'll even bring some back up."

My lips curl into a smile. "I spoke to him last night at the party before... you know. He said he was interested in seeing my art."

Roman raises his brows but doesn't reply.

"All I have is what I've done here, as well as your portrait, but I wanted you to be the first to see it."

He hesitates. "I might have a few hours tomorrow to pose—"

"No. No, it's complete." I draw back, grab his hand, and pull him to the other side of the room. "Look."

Roman follows me at a lumbering pace, he's still carrying the weight of last night's disaster on his shoulders. Guilt tightens my chest at bothering him with something as trivial as a portrait when he's under so much strain.

His feet make an abrupt stop. I turn around to stare into features slackened with shock.

My heart pounds, and the back of my throat goes dry. Jim always found a way to belittle my work, no matter how much a piece made me happy, and Mom would never acknowledge my talent. She always told me that mingling with artists was the fastest way to end up in the gutter.

I know that Roman's portrait is beautiful, but some people hate to see themselves through another's eyes. The man in the canvas is darkly handsome, with an aura of danger that conceals a lethal undercurrent of secrets. Despite his undeniable charm, I know there's more to him than the mafia Don. What I saw last night is still fresh in my mind.

"Emberly," he says, his words choked. "I suspected you were talented, but this..."

"What?" I whisper.

"This is fucking beautiful. You've made me look like the baddest motherfucker since Tony Montana."

"Tony who?"

He chuckles, the corners of his eyes crinkling with mirth. "Haven't you seen the movie *Scarface*?"

I shake my head.

"Say hello to my little friend?" He mimes holding a machine gun.

A laugh bubbles from my chest. "No? Does that even happen in the movie?"

"It's the best part." He shakes his head and exhales an exasperated huff. "Have you even seen *Goodfellas? The Godfather? Casino*?"

"No."

He wraps an arm around my shoulder. "I need to introduce you to the wonder of the organized crime genre."

"When does a man like you have time to watch movies?"

I ask.

"I spent twenty-two hours a day in a cell for five years. Those movies were one of the few things that kept me sane."

My stomach drops. "Oh, Roman, I'm so sorry."

He shakes his head. "Don't worry about me. Others had it much worse. So, are we going to this auction or not?"

"Yes, please," I reply with a smile. "Mr. Lubelli wanted to see the portrait. Do I have your permission to send him a photo?"

"Sure. I have an Art Purchase Agreement the family uses when buying paintings directly from the artist. It's in my office."

My heart skips a beat at the prospect of selling my work. I grab his bicep. "Let's go!"

With a chuckle, Roman guides me out of the pool house, across the garden, and through the patio doors that lead to a study of mahogany shelves framed with leather-bound books and a huge desk in the same dark wood that's topped with leather.

"Sit." He rounds the desk and sinks into a plush leather chair.

I perch on a seat opposite, feeling a little out of place. My gaze lands on a boardroom table at the other end surrounded by chairs. This must be where Roman holds court.

He opens a drawer, pulls out a folder, and slides it across the desk. "Read this carefully. Once you've signed it, I'll transfer the twenty-five grand into any account of your choosing and supply you with the new driving license and passport."

My heart drops at the prospect of this being the end of our agreement. Leaving means starting a new life in a different state, finding studio space, but most importantly, it means losing what I have with Roman.

Not to mention being hunted by Jim.

It's all too soon.

I glance down at the contract, my vision blurring, and I clear my throat. "Could I have some time to make sense of all the terms?"

"Of course," he murmurs. "I want you to be happy with what you're signing."

A knock sounds on the door. It swings open, and Cesare swaggers in wearing a black leather apron, his hands and face splattered with blood. Nausea churns in my gut, and I stagger to my feet.

"I'd better go," I murmur.

Cesare grins. "Don't leave on my account."

"Get out." Roman shoots out of his seat.

His younger brother backs out of the door with a scowl, and Roman sends me a pained grimace. "I'm sorry, baby. You weren't meant to see that."

"It's alright." I clutch the contract to my chest. "The studio needs cleaning up, and I still need to take photos for Mr. Lubelli."

Without waiting for him to protest, I scurry toward the patio door and bolt into the garden. It's not that I think Cesare is dangerous. At least not to me. He's always kept a respectful distance, as though not wanting to touch what belongs to his older brother.

But the man is completely insane.

Not because I saw him with that naked, tortured woman. It's his eyes. They're pale voids that could suck a person into an abyss of pain and mayhem. And his grin is so wide it could rival the Cheshire cat's.

I don't stop running until I reach the gallery, where I take out my phone and scan each page of the contract to create a PDF file.

I don't mistrust Roman, but after all that bullshit where I

ended up owing Gerard Lafayette money, I'm not taking any chances.

I upload the PDF to a website where legal experts can review the terms for a fixed fee. The cost is more than I can afford, but it's nothing compared to the twenty-five grand I'll get for selling the portrait.

An hour later, the expert messages to say that the Art Purchase Agreement transfers the intellectual property of my work to the buyer, which means they can make reproductions and print it on merchandise for sale.

Apparently, it's unusual for artists to relinquish the intellectual property of their works, even after they're sold. If I sign the contract, I would need permission from the buyer to even add a scan of the portrait to my portfolio.

"I'm okay with that." I sign the contract with a flourish.

Next, I send photos of all the paintings I've done, including Roman's portrait to the email address on Mr. Lubelli's business card.

If he doesn't like my work, I'll just try another gallery. I can't let that disaster with Lafayette put me off from launching my career.

My phone pings with an email from the MoCa Art gallery.

Emberly,

What beautiful artwork. May I have your phone number to discuss?

Regards,

Ernest.

I send a silent word of thanks to the universe that he didn't ask me to call him because my prepaid mobile has no credit. It takes a few minutes to find the number associated with my SIM, and I send him a reply.

The phone rings immediately, and the fine hairs on the back of my neck stand on end.

"H-Hello?" I rasp.

"Emberly? It's Ernest. I love your portfolio and adore the portrait. You've captured both his classical good looks and his brooding essence." He chuckles. "You're a natural."

"Thank you," I reply, my words breathy.

"I have a space in an upcoming auction, and I'd like to include one of your paintings. I think my patrons would bid highly on the blood-tipped roses."

"No," I blurt before I can stop myself. "I mean, can you buy it from me for a fixed fee?"

He hesitates for several heartbeats before asking, "Is there a reason why?"

"I'm not good with all the sliding commissions and just want to know what I'm getting without having to pull out a spreadsheet."

His laugh is deep and soothing. "Of course. How about twenty?"

I bite down on my bottom lip. That's more than I've ever gotten for my art until I met Roman. "The last painting I sold went for twenty-five."

"You drive a hard bargain, but I'm sure the fixed fees will work to my advantage. Meet me before my next auction to sign the paperwork. Bring Roman, if he's available."

The euphoria I felt when I completed the portrait returns. I rush out into the gardens and back through the patio doors leading to Roman's study and burst in.

He's sitting around the sofa with Gil and his two brothers, but I'm too happy to falter at the sight of Benito and Cesare. All the conversation stops, and Roman rises from his seat.

"Emberly?" he asks.

I leap into his arms and pull him into a kiss.

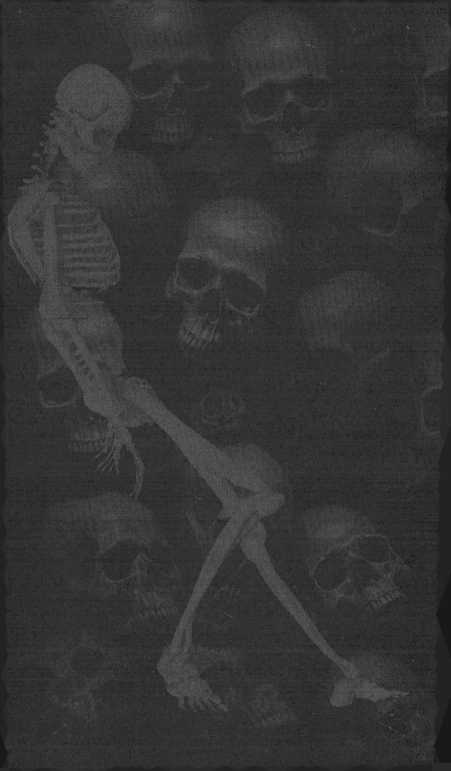

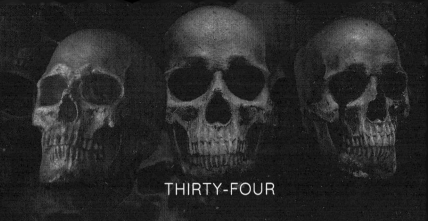

THIRTY-FOUR

ROMAN

Emberly's lips taste of promise and mint, drawing me into her allure. I pull her closer, my hands gripping onto her waist as I lose myself in an intensity that might consume my resolve. For this blissful moment, she becomes my possession, my entire world. I want to protect her from every bastard who means her harm, even if that bastard is me.

Someone wolf whistles. I don't need to open my eyes to know it's coming from Cesare. I ignore my little brother and lose myself in the feel of Emberly's mouth.

She's delicate and warm, yet her kisses are so demanding. This is what I like about her the most. She takes what she wants and doesn't stop until she's got it. And right now, all she wants is me.

I deepen the kiss, tasting and teasing, and tangling my fingers into her luscious curls. She's gasping, panting, grinding against me until her breath turns shallow.

Benito clears his throat. "Can this wait? We're sitting on a situation that needs sanitizing."

I groan, my mind returning to reality. He's right. No

matter how much I want to lose myself in Emberly, the Moirai group will keep coming with more and more assassins until we either force Tommy Galliano to end the contract or reduce the firm to rubble.

Emberly draws back and gazes up at me through glazed eyes. I haven't seen her looking so aroused since the night I edged her in the limousine.

"I'm sorry, baby. We have important business."

"It's alright," she murmurs. "I just wanted to show my appreciation. Mr. Lubelli wants to buy one of my paintings, and it's all thanks to you."

"Thanks to your talent." I press my forehead against hers.

"He wouldn't have been so interested in my work if you hadn't invited me to your party as your date."

"Roman," Benito says, his voice sharp.

My brother needs to shut the hell up and find some woman to fuck. Keeping Emberly sweet is the key to getting back hundreds of million dollars' worth of what was stolen.

Ignoring his impatience, I walk Emberly back toward the patio door. "As soon as I've finished with this business, I'll come see you."

She turns back to me with a sultry smile. "Can't wait."

For the next few heartbeats, I watch her saunter down the garden path. Everything about her is a wonder, from the swing of her hips to the way the sunlight turns the ends of her curls a bright shade of amber.

More importantly, she's nothing like any other woman I've met. Emberly is insanely talented, an untamable little wildflower. She's so full of surprises that a man could get lost unraveling all her beautiful layers.

"Back to the subject at hand," Benito grumbles. "I don't think the Moirai group will call off the hit in exchange for five hostages."

"Sounds like a good deal," Gil says with a shrug.

Benito steeples his fingers. "Perhaps for one hit, but Galliano paid for three."

The last conversation I had with the Moirai representative was with a low-level grunt, who claimed not to have the authority to negotiate. "Benito is right, but those bastards need to know that making an attempt on a Montesano comes with consequences."

Benito's gaze darts toward the patio doors. "How close are we to getting back the casino?"

I turn in the direction he's looking, making sure Emberly is out of earshot. "She's reviewing the Art Purchase Agreement and just came over to tell me that Lubelli wants to buy one of her paintings."

He nods. "Does he have the altered contracts?"

"Sending them over." I slide onto the sofa beside Gil and lean against the leather backrest. "When she's ready to sign, I'll be there to distract her from reading the fine print."

"Good." Benito's jaw tightens. "The moment we take back the casino, I want every Capello sympathizer working there terminated."

My lips lift into a smile. Benito might be the most level-headed of us, but he doesn't shrink from bloodshed. While I was locked up, I'd forbidden my brothers from moving against Capello and everyone who defected to the backstabber. All that pent up frustration from seeing the family legacy tainted by that unworthy prick is about to be unleashed.

Cesare leans forward in his seat, his eyes bright. "What else do we need to take back?"

I gesture at Benito for him to answer.

"We already have the cash in Capello's bank accounts," he says. "After the casino and its attached hotels, there's the stocks, the real estate portfolio, the loan company, and the contents of the safety deposit boxes."

Cesare rubs his hands and turns to me with a manic grin. "And then?"

"What do you mean?"

He flicks his head toward the patio doors. "When do we get to..." He slides his index finger over his throat. "I want her on my table."

The stench of burning flesh invades my memory, and the coffee and biscotti I snatched for breakfast curdles in my gut at the thought of my brother touching any part of Emberly.

I turn to Cesare, my chest burning with anger. "Emberly Kay belongs to me."

Cesare opens his mouth to protest, but Benito cuts him off. "Roman spent five years in prison while we lived here as free men. He's the one that gets to decide what to do with her."

A storm brews in my baby brother's eyes. He isn't used to being told no. "But I get to watch, right?"

I bare my teeth. "Keep your hands, eyes, and mind off Emberly, unless you want to lose them."

Flinching, he stares at me like a kicked puppy, not acknowledging or rising to my threat. Our glaring match continues for several moments until Benito breaks the tension with a loud clap.

"Gentlemen, we have more things to be concerned about than a woman. The leverage we have against the Moirai Group isn't enough to stop them from coming at us with more assassins. We need another plan."

Cesare's scowl deepens. "I say we take an army to New Jersey and kill the Gallianos."

"There's too many of them and too few of us," I mutter.

"Besides, it's going to be impossible to mobilize that many men."

"Then I'll sneak into his territory and put a bullet through his skull."

"No," I say.

He scowls. "But—"

"Galliano is too protected. If anyone's going to kill him, then we'll use a pro."

Cesare clenches his jaw, his chest rising and falling with the force of his anger.

I feel for my little brother. He was the closest to our mother, who left us to marry Galliano. Two years later, when she died during an unnecessary surgery, he fell into a destructive spiral.

He despises Galliano more than anything, but I can't risk him on what could be a suicide mission. Especially not for a woman who abandoned the family when we needed her the most.

"I doubt the Moirai group will accept a hit on Galliano." Benito's voice cuts through my thoughts. "Conflict of interest."

Humming, I tap a finger against my chin, trying to muster up a solution. Benito is right. We can always use our cousin Leroi. Anyone who can single-handedly infiltrate Capello's stronghold and murder his entire family can easily dispatch Galliano.

"Before you think of calling Leroi, remember he's still injured," Benito adds.

"I know," I growl. "We'll just have to conjure up another way to deal with the Moirai."

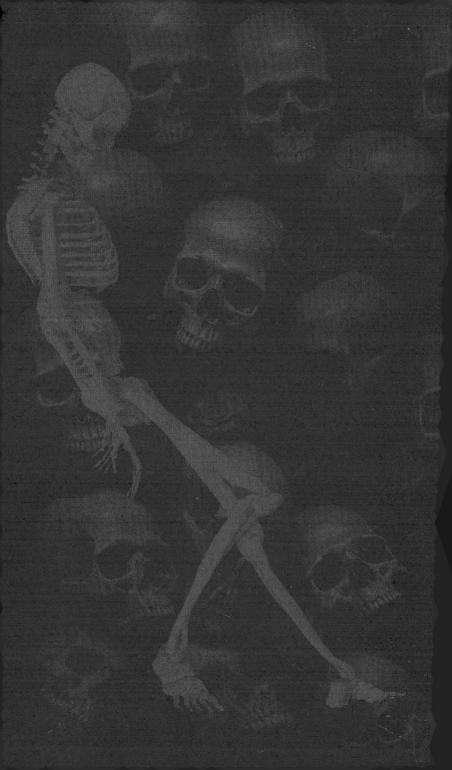

THIRTY-FIVE

EMBERLY

I might be floating on the clouds of artistic success, but Jim's third attempt to recapture me anchors me to reality. I can't sleep in the studio. It's too remote from the rest of the household, and the bed doesn't smell of Roman.

After signing the contract and completing another painting, I return to the main building. The patio doors to Roman's study are locked, so I walk around the ivy-covered mansion toward the front entrance.

I shower in Roman's master suite, change into one of his oversized nightshirts, and snuggle into his sheets. The pillow still smells of his cologne, and I lie on the firm mattress with my eyes closed, my mind filling with thoughts of him.

He's harsh on the outside and there's no doubt he's ruthless, but beneath the exterior of a mafia don is a man who cares deeply for those in his life. And somehow, through a miracle of fate, one of them happens to be me.

Warmth fills my chest at the thought of filling a spot in his affections. When I'm close to him, it's impossible not to feel special.

The door creaks open, and footsteps enter the room, only to come to an abrupt halt.

"This is a surprise." Roman's deep voice curls around my skin, infusing it with tingles.

"I can't sleep in the pool house," I murmur, my eyes closed.

He sighs. "You're always welcome in my bed."

I expect him to climb in and run his hands over my exposed skin, but he walks to the bathroom and turns on the shower. My heart sinks a little at what feels like a rejection, but I shake off that disappointment. Roman could be covered in blood. He's still dealing with the fallout from last night's shooting.

Just knowing he's only a room away sends me into a deep state of relaxation. As I'm drifting off to sleep, the mattress dips, and Roman curls up behind me and nuzzles my neck.

"Goodnight, baby," he murmurs into my curls. "I could get used to finding you in my bed after a long day of cracking heads."

He rubs slow circles over my belly, making my blood heat. I push my ass into his crotch, wanting to get something started, but he falls asleep.

I settle, remembering that he didn't go to bed last night and is probably still in pain from being hit with all those bullets, even if he was wearing lightweight armor.

It's not long before I join him for the most blissful sleep I've had since I escaped Jim's house.

———

Over the next two days, Roman wakes up before me and goes to bed after I sleep. He won't touch me out of guilt that

I got hurt. I catch glimpses of him through the day while he's in tense discussions with his brothers or his men.

From what I can glean from overheard snippets I hear, they might go to war with a rival in New Jersey who's encroaching on Roman's territory. And the man who shot Roman is an undercover cop, which is why everyone is on alert.

After lunch on the second day, Sofia brings me another box from the Dolce Vita boutique. She doesn't explain where we're going, but says Roman will pick me up at seven.

It's a deep red cocktail dress designed to show off my shoulders, tightly fitted around the bust and waist before flaring out at the hips. Thankfully, it doesn't drag on the floor.

Even the heels he provided are sturdy and easy to slip off in case I need to run. There's a little jewelry box containing a large pair of teardrop earrings with a green stone that might be emerald.

"This is far too generous," I whisper, my voice breathy.

But Roman is a multi-millionaire who owns several companies, and that's not including all the other illegal activities he doesn't declare to the public. An outfit like this won't even make a dent in his wallet.

I stand in his dressing room and gaze at my reflection in the full-length mirror. The woman staring back at me is a hundred miles away from the one who had to shop at thrift stores.

"This is just like *Pretty Woman*," I murmur.

Richard Gere helped transform a hooker to a sophisticated lady, and Roman is turning an impoverished artist into a socialite.

The door opens, and Roman steps into the dressing room with a towel wrapped around his waist.

I whirl around, my eyes widening, my gaze roving down the contours of his tattooed chest.

The last time I saw him shirtless, I made an effort not to focus on his body because I wanted to get a start on his portrait. That's a lie. I was so completely entranced by his huge cock and the way he stroked it to completion that I barely noticed all his body art.

Now that the towel is firmly wrapped around that distraction, I can focus on his tattoos. His left arm is encased by a sleeve of black designs. The head of a serene wolf stares out from his shoulder, its mane dissolving into a pattern of swirls. Beneath it are two smaller wolves, either fighting or playing. Their bodies merge into fur and feathers that end just below the elbow.

"Your ink is beautiful," I murmur, my fingers twitching toward his chest.

Roman grins. "You think I'm beautiful?"

"That's not what I said, but yeah. You are."

My gaze rakes over his chest, where a pair of wings take up the space beneath his collar bones, leaving a gap in the dip between his pectoral muscles.

"Is that complete?" I ask.

He shakes his head. "I wanted to add an angel in the middle, but then I got arrested."

My heart sinks. "Oh. Do you want to talk about it?"

"And ruin my night?"

"Sorry." I turn away, run a finger through my curls, trying to tame them into a semblance of an evening style.

Roman appears behind me and wraps his arms around my waist. "I didn't mean to be abrupt." He kisses my bare shoulder. "When I'm with you, I lose track of all my resentment."

"Really?" I ask.

He runs his fingers through my curls and twists them into a chignon. "Really. You're my safe space."

My chest flutters. The irony is that Roman is also mine. "How do you know what to do with my mane?"

He chuckles. "My mother had curls like yours. The only one of us who even close to inherited it is Cesare."

"Who ties his hair back."

"Curls look pretty on a woman. Not so flattering on a man."

"Where's your mother now?"

He releases my hair, letting it tumble down to my shoulders. "That's another sore subject."

I can't help putting my foot in my mouth and asking questions too painful to answer. Why can't I be more like Roman? He sees me at face-value and doesn't pry, yet he always seems to understand what I need.

Several minutes later, we're both dressed and sitting in the back of an SUV that Roman assures me is bullet proof.

I study his perfect profile and murmur, "You never told me where we're going."

He turns to meet my gaze and grins. "You already know."

"MoCa?"

He threads his fingers between mine and squeezes my hand. "I thought I'd better attend, since Ernest Lubelli won't stop using you as his messenger."

"He's just keen to have you in his gallery."

"Keen to have me spend money in his gallery," Roman mutters.

I rest my head on his shoulder and sigh. "Are you really that much of a patron of the arts?"

"You want the truth?" he asks.

"Go on."

"They're one of the best passive investments a man can

buy. Today's penniless art student can become tomorrow's superstar. Generations later, the family is sitting on a fortune more stable than any business."

"Are you serious?"

"Don't get me wrong. We also buy the pieces we think are beautiful. Otherwise, what's the point? You may as well just invest in stocks."

When we reach a gas station, the car drives into a car wash, where Roman makes us change vehicles, explaining that we're probably being followed.

The original SUV drives in one direction and our new car takes another. This would be exciting if I hadn't experienced an attack that left me near death or seen Roman gunned down by an assassin.

We make another change of vehicles before reaching the MoCa art gallery's back entrance, where a waitress ushers us through narrow hallways and into the viewing space.

Tonight, it's arranged like an auction room with rows of chairs facing a podium on a stage. Patrons in evening wear walk around the perimeter, examining each painting.

Roman leans into my side and murmurs, "None of these artworks compare to yours."

I place a hand on his chest. "You're just saying that to be kind."

He snickers. "No Montesano has ever had a maestro living under our roof. You're my little goldmine."

My cheeks heat at the implication that I might one day be as world renowned as Banksy, Damien Hirst, or David Hockney, who have reached the pinnacle of their careers. I love the thought of my art living on after I die.

Waitresses hand out canapés and glasses of champagne. Roman takes enough for us both, since neither of us has had dinner. As we eat, a few people walk up to Roman and congratulate him on his release. He's gracious in his replies and even introduces me as the next big thing in art.

"Emberly?" A woman places her hand on my shoulder.

I turn around and lock gazes with the blonde lawyer from the party. "Oh, hi. I didn't know you'd be here."

She beams. "I just love the arts. Have you thought about painting my portrait?"

Roman appears at my side and places an arm around my shoulder. "Miss Kay is more interested in working with the gallery."

She backs away and frowns. "If you change your mind—"

"She won't," he says with a bit of bite.

The blonde walks away, leaving me stunned. I whirl on Roman. "That was rude."

"How do you know she's not a cop?"

My jaw drops, and I glance at where she's pushing through the crowds toward the exit. Her business card said she worked for the Di Marco Law Group, but that's easily faked.

"You're right." I place a hand on my chest. "She didn't even stay for the main event."

He wraps an arm around my shoulder, plucks a flute of champagne from a tray and brings it to my lips. "That's why you need to stick with me. Cops come in all disguises."

By the time the auction starts, my insides glow with giddy excitement, and not just because I'm tipsy. This is what I had hoped for when I signed over my paintings to Gerard Lafayette. An introduction to the art world. As we take our seats, Roman hands me his untouched glass.

I turn to him and frown. "You're not drinking?"

"Alcohol and auctions don't mix," he mutters.

A giggle rises from my chest. Poverty is so ingrained in my consciousness that it would never occur to me to bid while drunk. I hand him my empty glass and take a sip of Roman's champagne.

Mr. Lubelli strolls onstage with a beaming smile. "Ladies, gentlemen, and honored guests." He nods in our direction. "Welcome to the MoCa art gallery's two hundred and fiftieth auction."

There's a smattering of applause. I sit straighter in my seat, my heart thrumming. These events are exclusive, with tickets only given to verified patrons or artists whose work is up for auction.

"I'd like to start today's show with the work of an unknown painter who will soon make waves in the art world."

Excited chatter spreads across the room. I take a sip of champagne to wash down the pang of envy rising from my chest at the thought of Mr. Lubelli giving some lucky devil his seal of approval.

"May I introduce *Blood Roses* by Emberly Kay."

A pair of assistants dressed in white, wearing gloves and face masks carry a familiar-looking painting onstage and place it on a stand.

Shit.

That's the one I painted of the mansion's rose garden. Mr. Lubelli mentioned wanting to sell my paintings in the future, but I never imagined it would be tonight. Auctions always take weeks to organize, if not months.

I turn to Roman. "Why am I being featured so soon?

He gives me a broad smile. "This is your time to shine."

Whatever Mr. Lubelli says is muffled by the pounding of my heart and the blood roaring in my ears. I sit dazed as the auction starts and people raise their paddles. Tears prick my eyes, and my chest fills with a mix of terror and elation. Every dream I ever had about being a recognized artist is about to come true.

I can't believe they're actually bidding. Bidding for my work. Bidding higher and higher and higher until the gavel strikes with a resounding crack.

The gallery owner's lips move, but I can barely hear it through my euphoria.

Applause fills the room, breaking me out of my shocked stupor.

Roman leans into me and murmurs, "Fifty-five grand. After paying the commission, you're netting over forty-nine. Not bad for your first time."

"Actually, it's twenty-five," I say.

"Why?"

"I sold it to him for a fixed fee."

Roman's features harden. "Oh yeah? We'll see about that."

My stomach drops.

I can't let him terrorize the best thing that's happened to my career.

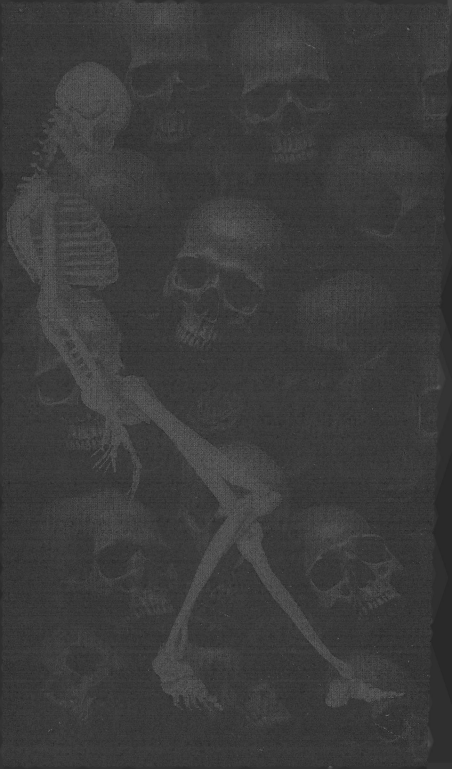

THIRTY-SIX

ROMAN

The applause is dying down when Emberly grabs my arm. "Don't say anything."

Lubelli already explained to me that she'd insisted on a fixed price for her paintings, but I need to demonstrate some amount of protest about her getting an unfair deal. Anything to distract her from asking questions about that blonde. How the hell did a high-ranking lawyer from the Di Marco group know I had control of their client's missing daughter?

"Bullshit," I snarl. "You're leaving twenty-four grand on the table."

"It's my choice," she hisses.

"Why?"

"You remember the gallery owner who framed me for assault, criminal damage, and the theft of his spoon?"

"What about him?" I ask.

"I signed a contract for the sale of five paintings, which he sold before the agreed date. After commission and some bullshit fixed fee, I ended up owing him money."

My brows crease. "Who did that to you?"

"The Elton John-looking asshole who runs Gallery Lafayette."

"Where are your paintings now?"

"Already with the buyers," she replies, her words bitter.

The assistants carry Emberly's painting off the stage, and the shill I sent to bid on it rises from his seat and follows them out.

While another pair of assistants carry in a second piece of art, I take Emberly's empty glass and replace it with a full one. She takes a long drag, her attention fixed on the stage, while I pull out my phone and look up Gallery Lafayette.

Her description of its owner is pretty accurate, and I forward a picture of Gerard Lafayette to Gil with a set of instructions.

Gil replies immediately to inform me he's on his way and will text back with updates.

I barely pay attention to the auctions, instead focusing on Emberly, who leans forward in her seat and gasps at the increasing value of bids. After each successful sale, I hand her another glass of champagne until she's drunk.

Fuck. I hate to be the bastard who plies a woman with alcohol to get what he wants, but I'll compromise my morals to get back our casino. That asset isn't just Dad's legacy, or even one of our most efficient methods of laundering money. The casino employs hundreds of employees needed to rebuild our ranks.

At the end of the evening, I walk Emberly to Lubelli's office, where he awaits with the bogus Art Purchase Agreement.

His room hasn't changed in the half decade I was away, with the same male nudes on the wall, framed in gold. Walking here is like stepping back in time.

Lubelli rises from an oak desk sporting a broad smile.

"Miss Kay, I owe you an apology." He places a gloved

hand on his heart. "When your painting arrived, I was so eager to show your work to my audience that I sold it without getting you to sign the agreement."

Emberly giggles. "I can't believe it reached that much."

He pushes a contract across the table. "Please sign. I can't collect payment from the buyer until I legally own the painting."

My fingers twitch to turn the sheets of paper to the final page, but I hold back, remembering what Benito said about needing her fingerprints. Lubelli's security cameras add a nice touch, as they'll record her consensual signature.

Emberly takes hold of the contract, and I stand at her back, wrapping my arms around her waist.

"You did so well, baby," I murmur into her chignon. "Hurry up and sign so we can celebrate."

"Okay." Emberly flips to the back page and signs.

Triumph slams into my chest with the force of a sledge-hammer, making my breath catch. Adrenaline courses through my veins, electrifying every nerve until they light up like the Fourth of July.

I burn with the urge to roar my victory at the top of my lungs that Emberly just signed over ownership of the casino. But when she spins around in my arms, the lust shining in her eyes makes me want to take her over the desk and fuck her and create our very own masterpiece.

"Wonderful," Lubelli says. "After each auction, I like to offer the bidders other works by the artist, if they're available. Do I have your permission to forward your photographs?"

"Of course," she says with a happy laugh.

"Look forward to hearing from me soon. In the mean-time, please carry on painting." Lubelli places the contract into a folder and leaves the room.

We need to stay here long enough for him to hand the

contract to my driver before I walk her toward the car. Emberly doesn't need to know that the other signatory on it will be me.

I place a stray curl between my fingers and pull it straight before releasing it to spring back. "You're everything," I murmur. "Beauty, talent, a brain that keeps me on my toes, and a body that makes me feral."

She presses her tits against my chest. "What are you going to do about it?"

I lean so close that our breaths mingle. "I could spread you over the desk and fuck you so hard you'll be tasting me for weeks."

She shivers. "What's stopping you?"

My phone buzzes with a text, most likely from Gil, confirming that he's finished.

"I have a surprise."

"What is it?"

I place a kiss on the tip of her nose. "It wouldn't be a surprise if I told you. Let's go to the car and see it."

Emberly and I walk hand in hand through the gallery's hallway, passing Lubelli, who gives me a significant look. I nod a silent word of thanks for helping me claw back the family casino.

We reach the back exit, where another bulletproof car awaits. Gil exits from the front and opens the door, where I usher Emberly inside.

She makes a strangled noise. "What's this?"

I sit on the seat and pull her onto my lap. "Don't you recognize him?"

It's understandable that she doesn't. Beneath the tinted glasses, frilly shirts, and colorful suits is a slug of a man who has no business swindling artists out of their work.

Gerard Lafayette is gagged, naked, and hogtied. I raise

my brows, impressed by Gil's finesse with ropes. Maybe spending all that time with Cesare has given him a fetish.

"Wait," she says, her voice breathy. "Is that..."

"The bastard who framed you for a crime you didn't commit?" I spit. "Here he is."

She claps a hand over her mouth to stifle a gasp. "For me?"

I nod. Emberly just sold me a casino for a pittance. The least I can give her is her revenge.

"You give me the best gifts!"

"No, baby. Watching you take back your power and kick the shit out of the asshole who scammed you is a treat. Give me a list, and I'll hogtie every man who's ever hurt you and place him at your feet as an offering."

She rises off my lap and kicks him in the gut, making him groan. "But why does he look unhurt?"

"And spoil your vengeance? He's your blank canvas to cover with bruises and blood."

Her breath quickens. "Won't he tell the police?"

"He won't say shit." I turn to the bound man and smirk. "Did you drop the charges against Miss Kay?"

He nods, his eyes streaming with tears.

"You caused us a whole lot of trouble with your theatrics," I say.

He squeezes his eyes shut and moans. I think he's finally understanding that he might not survive the night.

"What shall we do with him?" Emberly asks.

"This asshole forwarded your information to the police, practically hand delivering you to your ex. You have the rest of the journey to take out your anger on his ass."

I lean back, mesmerized by the sight of Emberly unleashing her wrath upon the bound and gagged man. Her punches are ferocious, her nails cutting through his skin like talons. The sounds of her little fists connecting with his tender flesh is doing something interesting to my cock.

Every part of me wants to touch her as she continues to unleash her wild, violent need for retribution. Any other woman would be satisfied with having the criminal charges dropped, but with her teeth bared and her hair curling like serpents, Emberly is the goddess of vengeance.

When she draws away and shakes out her hand, I pull her back onto the seat.

"Does it hurt?" I ask.

"I'm not used to punching," she replies through panting breaths. "And my fingers already ache from so much painting."

"Want me to take over?"

She turns to me, her eyes bright. "Would you?"

"Watch me."

Lafayette's eyes widen and the noise he makes behind the gag is pitiful. I pummel him with short and fast punches, until his pale carcass is covered in bruises and his face is a bloody mess.

"Untie his gag," Emberly says. "I want to hear him beg for mercy."

"You really like revenge, don't you?" I ask with a chuckle.

"Jim threatened to rape me in a police cell and kill me with an overdose. All because this scammer didn't want me to report him on social media."

Lip curling, I unbuckle the man's gag and let it fall to the floor.

"Please," Lafayette says, his words thick with agony. "I already got the charges dropped. What more do you want from me?"

"An apology?" Emberly asks.

"Yes." He inhales a shuddering breath. "I'm so, so sorry. And I deeply regret writing you off."

"You're only sorry because I have a protective boyfriend," she yells.

Boyfriend?

I must be more convincing than I thought. My chest swells with pride at the prospect of Emberly thinking of me as her anything. I'm just protecting my most precious investment—her capacity to continue signing contracts.

Lafayette curls into a ball and shudders.

I shake my head. This slimy bastard doesn't even know how to grovel. I appreciate the hustle, don't get me wrong. Maybe Emberly wouldn't have fallen into my lap so easily without his machinations, but he still tried to hurt what's mine.

"Where are the five paintings?" I ask.

"In my storeroom." He rolls onto his side and trembles.

"What?" Emberly screeches. "You told me they were sold."

He whimpers. "To myself."

I extract my phone. "What's its location?"

Lafayette rattles off an address that I enter in my maps app. I forward it to Gil, asking him to delegate the job of retrieving Emberly's paintings to whichever of our men is closest.

The car stops at a warehouse, where it's time to change vehicles to avoid getting caught up by any more Moirai assassins.

We're still holding four of their operatives, and that doesn't include Rosalind. The man I called doesn't seem to give a shit about them, so I've got Cesare persuading our hostages to release their locations. If the Moirai won't call off the hit, they can die.

Emberly and I enter the second car, which has a partition to give us privacy. I don't bother to tell her that one of my men will keep Lafayette in the warehouse for as long as it takes to extract him of everything he has of value. I certainly don't inform her I plan on having him drowned in a canal.

What I'm about to do is risky, but Emberly is already convinced of my good intentions. If it fails, I can always draw her back with sex. It worked last time.

"Our bargain is complete." I reach into my inside pocket and pull out a thick envelope containing a passport, driver's license, and fake utility bills. "Here's the ID you asked for, and the twenty-five grand is in your bank account."

"I don't want it," she says.

I laugh. "First, you're short-changing yourself on the sale of your painting and now you're refusing money? Get real, sweetheart."

"Not the twenty-five thousand." She slides her fingers into mine.

"Then what?"

"I don't need that fake ID."

My brows pull together. "What does that mean?"

"I want to stay... If you'll have me?"

Warmth fills my heart, and my lips curl into a self-congratulatory smile. With no warrant out for her arrest, she doesn't need to run.

I won't lose Emberly.

Jim Callahan's insane attempts to capture her means she doesn't even feel safe enough to leave. And the prospect of becoming a professional artist gives her an incentive to remain under my roof.

Everything has fallen into place with perfect precision.

I couldn't have planned this any better.

Emberly can stay with me for a lifetime. I no longer want to cut it short. It's ludicrous that I ever wanted her dead. Instead, I plan on doing everything in my power to make sure she never leaves.

"Of course, baby. Stay as long as you—"

Before I can even finish that sentence, her lips crash on mine in a searing kiss.

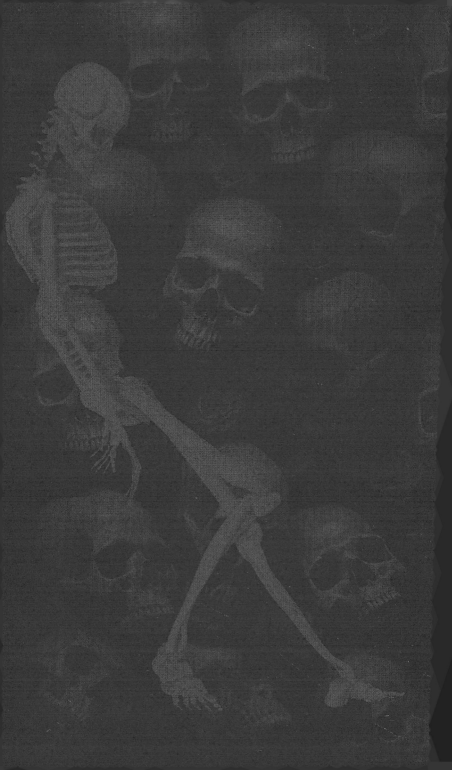

THIRTY-SEVEN

EMBERLY

I can't control my desire. My blood is still hot from the thrill of beating the shit out of that scammer, and it's all thanks to Roman. He's just so perfect. He's handsome, sexy, protective, generous—everything I've ever wanted. He destroys my enemies, makes dreams come true, and knows exactly how to melt my heart.

Straddling his lap, I join our lips in a kiss I never want to break. Roman is mine for as long as he wants me, and even beyond. I want him to know I have no plans on ever leaving a man who satisfies me so completely.

He makes a deep moan that goes straight to my pussy and stokes the flames of my arousal.

"Emberly," he murmurs into my mouth. "Keep going like that, and you'll ruin the second surprise."

I grab his wrists, trying to pin him down, but he grabs my ass and chuckles. "I don't want it unless it's you naked with a condom wrapped around your dick."

"Fuck," he groans. "How about all of that, but on a table at Chez Aquitani?"

My ears prick up at the name of New Alderney's most exclusive French restaurant.

"Do we have reservations?" I murmur into the kiss.

He squeezes my ass. "Those snobs wouldn't let you work there as a cleaner. Now, they'll grovel for you at the chef's table."

"You remember that?"

"How could I possibly forget the name of any asshole who hurt you? I want you walking into that restaurant like a queen."

My heart skips.

This really is the mafia version of *Pretty Woman*, and Roman is doing the utmost to exceed my wildest dreams. When I first came to Beaumont City, looking for work, the restaurant manager threw me out like I was scum.

"Thank you." I give him a peck on the lips. "And I want you to bend me over the table and have me for dessert."

He grins, his eyes sparkling. "Emberly. You're the only thing I ever want to eat."

I stay on his lap all the way to the restaurant's service entrance, where the same restaurant manager ushers us into an elegant dining room of dark wood floors, matching furniture, and white upholstery. Crystal pendant lights hang down from the ceiling, casting a dim light over a table set for two.

It's on the tip of my tongue to remind him of the time he threw me out, but I don't want to ruin my high. I've sold two paintings, kicked the shit out of Lafayette, and have the sweetest, sexiest boyfriend. Things don't get much better than tonight.

Roman orders the man to move the place settings together, so we're sitting at corners to each other with our knees touching.

We eat oysters, lobster, and the most tender wagyu beef

served with eggplant and fenugreek. Every mouthful is an explosion of flavor, but what I want most is Roman.

After the plates are cleared, our waiter comes in with the dessert menus. Roman orders a bottle of their finest sweet wine. I nearly choke when he informs us that it's thirty thousand dollars excluding tax.

The waiter inclines his head and disappears through the door.

"You can't be serious," I hiss. "That's too much."

"We're celebrating." Roman takes my hand and brings my knuckles to his lips. "Tonight has been my second happiest night since leaving prison."

"Which was your first?" I ask.

He casts me a side-long glance and smirks. "The one when you grabbed me by the lapels and kissed me."

I lick my lips, my gaze dropping to his perfectly formed mouth. "If kissing me makes you so happy, I could do it again?"

"That's the plan." He kisses each knuckle, sending zips of sensation up my arm and into my chest.

My heart flutters. "What did I ever do to deserve a man like you? You're perfect."

"I'm no angel," he says. "I'm a gangster, an extortionist, and a murderer. I take pleasure in other people's pain."

"Everyone has their faults," I murmur. "But you make me feel alive."

A knock sounds on the door, and the waiter steps in, holding a bottle of golden wine and two glasses.

"1865 Chateau d'Yquem," he says with a hint of pride as he pulls out the cork.

"Take the glasses and brighten the lights," Roman says. "We only need the bottle."

His face falls, but he bows, murmuring, "As you wish, sir."

"That will be all for the evening," Roman says just before the door clicks shut.

Moments later, the pendant bulbs shine brighter, bathing the room in light.

He brings the bottle to my lips. "Take a sip."

This is unusual. Wines normally need to be poured out to release the bouquet, but what the hell do I know about the drinking habits of the super rich?

I take a long sip, savoring the rich, sweet notes. The dessert wine is creamy, with hints of apricot, peach, and honey.

"Delicious." I lick my lips.

"Take another taste," he says.

"Aren't you going to have any?" I ask.

"Your mouth will be my decanter."

My eyes widen. "Oh."

He brings the bottle to my lips, and I let in a mouthful of the liquid, this time not swallowing it all. Roman moves so close, the warmth of his breath heats my already fevered skin.

"Kiss me again," he says.

I lean in, bringing our lips together and letting his tongue invade my mouth. Roman explores me with a hunger that goes straight to my core, tasting and swirling every crevice until he's stolen the last bit of flavor.

He draws back, leaving me out of breath. I don't know what arouses me more. The heated kiss or the fact that he finds me delicious.

The hunger in his eyes smolders so brightly that I shift in my seat, feeling like prey he wants to devour.

"More." Roman brings the bottle back to my lips.

This time, I take a large sip, which I keep in my mouth. When he kisses me, I push the wine between his lips, savoring the taste of our entwined tongues and the expensive liquid.

"You taste so good, sweetheart."

Roman pulls me onto his lap and we kiss like this until the bottle is half empty, taking breaks for him to lavish my neck with his lips and teeth and tongue. By the time he sets down the bottle, my pussy is aching and so wet with arousal that it hurts.

"Please." I grab him around the nape of his neck and raise my hips. "I want to ride your cock."

His deep groan goes straight to my swollen clit. "We haven't finished the wine."

"Later," I say. "We can drink it on the way home."

"Eager?" He flashes me a smile.

The last orgasm he gave me was days ago, after I trashed his guest room. Back then, I was too numb with shock to fully appreciate the pleasure because he wrapped his hand around my throat. Now, I want him so badly that I can barely restrain myself.

I slide a hand between our bodies and reach for his hard cock. "Come on," I murmur. "You want it too."

"You want me to make you come in this exclusive French restaurant who didn't think you were good enough to wipe their tables?" he asks.

"Yeah."

"Then stand, lift up your dress, and bend over."

My heart thuds so hard, its reverberations reach my clit. I scramble off his lap, stumble to the edge of the table, and seize the hem of my dress with both hands. Seconds later, it's up around my waist, exposing the lacy gold lingerie Roman included in the box.

He rises off his seat and positions himself at my back. "Good girl. Now rest your pretty head on the tabletop and spread your legs."

A whimper resounds in the back of my throat as I obey. I part my thighs to shoulder width, but Roman moves my legs further apart.

"I said spread them nice and wide, so I can see that pretty little pussy."

My breath catches, my legs tremble, and I arch my hips.

He runs a finger down my clothed slit, making me shiver with need. The muscles of my core clench, needing more. "Dirty girl. You're so wet."

"Please." The word comes out as an elongated moan, and I shift my hips from side to side.

Roman delivers a slap that resounds against my clit. "Who told you to move?"

"S Sorry," I wail. "Just please fuck me."

He brings his lips down to my panties and flicks his tongue over my covered clit. My breath catches, and pleasure radiates through my core. I buck my hips, my entire body shaking with anticipation.

"You like that, baby?" he asks. "You like it when I bend you over the table and make you expose that wet patch spreading out from your sweet cunt."

"Please," I rasp. "Take off my panties."

The laugh he makes is so predatory that the fine hairs on my neck stand on end. Roman's breath is hot, heavy, and hungry, reminding me of a slathering beast. If he wants to eat me on this restaurant table, I can't think of a better way to die.

He pulls at the waistband of my panties and breaks it with a snap.

"Roman!" I hiss.

"Don't worry, baby. I'll buy you five more."

My breathing shallows, and cool air swirls over my heated folds. Every time I've heard something along those lines, it's usually some bullshit a man says to get me undressed and to make himself sound like a baller.

Roman is the only man I know who stands behind his words. I've never needed to ask him for anything. He has this superhuman ability to anticipate what I need.

"You're dripping." Roman runs a finger up my inner thigh and scoops up the moisture, making me shift my hips and moan for more.

He leans close to my spread pussy and pulls its lips open with his thumbs. "I waited five years to get close enough to such a beautiful cunt. Now, I'm going to make it mine."

"What about that time in the limo?" I ask.

"It was too dark," he says, his heated breath fanning my folds. "Now I get to see you spread out across the table like my favorite dessert."

Need skitters up my spine and my breath catches when I feel the brush of his lips against my outer folds. Roman runs the tip of his tongue up my slit and gathers up my arousal.

When he reaches my clit, pleasure lights up every nerve ending and ignites a fire in my core. My pussy clenches around nothing.

"Oh, god," I moan.

"That good?" he asks with a deep chuckle.

"Fuck, yes."

He rewards me with a firm flick. After another, my legs buckle, and I cling to the wooden table for support.

"Roman," I groan, my voice strained.

He teases me with a few circular movements that make my toes curl and my eyes roll to the back of my head. Just when I think he's building up a rhythm, he surprises me by tracing his tongue down to my entrance, infusing my entire being with shivers of anticipation.

"Delicious," he murmurs against my folds. "Wet pussy always goes better with wine."

He reaches for the bottle, and I raise my head. "What are you—"

Cool liquid trickles over my asshole and slides down my slit. My hips jerk.

"Roman!"

"Are you going to deny me my dessert?" he growls.

"N-No," I say through panting breaths. "Never."

He licks and sucks, each stroke of his tongue delivering lashes of rapture. I moan and squirm against his hot mouth, wanting more, needing it, but his hands come up and hold my hips steady.

"If you keep moving like that, I'll stop, and you'll go home with an aching cunt. Is that what you want, baby?"

I shake my head from side to side. "No."

"No, what?"

"No, sir. I don't want that."

"Be a good girl and hold still while I drizzle this wine over your pussy."

I collapse on the table, determined to stay still, clenching my fists when the next serving of dessert wine pools in my asshole and then spills over to my entrance.

My anus clenches, and my heart pounds so hard that I swear it makes the wood beneath me tremble. Is Roman going to drink wine out of my ass?

His lips close in between my buttocks and he makes a noisy suck, followed by a swirl of his tongue that lights up every nerve like a firework display.

"Oh god," I groan.

"I'm the other guy." His tongue slides down my perineum and then he slurps wine from my pussy.

My back arches and my eyes flutter closed as he

continues to lick every drop and concentrates his efforts on my clit.

Roman continues pouring wine between my ass cheeks and licking me from anus to clit until I'm covered in sweat, jerking, begging, and crying.

After several moments of this sweet torture, he sets down the bottle and forces my legs further apart.

His tongue makes side-to-side strokes over my clit, pausing to occasionally suck the swollen bud between his lips. The pressure builds and builds, my walls clenching and quivering around his tongue.

"Come for me, baby," he murmurs around my clit and slides two fingers into my pussy. "I want to feel you come apart."

With a few more strokes of his tongue, an orgasm crashes through my system. Roman remains between my legs, licking and sucking until I scream, my body shattering into a million pieces.

When the waves subside into gentle spasms, he places one kiss on each buttock and rises to help me off the table.

I collapse against his chest, my body still trembling from the aftershocks. "You're the most exquisite dessert," he murmurs. "But I'm ready for another course."

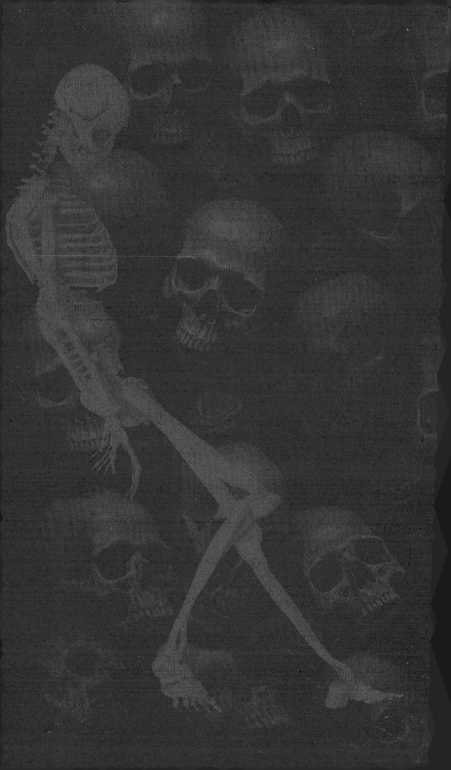

THIRTY-EIGHT

ROMAN

My cock strains at the sight of Emberly's peachy ass and exposed pussy that glistens with her arousal. She raises her hips, expecting me to take her from behind the way we fucked the first time, but I want more.

I want to see those green eyes dilate when I thrust into her, feel her tight heat as I fill her to the hilt. I want to see her pretty face contort with pleasure and need.

Sliding my hands beneath her shoulders, I pull her off the table, only to make her sit on its ledge. Emberly gazes up at me through half-lidded eyes, looking completely satiated from her first orgasm.

"You're going to spread those thighs for me like a good girl and hold on to my shoulders as I fuck you hard and deep," I say.

Her lips part, and her gaze darts toward the door. "Won't the waiters hear us?"

"Baby, you were already making plenty of noise. Besides, I want every motherfucker in this restaurant to know how much you enjoy my cock."

She giggles.

"By the time I'm done fucking that pussy, you'll be seeing Michelin stars."

"Oh," she says, her breath quickening, her thighs opening so wide I can see every fold of that sweet pussy. "You want me like this?"

"Just like that, baby."

My cock chooses this moment to push painfully against my zipper, trying to fight its way to Emberly's pussy. I finally put it out of its misery and let it out.

Emberly's eyes widen. "Oh my god. It's always a pleasant shock."

The corner of my lips lift into a smirk. "Nothing you haven't already taken before."

She shivers, and her chest rises and falls with the force of her excitement. I can tell how much she wants this, and it's been a long time coming. Emberly has lived under my roof for a week, yet this is the first opportunity I've gotten to fuck her since the night we met.

I hold her knees, positioning myself between them, and grip the base of my cock when she raises a palm.

"Condom?" she asks.

"Anything you want, babe." I reach into the inside pocket of my jacket, extract the foil wrapper, and tear it off with my teeth. "Put it on."

Emberly pulls out the condom with trembling fingers, her gaze never leaving mine as she rolls it over my length. Her delicate touch makes me groan so deeply that my entire chest vibrates.

"There," she says.

I grab her hips, position my cock between her slick folds, and slide past her tight entrance.

Emberly's eyes widen, and she pants through parted lips. "Oh, fuck."

"You got that right, baby."

Her eyes flutter closed as I enter her tight, wet heat. The muscles of her pussy clamp around my shaft, urging me for more. I press further until Emberly's back arches, and her fingers hold my shoulders in a death grip.

She throws her head back and groans. "Aaah. S-So deep."

"Eyes on me," I say.

Emberly whimpers, her eyes still shut.

"Open your eyes or I'll stop," I growl.

They snap open, and she gazes up at me, her eyes wide. "Don't stop. You feel so good."

"That's better." I slide almost all the way out before slamming back in.

She cries out, her eyes never leaving mine as I fuck her so hard that moisture gathers in the corners of her eyes with every thrust. Her ass moves further up the table.

"Hold on to my shoulders," I growl.

"A-Alright."

Each thrust into her feels like heaven with her pussy clenching and squeezing tighter with every movement. She gazes up at me through lust-glazed eyes and moans for me to pound into her with more strength.

When her legs wrap around my hips, it's like being welcomed into a connection that goes deeper than sex. For the first time since I began fucking women, I feel like I'm entering somewhere I finally belong.

It's almost like making love.

Emberly wants me just as much as I want her. Her inner walls clench and squeeze around my cock, pulling me deeper into a bond I can't deny.

She's perfect—talented, fierce, humble, and exciting. She appreciates all aspects of me, including my darkness.

Long-forgotten emotions swell in my heart at how

perfectly her personality delights mine. It's as though she was made for me. Emberly has enthralled me so completely that it's unnerving.

My balls tighten with the need to explode inside her exquisite pussy. I clench my teeth, summoning every ounce of willpower to hold back and concentrate on Emberly's pleasure. It's near impossible, since each time she cries out, her inner muscles spasms around my cock like she wants to milk me of every ounce of cum.

She gasps. "Roman, I'm going to come again."

"Together?"

She gives me an eager nod, her pretty green eyes gazing up at me like I'm the only man in the world who has ever given her pleasure.

Fuck. How can I resist?

I increase the speed of my thrusts, loving the way her lips parts and her eyes roll to the back of her head. Everything about this woman is perfect. Her passion, her artistic flair, the way she keeps me on my toes, and the way she warms my bed.

Sleeping beside Emberly is like taking the strongest sedative and waking up rejuvenated. Fucking her is like getting a taste of bliss. I sound sappy, even as I think this to myself, but she brightens the shadows in my soul.

When I look into her eyes, I no longer see her tainted blood. Being inside her makes me forget the burdens of leading the family to greatness. All that matters now is making her come.

My ears fill with her breathy moans, which drown out my thoughts. Right now, it's just Emberly and me and the intensity of our passion that grows stronger with each heartbeat.

I want to stay inside this woman forever. But from the

way her sweet pussy is squeezing my cock, I know neither of us will last much longer.

"Come for me, Emberly," I growl. "Now."

She tilts her head back and groans. In that moment, the hard shell encasing my heart melts into nothing, and I know with certainty there's no other woman for me but Emberly Kay.

Her eyes screw shut, and her entire body stiffens. I hold on to her, breathing her in like she's the only air I need. Emberly screams, and the sound goes straight to my soul, stirring up emotions I've never felt for a woman.

"Roman!"

Her pussy clamps tighter than a fist, sending electric shocks of pleasure straight to my core. My balls ache with the need to explode as she bucks her hips and clenches around me so hard that I come like I'm struck by lightning.

The orgasm rips through my entire body, sending white-hot pleasure to every corner of my being. My chest throbs with deep affection for this perfect woman who has unknowingly stolen my heart.

I roar, filling the condom with wave after wave of liquid euphoria, wishing desperately I could empty myself into her soul. Emberly's pulsing around my cock prolongs my pleasure, heightening my desperate need to keep her at my side forever.

"Mine," I growl into her neck.

"Yours," she replies.

When she finally collapses, I gather her into my arms and press my lips to her temple. "Good girl," I murmur. "You did so well."

"Hmm," she moans against my neck.

"You're more addictive than any drug, and I would gladly overdose."

She laughs, the sound throaty and rich. "Why do you always know just what to say?"

"No bullshit, baby. You're in my veins—the ultimate rush. I've never come so hard, but I'm still craving more."

"You're a poet now?"

"That's because you inspired me from the moment we met," I say, meaning every word.

Emberly might have once challenged me to think of creative ways to work around her volatile personality while trying to take back the family fortune. But now she inspires me to be the man she deserves.

I'm no longer satisfied with just keeping her alive or even keeping her within the walls of my estate. I'm consumed by an insatiable desire to possess her, to never let her go. No other woman could ever satisfy me except Emberly.

But what happens if she ever finds out what I'm doing or that I originally wanted her dead?

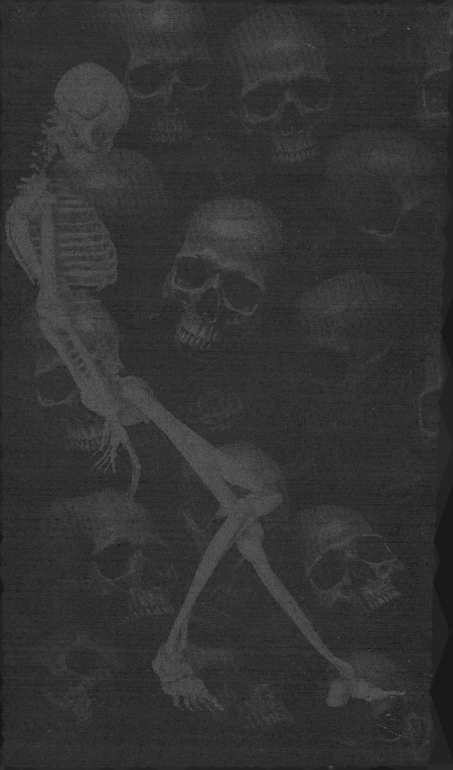

THIRTY-NINE

EMBERLY

My head spins. My skin tingles. My heart pounds so hard it might burst. Roman is so good to me that everything feels like a dream.

He's still inside me, his cock twitching against my quivering walls. His eyes looking so deeply into my soul that I'm certain he can hear my thoughts.

Roman is the first person outside of college that has supported my art, and I'm not just talking about the studio and free supplies. Because of him, I met Mr. Lubelli and I'm sure my painting sold faster because of Roman's influence.

And then the celebratory dinner at a restaurant that wouldn't even employ me to clean the floors? And the mind-melting sex?

More importantly, the praise? No one has ever called me inspirational, let alone addictive. I was always a nuisance at best, a burden at worst, and that doesn't even begin to describe how Jim treated me from the moment I fell under his control.

Roman isn't the kind of man to take advantage of a

woman's dependence on him. He encouraged me to start painting and invited the right people to his party to help further my career. He's the polar opposite to Jim, who treated me like a slave.

"Talk to me, baby," he murmurs, his warm breath fanning across my skin.

My legs tighten around his hips, trying to pull him in deeper. "I want to stay like this forever."

He smiles, the corners of his eyes crinkling, making him look so handsome my heart aches. "I want to spend the rest of my life with my cock nestled in your sweet little cunt."

A breath catches in the back of my throat. Why does that sound like he wants a long-term relationship?

My heart, which had calmed to a steady beat, picks up speed. Maybe it was just a figure of speech. Maybe I'm over-thinking things. Or maybe my paranoia is going into over-drive as usual to sabotage this beautiful moment.

Roman's eyes bore into mine, waiting for an answer to his unspoken question. With each shallow breath, the pres-sure intensifies until I'm certain my lungs will burst.

Does he want me to say the same? I already did. I part my lips, making no sound, but a sharp knock on the door forces him to break eye contact.

All the pressure escapes me in an outward breath. Roman holds his shaft at the base, eases out, and pulls me off the edge of the table, so my dress falls down to cover my thighs.

The knock sounds again.

"I told you not to disturb me," he snarls.

Whoever's behind the door clears his throat. "Sorry, boss. It's Gil."

"Come in," he says.

The door swings open, and the huge man lumbers inside with his gaze fixed to the floor.

Heat blooms across my cheeks at the thought of him knowing we weren't eating. I wrap my arms around my middle and try not to shuffle on my feet. Gil must have stood behind the door, listening to Roman fuck the life out of me while waiting for the right moment to knock.

"What is it?" Roman asks.

"One of the vehicles was attacked," Gil says. "We lost Sal."

"Shit," Roman hisses. "How the fuck did that happen?"

"They're saying it was automatic weapons." Gil grimaces. "And those bastards knew exactly what they were doing."

"Why do you say that?" he asks.

"There was a message saying that next time, they won't just blow up a lackey."

"The police?" I whisper. "How did they know you switched cars?"

Roman turns to me, his features tightening, his eyes conflicted. I don't think he wanted me to know that Jim's people were still trying to get me, but I'm glad Gil blurted out the truth. "Those corrupt cops don't give a shit if innocent people get murdered along with their targets."

"They want you to hand me over?" I ask.

He nods.

A shudder runs down my spine. "Wait. I thought the cars were bulletproof?"

"They are," Gil mutters. "But the moment Sal opened the door, the bastards had a clear shot. He didn't have a chance."

All the euphoria of the night drains away, leaving me cold with dread. What if Jim's people are watching us this very moment with weapons trained at our heads?

The food in my stomach turns to lead at the very

prospect, and I inch away from the window. I take a seat, not trusting my legs not to buckle.

The restaurant manager steps in with a clipboard that I can only assume contains the check. "Mr. Montesano—"

Roman holds up a finger, making the man's mouth click shut. He turns to me and asks, "Is that the man who gave you shit when you applied for a job?"

"Yes?" I rasp, wondering why Roman is asking about this when he should be more concerned about Jim and his lackeys murdering Sal.

"Do you remember this woman?" Roman asks the restaurant manager.

"Sir?" The other man frowns.

"She applied for a job at this restaurant, and you turned her away."

The manager's jaw drops, and his eyes widen. He stands frozen, his gaze darting between Roman and me.

Any other time, I would rise off my seat and chastise the man for being such a snob, but I'm still shaken by the news that Jim has escalated his attacks.

The manager clears his throat. "I see many applicants, sir. I cannot remember every single detail."

I roll my eyes. My interview was last week and just hours before my run-in with Lafayette.

Roman's nostrils flare. "You mean to tell me that my date was forgettable?"

He flinches. "Of course not. The young lady was inappropriately dressed and didn't have the required qualifications or experience."

My eyes narrow at the blatant lie. "Since when do you need a degree and a business suit to clean floors?"

Roman grabs the man's throat and slams him against the wall. "Big mistake," he growls. "You were too busy looking down your nose at her to recognize her talent. Now, I'm insulted."

He gasps. "Sir, I-I didn't realize—"

"Apologize to the lady."

The manager turns to me, his complexion matching the pristine white tablecloths. He places a hand on his chest and clears his throat. "I apologize profusely for any insult or discomfort you may have experienced."

My lips tighten at his passive-aggressiveness. What he said was another variation of I'm sorry you feel that way. He's only sorry that Roman took offense at his shitty behavior, but whatever. I don't give a damn.

Roman grabs him by the lapels. "You call that an apology? Get on your fucking knees and grovel."

The manager's features tighten. It looks like he wants to tell Roman to get lost, but he's smart enough to know it will result in disaster.

He turns to me, his eyes hard with resentment, and sinks to his knees. As he sucks in a deep breath to gather himself, Roman slams a hand between his shoulder blades.

"This is your last chance to crawl to the lady and grovel," he snarls.

My heart pounds, and I sit straighter in my seat. This is insane. It was only one snide incident among many, but Roman insists I should be afforded the same level of respect as a mafia don.

The manager crawls to me on his hands and knees, his breaths erratic. All traces of resentment slide off his face, replaced with terror. When he reaches where I'm sitting, his skin is already glistening with sweat. "I'm sorry." He stares down at my feet. "You came in with your hands covered with flecks of dried paint. Seeing you so happy stirred something in me—envy, I think, because I never had a talent for art."

My gaze darts to Roman's, who still looks like he wants to strangle the manager. I turn back to the man whose head rests on the floor by my feet and gulp.

"Please, forgive me."

"Stop making people feel inferior, and we're even," I say.

"Of course, miss," he rasps.

Roman flicks his head toward the door. "Crawl the fuck out."

As the restaurant manager scurries into the hallway like a desperate animal, Roman and Gil continue their conversation, discussing a strategy if our enemies tracked us to the restaurant, as well as the best route back to avoid getting blown to pieces.

I stop listening halfway because the pulse pounding between my ears drowns out all the sound.

Why the hell is this situation with Jim spiraling so desperately out of control?

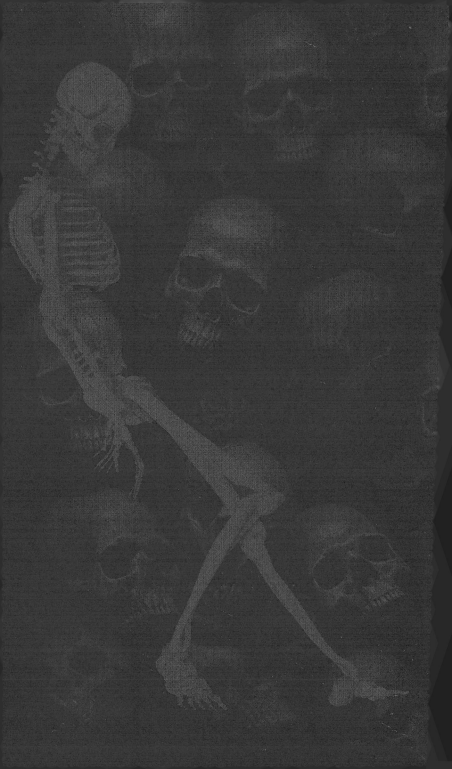

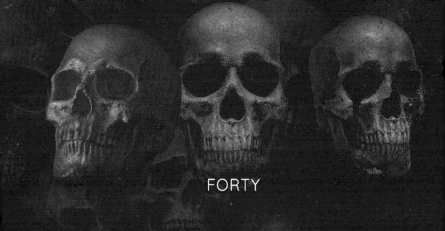

FORTY

ROMAN

Emberly was silent on the journey home, but relaxed the moment we stepped through the door. I understand why she was so shaken by the news of Sal's death. It was shitty of me to claim that Callahan's colleagues were killing my men to make me release her, but now she'll never want to leave.

The gamble I made by giving her a sense of freedom paid off, but what good is getting back our assets if we fall to those assassins? Something needs to be done about the Moirai Group before Emberly uncovers my bullshit.

I put her to bed, hugged her to sleep, and then spent several tense minutes on the phone with the Moirai bastards. They want me to release their operatives or else. I reminded them of their refusal to remove the hit on our lives and hung up.

Something tells me they won't stop coming after us until I've dealt with Tommy Galliano.

My spies tell me he's lying low, already anticipating our next strike, and will probably stay behind the closed doors of his hideout until all three of us are dead.

Fuck him.

There are more firms of assassins than the Moirai out there, and I've hired each of them to target Galliano. The moment he resurfaces, he's dead.

When I return to Emberly, she's facing my side of the bed, her dark hair spread over the pillow like curling cobras. I stand at the headboard and sigh.

If I'm the king of this operation, then Emberly is my dark queen. My heart swells at the memory of my pretty little gorgon kicking and punching Lafayette in the back of the car.

Emberly isn't like other women who only enjoy the rewards of organized crime. She doesn't just accept its brutal parts, but revels in them. Emberly has seen me murder twice, yet she's still here in my bed.

Violence is in her blood.

That's why we're so evenly matched. It's also why I made that asshole at the restaurant show her some fucking respect.

After undressing to my boxers, I climb into bed and wrap an arm around her waist. Emberly's head rests in the crook of my shoulder, and her hair drapes over my skin like silk.

I kiss her forehead, inhaling her cinnamon and vanilla scent. She smells of freedom, of comfort, of home. Being so close to this sweet creature almost makes me forget the years I spent on death row.

Emberly is mine, and no one will ever take her away.

———

Hours later, I'm still slumbering when Emberly stirs, withdrawing her body heat. I crack open an eye to find her sitting up in bed with her arms pulled up in a stretch.

As usual, her hair is a nest of tangles that enhances her wild beauty. Sunlight streams in from the balcony doors, lighting up her stray curls like a halo.

The cream camisole stretches over her breasts, offering me a tantalizing peek of her nipples. In response, my cock pushes against the fabric of my boxers, aching for another taste of her.

"Good morning, beautiful," I murmur, my voice still thick with sleep.

"Hey," she replies. "I wasn't expecting you to still be in bed."

"Why? What time is it?"

"Eight."

My eyes widen. "I haven't slept this late since before I got locked up."

"Are you serious?" she asks with a frown.

"It's just like I said last night." I pull her down into my arms, so her back lies flush against my chest. "You're better than any narcotic."

"Oh yeah. What are you going to do about it?" She pushes her plump ass into my erection, making me groan.

"I'm going to take my morning dose," I whisper against her neck, my hand slipping beneath the silk camisole to cup her breasts.

Emberly moans, her body arching against mine. "Condom."

"You know I always come prepared." I reach across to the bedside table and pick up a foil wrapper.

With one hand, I roll her nipple between my fingers. "Do you like that, baby?"

Emberly moans, "Oh, fuck. That feels so good."

My other hand holds the square package while I tear it open between my teeth. I sheath my cock, pull down her silk shorts, and position my tip at her entrance.

"Ready?" I ask.

"Always," she moans.

Any other time, I would make her beg, make her plead for my cock, but I want to be inside Emberly so badly that it hurts.

Holding her steady around the waist, I enter her from behind with a single thrust. Her pussy clenches around my shaft with the strength of a fist, making my entire body shudder.

Emberly gasps. "No matter how many times you fuck me, I don't think I'll ever get used to your girth."

I chuckle. "You can take it, baby. You're always so ready and wet for me, so impossible to resist."

"Then don't." She pushes back her hips.

I bury my face into her neck and pull back, only to push into her with a snap of my hips more powerful than the first. The air fills with our mingled groans as I fuck her hard and slow. Emberly rocks against my thrusts, deepening our connection.

"Oh God," she moans. Keep going!"

Somewhere in the back of my mind is the niggling thought that Benito is waiting for me to help take back the casino, but when Emberly grips my forearm and whimpers, I forget all about business.

I reach around, my fingers finding her swollen clit. "You feel so good, baby. Just like always."

Her tight heat continues closing in on my cock like a vise, and it feels like being welcomed home. The warmth of the sun on my back and the feel of her body against mine is everything I need.

I'm close to climaxing, but I hold back, needing Emberly to orgasm first.

"Come for me," I growl against her neck.

My fingers increase the pace of their strokes around her

clit, and I thrust harder than before. Emberly cries out each time I hit her g-spot, making my heart race.

"Just like that, baby." I push into her harder.

Finally, her breath hitches, and she releases a keening cry. "I'm coming."

"Good girl," I say, my voice tight. "Let it all out."

Emberly's scream rips through the air as her body stiffens, and her pussy clenches around my cock. Her inner walls ripple with each passing heartbeat, and I quicken my thrusts, reveling in the sounds of her pleasure.

"Roman," she screams.

"Say my name one more time," I growl.

"Oh, fuck. Roman!"

That's all it takes for me to explode within her. Pleasure rockets through my system, filling every nerve with an intensity that turns my vision white.

My body takes control, shooting jet after jet of cum into her until I collapse against the mattress, my muscles so relaxed that I go limp.

I have never come so hard.

Not even that first time, when all I saw in her was a conquest.

We're entwined, gasping for air in the aftermath of our lovemaking. Emberly is a goddess who ignites desires in me that consume my resolve. This is a dangerous game—I'm playing with fire and jeopardizing my revenge, but she's worth the risk of burning to ashes.

My phone rings, but I don't want to move.

"Don't you need to answer that?" she whispers.

"It can wait." I wrap my arms around her waist, squeezing her tight, and bury my face in her unruly curls.

Emberly's body relaxes against mine, her pulse still pounding. As we lie together, our heartbeats slow, then thrum in unison. I can't imagine a better sign that we are meant to be together.

My eyes close, and I'm about to drift into sleep when several sharp knocks echo through the room.

It's Benito.

And he's impatient.

The two of us set up an entire plan of action to take back the casino, where we would get revenge on the bastards who defected from our family to join Capello. And here I am, warming my cock inside the bastard's daughter.

"Ignore it," she murmurs. "Tell them to go away."

I kiss her neck. "This one can't wait, baby. I have to go."

She sighs, and I pull out of my little piece of heaven, wondering what's happening to my resolve.

For the past five years, I've fantasized about the moment I would escape the penitentiary to slice open chests and rip out hearts. Revenge was the only thing that helped me sleep through the injustice of being framed.

Now, one taste of Emberly is throwing me off kilter.

The knocks continue.

"Roman!" Benito growls.

"Coming." I shove on last night's clothes and walk to the door without a backward glance.

I can't let Emberly distract me from my mission.

Revenge will be mine.

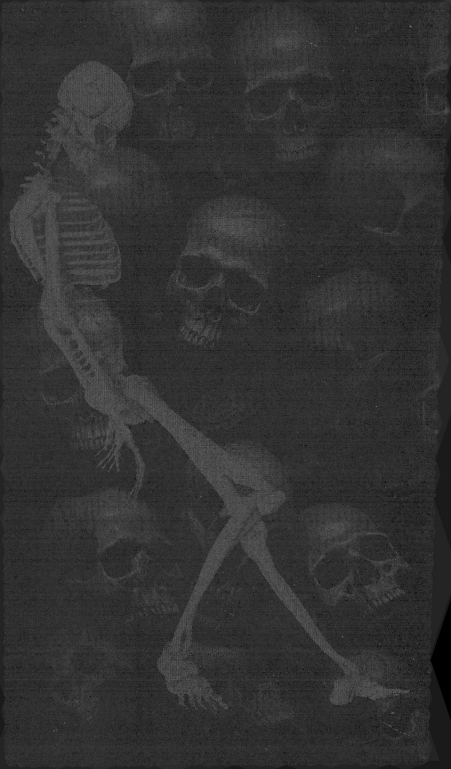

FORTY-ONE

ROMAN

When I step out of my room, Benito is only inches away from the bedroom door, and I nearly knock him on his ass. Today is the highlight of our plan for revenge, and I'm embarrassed that I'm late.

Emberly's allure will be my downfall. She's the embodiment of temptation.

"Where's Cesare?" I ask.

"Interrogating the assassin," he mutters.

We walk side by side down the hallway, passing a housemaid holding a stack of sheets.

"Which one?" I ask as we reach the grand staircase.

Benito gives me an incredulous look, as though the answer is obvious.

"Rosalind." I roll my eyes and descend the steps. "Cesare needs to keep his dick out of that woman and focus more on the threats hanging over our heads."

"Like you?"

My eyes narrow. "What does that mean?"

We reach the bottom of the stairs, where Gil leans

against the front door with his eyes shut and his arms closed, as though he's been standing there for hours.

Benito glances over his shoulder as though checking that Emberly is still out of earshot. "Our little guest has moved out of the pool house and into your bed."

My hackles rise, but I keep my voice even and continue crossing the entrance hall. "Can you blame her after nearly getting abducted under my roof by that cop?"

"That's not my point," he says.

"Then what is?"

"You're getting attached." He lowers his voice. "Giving her the illusion of freedom is one thing. Installing her in the master suite is another."

My feet stop. "How the fuck do you expect someone as cautious as her to sign over hundreds of millions worth of assets without passing each contract through an attorney?"

I don't wait for him to answer. "You use a woman's biggest weakness. Her need to trust the man she's fucking."

Benito stares back at me for several heartbeats, looking like he can see through the bullshit. The truth is, I'm catching feelings. Feelings are too inconvenient to complete my mission. I want her in my life, but I also want back what her father stole.

"Are you sure that's all it is?" he murmurs.

My brows rise. "What does that mean?"

Benito holds up his palms in surrender. "Never forget she's a Capello."

As if I could.

It's bad enough that Emberly has burrowed her way under my skin. Even worse, she's seeped into my blood-stream and is making her way into my heart. If I don't take control of myself, my need for her will extinguish my burning desire for revenge.

Gil opens the front door, and we step out onto the sun-drenched steps. Late mornings are another sign of Emberly's influence. By this time of the day, I should have already completed my morning run, read through the papers, and enjoyed a leisurely breakfast.

Emberly is making me weak.

Benito's gaze burns the side of my face. I turn to give his shoulder a hard squeeze. "I've thought of nothing for the past five years. No pussy could distract me from getting back what belongs to our family."

He nods, not seeming entirely convinced and looking like he isn't buying my explanation that fucking Emberly is just another way to stop her from scrutinizing the contracts. We step into another armored car and make our way to take back control of the casino and its attached hotels.

———

Half an hour later, our first stop is the Newtown Crematorium, a fine establishment that boasts four twin cremators. Its owner is a cousin who shares the same great-grandfather, but not the Montesano last name.

The cremation chamber's atmosphere is heavy with the mingled scents of burning metal and wood. Ventilators hum and gas burners roar, providing the perfect backdrop for a mass execution.

It's already cramped with eight of my men standing within its white-tiled walls among four gurneys containing cardboard coffins lined up at the entrance of each cremator.

In the middle of the room kneels a quartet of familiar-looking men with their arms tied behind their backs.

"Nicky Dellucci, Joe Napolitano, Val Esposito, and Vito De Luca," I say, "It's been a long time."

All four of them shiver, as they should. They were once

Dad's loyal lieutenants, who sided with Capello within days of my arrest.

I still remember a newspaper article that displayed a picture of Capello and his piece-of-shit attorney, Joseph Di Marco, cutting the ribbon of the hotel they built beside Dad's stolen casino. All four of these motherfuckers stood behind them, grinning like proud uncles.

"Status report," I ask Benito.

"We've had the cremators burning all night. All their underlings are nothing more than ashes," my brother replies, already sounding like the casino's new boss. "All that remains are these four, who we saved for you."

"Any last words, gentlemen?" I ask.

Three of them bow their heads, already knowing that nothing they say will save them from their fate. Vito De Luca is the only one who looks me in the eye.

"Believe me when I say I never betrayed your family. Enzo was dead and you were behind bars. Benito was away in law school and Cesare was busy in medical school. They were both too young to take the reins. The business had to continue." He squeezes his eyes shut and exhales a shuddering breath. "How was I supposed to know Frederic stole the casino from under your family's nose?"

I rub my chin, my gaze meeting Benito's, before turning back to De Luca's. "You mean to say that you thought you were still working for the Montesano family?"

He gives me an eager nod. "I swear to god."

"Ah." I nod back, my jaw clenching.

Nicky Dellucci chooses this moment to pipe up. "Roman, I've known you since you were a kid. This isn't like you. This whole situation is a misunderstanding."

The other two captives murmur their agreement.

"Then explain to me why you didn't reach out to my brothers the moment that bastard renamed the casino." I spread my hands wide, eager to hear what bullshit they'll spew next. "Or did you just miss the giant neon sign that flashed Capello Casino?"

All four of them fall silent.

It's exactly as I thought.

I turn to Benito. "Do you have anything to add before we put them to rest?"

"Capello took control of the casino because of cowards like you who switched allegiances," Benito says, his voice flat. "Now, you get to serve him in hell."

"Please," De Luca screams. "Don't do this."

I flick my head toward my men. "Put them to rest."

My brother and I step back to give our people space to lower the four betrayers into their cardboard coffins. Each of them snivels and begs for their lives, their voices adding a melody to the snap and crackle of the furnace.

"When you betray the Montesano family, you pay for disloyalty with your lives," I say.

Gil moves to my side. "Do you want them to tape down the lids?"

"No," I reply. "Let them get a preview of their fate."

The wails increase in volume, mingling with curses and pleas for mercy, even as the men slide the coffins onto metal rollers that feed them to the cremator.

The furnace comes to life, and flames spring out from both the top and bottom of the chamber. Heat shoots out from the mouth of the cremator, sending out bursts of warmth.

Benito and I stand shoulder to shoulder, watching the last of the betrayers disappear behind the flames. My ears ring with their shrieks, and I can almost imagine what it sounds like when they join ranks with the likes of Capello, Cain, Brutus, Judas Iscariot, and all the other betrayers in the inferno's ninth circle.

This is oddly satisfying.

A little voice in the back of my head whispers that I should join the backstabbers. Aren't I betraying Emberly? I worked so hard to earn her trust, yet I'm doing to her what Capello did to Dad. My shoulders tighten, and I tell the voice to back the fuck off.

This situation is different.

When the screams subside from within the cremator, I wrap an arm around my little brother's shoulders and smile. "Are you ready to take control of the casino?"

I turn to my men. "Let's go."

———

Less than an hour later, Benito and I pull into the casino's front entrance. Exposing ourselves is a risk with the Moirai still under contract to secure our deaths, but they've agreed to putting the hit on hold... At least until we return their operatives.

Construction staff are already removing Capello's ostentatious neon sign and replacing it with one that resembles the original. My breaths slow, and my chest expands with pride.

"Did you arrange that?" I sit forward in my seat, unable to take my gaze off our family name in lights.

"I commissioned the new sign the moment Leroi confirmed the date he was going to kill Capello," Benito replies. "What do you think?"

"It's perfect," I reply, my voice thick.

After half a decade, the casino is finally back in our hands.

Gil opens the car door, and we step out onto the pavement. Tiny droplets of water rain down on us from the fountains on the courtyard, transforming my dreams into a vivid reality.

"Welcome back, boss," Gil says.

I turn to him and smirk, unable to utter the words in case my voice cracks. This was Dad's pride and joy—the first thing I wanted to take back.

During my darkest days when I lay in my cell, I imagined all three of us brothers walking through the casino with AK-47s, gunning down our betrayers. This version of events is cleaner, far more dignified, and leaves no incriminating evidence.

Benito and I walk side by side through the grand entrance, where hundreds of employees stand in a line, applauding our return.

When we reach a podium in the middle, I place a hand on my brother's shoulder and step back. This is his moment. I promised him the casino and now it's time for him to take charge.

Gil and I stand at Benito's back as he delivers a well-practiced speech, informing the employees that the casino is under new management.

I zone out, making a mental note of what else we need to take back from Emberly. The stocks, loan company, the real estate portfolio, the contents of the safety deposit boxes. Four more paintings in exchange for four more contracts.

I promised to put a bullet through her head after taking back our assets, but the thought of hurting Emberly makes me want to put a bullet through my heart. But with the end in sight, I'm still no closer to working out how the hell I'm going to stop our relationship from turning to shit.

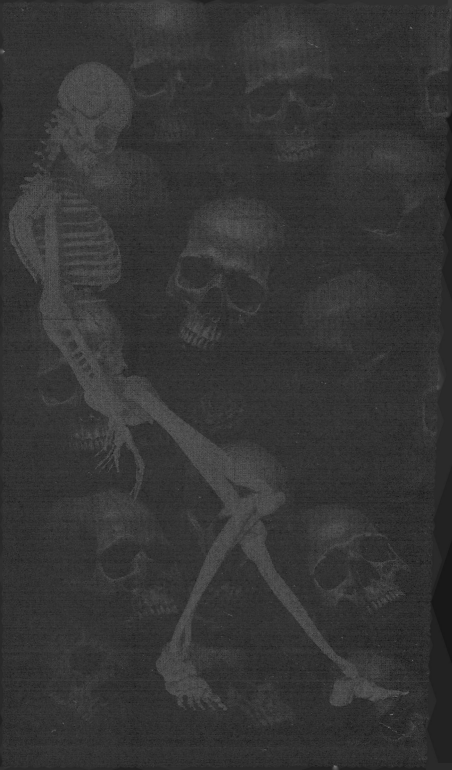

FORTY-TWO

EMBERLY

Last night, when Roman returned, he seemed troubled. He slid into bed and hugged me so tightly that I rose from my slumber. That urgent knock on the door yesterday morning must have been for some terrible emergency. I'm almost too afraid to ask.

It's morning now, and I hope his troubles have faded. I hold him around the middle with my head resting on his shoulder. When he's peaceful and asleep, I don't see our ten-year age difference. He doesn't look thirty-four.

All the worry lines are gone, replaced by a serenity that leaves me breathless. I can't bring myself to awaken this sleeping beauty.

"See something you like?" he murmurs.

"Actually, I do." I trail my hand across his chest.

Roman's deep groan resounds across his entire torso as I pepper his neck with kisses. I slide my hand down the curve of his pec toward his abs, but he grabs my wrist.

"What's wrong?" I ask.

"What's wrong with just wanting to cuddle?"

His arm around my waist tightens, and he tucks me closer into his side, so my chest lies flush against his ribs.

My brows pinch, and I scrutinize his perfect profile. "Are you okay?"

He hesitates for a heartbeat. "Yeah."

"Did something happen yesterday?"

"Like what?"

"I don't know... Maybe another of your employees got attacked by the police?"

He chuckles, but the sound carries no humor. "It's nothing like that."

I crane my neck to get a better view at his face, which is no longer looking so relaxed. A muscle in his jaw tenses and his mouth tightens into a thin line as though whatever he's keeping from me is terrifying.

My insides twist into knots. If it's worse than what he did to Dominic or that young police officer, I really don't want to know.

"I was thinking of asking Tony to take me to Simon's Pond," I say.

Roman stiffens. "What for?"

"Inspiration," I reply. "There's only so much I can paint around your estate before I run out of ideas. At least when I'm at Simon's Pond—"

"No."

A muscle in my face ticks. "Am I a prisoner?"

"I'll take you."

"Aren't you busy dealing with the cops?" I ask.

"Not today."

He releases his grip around my waist and eases us both up to sitting. When we're disentangled, he rises off the bed and walks toward the bathroom without a word.

I stare at his broad back, my teeth worrying at my

bottom lip. Shoulders sagging, I run through our entire conversation. Did I say something wrong?

This isn't like Roman at all.

Maybe I've overstayed my welcome. The arrangement was to leave after the portrait. He even got my charges dropped so I could start a new life in a new place with a new identity without fear of being hunted by the law.

Then what did I do?

I announced I was staying. To be another burden.

Oh, shit. How long until he switches up and starts resenting my existence like my mom?

He pauses at the doorway and flashes me a smile. "Are you coming?"

———

My concerns disappear during the steamiest shower of my entire existence, where Roman fucks me against the wall. Afterward, I select some clothes from the Gucci trunk that now resides in the dressing room.

Roman tells me to pack some art supplies and disappears through the door. I walk to the pool house, pick up the mahogany box filled with small tubes of oil paint, brushes and all the supplies I need to paint, and gather a small easel and a pair of canvases.

By the time I've finished selecting everything, Roman appears at the doors of the pool house dressed casually and holding a wicker basket.

"What's that?" I ask.

"Brunch." He glances at my bag. "Is that all you're taking?"

I nod, still not quite understanding why he's being so abrupt. The Roman I know is smooth, silver-tongued, self-possessed.

"What's wrong?" I ask.

"What do you mean?" He glances at a finished painting I made of a crimson iris dripping blood.

"You're blowing hot and cold. Am I overstaying my welcome?"

He finally looks me in the eye with an intensity that makes my breath catch. My heart stutters as he crosses the distance between us and stands so close that I flail under the weight of his attention.

"It's the opposite," he says, cupping my cheek. "I'm getting so attached to you that it will hurt like hell when you leave."

My brows draw together. "But I said I would stay."

His lips tighten, and I can already guess what he's holding back.

"You think I'm afraid of your dangerous lifestyle," I say. "But I like being with you. If I left, I would always have regrets."

Silence stretches out between us, and I continue looking into his eyes, trying to assure him of my sincerity. I might have kissed Roman to get away from Jim and hid here for protection, but I'm staying because I want him.

I like the person I am when I'm with Roman. I like being around him. Underneath the hard exterior is a man with family values, an amazing lover, and the protector I never knew I needed.

"Roman?" I whisper.

He sighs. "Let's go."

Our journey is mostly silent. I tire of his one-word answers and decide to leave him alone to brood. I try not to take it personally because I haven't done anything wrong.

Maybe all his responsibilities are taking their toll? Some people react differently when they're overwhelmed, especially when they don't have an outlet like art. There's a vast difference between being accustomed to death row and suddenly becoming responsible for a huge business. He's just trying to acclimatize to the change of circumstances. I need to stop being paranoid and thinking I'm some artist he's being forced to babysit.

When we leave the city limits and the roads narrow toward the woodland, Roman takes my hand and kisses my knuckles.

"Feeling better?" I ask.

"Too much on my mind," he mutters.

"I'm here if you want to talk about it," I reply with a smile.

He squeezes my hand in a silent gesture of appreciation and says, "I know."

Simon's Pond is a quarter-mile walk from a gravel parking lot that leads to a winding trail through tall trees and wildflowers.

Roman's shoulders loosen and his stance becomes more relaxed as we near our destination. A gentle breeze rustles through the leaves, and the air is alive with the melodic chirping of birds. It's as though nature welcomes us to this tranquil oasis hidden from the chaos of organized crime.

He pauses, his lips parting, his breath slowing. I follow his gaze to water so clear you can see the fish.

"What do you think?" I ask.

"I never imagined anything like this existed in New Alderney," he says, his voice breathy with awe.

"Don't you ever venture out into the forest?"

He shakes his head, his features forming a frown. "All my business is in the city."

"Let's make up for lost time."

I slide off my shoes and Roman does the same, and he tucks them into the outer pocket of the case containing my art supplies.

We hold hands, and I guide him to the water's edge, where there's a series of stepping stones that cut through the shallow side of the pond. They're cool and slick with moss, contrasting with the warmth of the sun.

Roman's eyes dance with wonder, making him look carefree. "How do you know about this place?"

"From other artists, and tourists," I reply.

"Tourists?"

"When I came to Beaumont City, the first thing I looked for was studio space." We reach the other side and continue up a small hill.

"Not an apartment?"

"The youth hostel where I stayed offered free accommodation for housekeeping staff, so I didn't have to worry about the expense. People visited from all over the world, which is how I learned about some of the more popular tourist sights."

He stares down into the side of my face but doesn't speak.

"When I found a studio I could afford, the other artists told me about the rarer beauty spots around the state. One of them was Simon's Pond."

We reach the top of the hill, which levels out into a grassy clearing surrounded by trees. There's a small opening that looks out onto the water that makes Roman whistle.

"They told me about this spot, too," I say. "No one ever comes up here."

While I set up my easel, Roman spreads a blanket over the ground and unpacks the picnic basket, revealing white wine, ciabatta, prosciutto, olives, and a variety of cheeses. There's even a panettone and fresh fruit for dessert.

"Sofia really prepared us a feast."

He pours the wine into plastic goblets and grins. "She knows how to keep us well-fed."

As I cut the bread and place it on the plates, Roman asks, "Why did you leave the youth hostel?"

"There's only so much sleep a person can get when sharing a bunk with eight much younger girls on vacation, so I found work with an agency that paid a lot more."

"Is that how you met the cop?"

My gaze drops to the pale slice bread. I add some prosciutto to it and shrug. "Yeah, I was cleaning the police precinct where he worked, and he asked me out for coffee. After a few weeks, we started dating."

Roman remains silent for several heartbeats longer than is comfortable, forcing me to meet his hard gaze. My stomach churns. I know he's thinking I'm a fool for letting myself get hurt by Jim.

"If you're wondering how I could have gotten mixed up with a psychopath, you need to understand he wasn't always like that. At first, he was goofy and endearing. Even a little shy. I thought he was a good guy."

"When did he switch?"

Bitterness coats my tongue, and I take a sip of the wine to wash it away. "It was more of a gradual descent. You know the frog in boiling water analogy?"

"Never heard of it."

"Frogs would leap out of hot water, but if you place them in cold water, they'll stay there, even if you increase the temperature as long as you do it slowly. Eventually, they'll boil to death."

His brows lower. "So you didn't notice the gradual changes until it was too late?"

My shoulders sag. "His manipulation was more skillful than turning up the heat."

"What do you mean?"

"When we first began dating, he would mention incidents where women had been attacked or raped by their roommate's boyfriends or guests, making me feel like where I lived wasn't safe."

Roman takes a long sip of his wine, his gaze dropping to the mozzarella.

"He would bring up arrests that took place close to my building, drug dens in the area... Everything that would make it sound like my only option in the world was to move into his suburb."

"With him," Roman says.

"Yeah." I sigh. "Even that started off slowly. When I stayed over at his house, he'd ask me to leave a few things. Then after each date, he'd drive me back to his place because it was more comfortable and private. Before I knew it, I'd already moved in."

"Sounds like a piece of work," he mutters.

"He was the perfect boyfriend for the first few weeks. He even turned his spare room into a space for me to paint."

Roman shifts on the grass. Maybe it's just me projecting, but he looks embarrassed for me that I didn't see Jim coming. I've changed so much from the naïve idiot who swallowed a man's bullshit without questioning his motives.

"He convinced me to give up my job and focus on becoming an artist."

"He did?" Roman asks, the words coming out pained.

My insides twist with revulsion at how I could have been so stupid. "I thought he cared," I say with a sigh. "In hindsight, it was a ploy to isolate me from my friends."

His brows crease with an unspoken question.

"No studio means no mingling with other artists."

He nods.

"Everything was going well until I exhausted my savings and had to rely on Jim for groceries. That's when he started chipping away at my sanity."

"How?" Roman asks with a grimace.

I chuckle because I can't believe I'm admitting this out loud. "Gaslighting, financial abuse, violence. Death threats. He was the full package, and I was his prisoner."

"How did you get out?"

"By stashing away a few dollars until I built a small nest egg. I needed to be careful about it because of the cameras."

Roman stiffens. "Cameras?"

"He used to watch me while he was at work to keep tabs on what I was doing. When I gathered enough cash, I waited for him the next time he got high on drugs, then left through a downstairs window to go straight to a women's shelter."

Roman stares at me, his expression so pained that I reach across the picnic blanket and grab his arm.

"It's over now." I force a smile. "When he caught up with me that night, you helped me escape."

He nods, but his eyes remain distant. "I wish I'd found you sooner."

"That would have been impossible."

His gaze darts to meet mine.

"You were in prison," I say.

Roman gives me a hesitant nod, as though he really could have helped.

"Stop looking so guilty." I squeeze his hand. "No one but you has ever given me so much protection. The day after being released, you faced down an army of cops. You killed Dominic, who'd been sent by Jim, and then you destroyed that horrible little cop who snuck into your party to bring me to him. You're my fucking hero."

His eyes soften. "You're a survivor."

"Damn right I am." I give him a sharp nod. "And so are you."

"What do you mean?" he asks.

"I couldn't survive five minutes of being locked up." I

shudder at the notion. "You were there for nearly five years. That makes you resilient."

He downs his wine and casts his gaze across the water with a non-committal hum as though he's still absorbed in my story.

"What was prison like?" I ask.

Roman shakes his head. "Something I don't want to relive."

"Roman? It's alright to talk about these things—"

"Drop it," he says with so much conviction that my jaw clicks shut.

We finish eating in silence until dessert, where Roman changes the subject to my art and poses for me in front of the water. Our conversation flows again, but it's superficial and light.

Roman hasn't been the same since that emergency the morning after the auction. Something is weighing on his mind, and I can't shake the feeling that it's related to me. Despite his assurances, I still feel like a burden.

That's what Mom used to call me every day.

Because of me, Jim won't stop sending people through Roman's gates and because of me, Roman has become a person of interest to the police.

I dab a little red umber onto the canvas to emphasize the ends of his hair, reflecting the way it's lit up by the sun. What am I talking about? A mafia don is always in conflict with the law.

Maybe my paranoia has morphed from thinking I'm Roman's prisoner to thinking I'm Roman's overstaying guest.

Or maybe it's none of that and I'm looking too deeply into his expression and constructing reasons to be unhappy. Maybe I'm finally succumbing to Mom's mental illness?

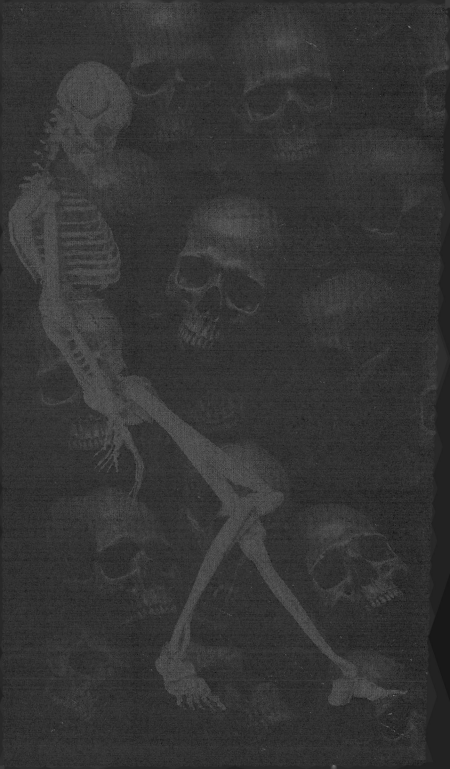

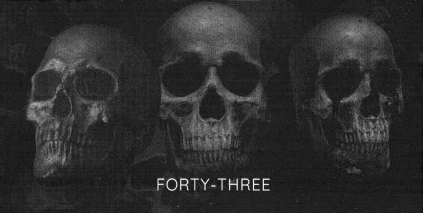

FORTY-THREE

ROMAN

Hours later, I'm lying in bed with my gaze fixed on streams of moonlight dancing on the ceiling. I can't stop thinking about what Emberly told me of her last relationship.

The man she described is me.

But unlike Callahan, I haven't yet dropped my mask. She got to see the violent, controlling monster beneath the cop's charming exterior, but she hasn't seen mine.

Emberly doesn't realize I engineered our meeting or that I have a game plan. Hell, she doesn't even know the identity of her father or how he's our family's greatest betrayer. She has no idea that I planned on putting a bullet through her skull.

With a heavy heart, I steal a glance at Emberly's sleeping face. Beneath the mass of curls, her long lashes rest at the top of her cheeks, with her pink lips parted. She looks so vulnerable, so innocent, so undeserving of being the pawn in a vendetta against a family she doesn't even know. My fingers twitch to brush a stray lock off her forehead, to feel the warmth of her skin against my fingertips, but I resist the urge.

I can't sleep beside her knowing that Callahan is out there still drawing breath, still plotting his next move to take her back. The situation with the Moirai group was more pressing, as well as the threat of war with Tommy Galliano. I needed the casino back and the chance to replenish our ranks.

Now that both situations are under control, I finally have the mental bandwidth to make sure the greasy cop never gets a second chance to hurt Emberly.

Carefully, I slip out of bed and get dressed, trying not to disturb her sleep. Then I navigate down the winding Alderney Hill drive while barking orders into my phone at my associates in Beaumont City. When I arrive at Gil's apartment, I ring his doorbell.

When he doesn't reply, I call his number.

"Boss," he says, his voice groggy with sleep. "What's happened?"

"Do you still have the blonde roommate?" I ask.

"Sure. Why?"

"I'm downstairs. Let me in."

The buzzer sounds, the door clicks open, and I step into the building's lobby and take the stairs all the way to the top floor. Call it claustrophobia, I don't give a shit, but I no longer care for confined spaces.

Gil waits for me at the door of his tenth-floor apartment. "Geez, boss. Why didn't you take the elevator?"

Ignoring him, I sweep through the door, making him move aside. "Where's the girl?"

"In bed. Why?"

"Bring her."

Gil's eyes flash with recognition. I'm sure he remembers telling me about the conversation he overheard of her trying to sell Emberly out to that cop. I walk into his living room, which he's set up as the ultimate bachelor pad. A large flat-screen TV hangs on the wall with surround sound speakers above a fully stocked bar.

I walk past the pool table, pour myself a glass of whiskey and sit in the leather armchair, just as the blonde shuffles in wearing a silk number that barely covers her pussy.

Whatever.

Monica Bellucci, Sofia Loren, Gina Lollobrigida, and Ornella Muti could walk in here naked and at the peak of their beauty, and I would still only have eyes for Emberly.

"Roman?" she murmurs and takes the seat closest to me on the sofa.

I toss a burner phone and a scrap of paper on the coffee table. "You're going to call Jim Callahan and tell him you just heard from Emberly. When he asks where she is, you'll say she's staying at this address."

The blonde reads the note and frowns. "You want me to lie to him?"

Leaning forward, I steeple my fingers and glare into her wide eyes. "I want you to do as I say."

Gil places a hand on her shoulder and squeezes. I can't tell if the touch is supposed to be reassuring or a threat. "Go on, sweetheart."

As the girl picks up the phone with trembling fingers, Gil instructs her to take several calming breaths. He even kisses the top of her hair. I'm not so anxious to murder Callahan to appreciate Gil's skill with the ladies.

I sit back and listen to the blonde's conversation with Callahan. He's naturally suspicious at first, but she impro-vises, saying she would like some cash to get her boobs done and a Brazilian butt lift. This makes the asshole chuckle, and he jots down the address.

When he hangs up, she asks, "What's this all about?"

I rise off the armchair, pick up the phone and the scrap of paper, and remove the SIM card. "You two are with me."

———

I don't normally bring civilians to these things, especially outspoken ones who will betray their friends for cash.

This one approached us more concerned about the missing rent than Emberly's safety. Any other time, I would put a bullet through her skull for attempting to hand Emberly to Callahan on a platter, but she serves another purpose.

The blonde's presence provides Emberly with the illusion that she has ties to the outside world. Now, she's going to lead that bastard into a trap. I'm aware of the hypocrisy of wanting Callahan dead for doing exactly what I'm doing to Emberly, but nobody fucks with her but me.

The blonde sits stock still in the back seat while Gil drives us across town to the address. At this time of the night, the traffic is thin, with only a smattering of cop cars.

My phone buzzes with a text to tell me that Callahan has taken the bait.

"He's there," I say to Gil.

He grunts. "That was fast."

"Bastard probably used his siren."

Callahan is the sort of coward to abduct a woman with backup, which is why I already have the house surrounded. Anyone who so much as sits in a parked car won't live to help that asshole.

Moments later, I receive more messages from my team, confirming that they've surrounded a police car and are incapacitating its two occupants with their own vehicle's exhaust fumes.

It's still dark when we reach the address, a small, run-down house in a less-than-desirable part of Beaumont City. The few streetlamps that still work flicker, signifying a place where it's wisest not to be out after dark.

After checking my weapon, I exit. Gil steps out and opens the door, letting out the blonde. She jerks forward, looking like she's about to bolt, but Gil's firm grip on her arm keeps her close.

When we reach the door, it opens a fraction, and a pair of eyes peep out from the darkness. Pale illumination glints from a gun aimed at my chest, but the man behind the door exhales and lets us in.

The house's interior is dimly lit and cluttered with mismatched armchairs. It's a former brothel with bedrooms that were occupied by so many trafficked women that the walls are coated with the stench of suffering, semen, and sweat.

When I was still behind bars, I ordered the operation dismantled, thinking it belonged to Capello. Recent intel suggests the legal owner is a company that belongs to Tommy Galliano.

"Where is he?" I ask.

"In the bedroom, boss," the man answers.

I nod and head for the stairs.

"Is she coming?" Gil asks.

"Yeah."

"What is this place?" the blonde whispers.

Gil murmurs an explanation, and the sound she makes is strangled.

We find Callahan lying naked on the floor of one of the bedrooms with two guns trained to the back of his head.

Good. He's unhurt.

"Jim," I say. "You have my permission to look up."

Callahan raises his head, meeting my gaze with eyes that burn with hatred. "Roman Montesano, the lady killer," he says through clenched teeth. "You have something that belongs to me."

I crouch in front of him and frown. "You sent one of your men after Emberly. That was unforgivable. But when you tried to bribe her friend into luring her out from my protection, you marked yourself for death."

The blonde woman gasps.

Callahan's gaze wanders to where she stands at the doorway. "Fucking bitch set me up."

"Look at me," I say.

He squeezes his eyes shut, his nostrils flaring.

"You imprisoned Emberly, beat her, and kept her as your own personal slave. That's a mistake you won't make twice."

He bares his teeth. "You don't know who you're fucking with, boy."

"You talking about your backup?" I ask.

His eyes snap open.

I smirk. "The two assholes you sent to watch the house have already died of carbon monoxide poisoning."

"Bastard," he hisses. "You think I don't know what you're doing? The moment Emberly gets her inheritance, she'll leave you the way she left me."

My smile falters, and dread drops into my stomach like a boulder. "All this time, I thought you were obsessed with her, but you just want her money."

"You're no different," he spits.

My veins pulse with angry heat, and my hands curl into fists that I itch to pound into his smug face. I'm nothing like this sadistic, opportunistic bastard. I never wanted Emberly's money, only the return of what was taken.

I turn to the only man not holding a gun to Callahan's head and say, "It's time. Bring the girl."

Gil ushers the whimpering blond toward another man holding a pre-filled syringe.

"Wait," she cries. "Why am I here? What do you want—"

"You're going to find a vein and inject your business partner."

"But we're not." She shakes her head. "I would never. I can't."

Gil massages her shoulders. "It's the only way you'll leave this place alive." He shoots me a glance. "Isn't it?"

I nod. "Do this, and I'll overlook your betrayal."

She sobs.

Callahan flashes his teeth. "Two-faced cunt. Touch me and every cop in the state of New Alderney will hunt you down. My friends will lock you in a cellar and fuck every hole until you bleed."

She shrieks.

My brows rise. "See what you tried to inflict on Emberly?"

"Do it," Gil says with a bit more bite. "Now."

She takes the syringe and crouches down to approach Callahan. One of my men grabs the cop's foot to hold it steady, while she injects its contents into his veins.

My man opens a box for the blonde to deposit the syringe. She's so preoccupied with her crime that she's failed to recognize that she's just handed over a murder weapon covered in her fingerprints.

I smirk. Gil will explain to her on the drive back that it's insurance to keep her in line, so she continues to play the role of Emberly's best friend without stabbing her in the back.

"What is that?" Callahan croaks.

"A lethal dose of heroin," I reply with a grin. "From what my people researched, it seems to be your drug of choice."

Callahan's eyes widen, and he opens his mouth to

scream but only produces vomit. He gurgles, chokes, and thrashes.

The blonde screams, but Gil clamps a hand over her mouth. I wonder if she's alarmed at the sight of a man dying or because she's just committed murder. It's interesting how she had no qualms about subjecting Emberly to an even worse fate.

"Roll him on his back to let him convulse in peace," I mutter.

The men comply, and Callahan shakes and spasms. After what feels like an eternity, his body goes still, his eyes glaze over, and he stops breathing.

I wanted his death to be more dramatic, but a detective found in an abandoned brothel having overdosed on his drug of choice is something they're more likely to cover up than investigate.

By the time I get home, shower, and slip into bed with Emberly, I no longer feel so unworthy of her affection.

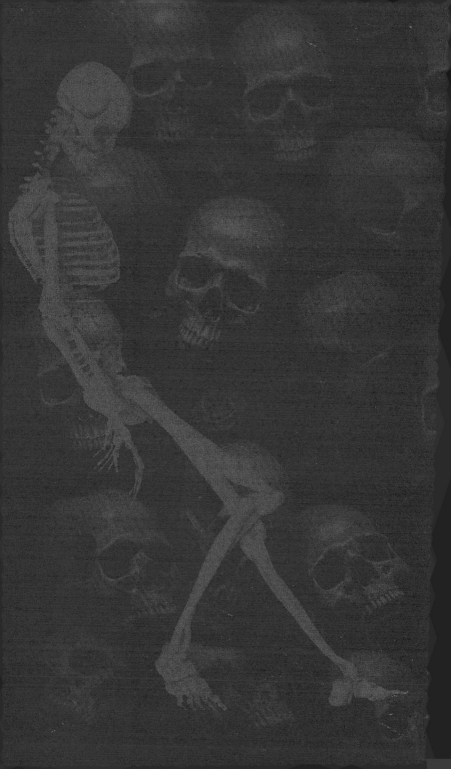

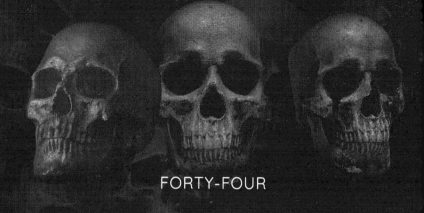

FORTY-FOUR

EMBERLY

Gentle morning light streams through my eyelids, and I wake up to Roman curled around me like a big spoon, peppering kisses along the nape of my neck. His erection presses into my ass, and he cups my breast.

I smile, my pussy flooding with heat.

"Good morning, baby," he purrs, his voice so deep and rich that my spine erupts into tingles.

"You're in a good mood," I say with a moan.

"Been doing a lot of thinking."

He rolls my nipple between his thumb and forefinger, making me gasp.

I press my ass into his thick length. "About?"

"You've been staying here for over two weeks, and I haven't formally introduced you to any of my family," he says. "That's going to change."

I turn around in his arms, my brow furrowing. Roman's face is so handsome in the dim light, with the lines and contours of his face standing out in the shadows. His features are serious, but there's no mistaking the way his eyes radiate with warmth.

"Are you sure?" I ask. "I mean, I see them around the grounds, and I don't want to impose—"

He silences me with a closed-mouth kiss, draws back, and says, "I want you to meet my brothers. Hell, I even want you to meet Gil."

"Your second in command?" I ask, remembering Annalisa's words.

Roman rolls onto his back and laughs, pulling me onto his chest. "Gil is a loyal friend who stood by the family through hell, but this organization has and always will have only one commander."

My chest lightens. Something has changed, and Roman is starting to open up. Maybe hearing about my past has brought us closer together.

"What about your brothers?" I ask. "Aren't you joint-leaders?"

"Benito is in charge of the finances. Cesare deals with other shit."

"What kind?"

"The kind you'd be better off not knowing." He places a kiss on the top of my head.

Roman is right, of course. I already saw enough of Cesare in action to know he enjoys inflicting pain. Benito seems to be the more reserved one of the trio, but I know very little about Gil.

"What does Gil do?"

"Anything I ask," Roman says. "While I was inside, he kept an eye on my brothers and made sure they weren't doing anything stupid."

"Even Benito?" I ask.

Sighing, Roman threads his fingers through my hair. "You've got to understand that my dad had just died under semi-suspicious circumstances. Then the same week, I get arrested for the murder of a woman I'd never met. And before the week is out, our mother moves to New Jersey and shacks up with Tommy Galliano."

I raise my head off his chest and stare into his dark eyes. "Isn't he from that crime family in New Jersey?"

"The very same," he mutters. "That's a lot of fucking provocation for even the most level-headed of people. Gil had to restrain them both."

"Where is your mother now?"

"Died during a breast enlargement," he says.

I lower my head onto the crook of his shoulder and wrap my arms around his waist. Maybe everything I read in the forums was wrong. Based on what I just learned, it looks like Mr. Galliano was having an affair with Roman's mother and set up Mr. Capello to look like the villain.

"I'm so sorry. Why does Tommy Galliano hate your family so much?"

"What do you mean?"

"It's obvious that he framed you, right? And if your mom remarried so soon after your dad died—"

"It wasn't him," Roman says, his voice tightening.

"Who else could it be?" I ask.

"Someone my dad loved like a brother," Roman says. "Unlike me, he made the mistake of elevating that man to his underboss and gave him enough power in the organization to stab us all in the backs."

Roman's heart accelerates beneath my ear, and his breath grows ragged. Tension radiates off his body like heat waves off asphalt. I want to ask if Mr. Galliano was working with Mr. Capello, but I'm afraid to dig. I know nothing about the underworld, but letting Roman talk about it might help release some of that pressure.

"Who framed you?"

Roman pauses for a moment and then releases a long, shuddering breath. "If I say the name out loud, it'll sour my mood."

"Are you going to deal with him?" I ask, trying to get him to confirm if it's Capello.

"He's dead," Roman replies with an exhale. "It happened when I was still behind bars."

So the forums were right. He's talking about the Capello Casino boss who died with his entire family at the hands of the gunman who detonated explosives around the house to escape the guards.

Roman's in such a talkative mood, and I'm not going to ruin things by stating the obvious. He probably doesn't want to admit he hired the assassin to take out his enemies.

"I've never heard of anyone on death row getting pardoned," I murmur.

"Exonerated," he says.

"What's the difference?"

"New evidence came to light," he replies, his voice bitter. "A recording of a man who obviously wasn't me murdering that woman."

"Didn't they look at fingerprints, DNA evidence, or anything to prove you weren't the killer?"

He laughs, but it doesn't meet his eyes. "Someone tampered with every piece of evidence that proved my innocence. The man who got caught claimed it was on my orders."

"And it wasn't."

"No," he snarls. "The bastard who framed me did everything he could to make me look guilty, down to bribing the judge. He made sure every appeal got shut down and even tried to bring forward the execution."

My hands curl into fists. "I'm glad he's dead."

Roman only cups the back of my head and places a kiss on my brow.

————

I spend the rest of the day alone in the pool house, reworking the painting I made of Roman by Simon's Pond. After our conversation, I cast his features in darkness and make his figure backlit by the setting sun.

The water's surface reflects rays of white fire, surrounding his figure in a full-body halo. I call this painting *'Out of the darkness comes the light.'*

It represents Roman's strength and his resilience in the face of such overwhelming tragedy and betrayal. It's a reminder that even in his darkest moments, he still found hope.

A knock sounds on the door as I'm starting a new painting. Roman walks in, holding a large box.

My eyes widen. "Another one?"

He grins. "What can I say? My love language is giving gifts."

Wiping my hands on a rag, I cross the room and place a quick peck on his lips. "Don't touch me. I'm wet."

Roman snickers. "You sure you're talking about the paint?"

He lets me pack away my supplies, wash away all traces of oil paint, and change out of my apron into a sundress.

We walk into the bedroom, where I open the box. I part the wrapping paper, expecting the shoe box inside to contain a pair of designer heels, but I pull out a newer version of my favorite shoes.

"What's this?" I whisper.

Roman chuckles and places a hand on the small of my back. "Keep going."

I pull out a flat box that contains a fitted denim dress from Diesel. It's one of those brands that isn't ridiculously expensive but is only affordable for me in a clearance sale.

"Roman!" My voice rises several excited octaves. "How did you know I'd like this?"

"You were wearing denim when we met," he replies with a smirk. "This seems more like your usual style."

The backs of my eyes grow warm. Every garment Roman has selected for me has been breathtakingly exquisite, but I've always felt like an impostor trying to fake Italian elegance.

This denim dress and the blocky heels are exactly the sort of thing I would buy.

"It's perfect," I say, my voice breathy with awe. "But I thought you would want me to dress up for tonight?"

He wraps an arm around my shoulder. "Not for family dinners," he murmurs. "Everyone wears whatever they want, and I want my brothers to see you, not someone with their personality hidden behind labels."

I bite down on my bottom lip. "You're my fucking fairy godfather."

Roman laughs, the sound as rich as whiskey. "Less of the fairy and more of the fucking. Now, open up the last gift."

The final box contains a selection of silk scarves from Pucci. I gasp at the vibrant colors and wild patterns.

"These are too much," I whisper, taking out one with pinks and purples and black.

Roman places a hand on my shoulder, infusing my body with warmth. "It adds a pop of color to represent your artistic spirit."

A giddy laugh bubbles up from my chest. Before I can stop myself, the words slip from my lips. "I fucking love you."

Roman stiffens, his eyes widening, and my stomach plummets.

My cheeks go hot, and my insides twist into painful knots.

I meant love in the other way. Not love *love*, but the appreciation of a larger-than-life personality who's irresistibly magnetic or a friend who tells the most eye-watering jokes. It's a strong like,. A deep affection, a fucking figure of speech.

Now, Roman's going to think I'm some clingy gold digger trying to manipulate him into saying it back.

"Roman, I'm sorry." I turn to him, my voice rising with a dizzying cocktail of panic and humiliation. "That came out wrong. I'm shit with words. It's just that I think you're really great."

He smiles, making the corners of his eyes crinkle, and pulls me into a hug so warm and tight that I can feel the beat of his heart.

It's fast, the way it was when he talked about the man who framed him for murder. Fast, just like when he's fucking me from behind and is about to climax. Fast, just like when what he's about to say next is emotionally charged.

His lips brush my ear, making me tingle. "I know what you meant," he whispers in my ear. "And I fucking love you too."

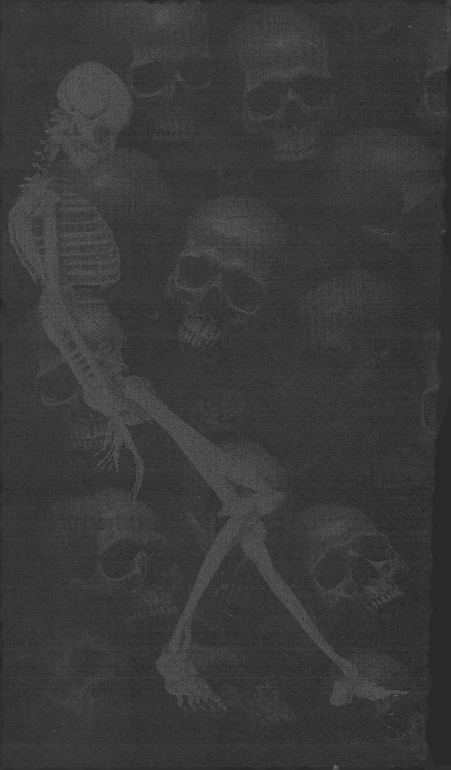

FORTY-FIVE

EMBERLY

He loves me?

Before I can even ask Roman what the hell that means, he cups the side of my face and kisses me so tenderly, my toes curl. My knees tremble, and I cling to his arms, all doubts and thoughts and confusion evaporating into the ether.

Maybe his declaration is just a manner of speech.

I like him. A lot. When I'm with him, I feel seen. He appreciates all aspects of my craziness and doesn't try to make me feel small. And I find him more than attractive. Sex with him is always beyond satisfying, and he takes an interest in my art.

The broken part of me that never thought I would find love reminds me that Roman is the only man who can protect me from Jim. What more can a woman ask for?

Roman's arm wraps around my waist, and his deep groan makes my body melt against his chest. Our kiss is gentle, slow, and so filled with emotion that I could drown and never want to come up for air.

Okay. Maybe I more than like him. Maybe what I feel for him is close to love. It's so difficult to tell. I've been infatuated, but never in love. Every man I've been with has been a user.

Jim only saw a person he could control. The guy before that was another artist who used my affection for him as free labor to launch his career. He got me touting his work from gallery to gallery when all he did was criticize mine. Then he dumped me for 'bringing down the vibe' when Mom committed suicide.

Things are different with Roman. Maybe not at the beginning, when I grabbed him to get away from Jim, but I've seen the kindness beneath his tough exterior. I love his strength, I love his comfort, I love his stability. When we're together, I feel like the center of his world. When we're apart, my thoughts always drift to him.

The kiss deepens, and I tangle my fingers through his hair and pull him closer. Roman tastes of whiskey and mint, of protectiveness and strength, of something addictive and primal that overwhelms rational thoughts with pure desire.

He sits me on the edge of the bed, arranging my knees on either side of his legs. I recline with my weight resting on my forearms and my gaze sweeping down to the thick erection straining in his pants.

Lifting my sun dress to my waist, he rasps, "If I'm not inside you in the next ten seconds, I'm going to die."

"Then you'd better hurry." I pull the rest of the garment over my head and toss it onto the floor. Cool air circulates over my heated skin, making my nipples tighten.

Roman's gaze scans my naked form.

"No underwear?" he growls.

"You know me," I say with a grin. "Always wanting to be free."

His deep groan goes straight to my clit. "I love that about you... You're a free spirit and always so wet."

This time, I'm not so startled by the word love. It's just a figure of speech. There are more things I love about Roman than I could possibly count.

He slides his finger between my wet folds and pinches my clit, triggering an explosion of electric ecstasy. "I'm torn between wanting to taste you and wanting to bury myself inside your sweet cunt."

"Let me pull out your cock and I'll decide."

Roman gifts me with a grin so dazzling I almost forget to breathe. It's only when he rocks forward and I feel his hard length, that I run my hands down his clothed chest and unzip his pants.

His erection springs free, and I curl my fingers around its thick shaft. It's covered in prominent veins, culminating in a bulbous head already leaking clear fluid. I slide my hand up and down, making Roman pant.

"Are you going to let me get on top?" I run the pad of my thumb over his slit.

He releases a guttural groan. "You want to ride my cock, then you earn the privilege."

"I'm so fucking ready. Give it to me now."

Roman reaches into the inside pocket of his jacket and takes out a condom. "Start by wrapping it up."

I take the foil wrapper, rip it open with my teeth, and roll the latex down his length, making sure to move my fingers in delicate circles to make him shiver.

Once he's fully sheathed, I ask, "Now, can I get on top?"

"It's all yours, baby."

Roman lowers himself beside me onto the mattress. I rise up on my knees, hold his shoulders, and straddle his thighs. He gazes up at me, his dark eyes shining with so much affection that my heart sputters. It's too much. I'm overwhelmed, yet the sight of him beneath me, hot and hard and ready, heats my blood until it sizzles.

"Come on, baby," he says through his teeth. "I thought you wanted to ride my cock?"

"More than anything." I reach down, grip him by the base, and line up his tip to my pussy.

"Then take it," he growls.

I lower myself onto his shaft, feeling the incredible stretch as I'm filled to the point of pain. His hands are warm and gentle on my waist, barely guiding my movements, as though he wants me to take control.

As soon as he's completely sheathed and I'm sitting on his lap, Roman tightens his grip. "Stay like this a little longer," he says, his dark eyes boring into mine. "I want to savor this moment forever."

"A-Alright, but this angle—"

"Take your time."

I study Roman's features, wondering what I ever did to deserve a man so classically beautiful. His eyes are deep pools of desire, darkened by his strong brow. His chiseled jaw is more handsome when covered in stubble that I can't help but trace it with my fingertips.

"You're so thick."

Roman's shaft swells inside my pussy, making the walls clench. Our combined moans fill the room as pleasure radiates through my core.

"You can take it," he rasps.

I swallow hard, the muscles of my pussy tightening around his shaft.

"That's it," he rumbles against my chest. "Squeeze my cock with your cunt. Take what you need. It's all yours."

I grab on to his shoulders, my pussy giving him one last squeeze before I raise my hips and begin a slow, steady rhythm.

Being in control of my pleasure is incredible, but even that pales in comparison to having Roman's full attention. He has a way of making me feel like I'm his everything. Like I mean more to him than oxygen.

The pleasure on his features is feral. I feel so powerful and beautiful reflected in his gaze. "Fuck, Emberly," he groans. "I love how you feel around my cock."

Roman meets my downward slide with an upward thrust, his fingers gripping my waist. "So. Fucking. Tight."

My nipples brush against the silk of his shirt, infusing my nerve endings with tingles. I squeeze my eyes shut, feeling so lost in ecstasy that I barely remember my name.

"Look at me," he growls.

My eyes snap open, and I'm met with the intensity of Roman's gaze. His eyes are hooded with pleasure and his teeth are bared, as though trying to hold back an explosion of pure lust.

"You're so beautiful," he says, his voice thick with desire. "When your hair curls like that, they remind me of baby snakes."

"What does that make me, Medusa?"

"You're the fourth Gorgon sister, the one no one ever talked about because her beauty turned cocks into stone."

I giggle. "You're so full of shit. You just made that up."

"No, baby. I'm looking at a goddess right now."

Warmth fills my chest and spreads across my cheeks. How on earth can he get me to blush during sex?

"Now, my little Medusa, let me feel you come around my cock."

Roman's fingers dig into my hips, anchoring me as he thrusts up with unrelenting power. His thick length hits every pleasure spot, including a few I never knew existed. An orgasm builds, threatening to overwhelm me with its intensity.

I cling to his shoulders. "Roman," I say through ragged breaths. "Don't stop."

"Never." Growling, he pushes me without mercy or restraint to the brink of ecstasy, pounding and grinding.

With each thrust, the sensations build until every muscle trembles and my body can hold out no longer. A powerful wave of rapture crashes through me, leaving me breathless and shaking around his thick cock.

His body tenses, and his muscles grow taut. He convulses beneath me and roars, "Fuck!"

He bucks his hips, holding me so tightly that the world around us disappears. In the throes of our combined climax, I can't imagine why I ever thought loving him could ever be just a figure of speech.

We sit together for several heartbeats, basking in the afterglow of our shared connection. Roman's peculiar behavior from yesterday is forgotten, along with all the craziness associated with him being a mafia boss. When we're alone, nothing matters except me and him.

I'm still trembling from the aftershocks of my orgasm and gasping for breath when Roman's voice breaks through my lust-filled haze. "Ready to meet my family?"

———

Less than ten minutes later, I've changed into my new casual clothes, and Roman looks immaculate and composed, while I'm still flushed from our intense lovemaking.

My heart pounds as we cross the garden hand in hand, which is stupid because I've seen Roman's brothers multiple times around the estate and even exchanged a few words with Benito.

"Are you sure I look alright?" I ask, my fingers fussing with the Pucci scarf.

"Perfect." Roman releases my hand and wraps an arm around my waist. "They will love you."

His tone of voice implies that his sentence ends with a silent 'or else.'

We walk through the patio doors of his office, down the hallway, and into a chandelier-lit dining room large enough to sit twelve. Like the rest of the house, the walls are decorated in pale colors to match the marble floors.

A huge portrait hangs on the wall of a family enjoying a meal. The subjects all face forward, just like in da Vinci's *Last Supper*.

Benito sits alone with his gaze fixed on the screen of his phone, engrossed in a video. To his left is an empty place for his date, and the two seats beside him are occupied by Annalisa and Gil.

My steps falter at the sight of my former roommate.

Annalisa's back-combed blonde hair almost balances out the way Gil's tailored suit shows off his bulky frame. She wears a teal dress with puffy sleeves that I'm sure I recognize from one of her fashion magazines.

The glare she shoots me is so venomous, I glance over my shoulder to make sure she's really looking at me.

"Where's Cesare?" Roman asks as we walk to the unoccupied side of the table.

Benito glances up and shrugs.

Gil clears his throat. "Having trouble with his date, boss."

Roman nods, his gaze turning to Benito. "Where's yours?"

"Working on the bruschetta," he mutters.

We walk to the head of the end of the table, where Roman pulls out the chair opposite Benito's empty place and motions for me to sit.

I sink into the seat and rest my damp palms on my denim dress, while Roman sits opposite Benito.

"You should be at the head of the table." Benito flicks his head toward the empty chair at the end.

Roman shifts, his jaw tightening. I rest my hand on his, already guessing that the last time he ate in this room, his father was the head of the family and still alive.

The click-clack of heels and the jangle of chains makes me turn to the door, where Cesare walks in with the woman he had gagged and strapped to the torture chair.

And she looks furious.

The dress she wears has a bodice that's more like lingerie, made of sheer fabric with thick boning to conceal her nipples. It's worn with a leather pencil skirt so long and narrow that each step comes with a struggle.

I snatch my gaze away from her outfit in time to notice her stilettos are joined together by chains.

"Really?" Benito says, his voice flat. "You're bringing that to our family dinner?"

Cesare's vicious grin makes the fine hairs on the back of my neck stand on end. "It's her last supper."

My gaze darts around to check everyone's response because I'm not sure if he's joking.

"You know," Cesare adds. "Before she..." He runs his index finger over his neck with a slicing motion that makes Annalisa squeak.

"Don't explain." Benito purses his lips and turns his attention back to his phone.

My stomach plummets. What the actual fuck? I glance at Roman, whose jaw is set so tightly that it looks like he might snap. He doesn't say a word, but there's no mistaking his suppressed fury.

Leaning against his side, I whisper, "Is he joking?"

"Yes," Roman says through clenched teeth.

"I'm not hungry," the woman mutters, presumably because she doesn't agree with Roman's assessment.

Cesare leans into her and whispers something that makes her shudder. Maybe I'm looking into things too deeply, but something tells me she didn't consent to being paraded around like a fetish model.

I nudge Roman, but he shakes his head and sighs.

"Roman," I hiss.

"He's..." Roman shakes his head. "They're kinky."

Across the table, Gil shoots Roman a look that seems to say, see what I mean?

Sofia comes in with a trolley laden with dishes. After placing two large plates of bruschetta on the table, she walks around to the other side and takes the empty seat between Gil and Benito.

"Sofia's your date?" Cesare asks with a cackle.

"Better than picking up any old trash from the basement," Benito replies with a sniff.

Cesare rises out of his seat. "What did you say?"

My gaze darts to Roman, whose tight features seem to agree with Benito. I'm still trying to work out if the woman is a prisoner or a bratty submissive.

"Sit the fuck down," Roman snarls. "Sofia is always welcome at this table."

Cesare lowers himself onto his seat and mutters an apology to the housekeeper.

Another member of staff comes in with bottles of white wine, and we pass around plates of bruschetta and bowls of caprese salad, each taking as much as we want.

While tensions are high and nobody speaks, it really feels like I'm dining with a family. A family who may not all get along all the time, but it's obvious that this room is full of loyalty and love.

The next course is a creamy orzo pasta served with an

eggplant parmigiana that makes my mouth water. As I take a heaping serving, Annalisa's high-pitched laugh grates on my eardrums.

"Denim at dinner?" she says with a smirk. "You could have at least dressed for the occasion."

My stomach tightens. I'm about to defend my outfit when Roman slams his fist on the table, making everyone startle.

"Get out," he snarls.

My gaze snaps to Roman, who didn't say a word while his brothers insulted each other and only said half a sentence about Sofia. But now he's outraged? This reminds me of the time he made the restaurant manager crawl.

Annalisa's features falter. "Who, me?" She makes a nervous giggle and glances from Sofia to Cesare's date for support. When they glare at her, she turns to meet Gil's furious scowl. "Come on. It was only a joke. We talk like this all the time. Don't we?"

My lip curls. "If you're referring to the veiled insults, that's only you."

Roman rises off his seat. "Nobody insults my woman more than once and gets to keep their tongue. Get the fuck out of my house." He bares his teeth. "Now."

I glance around the table, seeing all the furious glares directed at Annalisa. Even Cesare and his date look disgusted at the jab.

This is the first time someone has recognized a barb made against me, let alone risen to my defense. Something in my chest loosens and my heart floats free. I feel vindicated for all those times people like Annalisa gaslighted me into thinking I was being oversensitive.

Maybe the Montesano family is where I really belong?

Gil nudges Annalisa, making her rise off her seat and walk to the exit on trembling limbs. Her shoulders sag and she bows her head. I wait to feel the usual guilt she elicits whenever I've tried to call her out, but it's absent.

It looks like I'm finally learning that attacking me is never acceptable, even if it's only with words. How could I not when I finally see my own self-worth? I always defended myself, but never truly followed through because I was riddled with doubt.

That part of me is dead.

As she reaches the door, she turns to Gil and asks, "Take me home?"

Gil snorts. "You insulted the boss's woman. That's worse than insulting the boss."

Everyone around the table nods.

"But how am I going to get back?" Her voice trembles.

"Work it out," he rumbles. "And you're no longer welcome in my apartment."

I tune out the rest of the conversation, focusing only on Roman. Loving him could never be a mistake.

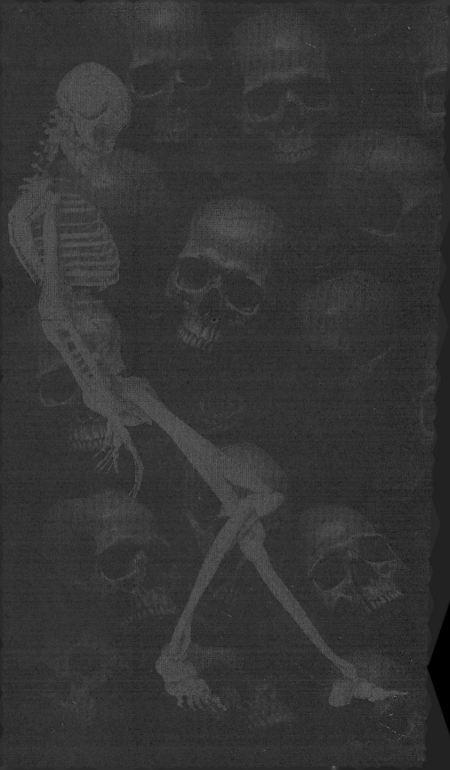

FORTY-SIX

ROMAN

Things are quiet on the business front for the next two days, so I spend each morning proving to Emberly that I meant every word. She's my woman and I love her.

I. Love. Emberly. Kay.

There. I said it.

Despite this, my loyalty will always remain with my family, which means I'm still buying her paintings via Lubelli. We've clawed back the loan company and the real estate portfolio, which only leaves the stocks and vaults.

Emberly doesn't know she's safe from the cops. Someone reported finding Callahan's colleagues dead at the wheel, but the police haven't yet broken into the brothel.

I don't give a shit how long it takes for them to track down that asshole's corpse. By the time they do, it will look like he overdosed with a trafficked prostitute, leaving Tommy Galliano no choice but to close down the operation.

The biggest threats facing us now are the Galliano brothers and the Moirai Group. Since those slimy bastards have now gone undercover, we'll have to deal directly with the assassins.

That's why Cesare and I are standing in a parking lot on the outskirts of Beaumont City, dressed in bullet-proof armor. We're waiting for representatives of the Moirai to arrive to retrieve their hostages.

Sunlight peeks in through the gaps in the warehouses, casting long shadows across an empty courtyard. Cesare and I are outside, facing the road with our backs against a van containing four individuals.

"Dinner the other night was good," he says.

I grunt.

"It was almost like old times."

The corner of my mouth lifts into a smile. "But without Dad telling us to shut the fuck up and appreciate the good food."

"That's you, now."

I exhale a long breath. "You think?"

Cesare nudges me in the arm. "You were just like him when you kicked that bitch out for insulting your woman. Remember how Dad used to react when you and Benito talked back to Mom?"

"Yeah." My jaw clenches.

I was never close to our mother. She left our Aunt Clarissa to tend to us kids. Then our uncle died, and our aunt left with our cousins, Leroi, and his little sister, Jennifer. Mother was only close to Cesare. Maybe because he was so much younger or the only son who resembled her, while Benito and I look more like younger versions of Dad.

Now isn't the time to dwell on how she abandoned us, leaving Sofia to hold the family together. Cesare took it the worst and dropped out of medical school in a depression.

When Cesare had that drug problem, she and Gil took care of him while he went cold turkey. According to Gil, it was Sofia who dragged Cesare out of bed, and made sure he was recovering, making me the meals I ate in prison at the same time. Benito set back his ambitions to become a lawyer to take care of the businesses Capello didn't steal. While the entire family went to shit, our mother commiserated in the arms of Tommy Galliano.

"Roman?" Cesare's voice slices through my resentment.

"I remember," I mutter.

"What's the deal with the crazy balcony woman?" he asks with a chuckle. "Are you making her fall for you just to break her heart?"

My breath catches. I turn to look at him through his visor. "Is it that obvious she's in love?"

"After you stood up for her, she leaned against you the entire evening like you were some kind of knight."

My chest swells at the confirmation of her emotions, but I play it cool and raise a shoulder. "Maybe she was just grateful."

"I'll bet she showed you her gratitude after dessert," he says.

I smirk. Emberly had dragged me upstairs before I'd even finished coffee, and spent the rest of the evening fucking me breathless. If women rewarded knights like that all the time, there'd be no organized crime, only chivalry.

"Can I be the one to tell her everything was a scam?" he asks.

Cold annoyance seeps into my gut, powered by Cesare's words. I grit my teeth and spin around to face him, but his features are hidden behind the bulletproof helmet.

"What?" I hiss through clenched teeth.

"I just want to see her reaction."

Heat surges through my blood, and I breathe through flared nostrils. My jaw tightens so hard that my molars grind.

I curl my gloved hands into fists. "Stay away from Emberly."

Cesare huffs. "At least let me join in when it's time for her to die."

Something inside me cracks, and I spin around, grabbing the straps of his bulletproof vest. "How many times do I need to tell you that Emberly Kay is mine? There will be no ambushing, no killing and no fucking spectacle."

Cesare's eyes widen behind the helmet, and he raises both palms in surrender. "I was only joking."

"You're not listening." I give him a hard shake. "She's not a toy. She's mine. Stay the fuck away."

"Okay," he says, his voice oddly low. "I won't go near her."

"There's a truck approaching from the freeway." Gil's voice fills my earpiece.

I release my little brother, leaving him leaning against the side of the van, and we both turn our attention to the road.

"Get ready." I shove my elbow into the side of the van, alerting its occupants.

A medium-sized truck turns onto the deserted road, making my heart race with anticipation. From what Cesare's little assassin said about the Moirai Group, they're not likely to bazooka us while we're standing so close to four of their operatives.

She added that they would shoot us in the heads, which is why we're wearing so much armor.

As the truck approaches our van, I catch the first glimpse of its driver. He's a nervous-looking young man, who I assume is hired help or an apprentice. Cesare has learned through his interrogations that the Moirai recruits its assassins young and organizes itself like an academy where only the strongest survive.

The truck stops, and its back doors open. Four masked figures step out, each dressed in bulletproof vests and holding automatic weapons.

"Where are they?" the shorter of them asks.

Cesare walks to the back of the van and opens its doors, revealing four of my men wearing large sacks over their upper halves.

"Walk them over," their leader says.

My brother leads them out of the van and lines them up, letting them hobble across the road to the assassins.

"Tell your boss this ceasefire is bullshit. He needs to call off the hit," I say.

The leader doesn't reply, seeming more interested in the captives.

"An answer would be nice," I say.

"We'll be in touch," he mutters.

The other three operatives lead the fake hostages into their truck, step inside, and shut the door. Cesare and I retreat behind the van and break into a sprint.

Another thing Cesare learned is that the Moirai will turn deadly the moment they retrieve their hostages. That's why Cesare and I are running for our lives. Sure enough, our van explodes with a deafening boom. Debris hits us from all directions, cushioned by our armor.

"Those fuckers," Cesare growls.

I grab his shoulder. "You okay?"

He laughs. "Yeah, but why are they so predictable?"

"Wait for it."

Gunshots resound down the road, and the truck skids to a halt. I hold my breath and wait beside my brother for the door to open.

When it does, it reveals our men dragging out unconscious Moirai operatives.

"Looks like they underestimated us," Cesare says.

I nod. "They won't make that mistake again."

An armored truck trundles to meet us, where Gil is ready to load six more Moirai hostages to add to our original quartet.

After stripping them naked and inspecting them for trackers and hidden weapons, I call their leader and ask if they're willing to renegotiate.

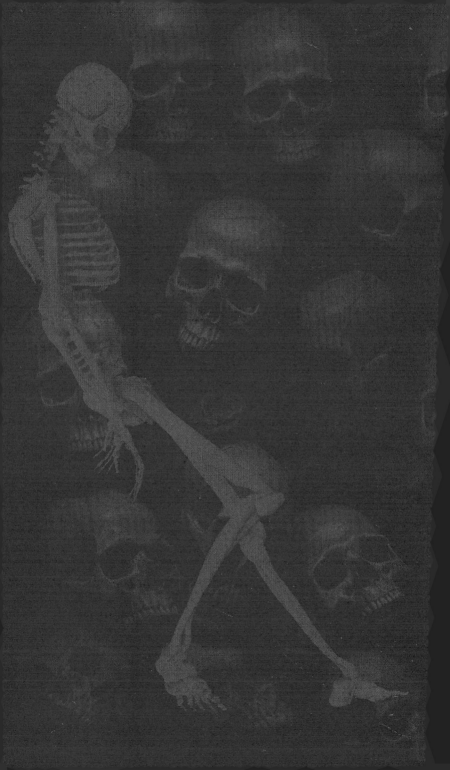

FORTY-SEVEN

EMBERLY

Everything I sketch includes a male figure with Roman's physique. Sometimes, he's floating on water within a fantasy landscape. Other times, he's cast in shadow against different sources of light. Ever since we exchanged '*I love yous*', Roman has become my muse.

The grounds of his home extend beyond the tall walls and electrified fence. His great-grandfather purchased all the plots around the one they occupy, so they have no neighbors. Wildflowers and tall trees cover acres of unused land, dotted with the occasional guest cottage. It's their own personal forest.

When Roman isn't around for protection, Tony accompanies me whenever I venture out, along with someone else to hold my supplies. I'd like to say it wasn't necessary, but there's no telling when Jim and his cronies will make their next move.

A few days after the family dinner, I'm sitting under the canopy of a cypress tree, sketching a cluster of fungi that resembles orange peels, when Tony hands me a phone.

"Hello?" I ask into the handset.

"Meet me at the front gates," Roman says.

I smile. "Why?"

"It's a surprise." He hangs up.

With Tony's help, I gather my belongings, and we trek up the hill, cutting through the woods to bypass the winding road that leads to the estate's tall iron gates.

The men guarding them nod in acknowledgment, which they didn't do before Roman declared I was his woman. Before that, they went from laughing and smirking after the incident on the balcony to ignoring me completely after Roman and his brothers shot bullets into Dominic's corpse.

On the other side of the gates, Roman lounges beside one of his usual bulletproof vehicles, dressed in black and sporting a wide grin.

"What's the surprise?" I rock forward on my tiptoes and kiss him on the lips.

He opens the back door and gestures for me to get in. "You'll see."

My stomach rumbles, and I lower myself into the back seat. "Will there at least be snacks?"

"As much as you can handle, baby." He slides in beside me and squeezes my thigh.

"Somehow, I don't think you're talking about food."

He answers with a long, deep kiss. "You can snack on these nuts."

I draw back, ready to make a joke when he reaches into a drawer and extracts a jar containing almonds, hazelnuts, and pistachios.

"Oh." I place a hand on my chest. "Actual snacks."

As the car pulls out into the road, Roman leans back in his seat and smirks. "If you prefer the other kind, I'd be happy to oblige."

"Maybe later." I unscrew the jar of nuts and take a handful.

"How is the art going?" he asks, his eyes softening.

I launch into a summary of what I'm planning for the next painting. It's going to be a massive canvas featuring a close-up of male perfection sinking into nature. I want something more intricate than wildflowers, which is why I'm taking time to study every kind of fungi growing in the forest surrounding the house.

Roman listens attentively with a smile, as though basking in my enthusiasm. I can't help but preen under his attention. "You're the first person who has ever supported my work."

His brows pinch together. "Surely your parents noticed your talent."

"My mom had too many demons, and I didn't know my dad."

"She never told you about him?"

I bite back a bitter laugh and grab another handful of nuts.

"What is it?" he asks.

Almonds and hazelnuts crunch between my teeth, soothing my banked resentment. "The only time she talked about him was whenever I got into trouble at school."

"What did she say?"

"You're just like your father," I recite in a monotone. "Always selfish. Always thinking you're above the rules. Always so violent. This is why I have to keep you away. To stop you from becoming a monster."

"Monster?"

I shake my head. "Sometimes, she made him sound like a serial killer. Other times she'd call him a thief and a bum. She couldn't decide whether he was a bottom feeder or a psychopath."

Roman's hand finds mine, and he gives it a squeeze. "I'm sorry."

"The most infuriating thing was that if I ever asked her a direct question about him, she'd clam up and say I was better off not knowing."

He reaches over to brush a stray curl behind my ear. "Did you ever investigate or gather any leads?"

I raise my shoulders. "Even my birth certificate doesn't list my father. I once did a DNA test to find some relatives, but it was a scam."

"How so?"

"They never sent back the results. When I asked for a refund, they offered me a digital copy. The file they sent was corrupted and crashed my computer."

"Your mother never dropped a hint?"

"She ended her life before I graduated from art school, so she took the secret to her grave."

Roman's expression darkens, and he pulls me into a hug. "That's rough," he murmurs into my curls. "Did you have to go through that alone?"

"Yeah," I reply with a long sigh. "It always used to be the two of us. She worked so hard to put food on the table, even though she thought she was being stalked."

"And she wasn't?" He pulls back and gazes into my eyes with a frown.

"No." My shoulders sag. "I can't even be angry with her because I know she was mentally ill."

"With what?"

"Well... she was never formally diagnosed. I just entered her symptoms into an online quiz and the results pointed to paranoid personality disorder."

"Then how did you know she was really sick?"

"She kept moving us from place to place, running from some imaginary bogeyman. Mom didn't have the mental bandwidth to concern herself with something as trivial as my art."

Roman cups my face with both hands, his dark eyes softening. "You're not alone anymore. You have me, and you have a family."

My breath slows, and my heart fills with warmth. Roman's words are full of sincerity, as is his touch. I've finally found a man who understands me and accepts me for who I am and doesn't want me to change. I rest my head on his chest, feeling safe and loved.

"What are you thinking about?" he asks, rubbing circles on my back.

Tilting my head, I gaze into his dark eyes and smile. "That I'm the luckiest woman in the world."

Roman smiles back, but it's one of those pained expressions that makes my heart clench.

"What's wrong?" I ask.

He inhales a deep breath. "I didn't bring you to my home for the right reasons."

I draw back, my brow furrowing. "What do you mean?"

"It was revenge."

"Huh?"

He glances away and falls silent for several moments, his jaw clenching and releasing as though trying to fathom how to force out an unspeakable truth.

Dread trembles along the lining of my stomach and the fine hairs on the back of my neck rise. It feels like I'm dangling over a precipice, waiting for the ground to crumble beneath my feet. At any moment, I could tumble into an abyss of rejection and despair.

What horrific truth could he be struggling to reveal?

When he sucks in a breath, my entire body tenses like I've leaped off that balcony and am hurtling toward certain doom.

"When I saw the man who wanted you was a cop, I took you to spite him," he says.

"Because of your wrongful imprisonment?" I ask.

"Yeah," he rasps.

"Okay..." I wait for him to say something devastating, but he continues staring at me as though expecting an explosion. When I realize that's all there is to his confession, I grab his hand. "You saved me."

Roman drops his gaze.

I squeeze his hand, making him finally meet my eyes. "Listen to me. That night, Jim would have put me in a cell, raped me, and maybe even let his buddies at the police precinct have their turn. After that, he planned on injecting me with hard drugs so I would die of an overdose."

He doesn't answer.

"You fucking saved me, Roman." I give his hands a shake. "Who was there when Dominic tried to strangle me to death? Who ran after me when that cop wanted to abduct me for Jim?"

The corner of his mouth lifts. "Me."

"Are you still keeping me out of a sense of revenge?"

He smiles. "No."

"Then stop feeling guilty." I give him a few swats on the arm to emphasize my point. "You're my fucking hero and I love you. Do you understand?"

His eyes widen, and his smile vanishes. "What did you say?"

"You're my hero?" I ask with a smile.

"The other part."

"I love you, Roman Montesano."

"Say that again."

"I love you."

Roman's lips press against mine, infusing my body with

sparks. With a jolt, I scramble onto his lap and wrap my arms around his neck.

His hands roam down my back and cup my ass, and I grind against his growing erection.

Pulling back from the kiss, he says, "I love you too, but we've got to stop."

"No." I cling onto him like a koala in the throes of separation anxiety, but he lifts me off his lap.

I reach for his chest, but Roman grabs me by the wrists and chuckles.

"Emberly, behave."

"Why?"

"Because the owner of the Dolce Vita boutique is glaring at us through the window, waiting for you to come in so she can finally close up."

My face drops, and my gaze darts to the tinted window, where I catch the gaze of the most elegant woman I've ever seen.

"What?" I whisper.

"Come on." He takes my hand and turns toward the door. "I've shut down the entire boutique. And she's even provided snacks."

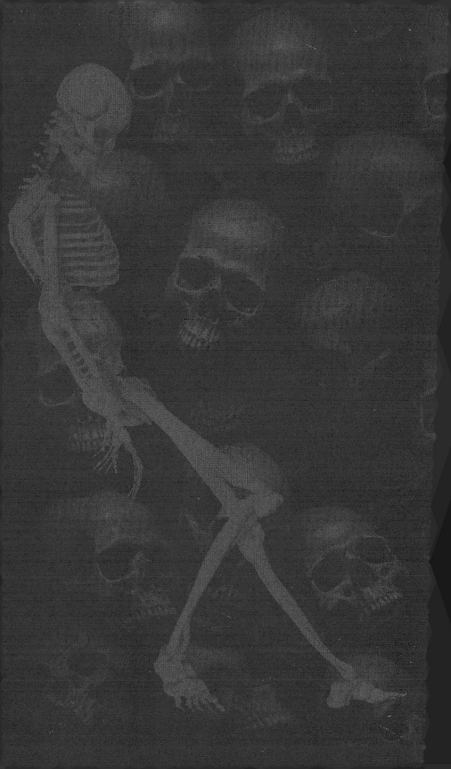

FORTY-EIGHT

ROMAN

I open the door and step out into the fresh air, my heart pounding so hard I want to punch it back into my chest. Maria from the Dolce Vita steps back and welcomes us, but I'm too riled up to hear her words.

Being in Emberly's presence is like stepping into another world where nothing else matters, including my bullshit. She makes me feel so accepted that for a moment, I dropped my façade and almost confessed.

Fuck.

My love for her almost made me spill my guts. I would have told her everything and ruined the best thing that's ever happened to me. I turn back to the door, offer my hand, and help her out onto the street. She gazes up at me through concerned green eyes because she thinks I'm wracked with guilt.

She'd be right about the emotion, but wrong about the reason.

Sure, I got a thrill from taking her away from Callahan,

but I wouldn't bring so much trouble to my doorstep just to intervene in a cop's domestic dispute.

But I would if it meant taking back a fortune.

That's the reason I'm a bastard. I started off using her affection as a way to take her attention from the bogus contracts. Now, I can't imagine life without her.

I place a hand on the small of her back and make the short walk to the boutique. It's one of those exclusive establishments set up like an old-fashioned boudoir with chandeliers, velvet chaise lounges, and mirrors.

Maria only displays one of each outfit to maximize the aesthetic. I've been a patron of the boutique for years, but this is the first time I've brought a woman I love.

Emberly gasps. "This place is so beautiful!"

Maria beams. "Welcome to the Dolce Vita."

Two young assistants emerge from the back room, holding silver trays. One contains flutes of champagne, and the other is laden with frou-frou canapés.

I lead Emberly to the nearest seat and make sure she's comfortable before accepting two glasses.

"Is this all for us?" she asks, her eyes wide, her face flushed.

"Tonight's all about you, baby. Pick anything you want." I reach into my pocket and pull out an ebony card engraved with her name.

She raises her palms. "I can't accept this."

"Do you want to get spanked?" I slide the card into the cup of her sundress. "Give it to Maria and use it to pay for a new wardrobe."

"But why?" she whispers. "You've bought me so much already."

I tap her thigh. "Because I dressed you up like my own personal doll and you looked beautiful. Now, I want you to have a wardrobe suited to your taste."

"You think I have good taste?" she asks, her voice lowering.

"You've got more flair in your little finger than most people do in their entire body. Now drink up, have a snack and shop."

Flushing, she drinks half a glass of champagne as though needing to cool down. Then she walks over to the nearest rack. Maria follows her, offering advice on cuts and color combinations.

I sit back and watch Emberly take control, describing her preferred colors and shapes, all the while snacking from the tray of canapés.

Warmth fills my chest at the sight of her looking so confident and in command. Emberly may not have been born into money, but her mastery of art gives her authority among other women.

Maria sends a third assistant back and forth to the stock room and takes notes on alterations, and the guilt festering in my gut expands until it crushes my throat.

Emberly won't stay ignorant forever. The moment she discovers our relationship was built on vengeance and lies, she will want to leave. And I can't let that happen. The episode on the balcony proves that she would rather chew off her arm than remain a prisoner.

I need to find another way to keep her at my side.

"What do you think?" The brightness in her voice pulls me out of my thoughts.

I turn to find Emberly holding a cropped top in a black and pink geometric pattern to her chest.

"Anything on you would be perfect," I reply, my voice hoarse.

Her smile is so radiant that it takes every ounce of self-restraint not to pull her close. She hands the top to one of the assistants, who takes it to the storeroom to get the right size.

I watch her in the mirror as she admires herself from all angles. The art studio won't be enough to keep her now that she's earning money from the paintings and can pay for her own supplies. Eventually, news will spread of Callahan's death, and she won't even need me for protection.

How do I trap a spirit that will do anything to be free?

She places a hand on her navel, demonstrating how she wants a pair of pants to hang low on her hips and expose her belly.

The answer hits me like a lightning bolt.

I need to get her pregnant.

It should be easy enough. She's not on birth control and insists on condoms. I just need to make sure they fail and fuck her at least twice a day to increase my chances of conception.

Once she's pregnant, she won't want to run, even when she discovers I swindled her out of her inheritance. I'll explain that it will all belong to the baby.

Our baby.

My heir.

I sit straighter, already imagining Emberly's flat belly rounding with my baby and her perfect breasts swelling with milk. My cock stirs at the thought of filling that tight pussy with enough seed to produce a child.

My lips lift into a smile. Pregnancy will keep her with me, exactly where she belongs, and she'll never even think about leaving. She'll finally have a real family.

"Roman?" she says, her voice light. "What do you think of this?"

Emberly holds up a mauve bra with transparent cups and a matching thong.

I rise from my seat, not giving a shit that my cock is bulging through my pants. What I'm about to do next is even more important.

"Put it on." My voice lowers several octaves.

I stalk toward her, my heart beating faster with each step.

Adrenaline courses through my veins, combining with a surge of testosterone. The entire boutique and all the women in it fade into insignificance, leaving just Emberly and me and my urge to breed.

"Show me how it looks," I growl.

Emberly's gaze darts to Maria, who directs us to the door next to the stockroom, which reveals a fitting room that looks even more like a boudoir than the rest of the store. It's dimly lit with one red wall and three made of mirrors. The seating is a seven-foot-long daybed that lies completely flat and is just about wide enough for two.

Electricity charges the air as though even the molecules know we're about to create new life. My sweet Emberly will soon be bonded to me forever.

"Take it off," I say, my gaze roaming up and down Emberly's sundress, already picturing her naked.

She glances at the door. "You can't fuck me in here," her voice lowers, sounding scandalized. "Maria and the others are right outside."

"Baby, this room was designed for fucking." I reach for her hips, pull her into my chest, and grind my erection into her belly. My lips brush her earlobe as I murmur in a low voice, "Why do you think they supplied a bed?"

"It's a chaise," she replies with a giggle.

"This boutique caters to rich men who buy their women lingerie and stupidly expensive fashion. And the highlight of a shopping trip for a man is that he gets a semi-public fuck."

Her cheeks darken, and she breathes fast through parted lips. She's tempted. It will only take a little more persuasion to get her on her hands and knees.

"Maria won't throw us out?" she whispers, her voice urgent.

"Why do you think she led us to this room instead of a smaller one with a mirror and a chair?"

I reach behind her back and pull down her zipper, loving how she shivers with anticipation. When all she does in response is inhale deeply, I answer my own question.

"She knows we're going to need the space to fuck."

"Oh."

The word is so breathy, I can almost feel her skin tingling.

I slide the straps of her dress off her shoulders, letting the garment fall to the floor.

She wears nothing but a pair of black panties, and the sight of her slender body fills me with a possessive rage. She spent the entire day braless and frolicking through the trees with my guards?

I need to mark her, make her mine, fill her belly with my child.

"Does exhibitionism turn you on, baby?" My teeth close down on her earlobe. "Does the thought of those women hearing you get fucked into oblivion get you soaked?"

Emberly trembles and moans in my arms but doesn't speak.

My hands travel down her back to cup her perfect ass, and it's me who has to bite back a moan. She's so soft and warm, I want to stay nestled inside her forever.

"Answer me, or I'll leave you unsatisfied."

"Yes," she whispers.

"Yes, what?"

"Yes, sir. I love the thought of those women knowing that you're mine," she says, her voice barely audible.

"Good girl," I growl. "Are you wet for me?"

"Roman." She bites down on her bottom lip and gazes

up at me with a look of pure desperation that makes my cock jolt.

I chuckle, my other hand reaching down to cup her pussy. Her gasp only makes me harder.

"Never thought you would be so shy," I murmur.

She glances at the door, and I cup her face, turning her gaze back to mine. Her eyes smolder, but her short, shallow breaths tell me she's conflicted.

"Think of what's about to happen as an exhibition," I say. "And you're about to put on a show."

She chuckles. "That's so silly."

"Is it?" I peel down her panties, making her exhale a shaky breath. "Do you want me to stop?"

"No," she whispers.

"Louder."

"Please, don't stop."

"Good girl."

I slip my finger between her folds, finding her already dripping wet. Emberly dips her head, trying to hide her flush in my shoulder, which only makes me grin.

"You're soaked." I rub slow circles over her clit, enjoying how it swells beneath my finger. "Turns out you're a little exhibitionist."

She whimpers.

I quicken my strokes, making sure they're too light to get her off. She circles her hips to increase the friction.

"Yes," she hisses. "Just like that."

"That's it, baby," I murmur. "Let them hear your pleasure."

"More," Emberly cries out, her moans growing louder.

She reaches for my fly and pulls out my cock, stroking it with her agile fingers until it aches. I pepper her neck with kisses and continue teasing her clit to bring her to the edge.

"Do you want to come?" I ask.

"Please."

"Then get on your hands and knees."

Emberly releases my shaft and scrambles onto the daybed, presenting her round ass. Arousal surges straight to my already hard cock, making me light-headed.

This is almost like our first time, when I got her to hold on to the headboard. Back then, I didn't want to see her face. Now, I don't want her to see my cock.

"Condom," she says.

I reach into the inside pocket of my jacket and pull out a foil wrapper. Our gazes meet in the mirror and Emberly watches me tear it open and roll the latex over my shaft.

Fuck.

How am I going to sabotage the condom without her getting suspicious? An idea springs to mind from our first fuck, and I grab the hair at the base of her neck and pull her head backward.

"I'm going to fuck you hard and deep," I growl. "Just the way you like it."

"Yes," she moans.

With her head held high and her gaze to the ceiling, I'm free to nick the latex until I feel a small tear.

I line the head of my cock up against her slick entrance, already feeling the heat of her pussy against the exposed part of my crown. Next time, we'll fuck in the dark, and I'll toss the condom away before I enter her. I'll tire her out, so she won't even notice she's full of cum.

Emberly arches and I slide inside. Her pussy closes in around my shaft, drawing out a guttural groan.

"Fuck, baby. You're so tight."

I drive into her in long, deep thrusts, feeling my hips collide with her ass with each stroke. She pushes back in counterpoint to my movements, giving as good as she gets.

Fucking Emberly is like riding a wild horse. No matter which position I take her, she always wrestles for control.

She's unrestrained, spirited, free, and all that is about to change.

"You like that?" I ask, with a hard snap of my hips.

"Fuck, yeah." Her inner walls clamp hard around my length with a strength that makes my balls ache for release.

My breath comes in ragged gasps. I can't last much longer, not knowing that I'm about to make her mine forever and not with the way she's milking my cock.

"Come for me." I reach around her hips and rub her clit, this time with vigorous strokes. Emberly's pussy clamps so hard that my thrusts become shallow.

"That's it, baby," I growl into her ear. "Squeeze my cock."

She quivers and shakes, her hungry pussy pumping me with a desperation that nearly brings me to my knees.

My eyes roll to the back of my head. At this rate, she'll make me come too soon.

My fingers quicken their pace over her swollen bud, and I feel myself reaching the limits of my control. I focus on the ceiling, the red wall, anything to last even just a moment longer.

"Let go, Emberly," I snarl.

Her pussy spasms, and the cry that tears from her throat makes my ears ring. I come in a hot rush, spilling inside her unprotected walls, claiming her as my own.

We collapse on the daybed, still trembling from our climaxes. The usual sensation of trapped cum pooling around my tip is gone, and I'm convinced that my sperm is already marching their way to her egg.

When I pull out, there's a third less of the usual amount of cum left on the condom's tip. I wrap it up in a tissue along with the foil packet and toss it into the trash.

Emberly finally leaves the fitting room to continue her shopping. The door clicks shut, and I grab a pin from the dressing table and puncture my remaining condoms with holes. Cum will drizzle out, but not enough to be noticeable.

On the way home, I fuck her again with the sabotaged condoms, dreaming of her being so swollen with my baby she won't even be able to leave my room. The roads are so dark and windy that the car drives up at a glacial pace, giving me time to fill her up before we reach the top.

When we round a bend for the final stretch before the estate, there's a commotion at the gates. Someone wearing a uniform has parked outside and is trying to argue their way inside.

I recognize that outfit. I also recognize the woman wearing it.

It's Officer McMurphy with the double-Ds. The last words she said to me as I left death row were not to be a stranger.

It looks like my pet prison officer still thinks she can keep me in line.

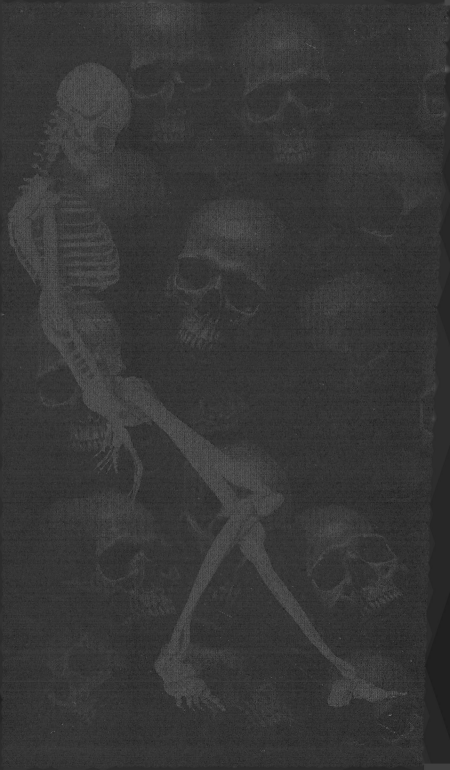

FORTY-NINE

EMBERLY

I slump on the back seat, drunk on champagne and pleasure, my pussy so wet that I'm still dripping. Who knew rich men found buying women lingerie so arousing?

My new purse sits beside me, empty save for an ebony card I don't intend to use. As much as I love Roman, I need my independence. The days of being financially beholden to anyone are gone. Thanks to him, my paintings provide me with an excellent source of income.

The car slows toward the iron gates, where a woman in blue blocks the way with her vehicle.

Roman snarls.

"What's going on?" I ask.

The woman turns around. She's about my height, maybe a little taller. She's wearing a black eye patch along with some kind of uniform, and looks furious.

My spine stiffens. What if she's associated with Jim? "Is that a police officer?"

"Corrections officer," he mutters. At my blank stare, he adds, "Prison guard."

Relief whooshes from my lungs, but only for an instant. "What's she doing here?"

Roman's jaw tenses. "She's here to see me."

"Parole violation?" The words slip from my lips, even though nothing about this situation makes sense. Roman was exonerated.

"Stay here," he says and turns toward the door.

"Wait." I grab his arm.

Roman pauses to gaze back at me, his expression unreadable. It's obvious he doesn't want me to listen to their conversation, and I want to know why.

"Who is she to you?" I ask.

"Nobody," he says.

"Random corrections officers don't just turn up at the gates of men who were falsely imprisoned. You know her."

"I do," he replies, his voice flat.

"Did you sleep with her?"

He hesitates. "No."

My eyes harden. I can tell by the expressions of the men around the gates that whatever was between the police guard and Roman was sexual.

"But something happened between you," I say.

His jaw flexes. "Yes."

"Tell me."

Roman grinds his teeth, looking like he isn't used to being interrogated by women about his love life. I really don't give a shit, considering I laid out my entire history with Jim Callahan. My grip around his arm tightens to let him know I'm serious.

"She was my mule," he replies.

"What does that mean?"

"I had a financial arrangement with her to bring in Sofia's cooking, so I didn't have to touch the prison slop."

My brows pinch. "What else?"

The woman rushes at our car and bangs both fists on the window, making me flinch. Someone must have jostled her eye patch because it's now hanging halfway down her face.

"Montesano," she screeches. "Where are you?"

Roman grimaces as a man in armor lifts her off her feet and carries her to the roadside. A few others jog close to watch the spectacle.

"Are you sure you didn't have sex? She seems awfully invested," I say, my gaze bouncing between Roman's attempts to be stoic and the guard manhandling the squirming woman. "Or did you make her promises you can't keep?"

His head snaps in my direction and he shoots me a hard glower. "That's not how it happened."

"Then how, Roman?" I ask through clenched teeth. "Because you're a very easy guy to fall for. After five years of togetherness, I can imagine she'd feel abandoned."

His lips flatten, and his nostrils flare. "Is that what you think? That I led her on?"

"Well, did you?" I snap.

"Never," he rasps. "Officer McMurphy was assigned to me because I was a high-risk prisoner."

"High risk of what?"

"Escaping," he replies and turns his gaze back to the front. "Cesare had a plan to fly a helicopter into the courtyard and break me out. A lot of inmates were still loyal to us and willing to take out the guards. Benito, Gil, and my cousin all worked together to make the warden assign me someone who wouldn't be a pain in the ass."

"Alright..." I scrutinize his profile, my patience fraying. "When did the relationship turn romantic?"

He shakes his head. "It wasn't like that."

My temples throb with the force of my frustration. Roman can't talk his way out of this situation. I won't allow any bullshit. Exasperation tightens my chest, and my voice becomes sharp. "Then when did the sex start?"

A muscle in his jaw flexes. "One morning when she served me breakfast, she got on her knees and crawled beneath the table."

"In the middle of the prison cafeteria?" I ask with a gasp.

"I was on death row. We eat in our cells." He pinches the bridge of his nose. "I knew we were playing a dangerous game, but it had been months since I'd had a woman, and I wasn't interested in any of Gil's whores—"

"Wait. There were prostitutes?"

His gaze shifts to me, his expression incredulous. "Anything is available in prison for the right price."

"Oh." I wait for him to continue, but he doesn't. "So, she just volunteered to blow you under the table without an explanation?"

Roman glances out of the window to where a small crowd has formed around the woman. I can't see her behind the wall of amused men.

"What?" I ask.

"I used to jerk off to Gil's stupid magazines and..."

"She watched and got turned on at the sight of you stroking your cock," I say, my voice bitter, my cheeks heating.

My mind dials back to the display of Roman masturbating in the studio while I was trying to paint his portrait. I don't need the rest of the story because I experienced it first-hand. The man is the embodiment of temptation.

"She fucking took advantage of you." Roman stiffens, and I grab his shoulder. "Is that how it happened?"

"Emberly..." he says, with an exasperated sigh.

"Now she's back for more?" I shuffle to the other side of the seat and reach for the door handle.

Roman grabs me around the waist and pulls me into his chest. "What are you doing?"

"She abused her authority," I hiss.

"Stop this."

Now, I'm the one who's squirming. "Let go of me. You were stuck in that cell all day and she took advantage of her authority over you to molest your cock!"

His chest shakes, its vibrations rumbling against my back.

My eyes widen. "Are you laughing?"

"No," he says, his voice light. "Are you jealous?"

"You're mine." I thrash within his arms, desperate for him to release his grip.

We tussle in the back seat, with Roman's hands wandering over my body, squeezing and groping at every opportunity. My rage mounts, and my skin breaks out in a sweat. I'm trying to break free and tell his prison bitch to back off, and Roman seems to think this is a game.

This is infuriating. He's stronger, faster, with infinite amounts of stamina. I can't fucking win.

"Why are you so mad?" he asks, still chuckling. "It wasn't cheating."

"This isn't a joke," I yell. "Would it be so funny if the guard was male and the prisoner was female? If some poor woman was masturbating in private, and a male officer entered like it was an invitation?"

Roman sobers, and his grip around my body loosens.

He might be finally understanding the situation.

"Answer this question truthfully," I say, my voice breaking. "Would you be interested in her if she approached you at your club?"

"This isn't the same."

"Because you're a man? How is it different if she was the one with all the power?"

"It's different, baby. Nothing like what you're thinking. You weren't there."

"What do you think happened when I was Jim's prisoner? Same fucking thing that happened to you, and now she's coming back for more. You protected me from that bastard. Let me do the same for you."

He sighs. "Believe it or not, she kept me sane."

"With fellatio?" My voice wavers.

"I was strong on the outside, but on the inside, I was losing hope. They let me have visits every day, but there were limits on what I could do to stop the family from crumbling."

My muscles weaken, and I slump against his chest. "You must have felt powerless."

"For the few minutes each day when she sucked me off, all I concentrated on was that hot mouth around my cock," he murmurs. "I could close my eyes and imagine I was somewhere else, then afterward dine on a breakfast cooked with Sofia's love."

My throat swells. I wouldn't last a day in a cell. Nothing and nobody could compensate for the terror of being confined.

"Sorry. I can't even imagine what you suffered."

"And I'm sorry for not taking you seriously," he rasps. "Being trapped by that asshole had to be hell."

He kisses my temple, and we fall silent for several moments. Maybe I was projecting. If I had been in that prison and an officer came into my room for sexual contact... I don't want to dredge up all that shit I went through with Jim.

"You must have talked," I say. "Did she ever ask for a

future?"

His hug tightens. "There's only one future for a man on death row."

Realization hits me like acid. Heat rushes to my eyes and I close them before they produce tears. "That's so... I can't believe you're still functioning."

"The day I was exonerated, she asked me not to be a stranger. She's still getting paid to be a mule."

"She wants a relationship," I mutter.

"What I had with her was strictly business," he says.

"And me?"

Roman draws back and stares down at me with a frown. "What do you mean?"

"You admitted earlier that you only took me in to spite Jim because he was in the police."

He gazes down at me with an intensity that makes my heart pound hard enough for us both. "Emberly, I have never brought a woman to my family home, never spent the night with a woman, let alone slept beside her."

My breath shallows, and every butterfly in my stomach takes flight. "Oh."

"I've never hidden a fugitive who wasn't a blood relative and never risked going back to prison by murdering a cop to protect a woman."

"Okay." I gulp.

"And I've never told a woman that I loved her. I did all those things for you because you're the only person in the world who makes me feel alive."

"Really?" I rasp.

His dark eyes soften, and he cups my face with both hands. "Being with you is like soaring the kite-tails of freedom." He pauses to brush his thumb over my cheekbone. "It doesn't matter if you're sleeping, painting, or freaking out, each moment with you is fresh, exciting, and new. You make me feel every emotion under the sun."

"Why me?" I whisper.

"Because you're the most unique person I've ever met, and the opposite of what I expect. Everything about you is addictive. I would kill for you, maim for you, and step over a pile of twitching and dead bodies if it meant keeping you by my side."

"Oh," I say with a breathy sigh, not knowing how to respond.

"And thank you."

"What for?" I ask.

"No woman has ever fought to protect me."

Before I can ask if he's excluding his mother, his lips find mine, and I melt into the warmth of his kiss. I dig my fingers into his shirt. This kiss is different from all the others and carries an urgency I'm not sure I understand.

It's as though he's afraid of losing me, even though we've had much worse spats. I kiss back, trying to assure him I have no intention of ever leaving.

Still joined to his lips, I whisper, "I love you, too."

He draws back, his gaze dropping to my mouth before meeting my eyes. "I never get tired of hearing that."

"Anytime your honor needs defending, I'll be there with a craft knife."

He chuckles. "I'll be sure to order you an extra supply."

I give him a firm nod.

"Now, will you please stay in the car and let me get rid of this pest?"

"Fine," I mutter as Roman opens the door, letting in the sound of her yelling.

As he steps out into the night, I sit back, my mind reeling, and my pussy unusually wet. What part of wrestling

Roman was a turn on, or did I just get over excited from the memory of him touching himself as I painted?

I shake off that thought and resolve to make more of an effort not to overreact. Roman was telling the truth about his association with the officer.

There's no need to concern myself about other women, regardless of what else he might be doing.

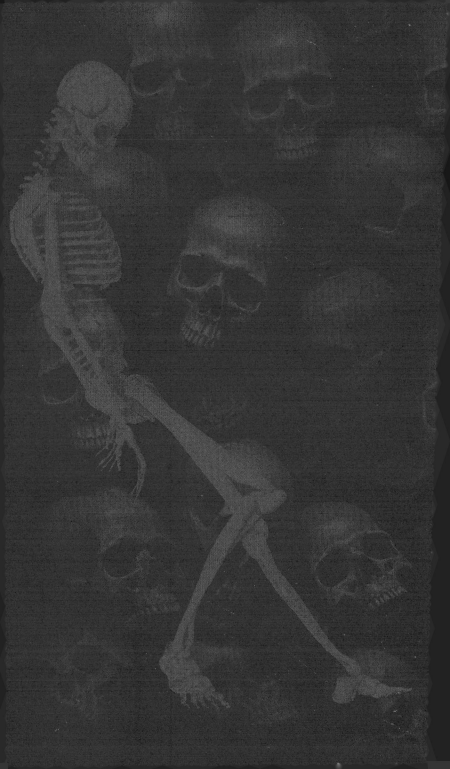

FIFTY

ROMAN

One evening, after sorting out the mess Capello made of the loan company, I approach the pool house with a gift, my stomach twisting with dread. It's been a week since Officer McMurphy made that scene at the gates, and nothing has been the same.

Seeing myself through Emberly's eyes was the bucket of ice water that snapped me back to reality. The way she rushed to my defense opened my eyes to the depth of her compassion. I'm not worthy of her empathy, let alone her love. After everything she's suffered, how the fuck can I condemn the woman I love to an unwanted pregnancy?

I enter her little art studio, letting out a cloud of paint and turpentine fumes. Emberly sits hunched over a small canvas with her lips tightened, seeming too focused on her work to even notice my presence.

"What are you painting, baby?" I cross the room and place my arms on her shoulders.

She turns around, her face a mask of calm. "Just a few toadstools that will end up in the larger painting."

"I brought you a gift."

"Oh, thank you," she says, her voice flat.

Frowning at her lack of enthusiasm, I open the box, revealing a wooden mask. "This is for you."

Her jaw drops. "Is that—"

"A Roger Thango original. You once mentioned liking his art."

Her face crumples, and tears run down her cheeks. She stares down at the mask, her breath turning ragged. "You remembered. It's so beautiful. What did I do to deserve you?"

I place a hand on her arm. "Are you okay?"

"Yes," she says, her voice choked.

My jaw tightens. This isn't like Emberly at all. She should be crying happy tears, not looking pained. "Tell me what's wrong."

"I just feel weird." She bows her head.

"You need a doctor?"

She shrugs. "It's just a period thing, I guess."

My heart skips a beat. "You need some tampons or something?"

"No, it's late, and I'm feeling off."

Dread punches me hard enough to silence a roar of triumph. Massaging the knots out of her shoulders, I tell myself that it's impossible to knock her up after one try. I know I'm potent, but even that's a stretch.

"It's probably stress. A lot of shit has happened this month, it could have thrown off your hormones."

She gives me a watery chuckle. "What do you know about the menstrual cycle?"

"When all you've got is time and the prison library is shit, you'll read anything, including anatomy and physiology."

Emberly sets down her brush and stands. I take a step

back, giving her space to move. When she gazes up at me, her eyes shine with remorse. "Sorry for being so off recently."

I shake my head. "Changes in mood are all part of the beauty of womanhood."

"Did Officer McMurphy have mood swings?" she asks, her brows rising.

"Emberly," I say with a sigh. "If that woman meant anything to me, I would have invited her to the club the night of my release and would never have met you."

She lowers her lashes. "I don't know why I said that."

My chest fills with warmth. She's still jealous. That's an excellent sign. It means she plans on sticking around.

"Come here," I say.

She steps back. "I'm covered in paint."

"Do you think I give a damn about that?" I pull her into a hug and kiss the top of her head. "It will always be you, baby. No matter how many women come to my gates thinking I owe them attention, the only one I will ever love is you."

She giggles. "Stop it."

"No bullshit," I say. "You're the one for me. My one and only."

Emberly melts against my chest, smearing my shirt with paint. I close my eyes, wanting to savor this closeness. A gunshot rings out and we both jump apart.

"Get into the bedroom."

"Roman, what's—"

"Now!" I bark.

As she darts behind a canvas, I pull out my gun before making my way to the French doors. Gil sprints toward us from the side of the pool, his features a mask of determination.

I meet him at the door. "What's happened?"

Gil flicks his head toward the mansion. "It's the cops."

Behind me, Emberly whimpers, and my stomach drops. I told her to stay in the bedroom. Of all the fucking times for the cops to return, did it have to be when I was finally making inroads with her?

Someone must have found Callahan's corpse and now they're throwing shit and trying to see what sticks. Emberly can't know he's dead. At least not until after I've worked out a way to explain why I withheld the information for so long.

She crosses the room and buries her head in my chest. "It's Jim."

I cup her cheeks and stare into her terrified green eyes. "He won't come through the gates, even if he has a warrant."

She shivers. "You don't know what he's like."

"And you've forgotten that Lafayette dropped the charges. You're no longer a fugitive."

The words tumble out of my mouth before I can stop them. I cringe, knowing I've fucked up. I've just given her a shot of courage.

She straightens, the fear on her features morphing into something fierce. "That's true. Jim can't hold that bullshit over me, so what the hell does he want?"

"Let me take you to the kitchen, where someone can make you a nice drink. I'll even station some men at the door. What do you want? Iced tea? Hot chocolate?"

"No." She takes my hand. "I want to confront him."

My stomach drops like an iron ball and sweat breaks out across my brow. The moment she reaches those gates and discovers Jim is dead, I'm screwed. I wrack my brain for a way to convince her to stay back, but the love I have for her is fucking with my ability to churn out smooth lies.

"They want to speak to the boss," Gil blurts.

"Yes," I say, my mind still scrambling for a solution. "Stay here. Let me protect you."

"Why is it okay for you to fight my battles when I can't fight yours?" she asks, clearly referring to the incident at the gate with Officer McMurphy.

"Emberly, please," I reply with a sigh.

"I'm coming with you." She marches to the door, her hands balled into fists. "I want to know why he paid Dominic and sent that new recruit disguised as a waiter."

"And let it slip that I shot him in the head?"

She whirls around and meets my gaze with wide eyes. "What?"

"Gil said they wanted to speak to me. It's probably about that missing cop. If you march over to the gates accusing Callahan of sending him, it won't take long to give them probable cause to get a warrant."

"Shit," she whispers.

"Now, will you go back to the house and get a drink?"

She nods. "Maybe a whiskey."

No way in hell a potentially pregnant woman will drink alcohol under my roof.

I wrap an arm around her shoulders and walk her out of the pool house. "Nah. You don't want booze."

―――――

Half an hour later, after I've calmed Emberly and talked her out of drinking alcohol, Gil drives me to the gates. My heart still pounds at the prospect of her nearly uncovering my lies. I'm slipping, and I need to keep better track of my own bullshit, especially when she's so unpredictable.

The floodlights are on, illuminating the small army of cops at the gates. As usual, my men have parked all kinds of vehicles in the driveway and are recording the police on their phones. Social media wasn't as powerful before I got arrested, but I appreciate any opportunity to make them look like idiots.

I step out of the car and walk past the barricade of vehicles to the gates, where I spot the detective in charge. He's a mustached motherfucker with a paunch that could rival Saint Nicholas and has the nerve to look me up and down before speaking.

"What do you want?" I ask. "You're interrupting my evening hot chocolate."

"We're here to investigate a murder," he says.

"And you are?" I raise my brows.

"Detective Stanley Bradford from homicide." He holds up his badge.

I nod. "Are you finally going to open the murder investigation you guys fucked up? Because I spent nearly five years behind bars while the real killer is still out there, murdering other women."

Bradford shuffles on his feet. "The body of Detective James Callahan was found an hour ago. We're here to question you and take a look around."

I huff a laugh. "You got a warrant?"

He scowls. "We were hoping you'd cooperate on a murder investigation."

"And why would I do that?" I ask.

"Cut the bullshit. Callahan was investigating you."

"For kissing his ex-girlfriend?" I ask. "I know it's been decades since anyone has seen your cock, but since when was it a crime to have charisma?"

My men burst into cheers and laughter, but I keep my face impassive. Bradford glances at one of the detectives at his side for support, but they avert their gazes.

It looks like no one wants to go viral for harassment.

I raise a palm, motioning for my men to be quiet. When

the laughter dies down, I ask, "Where did you find Detective Callahan's body?"

"We're not at liberty to say," he mutters.

"So, not on my grounds?"

He jerks his head to the side, unable to meet my gaze.

"I'll take that as a no, otherwise you'd have a warrant. Since I was at home all day, minding my own business, I'll thank you for not wasting any more of my time and let me get back to my hot beverage."

Turning around, I walk back to my car.

"Mr. Montesano, we're not done," the cop yells. "Where were you seven to ten days ago? We need to confirm your alibi."

I pause to spare him a glance over my shoulder. "You should know better than to ask such vague questions. If this is part of an official police investigation, you may contact my attorney. Someone give him a card."

Bradford yells something else, but it's swallowed up by all the raucous shouting. I slide into the car's front seat and let Gil drive me back to the house.

Eventually, forensics will narrow down Callahan's accurate time of death and its cause. Fortunately for me, Benito has arranged ample security footage of us at the casino that can prove my alibi.

I make a mental note to get someone at the coroner's office to obtain the autopsy results. Anyone with half a brain will spot the scarring on Callahan's feet and realize he was a long-time user.

In the meantime, I'll withhold the information on Callahan's death from Emberly and let her keep thinking that she still needs my protection. There's one more thing I can do to make sure Emberly never leaves, but that is going to involve the casino.

It's going to be my most audacious scam.

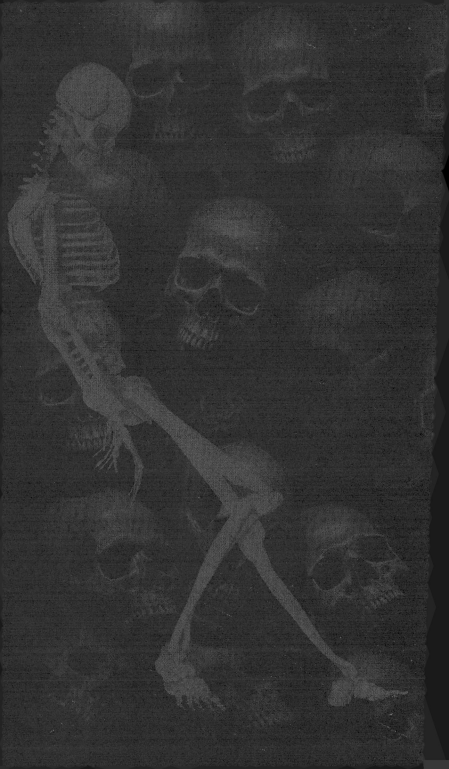

FIFTY-ONE

EMBERLY

The next morning, I'm staring at the wooden mask, awestruck that Roman remembered the name of my favorite artist. Gratitude swells in my chest, and my eyes mist with tears. After everything he's done for me, I almost confronted Jim about that dead cop.

My skin warms with the memory of being sprayed with blood and brain matter. Then my stomach churns with a surge of nausea. I need to focus on my art and stop thinking about gore.

Bright sunlight streams through the pool house's windows, illuminating the canvas of the painting I made of Roman bathed in light and shadow. Two more completed canvases hang on the wall, but this one is my favorite by far.

A knock sounds on the door, and I flinch. No one ever comes here except Roman, who hardly ever knocks.

"Who is it?" I ask from behind the canvas.

"Ernest from the MoCa gallery," says a deep voice. "Is now a good time?"

"Oh." I place a hand on my chest. "Come in."

The door opens, and Mr. Lubelli strides in, holding a leather folder and sporting a dazzling grin. As soon as our gazes meet, his steps falter, and his dazzling smile fades to a concerned frown.

"Are you alright, my dear? You look awfully pale."

I pull my features into what I hope is a reassuring grin. "Just a little tired. I didn't get much sleep last night."

His eyes twinkle. "If I shared a bed with Roman Montesano, I wouldn't waste a minute on slumber."

My cheeks warm, and I dip my head, letting my stray curls fall over my face. Ever since we fucked in that changing room, Roman and I have made love at least twice a day. He's either trying to convince me that it's me he loves and not that prison officer, or he's distracting me from worrying about Jim.

"Thanks for coming to visit," I murmur. "I hope you find something you want to sell in your gallery next."

Mr. Lubelli walks over to the canvases, his eyes brightening. He points at the painting of Roman's body and sighs. "This one is exquisite. You have a talent for capturing the male form."

"Thanks," I reply with a smile.

Any other time, I would dance with joy at the praise, but I'm so nauseous and exhausted that my body can't muster up the right emotions.

He moves onto the other two and studies them each with his hand over his mouth. "These are all very good. I think they'll sell well in my next auction."

A wave of tiredness sweeps over my senses, and I yawn.

Mr. Lubelli turns around and laughs. "That's not quite the response I was expecting."

"Sorry." I rub my eyes. "Which one do you want?"

"Ideally, all three."

My heart skips several beats. "What?"

"But I imagine Roman might want to purchase that one." He nods toward the first painting. "So, I'll take the other two off your hands and you can contact me next month to let me know if you're interested in selling the third."

I haven't spent a penny of the seventy-five thousand I made from Roman's portrait and the last two paintings I sold to Mr. Lubelli. Now, I'm going to get another fifty.

"Thank you," I say, my voice breathy with excitement. "That's very generous."

"Are you sure you want to sell them at a fixed price? I could revert to a commission-based structure—"

"No," I blurt. "I'm happy with what I'm getting."

I force back memories of that disastrous contract I signed with Lafayette and what we had to do to make him drop the criminal charges. If my career takes off, I can ask for a higher price, but this amount is already beyond my wildest expectations.

Mr. Lubelli extracts some papers and glances around for a clean surface. He strolls to the kitchen area and sets down his folder. "If you'd like to sign these two contracts, I can have the paintings wrapped up and delivered to the gallery."

Wiping my grubby hands on my apron, I trudge across the room and stifle a yawn. As soon as Mr. Lubelli leaves, I'm going to retreat to the back room for a nap.

———

Hours later, I wake with Roman curled at my back, his arm draped over my waist. One of his hands cups my breast, his thumb brushing back and forth across my nipple.

"Thank you for the mask," I murmur.

"You're welcome, baby."

"How do you do it?"

"What?"

"You always know my heart's desire."

He kisses my neck. "You're my obsession. Everything I learn about you is a revelation. Making you happy is an addiction I never want to lose."

I snuggle into his chest, my body warming at his touch. "What time is it?"

"Eight."

"At night?"

He chuckles. "Yeah."

I yawn. "Damn. I hadn't meant to fall asleep for so long."

He nuzzles my shoulder. "You've had a lot on your mind. I'm glad you got the chance to rest."

Another yawn escapes my throat. "I sold two paintings today. Mr. Lubelli wanted to buy a third, but he said you might want it for yourself."

"The other portrait?" Roman asks.

"Uh-huh."

"Fuck yes," he growls and peppers my neck with soft kisses. "I'll get a copy of the same art agreement as before."

"Don't be silly." I turn around in his embrace and melt into his smile. "It's a gift. Just like that mask."

Roman's features form a deep frown. "No woman has ever given me such a valuable gift."

"Good, then I'll be the first."

Something flickers across his features. A mix of frustration, tinged with guilt. "How are you ever going to have a thriving art career if you keep giving away your paintings?"

I lean into him and kiss him on the lips. "How much money have you spent on me?"

"What's that got to do with anything? I don't keep score. Besides, you're my woman."

My face flushes, the warmth spreading down to my chest and filling my heart with joy. Hearing this feels even better than the last time, when he claimed me at the family dinner in the heat of the moment.

"Say that again," I murmur.

His eyes shine in the semi-darkness. "You, Emberly Kay, are my fucking woman and I fucking love you."

I giggle. "Seriously?"

"I'm never letting you go," he snarls.

"O-Okay..." When he doesn't elaborate, I press my forehead against his and sigh in contentment. "And I love you, too."

Roman pulls me into a hug. "You're going to sell me that painting."

"It's a gift."

He spanks my ass. "I'm serious."

"Alright then," I say with a giggle. "You can have it in exchange for a kiss."

"Emberly," he growls.

"Roman," I growl back.

He pulls away from the hug, looking me dead in the eye. "How about I pay you twenty-five grand and you use the money to take me out on a ridiculously expensive date?"

I huff. "Drop it, Roman. For once, I want to be the one giving you the gift."

He rolls me onto my back and pins my hands over my head. "Are you sure about that, baby?"

"Yes." I arch into his chest. "Accept the gift, asshole."

His eyes darken, and he parts my thighs with his knees. "Your paintings are valuable investments, not gifts. Sign the fucking agreement and accept my money."

"Make me."

He flashes his teeth, looking like the sexiest kind of predator. My stomach flip-flops, not knowing whether to be afraid or aroused.

"Hold on to the headboard," he growls.

As my fingers cling to the cold metal, Roman reaches to the corners of the bed and pulls out some white rope.

"Where did you get those?" I ask.

"They were tucked into the sheets," he murmurs. "You never know when you have to tie up a brat."

He binds my wrists together with the rope, which feels like it's made of hundreds of silk fibers. My nipples tighten at the new sensation, and heat radiates from my core.

After securing the rope to the headboard, he stares down at me with a grin. "Now, will you sign the agreement?"

My lips quirk into a smile. "Never!"

"I hoped you would say that." He hops off the bed, jostling the mattress.

The fine hairs on the back of my neck stand on end. I raise my head and glare at his retreating back. "Where are you going? Roman?"

"Wait there." He disappears behind the door.

As soon as it clicks shut, my insides coil with a tight knot of dread. My heart pounds through the silence, drowning out the sounds of my frantic breathing. Panic grabs me by the throat, its grip cold and suffocating. I gasp for air, trying to calm my racing thoughts.

It's like I'm trapped in a prison and there's no escape. Deep down, I know this is only temporary. It's only a form of bondage. It's nothing like being locked up in a burning apartment. Roman will return soon with something like a dildo.

Stay calm. Stay calm. Stay calm.

My hands curl into fists.

Seconds pass. Maybe minutes. My brain knows he hasn't left for long, but my fight-or-flight response is going into overdrive and screaming at me to run. Every nerve becomes over-sensitized, with sweat rolling over my skin like balls of mercury. I thrash my arms, struggling to break free, but the rope only tightens around my wrists.

No matter how many times I try to reassure myself, every instinct screams red alert. My nostrils fill with the remembered scent of smoke, and I cry out.

"Roman?"

Nothing.

"Roman!"

The door swings open. Roman returns holding a piece of paper, his eyes wide. "You okay?"

Shudders seize my bones, and I squeeze my eyes shut. "Fuck."

He scrambles onto the bed, his hands working through the ropes with an urgency that matches my racing pulse. "Emberly, talk to me."

"I'm okay. I'm okay. I'm..." I gulp. "I'm okay."

"You're not." He releases my wrists and pulls me into his arms. "You're trembling, and your heart is pounding. Tell me what I did, baby?"

"Nothing," I say with a sigh, my muscles finally relaxing. "It's just me."

Roman's strong arms tighten around my waist and shoulders, and he rocks me from side to side. His heart pounds as hard and fast as mine, as though my panic attack shook him to the core.

"Was it the bondage?" he asks.

"No, that was really hot," I say, my voice still shaky.

"Then what?"

"You left me tied up."

He rubs circles over my back. "Did you think I would leave you there all night?"

"No," I rasp. "My mind is fucked. This is a new fear unlocked."

"You've never been tied up?" he asks.

I shake my head. "This was my first time. It was fine when you were on top of me. I knew you would eventually let me go, but the moment you left the room, my mind went into overdrive."

"I'm so sorry, baby," he murmurs, his lips pressing against my ear. "We won't do this again unless you ask. I wasn't even thinking."

"Roman, it's not your fault." I throw my arms around his shoulders and squeeze him tight. "Now, give me that contract and let me take you out on a nice, expensive date."

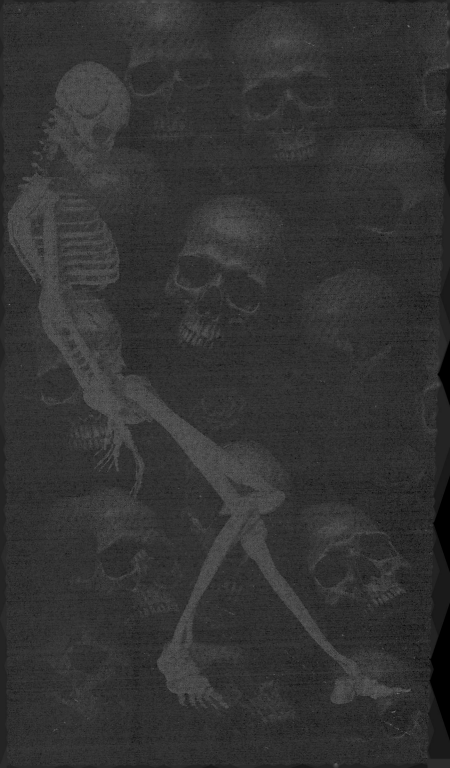

FIFTY-TWO

ROMAN

I'm officially an asshole. An asshole driving us both to a dangerous precipice in a car with no brakes, careening toward the edge of a cliff. I'm too obsessed with Emberly to let her know the truth. Too selfish to let Emberly jump out and save herself from being tied to me for life.

But I'm a determined bastard who's willing to risk everything to make her mine. By the time Emberly discovers what I've done, she will hate me with the firepower of a thousand automatic rifles, but she won't be able to leave.

As the limo approaches the casino, her loud gasp pulls me out of my funk. "It's beautiful!"

I smile, relieved that she's impressed. When the front entrance is lit up at night, it's one of the most spectacular sights in New Alderney.

"Casino Montesano?" she asks.

"Great-Grandfather Paolo built it in 1951 based on similar archeological principles as the mansion," I reply, my chest inflating. "It was the Salerno back then until my dad renovated the casino, added a hotel, and named it the Montesano."

Whatever pride I feel is bittersweet, considering that one of the buildings behind it is the Hotel Marisol, which that bastard built. The limo passes the grand entrance and stops at a side door reserved for VIPs.

"The man had great taste," she murmurs, her voice breathy with awe.

"It's a common trait shared by all Montesano men," I say, my gaze skimming over her outfit.

She wears one of the dresses I chose for her: a strapless, red gown that showcases her curves and long legs. Her curls are piled atop her head with her pretty face framed with stray tendrils.

If this date wasn't part of a plan to keep her at my side forever, I would take her back home and fuck her until those curls lay straight.

"Shall we?" I offer her a hand and lead her out of the limousine.

A host leads us through the chandelier-lit VIP entrance, which has a glass-paneled walkway that takes us over the main floor. It's bustling down there with thumping music and crowds around the slot machines.

Emberly clutches my hand, her gaze darting from side to side, her breath growing fast and shallow. From the smile flickering on her beautiful features, I'd say she was awestruck.

"Is this your first time at a casino?" I ask.

She laughs. "I never had enough money to gamble away. Why are there so many slot machines?"

"Would you believe we make more money from those than from the tables?"

She shakes her head, her lips parting with a gasp.

"Come on." I wrap an arm around her waist and tuck her into my side.

The host leads us to a private dining room with glass walls that offer a panoramic view of the casino's tables. I called ahead, informing the staff that my guest wasn't allowed booze under any circumstances. If Emberly orders something alcoholic, they will shut their mouths and replace it with something else.

"This is incredible," she whispers as I settle her into her seat.

I place a kiss on her lips before returning to my place. "This casino was my father's pride and joy."

"What happened?" she asks. "Last thing I heard, it was called the Capello Casino, and now—"

"It's back where it belongs," I say, my smile tight.

She nods but doesn't comment. Emberly is intelligent enough to put two and two together and work out that the man who framed me for murder also stole our casino.

I'm betting everything on the house that she doesn't figure out where she fits into this mess. At least not until it's too late.

A waiter comes in to take our order, and she selects the tasting menu, which provides a different wine with each course. I get the same in case she complains about the vintages because the staff will replace everything with alcohol-scented juice.

The first course is a foie gras terrine with what's supposed to be a light Pinot Gris. She takes tiny bites, savoring each morsel, and I'm enchanted by the way she eats.

"What?" she bats her eyes.

"Nothing." I shake my head and smile. "I just like watching you enjoy your food."

She dips her head. "This is pretty good, but I still can't

work out how on earth you clawed back a whole casino. Did you have to take it over with all your men?"

"Like an invasion?" I ask.

"I really can't imagine how else it could happen."

"We have a very talented lawyer."

She gasps. "That's all it took?"

A knot forms in my gut as I think about all the plans I had for divesting Emberly of her inheritance. Murder, imprisonment, humiliation, coercion... all because the father she never knew was scum.

Holding my features in a neutral mask, I swallow a mouthful of non-alcoholic wine. "Sometimes brains trump brawn."

She laughs. "That's something to remember for the future. What else did you get back from the Capello family?"

I take her hand. "Tonight is about celebrating you and your rise to the top of the art world."

She lowers her lashes, her cheeks turning pink. "I couldn't have done it without you."

"Nonsense," I say. "Your talent speaks for itself."

Emberly sets down her fork and sighs. "I spent years struggling to afford painting supplies and just as much time trying to get noticed. It's so competitive out there and nearly impossible to get a break."

The tension in my belly loosens now that she's no longer asking dangerous questions about her family. Exhaling my relief, I give her hand a gentle squeeze. "That must have been hard."

"It was." She glances up, her eyes shining with unshed tears. "But then one introduction to the right person made all the difference."

"That was all you, baby," I murmur, my hairline breaking out in sweat. "You and Lubelli were in the right place at the right time. You took the initiative and made things happen."

"Stop being so modest," she says with a bright smile. "Mr. Lubelli might never have taken me seriously if I hadn't walked in on your arm."

The words hit like a punch, bringing up a reflux of guilt. Adrenaline surges through my veins and tension winds around my chest, forcing my breaths to shallow.

She isn't accusing me of engineering a meeting with the owner of New Alderney's most prestigious art gallery to swindle her out of her inheritance.

She's just talking.

Just expressing her gratitude.

She doesn't know she's a pawn in a grand scale game far beyond her understanding.

Right?

The next course arrives, a seared scallop with a buttery Chardonnay. When Emberly breaks eye contact to take a bite, I take in a deep breath and pull back my shoulders. It's time to change the subject away from the casino, her art, or anything else related to the stolen assets.

I take a bite of the scallop, barely able to appreciate its delicate flavors when all I can taste is dread. Emberly needs to be distracted in case I fumble tonight's plan and lose her forever.

"Can we talk about what happened tonight?" I ask.

She pauses, mid-chew, her eyes widening. "What do you mean?"

"Your panic attack," I say.

Her features fall and her shoulders droop. "That was just a misunderstanding, and we talked about it already."

"Perhaps." I take a sip of the non-alcoholic chardonnay. "But we also haven't talked about what happened on that balcony. Are they related?"

She swallows her mouthful and downs her glass. My eyes narrow, and I remind myself to remove all traces of alcohol from around the house in case I've managed to get her pregnant.

"I just don't like to be stuck," she mutters.

"You're claustrophobic?" I ask.

Her nose wrinkles. "Not really, although I'd probably freak out if I was put in a box."

"Understandably," I mutter. "But that's not what I meant. What did you mean when you said you didn't like feeling stuck?"

She picks up her napkin and twists it around her fingers. "It's hard to explain."

"Do you feel trapped in our relationship?" I ask.

Her eyes dart to mine, and she gives her head a vigorous shake. "Of course not."

"Then what is it?" I lean across the table and place a hand on her shoulder. "You can tell me anything, baby. All I want is to make you happy."

"I have cleithrophobia."

"What's that?"

"A fear of being trapped."

"From being locked up?"

Emberly ducks her head, inhales several deep breaths and tightens her jaw. "I was four years old, maybe five." She swallows. "Mom used to work all day and lock me in the studio apartment. She couldn't afford childcare, but she also kept thinking that the people out to get her would take me as a hostage."

My heart sinks into my stomach as I picture a little girl with wild curls stuck in a cramped room, comparing it to the freedom I had as a kid on a huge estate with two brothers to play with, cousin Leroi, his little sister, and Capello's twin sons.

"She kept you there all day?" I ask, my brows furrowing. "No neighbor to check up on you? What did you even eat?"

Emberly wipes her brow. "I got used to the confinement. Mom always left sandwiches on the table and a big bottle of water. I got to watch TV, draw pictures, and play with toys."

"I'm sorry, baby. I had no idea."

"That's not the worst."

A lump forms in my throat. "Something happened?"

"One day, I got sick of cold sandwiches and tried to use the toaster oven. I don't know what I did wrong, but I started a fire." Her voice trembles. "The room filled with smoke, then the alarm sounded. The windows were locked, and I was trapped. The place was so cluttered that the fire spread across the kitchenette. I broke a window but didn't have the guts to climb out. All I could do was lean against the door and scream for help."

"Fuck," I whisper. "How did you get out? Were you hurt?"

"No... Not really."

"Emberly?"

"A neighbor heard me and used one of those fire axes to make a hole in the door, so I could crawl into the hallway. I went to the ER for smoke inhalation and then Mom got arrested for child endangerment." Her voice cracks and tears stream down her cheeks.

"What happened next?" I ask.

"I was trapped in a hospital for days with an oxygen mask and tubes coming out of my arms. Nobody would tell me what they'd done to Mom, and I was terrified I'd never see her again."

My heart aches so much for her I can't even form the right words. Guilt squeezes my chest for making her dredge up something so painful just to distract her from asking about Capello.

Pulling her onto my lap, I hold her close as she cries. "How long until you were reunited with your mother?"

She shudders. "A month. I had to stay in a foster home with a woman who locked me in a closet when I cried. Then she'd get mad at me if I peed myself. At least Mom gave me free rein of an entire apartment. When CPS finally reunited us, Mom moved us to a new town."

"I'm so sorry, baby," I whisper into her hair. "You're safe now. You never need to be afraid again."

She clings to my neck, her body trembling with sobs. I stroke her hair, trying to soothe her pain.

"Tell me what you need," I murmur. "Counseling? Therapy? I'll do whatever it takes to help you heal."

Eventually, her breathing evens out and she looks up at me with red-rimmed eyes.

"You've already done so much," she rasps. "I don't know how I could have survived these past weeks without you."

Guilt grabs my throat, urging me to say something to ease her burden. I should tell her Jim Callahan is dead, but I can't risk setting her free.

The waiter enters with the next course, but I raise a hand. "We'll finish the meal in our suite. Tell the host to check us in."

Moments later, one of the casino's longest-serving officiants, Reverend Johnson, walks in wearing the uniform of a host. Sweat glistens on his forehead, and he fidgets with his collar.

"Good evening, sir and miss," he says, his words stilted. "I understand you wish to retire to your suite?"

I don't know what the consequences are of marrying a woman without her knowledge or consent, but the good reverend stands to have his gambling debts forgiven if he can pull off this wedding ceremony.

The last shreds of my morality pound at my heart. My

conscience screams a warning not to take advantage of Emberly's vulnerable moment to trick her into signing a marriage certificate. It wants me to think of the consequences, and the chances of earning her unending hatred.

But if I listened to my conscience, I would never have joined the fucking mafia. In fact, I would have made sure every member of my family and loyal friends was behind bars for crimes against the good people of New Alderney. Nobody ever got what they wanted out of life by playing nice, and I won't let Emberly slip away from my fingers.

Determined to tie her to me forever, I brush that fucker aside. My obsession with Emberly has reached the point where the thought of her leaving tears a cavity in my chest.

I can't let her go.

Not now.

Not ever.

"Mr. Montesano," the reverend says, his voice unsteady. "Your suite at the Hotel Montesano is ready. All we need is your signature on the check in forms and we'll escort you upstairs."

He slides a clipboard on the table, with the details of the marriage certificate covered by hotel documentation.

Cupping Emberly's cheeks, I gaze into her shimmering eyes. "You're mine, Emberly Kay," I say. "And I'll take care of you until my dying breath. Do you understand me?"

She sniffles. "I do."

"And I'm yours." I place a soft kiss on her lips. "What did I just say?"

"Mine," she says with a smile.

"That's right, baby. Forever."

Reverend Johnson clears his throat. "If you could just sign here, I will complete your check in."

I sign the form and hand Emberly the pen. "Right here, baby."

"But I'm still paying for tonight's date," she says.

"Anything you say."

Holding my breath, I send out a prayer to every saint, sinner, and supernatural being that she's too distracted to pull out the sheet of paper and realize she's about to sign a marriage certificate.

I place a kiss on her cheek. "Come on, let's go upstairs so I can eat you in the suite."

She signs her name with a flourish, and both the officiant and I exhale relieved breaths.

Reverend Johnson snatches up the certificate. "Congratulations and welcome to the Hotel Montesano's honeymoon suite. I hereby declare you checked in."

Emberly wipes at her eyes, too absorbed to notice that the officiant just pronounced us man and wife.

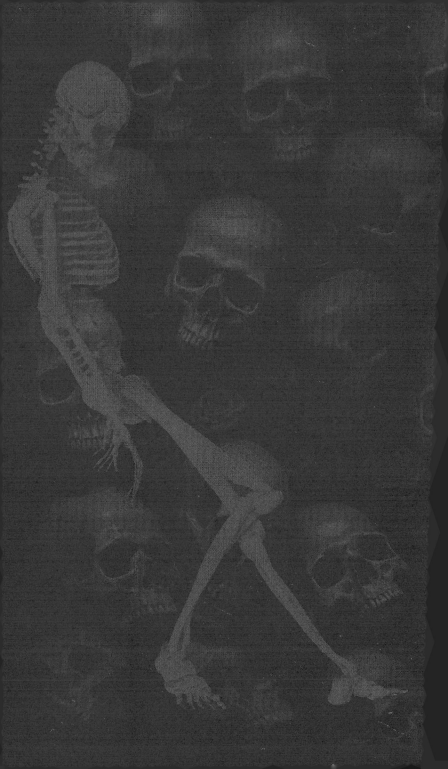

FIFTY-THREE

EMBERLY

I rise off the seat and stumble toward the door. Roman catches me by the waist with his strong arm and pulls me into his chest.

"Are you okay, baby?" he asks, his deep voice laced with concern.

"I-I don't know."

Maybe it's the excitement, maybe it's the wine or maybe it's all that uneven sleep, but I feel so giddy. Tonight, I've experienced more emotions than I have in an entire week.

I've never opened up to anyone about the reason I don't like to feel confined, but Roman made me feel safe enough to confide to him about Mom.

He doesn't just know the right things to say, but backs them up with actions, even if it means filling a man with bullets. Roman is the protector I never thought I needed.

As we reach the door, Roman scoops me off my feet, making my stomach lurch. I shriek, but he only chuckles, carrying me bridal style through the exit and all the way towards the elevator.

"Put me down." I wrap an arm around his neck and bury my face in his shoulder.

"What's wrong?" he murmurs. "You suddenly feeling shy? I want the whole fucking world to know that you're mine."

My heart flutters, and heat spreads across my chest and travels between my legs. Once again, he's claimed me as his. I peek up at him through my lashes and meet his searing gaze.

"I'm not shy," I say with a giggle.

Roman raises a brow. "Then what are you?"

My breath shallows, and I look straight into his eyes. Roman's full lips curl into a dazzling smile as though he's just won an argument or made some kind of point. When he looks at me like that, I'm weak. Completely under his spell.

I inhale a deep breath, eager to match his intensity. "I'm yours."

Roman captures my mouth in a kiss so searing that I almost forget we're walking through a hallway made of glass. Even the hotel manager following us fades into the background as Roman's tongue twists around mine and he threads his fingers through my hair.

"I love you, you know that?" he says.

"Mmmmm."

"And I will never let you go."

We reach the end of the hallway. When the elevator dings, Roman carries me inside. I cling onto his broad shoulders, letting him devour me with his kisses.

The doors slide open, and the man accompanying us guides Roman down a set of hallways, through another door, and up another elevator. Roman continues kissing me until I'm only vaguely aware that we're no longer in the casino.

"Where are you taking me?" I whisper against his lips.

"Welcome to the Hotel Marisol," Roman replies with a smirk. "We're about to step into its best suite."

The hotel manager slides the keycard into a lock, letting the door click open. Roman carries me inside and finally sets me on my feet.

The first thing I see are floor-to-ceiling windows over-looking the bright lights of Beaumont City. My breath catches, and I reel back on my feet.

"This is—"

"Beautiful?" Roman asks.

I whirl around in his arms and gaze up into his hungry, dark eyes and all the words die in my throat.

Roman lowers his head, his lips hovering so close to mine that I smell the wine on his breath. "There's nothing in this world I want more than you," he says, his voice low. "I would lie for you, steal for you, kill for you. I'll do whatever it takes to keep you at my side."

The pulse between my legs quickens at his words, and heat rushes into my core. How can the most perfect man I've ever met be so terrifying and thrilling?

"Well, you're mine, too." I grab his lapels and yank him down to meet my lips.

With a growl, Roman deepens the kiss. I hook my arms around his neck and hold him close. Tonight feels like a new beginning for us because Roman accepts me with all my flaws.

I'm the girl who never knew her father, the burden who set Mom's possessions on fire, the fuckup who allowed herself to get abused by a sociopath, and the woman who can't stay a minute in a locked room without regressing into a panicked child.

He doesn't judge me for my weaknesses. He doesn't see me as a fuckup or even a burden. He sees beyond all that and into my soul.

When we break the kiss, the thick curtains cover the tall windows, giving me a chance to appreciate the room. A huge king-sized bed takes up its center with a headboard made of silver bars. All the furniture is either pewter or mirrored and upholstered in silver.

My gaze rises to the mirrored ceiling, and my breath hitches. I remember how Roman wanted to experiment with bondage earlier, and how I ruined what could have been something special.

Sliding my hands down his broad back, I place both hands on his ass and squeeze.

Roman groans. "You're so fucking sexy when you take control. Do you see something you want?"

"Yeah," I murmur. "I want you to tie me up."

He pulls away, his eyes darkening. "Why?"

"I want to see if I can do it."

"You sure about that, baby?"

I give him an eager nod. "I trust you. Just stay with me the whole time, okay?"

He nods back, his features turning serious. "I won't leave you alone for a second."

"Alright."

Roman takes my hand, pulls me toward a silver sofa, and guides me down to sit. "Stay here for a moment while I get everything ready."

Anticipation skitters across my skin as I watch Roman move across the room to a chest of drawers and pull out a black box.

"What's that?" I ask.

"Every suite charging over ten grand a night comes with its own box of toys."

He sets it down on the low table and breaks open its seal to reveal two sets of leather cuffs, black ropes, a blind-fold, a vibrator, a butt plug, and a pack of textured condoms. Each item is shrink-wrapped in its own sterile package.

My eyes widen. "It's brand new."

He chuckles. "Anyone who opens the room's toy box gets charged for the entire contents, so they're all yours. What do you want to try?"

"Everything except the blindfold," I reply.

"You want to watch?"

I nod, my breath quickening.

Roman's features harden. "Then stand up."

"What?" My stomach flips.

"You want me to tie you up, then be a good girl and take off that dress."

My heart skips a beat. "A-Alright."

"It's 'yes, sir,'" he growls.

"Y-Yes, sir!"

"Good girl." His gaze sweeps down my dress. "Now, stand up and take off your clothes."

I get up, my thighs trembling, the pulse between my legs beating so hard that its vibrations hit my core. Roman stares at me as I unzip the back of my dress and let it slip down my body.

Pulling back my shoulders, I stand before him, wearing nothing but a pair of heels and a lacy thong. The air conditioning sends shivers across my skin, making my nipples tighten.

Roman's heavy gaze skims every inch of exposed skin.

"Untie your hair," he says, his voice thick with desire.

"Yes, sir." I take the pins out of my chignon, letting my curls fall around my shoulders.

Roman's nostrils flare, and the bulge in his pants forms a tent. "Beautiful." His gaze drops to my nipples. "Now, crawl to the bed."

My breath shallows, and I sink to my hands and knees.

Roman picks up the box and steps back to watch me crawl across the marble floor toward the bed. Heat flushes across my skin as my breasts and hips sway with each movement.

When I reach the bed, I sit back on my heels.

Roman reaches out and runs a finger down my cheek. "You look so perfect on your knees. So sexy."

My cheeks heat, and he smirks. "What do you say?"

"Thank you, sir," I murmur.

"Are you ready to be tied up and used?"

I swallow hard. "Yes, sir."

Roman pulls out the cuffs and smiles. "You're going to earn that privilege."

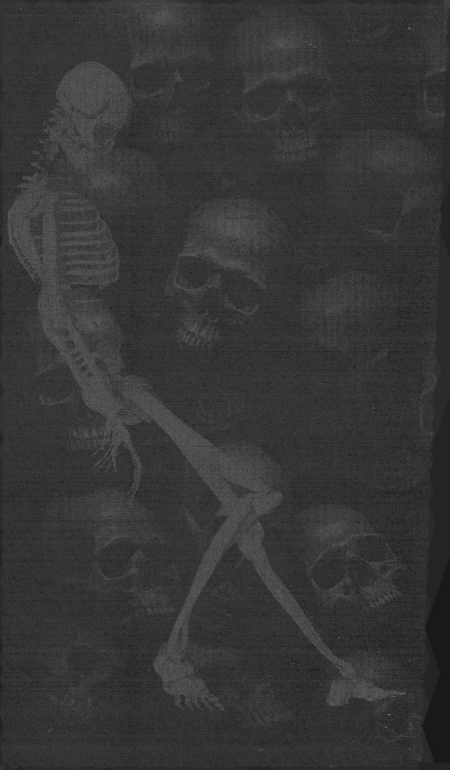

FIFTY-FOUR

ROMAN

All I want from Emberly now is her. Her body, her mind, her soul, and her tight little holes. She kneels before me, her body trembling, her eyes shining with desire. She trusts me so much that she's willing to let me tie her to the bed and use her however I please.

The sight of her submission sends a rush of desire that overpowers my guilt, and my cock aches to be released.

"Give me your hands."

Emberly raises both arms, and I secure the first cuff around her wrist. She watches as I thread the leather strap through the steel loops, making sure it's tight before buckling it in place.

When I'm done, I fasten the second cuff and walk behind her and clip together the metal rings, so her bound wrists are resting on her ass.

She pulls back her shoulders, her chest arching forward, and her nipples pebbling in invitation. My cock throbs so hard I'm forced to release it from the confines of my pants.

Emberly's pupils dilate, and a blush spreads across her

cheeks. She parts her lips, her pink tongue darting out for a taste.

"You have no idea how sexy you look right now," I rasp.

She pants hard, her chest rising and falling with rapid breaths. The part of me that's always longed to see her on her knees, with my cock down her throat, takes over my good sense and rears to the front.

I grab my shaft at the base and slide my tip over her lips. "Lick."

Emberly swipes the tip of her tongue over my head and laps up the bead of precum. Her touch sends a shiver down my spine.

"Good girl," I groan. "Now, open."

She obeys, and I push my way inside her warm, wet mouth. She sucks me deep, her tongue swirling around my shaft as if it's the next course on a taster menu.

A curtain of dark curls falls over her face, and I grab a handful of it so our gazes can meet.

"Eyes on me," I growl.

She sucks me harder, causing a surge of liquid ecstasy that makes my knees buckle. I thrust my hips back and forth, driving into her hot mouth.

"That's it, baby. Take it all."

Emberly's mouth relaxes, letting me slide all the way to the back of her throat. The muscles tighten around my cock head, and I let out a guttural groan.

Her eyes water, and tears spill down her cheeks. She's completely at my mercy, and it's the most incredible feeling in the world.

When my balls draw up and I'm on the brink of coming, I pull out of her mouth.

Emberly gasps, her eyes glazed with lust, and she licks her lips.

"Stand up," I growl.

She scrambles to her feet, her chest rising and falling with rapid breaths. Her cheeks are flushed, her lipstick is smeared, and her curls are a wild mess.

She's never looked so beautiful.

I turn her around and unclip the metal rings. "Take off your panties. Keep the shoes."

She dips her fingers beneath the lace, slides her panties down her hips, and lets the fabric fall to her feet.

My gaze drops down her gentle curves. She's so fucking perfect, and she's all mine.

"Get on the bed, lie on your back, and spread your legs."

She obeys, her eyes never leaving mine. I kneel between her thighs and drink in the sight of her glistening pussy.

"Are you wet for me?" I ask.

"Yes, sir," she whispers, her breathing ragged.

"Want me to lick that sweet cunt?"

She arches her back. "Please."

"Then hold on to the headboard, sweetheart, and don't let go."

As she curls her fingers around the metal bars, I pull out one of the ropes from the box and secure the cuffs to the headboard. This way, freeing Emberly will be as simple as loosening a buckle.

"I'm so proud of you, baby."

I move down the other end of the bed, bind each ankle with the second pair of leather cuffs, and attach them to the metal footboard with ropes.

She looks utterly helpless now, and my cock aches at the sight of her at my mercy.

"Good girl," I say again, stroking her cheek. "You're doing so well."

She smiles, her face flushing as I plant kisses along her neck and shoulders. Each time my lips brush against her skin, she shivers.

"More," she moans. "Please."

My kisses travel lower, exploring every inch of the smooth skin over her breasts, her ribs and down to her pussy.

After several minutes, Emberly's breathing grows ragged. She writhes against the mattress, her hips rising to meet my mouth.

"Pretty girl," I murmur as my lips slide down to her pussy. "You look so delicious."

As I flick my tongue over her swollen clit, her thighs try to pull together, but her ankles are spread so wide that she can't trap my head.

I continue to lick and suck until she's trembling and panting. When my ears fill with her cries, I pull back and blow a cool stream of air over her clit.

"Don't stop," she says, her voice hoarse.

"Lift your hips for me, baby," I growl.

When she does, I gather the moisture from her pussy and spread it over her tight little pucker, making her moan.

"You like that, sweetheart?" I ask.

"Oh, fuck." Her ass cheeks tense. "Roman, I've never—"

"Relax, baby. I'll take care of you."

And I mean every word. Emberly is my wife, and I take care of what's mine.

I reach for the box of toys, unscrew a tube of lube with my teeth, and squeeze a generous amount on my finger. To help loosen Emberly up, I rub circles over her asshole and synchronize the movements with slow licks over her clit. After a few moments, her muscles relax, as does her breathing.

"Ready?" I position my fingertip at her entrance.

"Yes," she moans and pushes up her hips to meet the digit.

I slide my finger into her tight little ass and let her get

used to the sensation before pulling out. Her walls clench around my digit as though desperate to keep it inside.

"How is that?" I ask, while still applying a little pressure to her clit.

"Feels nice," she says through panting breaths.

"Good girl," I mumble around her swollen bud. "Take my finger like a good little wife, and I'll give you one more."

She's panting so hard that she either misses what I said or is too steeped in pleasure to understand the significance. I slide in a second finger and lick her clit until she's rocking back and forth, desperate for more.

I add a third lubed finger and hold my digit still, letting her fuck my hand with her ass. Every instinct in my body screams at me to claim that virgin ass, but I can't take what I want until she's nice and loose.

"Come for me, baby," I murmur from between her legs.

Her back arches, and she cries out, her body quivering and jerking within the restraints. Her asshole squeezes and clenches around my fingers, and my cock pulses in response.

I want to bury myself to the hilt while she shatters, but I hold off that urge until her ass is fully stretched and ready to take my girth.

"Fuck, Emberly. I love you so much."

"Kiss me," she murmurs.

I pull out my fingers, wipe them clean, and extract the butt plug. After covering the rubber object with lube, I position it against her ass.

"Are you going to be a good girl for me and take this?" I murmur against her mouth.

"Yes, sir." She captures my lips.

I press the plug into her ass, making her moan around the kiss. Its widest part is thicker than my cock, so I take my time pushing it all the way in. Emberly arches and gasps beneath me, whimpering into my mouth as I stretch her tight little anus with the rubber toy.

"What's that, baby?" I ask.

"So big," she says, her voice guttural.

"Be a good girl and take it."

I reach into the box and pull out a silicone object shaped like a rose. From the opening within the bud, I can only assume it goes over the clit. After turning it on and making it vibrate, I press it against her sensitive nub.

Emberly gasps, her eyes widening, her back curving off the mattress. She writhes and moans within her restraints, breathing so hard and fast that my cock aches to add to her pleasure.

"P-Please, take off your clothes," she says. "I need you."

"You're so perfect," I moan. "Is that all you want from me?"

"Fill me up," she cries.

"Anything you want." I pull away from the kiss, my gaze never leaving hers, and ease off my clothes.

Emberly pushes against her restraints as though she wants to strip me naked with her teeth. With a chuckle, I climb onto the bed and kneel between her spread legs.

"How much do you want this cock?" I slide on a condom.

"More than anything," she replies, her voice hoarse with need.

I raise my chin. "Tell me."

"Please." She squeezes her eyes shut. "Fill me up. Make me yours."

A groan fills my chest. How the fuck can I refuse such a request?

I position myself between her legs and slide into her slick heat, inch by inch, feeling every ridge and contour of her tight cunt, made tighter by the plug in her ass.

She squeezes, clenches, and wraps around my shaft, her breaths coming in shallow gasps. Sensations overwhelm my senses, and my eyes roll to the back of my head.

"I'm home," I rasp. "This pussy is where I belong."

"Roman," she cries. "You really mean that?"

"Every goddamn syllable," I growl. "You're mine, Emberly, and I'm never letting you go."

I push into her until I'm fully embedded. She's hot and tight and wet. My perfect match. I thrust slowly at first, building up a steady rhythm, taking her higher and higher until she groans.

"Oh, Roman," she cries.

"That's right, sweetheart. I'm the only one you'll ever worship."

The pressure builds, and I move faster, harder, until I'm pounding into her with abandon. She cries out with each thrust, her body melding against mine.

My heart races as her tight muscles clamp down around my shaft, squeezing and milking until I'm sure I'm going to explode.

"Oh, god," she screams, her body trembling. "I'm going to come!"

Her pussy ripples around me, and I feel my own pleasure cresting. I can't hold back much longer.

"Yes, baby," I whisper, pushing deeper and deeper. "Let it all out."

My orgasm tears through me until my mind blanks and I collapse onto her body. We lie together, panting and trembling, until I can finally move.

"I love you so much, baby," I murmur into her ear. "As soon as I get hard again, I'm going to claim every hole, including your sweet ass."

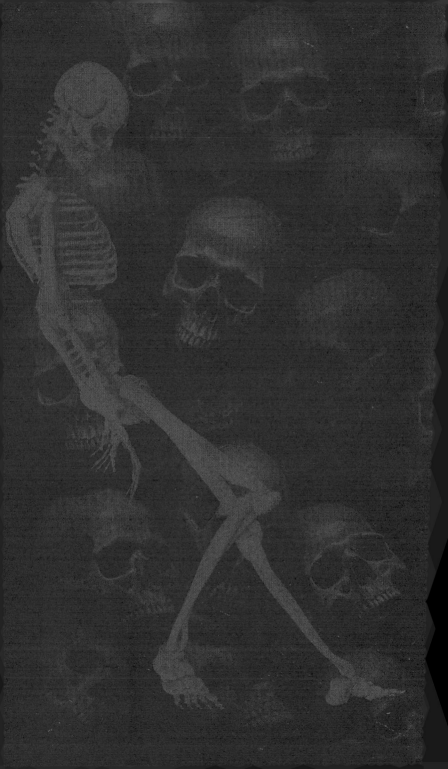

FIFTY-FIVE

EMBERLY

I slump back against the mattress, my heart beating in unison with Roman's, and our breaths mingling. Tonight is one of many firsts: the first time I've ever felt so close to a lover, the first time I've felt so accepted, and the first time I've ever submitted so completely to a man.

The bond between us is so natural that all previous sexual experiences now feel like obstacles I had to navigate to find my way to Roman. He's my perfect match.

Something about the way he made love to me was different. More tender. More loving. More connected. It's so hard to explain, but it felt like being owned and even claimed. Maybe it's just me projecting, but I got the impression that he wanted to convey the depth of his emotions with every thrust.

My pussy twitches around his softening cock as though never wanting him to withdraw. This is exactly where he belongs.

"I love you, too," I murmur as my eyelids flutter closed.

Roman says something else, but I feel so relaxed that his

words fade into a gentle hum. I'm so deeply steeped in bliss that nothing else seems to matter.

Somewhere on the edge of my awareness, Roman's larger body drifts inches away from mine. The pressure eases off my wrists and then off my ankles, and he rearranges our bodies, so I'm cradled in his arms with my head resting on his chest.

His lips touch my brow, and his arms wrap around my waist like a protective shield. Roman's breathing slows, and I fall asleep to the steady rhythm of his heart.

———

Hours later, soft kisses pull me out of slumber. Roman's hands roam down my waist and rub circles over the curve of my ass.

Sensation skitters across my skin, awakening my senses, leaving me tingling with anticipation. Shifting, I brush my thigh against his hard cock.

"Good morning, baby," he murmurs into my ear.

"I had the craziest dream last night," I say.

His deep chuckle rumbles from beneath. "Tell me about it."

I giggle. "You and I went to a casino in Las Vegas—"

"New Alderney."

I give him a playful swat. "Are you telling this story, or am I?"

"Sorry, baby."

"We had dinner and met Elvis."

He snorts.

"Of course, it wasn't the real Elvis, but an impersonator."

"Did he sing Jailhouse Rock?"

"Okay, you're pissing me off," I say with a laugh.

"Please continue."

"Elvis took us to a little chapel, and you sang some wedding vows. I was your backup singer. At the end, he told us to kiss, and we were married." I wait for Roman to laugh or make a sarcastic comment, but he falls silent.

"Roman?"

"Would you marry me?" he blurts, his heart beating fast.

I release a shocked laugh, but he remains quiet.

Silence stretches out for several heartbeats more than I can bear. I crack open an eye to meet his gaze.

At this time of the morning, tiny slivers of sunlight stream in through the curtains, casting a golden sheen across the contours of Roman's face. My stomach flips at the intensity in his dark eyes. I've never seen him look so serious.

"Hey, I wasn't trying to hint anything. It was just a funny dream, and—"

"But would you?" he asks, his voice rough.

My brows pull together. It's on the tip of my tongue to say yes, but bitter experience has taught me not to get carried away by the first flush of love. No matter how perfect Roman might be for me, we need to take this slow.

"Why are you bringing up something as serious as marriage?" I ask. "We've barely known each other for a month."

He flashes me a smile that feels more like a grimace. "The question was hypothetical."

I flop down on the mattress and close my eyes. Of course. It was probably just a slip of the tongue, like the first time I declared my love. Roman just got caught up in his emotions. It's no big deal.

Keeping my voice measured, I say, "That's the sort of hypothetical question I'd like to consider in about a year's time."

"You're right," he says, his voice softening. "I got carried away."

He slides his fingers between my ass cheeks, which tighten around something thick and rubbery. All thoughts of dreams and marriages and hypothetical proposals vanish.

My eyes snap open. "Why do I still have a huge toy in my ass?"

He smiles, flashing perfect white teeth. "I wanted to make it easy when I claim your virgin hole."

Heat blooms across my cheeks, and warmth spreads down my chest and settles between my legs. Any awkwardness between us is gone, replaced by our usual playfulness.

"Excuse me?"

Roman holds me by the waist and squeezes my ass, making me squirm in his grip. "You're going to let me stick my cock in your tight little ass."

I reach between our bodies and wrap my fingers around his shaft. "But you're too big."

Roman groans. "If you can take the plug, you can take my cock."

Electricity skitters down my spine, lighting up every nerve ending before reaching my clit. Roman tilts up my head and peppers soft kisses on my neck. This is what I adore about our relationship. He doesn't just push my limits. He makes everything so tantalizing and erotic that I'm left breathless.

"Last night, you fucked my fingers while still begging for more," he growls against my skin. "Now, that greedy ass of yours is ready for my cock."

My pussy clenches, as do the muscles of my anus. I bite my lip, trying to slow down my breath. Roman's fingers slide between my legs and rub my clit until it aches.

Squeezing his cock, I rub the pad of my thumb over his

slit that elicits a moan deep and rumbly enough to reach the marrow of my bones.

"Alright," I whisper, "But if it hurts—"

"Then you'll tell me to stop," he says.

"Fine."

Roman rolls me off his chest, so I'm lying face-down on the mattress. I turn my head toward his side of the bed and watch him reach for the black box.

"What are you doing?" I ask.

"Lubing myself up." He pulls out a tube.

"Don't forget the condom."

Roman hesitates for a second before reaching back into the box and pulling out a foil wrapper. As he rips it open, I hold out my hand.

"Let me do it."

He hands me the condom, and I roll it down his thick, hard cock. Roman squeezes lube over the rubber sheath, letting me spread it over his shaft. The skin beneath my fingers is warm, and his veins pulse at my touch.

I swallow back a moan. Everything about this man is exquisite, and being in bed with him is dreamlike.

His dark hair is tousled, and his skin glows in the morning light. When he stares down at me through those thick lashes like I'm the only woman in the world, there's a part of me that can't believe he's mine.

"All done." My gaze slides down his muscular chest and tight abs, before settling on his impossibly large erection.

Roman eases me back down onto the mattress, so my weight rests on my knees and elbows. His chest hovers so closely over my back that I swear I can feel the beat of his heart.

One of his hands reaches beneath my belly, where he flicks my clit. Sparks of pleasure ignite in my core, and I arch up into his touch.

"Relax, baby," he says, his slippery cock brushing against my inner thigh. "I promise this will feel good."

My ass cheeks clench around the butt plug, and I whimper. He pulls at the rubber toy, sliding it out inch by inch. It's shaped like a diamond with a middle point that stretches my hole, but Roman's fingers on my clit only intensifies the pleasure.

When he finally extracts it with a soft pop, I'm left feeling empty, hungry, and desperate.

"Roman," I whisper, my hips rocking against his hand. "Please."

"You look so beautiful beneath me with your legs spread wide, begging me to fuck your gaping hole."

My skin flushes with heat. He's so wonderfully filthy.

"Tell me how much you need it, baby," he growls, his hand sliding down my spine.

Moaning, I arch my back. I'm so overwhelmed with need for this man that I can't form a full sentence. My voice breaks. "Just fuck me."

He lines his cock at my asshole and presses forward, its thick crown stretching me open. A pulse flutters at my entrance, it's muffled as he slides into my back passage, inch by incredible inch.

The stretch as he fills me so intimately makes my eyes water. My breath comes in shallow pants at the depth of our connection, and my limbs tremble at the intensity of his invasion. I shove my head into the mattress and moan.

"Oh, fuck," I groan. "Don't stop."

"Never," he growls between clenched teeth as he enters me so intensely.

Roman's chest lies flush against my back, his heart beating hard enough for us both. He groans so deep and low that every nerve in my body vibrates. Love radiates from him in waves, submerging me in security and warmth. His arms wrap around my waist and holds me close as he continues to thrust. I cling onto him like he's the only thing keeping me afloat.

Once he's fully sheathed, he gropes around in the toy box and pulls out another device. I'm so immobilized by the unfamiliar sensation of his cock in my ass that I can't even raise my head to pay attention.

"What are you doing?" I whisper, my voice trembling with anticipation.

"You're taking my cock better than I thought." He tears open the plastic wrap and makes something buzz. "Now, you're going to take two."

Roman pulls back and positions the vibrator at the entrance of my pussy. I'm so relaxed and wet that it slides inside with ease.

Vibrations spread through my core, making my clit swell to what feels like twice its usual size. Roman rocks into my ass with long, smooth strokes, all the while holding the toy in my pussy.

Electricity infuses my veins, and every nerve brightens like lights on a Christmas tree. I can't believe he's convinced me to take both his cock and a vibrator. I can't believe it feels so good.

As the vibration spread through my core, I almost regret turning down his proposal. Roman is everything. I can't remember ever being so complete. No man in my entire existence has ever made me feel so pleasured, so wanted, so loved.

"Oh, god," I moan.

He laughs, the sound harsh. "God can't save you now, baby, but I still want you crying out for mercy."

Roman increases the speed of his thrusts, fucking me deeper, harder, and with so much raw power that my body jerks forward.

"Fuck," he groans, his hot breath tickles the back of my neck. "You were made for this. Made for me. Made for my cock."

"Aaah yes!"

"Say it," he growls, punctuating each word with a thrust. "Tell. Me. How. Much. You. Love. This. Cock."

Sweat pours down my brow and into my eyes. I squeeze them shut and gasp. I'm panting, shaking, my pussy quivering around the toy and every molecule in my body thrumming with rapture.

"Say it, or I'll stop," he snarls.

"I love your cock," I cry. "I love it, I love it. Don't stop!"

With a satisfied grunt, he quickens his pace, pushing us both closer to the edge. The only thing stopping me from crashing into the headboard are my elbows sinking into the mattress and the arm around my hips still holding the vibrator in my pussy.

Every inch of my body feels like a raw nerve. When Roman's teeth sink into my shoulder and he positions the toy on my G-spot, I implode.

Pleasure spirals through my system, and my eyes roll to the back of my head. My muscles tense and jerk around the vibrator and his thick cock, sending me into a frenzied state of euphoria.

"Roman." I scream, and he roars in response.

His arms tighten around my middle as his body shudders with the force of his orgasm, and we both collapse into a tangle of limbs. Lying together, we catch our breaths, our hearts slowing in sync.

I'm consumed by the intensity of our connection. It's euphoric, electric and entirely exquisite. Roman cups my face and gazes at me with such adoration that it steals my breath. I swear it's like he's looking into my soul and not only liking what he's seeing, but claiming it as his most treasured possession.

"That was... Wow," I whisper.

"Yeah, baby," he murmurs. "I know."

Several moments pass, filled by the sound of our breathing. We luxuriate in the warmth of each other's bodies, and it feels like floating on clouds of bliss.

Roman pulls out the vibrator and tosses it aside. At some point during our vigorous lovemaking, it either got turned off or broke. I let that thought drift away and focus on the moment.

Someone is pounding on the door with such force that it seems like they've been trying to get our attention for a long time.

Roman groans. "Only one person would have the balls to interrupt me at a moment like this."

"One of your brothers?" I ask.

"Benito."

"How can you tell?"

"He runs the casino and its hotels," Roman mutters. In a much louder voice, he yells, "What?"

"It's urgent," Benito replies.

Roman kisses me on the cheek. "Go to the bathroom and fill the tub."

He grips the base of his cock and pulls out before rolling to the other side of the mattress.

As I scramble off the bed and walk to the bathroom, I pause at the door to glance at Roman pulling on his pants.

Benito continues knocking, making Roman bellow, "I'm coming."

The bathroom looks like a luxurious spa, with a huge television above a soaking tub large enough to accommodate six. After turning on the taps, I pick up the remote and point it at the screen. A news reporter stands outside a church among a crowd and other members of the press.

A female voice says, "Although Detective Jim Callahan's body was found in the building where two of his colleagues took their own lives, investigators insist there was no foul play."

The camera switches to eight uniformed officers walking into the church carrying a coffin draped in the American flag.

"What?" I whisper.

Jim's official picture appears on screen with his date of birth and an approximate date of death.

"This is Brenda Davis, from News 4, reporting live from St. Clement's church," says the reporter.

My jaw drops.

Jim is dead.

And his funeral is happening right now.

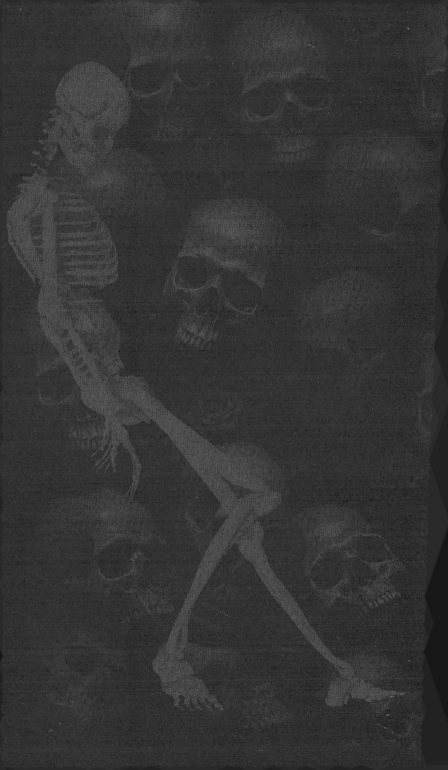

FIFTY-SIX

ROMAN

I slip out of the suite to find Cesare and Benito waiting in the hallway. Benito wears an elegant suit, while Cesare wears bulletproof armor with a couple of guns strapped to his belt. Tony, Gil, and a few others stand behind them, their expressions somber.

"What's happened?" I ask.

Cesare pushes forward. "Those Moirai bastards finally agreed to a time and place."

My gaze snaps to meet Benito's. "What do they want?"

"The hostages in exchange for calling off all three hits," Cesare answers with a touch of pride.

I turn my attention to my baby brother, wondering why the hell Benito allowed him to negotiate with the Moirai. Cesare squares his shoulders as though expecting a reprimand, but I don't have the heart. If he's finally stepping up, then who am I to discourage him?

I clap him on the shoulder. "Great job."

Cesare grins. "Drop off point is across town, and we need to get there within the hour. You coming?"

I hesitate. After the shit Cesare and I pulled last time with the Moirai group, we could be walking into an ambush. I can't leave Emberly waiting for me all day in a hotel room, and there isn't enough time for me to take her back to Alderney Hill.

My gaze flicks to Tony and Gil. "Hang back, you two, and take Miss Kay back home."

"Sure thing, Boss." Gil pushes his way forward and hands me a duffle bag. "Brought you something to wear."

"Thanks." I place my hand on the doorknob. "I'll be ready in ten."

Cesare heads toward the elevator, and I'm about to step back into the room when Benito grabs my arm.

"Can I talk to you in private?" he asks, his voice low.

I walk to the other end of the hallway, my brow furrowed. "What is it?"

"Did you get married last night?" Benito whispers.

My gaze darts over my shoulder, where Cesare and his entourage stand by the elevator, leaving Tony and Gil by the door, deep in conversation.

"Why do you ask?" I whisper back.

"Reverend Johnson asked me to witness your marriage certificate, saying you've written off all his debts."

"That's right."

Benito's jaw tightens, and his eyes narrow into slits. "And that's why you took my best suite without clearing it with me first?"

My eyes widen, and I study my brother's disgruntled features. I wouldn't have thought interfering with casino business would piss him off more than the fact that I married Capello's daughter, but this is unexpected.

"You're griping about a hotel room?" I ask with an incredulous laugh.

"It's reserved," he replies with a sniff.

"For who?"

"Doesn't matter. My guest is waiting for the suite, and you need to vacate it by checkout today."

"The special guest you didn't invite to the family dinner?" I ask, remembering how he stared into his phone the entire time we were supposed to be eating.

Benito inhales a deep breath and rubs the back of his neck. He shuffles on his feet, refusing to meet my gaze. "Roman, please."

"Fine." I shake my head. "But you're going to tell me all about her later."

"So, you married her?" Benito raises his brows, looking like he's trying to deflect. I get the message loud and clear. Don't ask about his mystery woman and he won't poke around my relationship with Emberly.

I shrug. "It's a preemptive measure. If anything happens with the contracts, then I can tell the judge she was my lawfully wedded wife."

"But you love her," Benito says, leaving the rest of the sentence hanging.

I was supposed to romance her out of the stolen assets and put her six feet under. Now, I've made her my wife and we're celebrating the union in our hotel's honeymoon suite. The answer to that question should be obvious.

"Do you want me to vacate the room or what?" I brush past him, toward where Gil and Tony are waiting by the door.

If Benito is as defensive about this mystery woman as I am about Emberly, then she'll probably be someone we'll despise. I shake off that thought. No one can be a worse choice than Cesare's little assassin.

Thirty minutes later, after kissing Emberly goodbye, I'm sitting within a convoy of armored trucks heading toward an underground parking lot outside Beaumont City.

By now, Emberly should have reached Alderney Hill, but when I check the surveillance app, she isn't in my bedroom or the pool house. I fire up a second app that tracks the location of her phone to find it moving through the winding roads that lead up to the mansion.

I pull at the collar of my bullet-proof jacket. Maybe there was heavy traffic, or she stopped to make a detour.

She even could have stayed a few minutes extra to finish watching TV. By the time I found her in the bathroom, she was too absorbed in the weather report to get upset that I was cutting our romantic morning short.

I'll make it up to her tonight.

"We're close," Cesare mutters, his voice tense.

My gaze snaps to the window, where our vehicle passes through the parking lot's ground-floor entrance. The building is covered in graffiti, and its windows are boarded, yet the security machines are still in working order.

I lean into Cesare and whisper, "You sure this is their headquarters?"

He nods, his features tense.

I'm not a control freak, but this is the first time my little brother has taken the lead in organizing anything so vital.

"Helmets on," he mutters.

Our vehicles stop twenty feet away from the entrance, and shutters roll down from the boarded-up windows.

After putting on my helmet and checking my armor for any weak spots, I check my brother's, then he checks mine. When we're sure we're both ready, I nod.

"Let's do this," he says and opens the back door.

The last set of hostages sits in the back of the second truck. Rosalind and the four we captured at the party sit in our smaller vehicle, their heads covered with hoods. They're each blindfolded, wearing earplugs, and cuffed at the wrists and ankles.

"Roman Montesano," a voice says from the loudspeaker. "Release the hostages."

I smirk.

Cesare pulls off one of their hoods, yanks off the blindfold, and gestures to him to get out. My brother explained already that he's primed this hostage to do our dirty work.

The young man stumbles out, hobbles to the second van and opens the door.

Four figures in black rush forward from the shadows to liberate five hostages from inside the vehicle, while the one we freed hobbles away with his comrades.

"That's six," the voice says over the loudspeaker. "Where are the other four?"

The man driving the other vehicle also steps out, making seven.

My heart pounds hard enough to break through my armor. This is the part where Cesare's plan becomes dicey because there's no way in hell the Moirai Group would renege on a contract Tommy Galliano placed on our heads.

We grab the three hostages nearest to the door and toss them out into the darkened parking lot. They each fall on their faces and struggle to get on their knees with their arms still cuffed behind their backs.

As I glance at the fourth, Cesare slams the door shut and places her on his lap. We buckle up just as bullets rain down on our vehicle.

Cesare pounds his fist on the divider, and our driver reverses at incredible speed. I pull out the remote and wait for the signal.

We burst out of the parking lot, through the metal shutters, and onto the open road, leaving behind the sound of chaos.

"Now," my brother roars.

I press down on the red button, triggering an explosion that shakes the ground, sending our vehicle swerving to the side as our driver wrestles for control.

"Shit," I say through clenched teeth. "What the hell kind of bomb was that?"

Cesare grins, his eyes dancing. "Just a little extra power from Dr. Cortese and her team. It meant slowing down this week's production of meth, but it was the only way to make sure the explosives reached their lower levels."

My gaze drops to the slender figure squirming in his arms. "And the last hostage?"

Cesare squeezes her breast, making her yell. "I've decided to keep her."

"Of course you have." I don't even bother to roll my eyes. "Just keep her out of trouble."

"Nick Terranova came by the house this morning," Cesare says.

"About what?"

"He dropped off some documents he wants you to sign to access the safety deposit boxes."

I nod.

The vehicle makes a sharp turn before shifting out of reverse.

"So, we have the casino, the loan company, the real estate, bank accounts, the stocks, and now the safety deposit boxes. Are you going to..." He takes his index and middle fingers to form the shape of a gun and then points them at the woman's temple.

I try not to bristle at the suggestion of killing Emberly. "No," I say, keeping my voice even. "I've decided to keep her."

With a nod, my little brother tears the hood off her head, revealing Rosalind's flushed face. She wraps her arms around his neck and kisses him like he's the last man on earth.

I pull out my phone and fire up the surveillance app, where Emberly sits behind her canvas.

It looks like all three of us brothers are in controversial relationships.

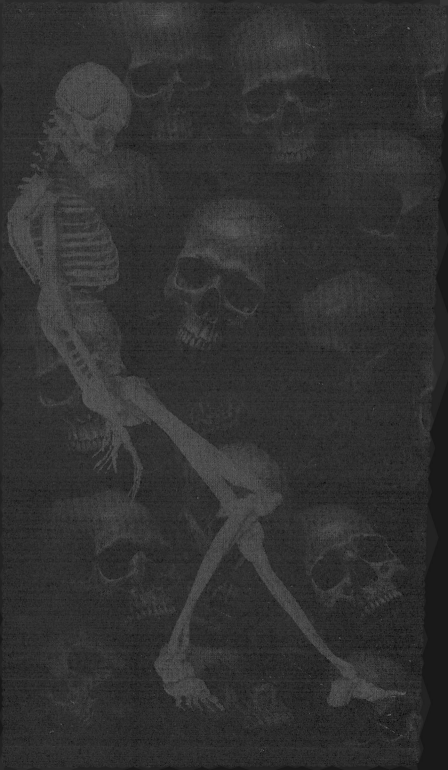

FIFTY-SEVEN

EMBERLY

I sit on the edge of the tub, staring at the TV screen long after Jim's official photo has disappeared and long after the two presenters at the studio speculate on whether his death is connected to the squad car suicides.

As Bill Mayhew reads out today's weather report, Roman slips into the bathroom and takes hold of my shoulders.

"Baby, something's come up," he murmurs into my ear.

"Huh?" According to Bill, it's a nice morning for an outdoor funeral.

"Tony and Gil are outside to take you back home." Roman kisses my temple. "I'll make it up to you tonight."

"Right," I murmur.

Whatever Roman says next fades into insignificance compared to the shock of discovering that Jim might have been dead for nearly two weeks. That all this time, I've been drowning in this unnecessary worry of being hunted.

My throat tightens.

What if the news report is part of an elaborate scam to lure me out of hiding?

I shake off that thought. It's far too paranoid.

But what if Jim concocted this fake death just to smoke me out? He isn't that powerful, is he? The more likely option is that Roman intercepted another of Jim's attempts to abduct me from his grounds and put an end to that threat.

My legs straighten, propelling me off the tub. "I've got to see this for myself."

Roman's cologne is only a memory in the room by the time I fling on the strapless red dress and matching heels. He would probably want me to keep far away from the police, but I'm too riled up to care about earning his disapproval. I step out into the hallway, making both Tony and Gil jolt out of their conversation.

"You ready, Miss?" Tony asks.

I run my fingers through my curls. "Yeah, but we're taking a detour."

Ten minutes later, we're pulling into the courtyard of St. Clement's Church, where most of the mourners are already leaving in an array of police vehicles. I sit up in the back seat, seeing no sign of a casket, and glare into the establishment's double doors.

"I'm going inside," I say.

Gil glances at me over his shoulder. "The boss won't like this."

"What does the boss know about this funeral?" I ask.

His jaw tightens, which is an answer in itself. The only thing I'm mad about is that Roman didn't tell me Jim was dead.

"You sure about going inside?" Tony asks.

"Yeah." I reach for the door handle and step out into the cool morning.

Adjusting my dress, I take a deep breath before walking

toward the church entrance. My spine straightens at the sound of two car doors opening and closing, and I pull back my shoulders.

With Tony and Gil at my back, I can face those bastards.

The two men flank me on both sides and push open another set of heavy wooden doors, allowing me to step inside the church.

By now, most of the pews are empty, save for some stragglers deep in conversation by the walls. Up ahead, two officers I recognize as Jim's colleagues stand in front of an open casket.

My heart skips several beats, but I force myself to approach them, the click-clack of my heels against the wooden floors making them turn around.

I lock gazes with Jim's boss, Stan Bradford, who stares at me with his mouth agape. He notices my two companions before allowing his gaze to flicker over my outfit.

This asshole once laughed like a donkey when Jim backhanded me for serving him coffee with only two sugars, so I don't give a shit about what he thinks of my dress.

"What are you doing here?" he hisses.

"I came to send my regards," I snap.

Bradford's oversized face turns purple. "Show some fucking respect—"

Tony and Gil lurch forward, but I grab both their arms. "We're not here to start a fight," I say. "Just let me see his face."

Two more officers join Bradford to square off with Tony and Gil. I walk around the testosterone-fest and approach the casket.

Jim lies inside, his features frozen in an expression of peace. I study his artificially smooth skin and the way his red hair has been carefully arranged to make him look respectable. Now he looks like a waxwork.

My hands curl into fists. I want to scrape off that veneer and expose the real Jim Callahan. The monster who broke me down until I was a shell.

"Enjoy hell, you worthless motherfucker." I ball up my saliva, ready to spit in his face.

"You've got a nerve, coming here dressed like a whore," a voice croaks from behind.

I turn around and lock gazes with a much older version of Jim. "Mr. Callahan?"

Jim's father is in his sixties, frail from getting shot while on duty. He exists on a liquid diet, the alcohol turning his skin into a network of broken capillaries.

His lip curls. "My son took you in and put a roof over your head and you left him the moment you struck it rich."

I flinch. "I left Jim because he was abusive."

He shakes his head. "That law firm came knocking with news of your inheritance and you bolted."

My brows pull together. "Have you been hitting the scotch again? What are you talking about?"

"Your father died, and the lawyer gave you millions, then you forgot all about my Jim," he says.

"You're drunk." I glance over my shoulder to where Tony and Gil are surrounded by officers.

My stomach drops. One of these bastards must have called for backup. I need to leave now before either of them gets hurt. As I turn around, Mr. Callahan grabs my arm with a surprisingly tight grip.

"You owe us for all the money Jim poured on your ungrateful head," he hisses. "They're saying you're worth over a hundred mil. So why the fuck are you shacking up with the man your father framed for murder?"

Blood roars in my ears, and I remember every time this worthless old bastard swung a punch at me, trying to punish me for the sins of his ex-wife. Worse still, his successful attempts at goading Jim to violence. This drunk taught his son to be a monster, and I'll be fucked if I put up with another moment of his abuse.

Whirling around, I shove Mr. Callahan hard in the chest, and he falls against the casket. It crashes to the ground with a heavy thud and Jim's body rolls out onto the floor.

Jim's face is no longer a mask of peace, but a mess of broken wax and decomposed flesh.

My senses turn numb with shock. I gasp, my hands flying up to my mouth.

"My son!" Mr. Callahan screams, his voice echoing across the church.

The officers surrounding Tony and Gil rush over to the commotion. I turn on my heel and run, every muscle in my gut heaving. My two companions jog after me, filling the walls with their laughter.

Once we're outside, a wave of nausea forces me onto my knees. I collapse against the car and vomit, my mind replaying the horror of Jim's dead, mangled body. Gil holds me up as my stomach ejects its contents. Afterward, he bundles me into the back seat of the car, and Tony speeds down the street.

———

Despite Tony and Gil's assurances that I'm some kind of fucking hero, Jim's broken body haunts me for the entire journey home. I wanted to spit in his face but ended up desecrating his corpse. I can't think through their raucous laughter, and my stomach won't stop churning.

Once the two men fall quiet, I think back to my conversation with Mr. Callahan.

Jim's father was an alcoholic who used to get drunk until he blacked out. At least once a week, Jim's mood would be soured by a late-night phone call from some precinct informing him about his dad's latest antics.

On the few occasions Jim allowed Mr. Callahan to sober up in his house, the old man would spew violent diatribes about Jim's gold-digging mother who ran away in the dead of night.

I lean forward on the back seat with my head against the cool window and groan. Mr. Callahan must have been confused, because the paintings I sold makes me worth a few hundred grand, not millions.

"You alright, Emberly?" Gil asks.

I raise my head. "Still grossed out."

"Who was that old bastard, and why did you push him into the casket?"

"My ex's father," I mutter. "He's a former detective. He wouldn't let go of my arm, so I shoved him."

The two men erupt into snickers, presumably at the same subject they found so funny: how I wrecked the funeral of a cop. As they fade, Gil turns around, his features grave. "What was he saying?"

"Just the usual bullshit about me being an ungrateful bitch." I shake my head, trying to forget that entire incident. "Then some tirade about money."

Gil stares at me for several heartbeats too long, making me squirm in my seat.

"He was just a crazy drunk," Gil says with a nod. "You got that?"

My eyes narrow at his inflection. Why is he trying to convince me of what I already know? More importantly, what does he want me to forget?

"Right," I say, my mind running through Mr. Callahan's rant.

What the hell did he ramble about? A bunch of made-up nonsense, conflating me with his ex-wife. I can't even focus properly because my blood sugar is six feet in the grave and all I can see is the face of Jim's broken corpse. But Mr. Callahan also spewed a lot of bullshit that needs sifting.

I dressed like a whore.

I'm an ungrateful whore.

I left his precious son for a richer man?

No, that's his ex-wife. I squeeze my eyes shut, dig my fingers into my scalp, and force myself to remember.

Mr. Callahan said *I* was rich. That I walked out on Jim the moment I came into money.

That can't be right.

The car pulls off the highway and heads up the slope that winds around Alderney Hill. I press on the button to lower the window and let in the fresh scent of juniper.

Filling my lungs with cool air helps to clear my head.

Mr. Callahan mentioned an inheritance. And a law firm, but which one? I try to remember what else the old man spewed, but my mind dredges up the image of Jim's face breaking against the marble altar in an explosion of cosmetic wax, revealing a decomposed corpse.

My stomach roils, and I clap a hand over my mouth, trying not to dry heave. I know a lawyer. Sort of. We've only spoken twice.

That night I met Mr. Lubelli, his date asked me for a portrait. I don't remember her name, but she handed me a business card that said she was an attorney. She also tried to speak to me at the auction, but Roman chased her away.

It's a long shot, but maybe I can give her a call and see if she can reach out to one of her contacts?

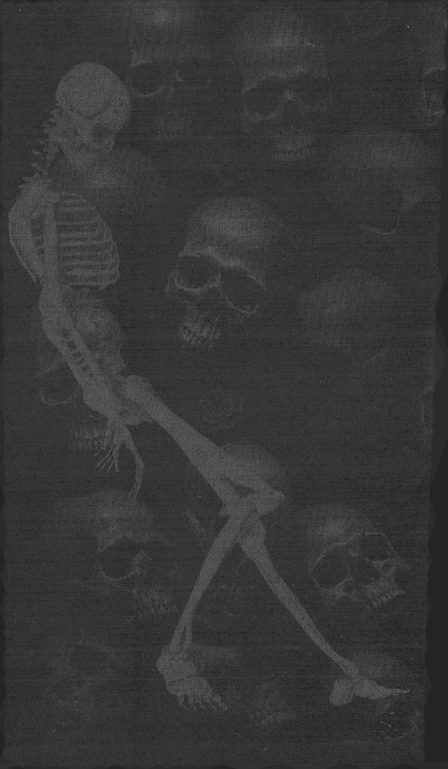

FIFTY-EIGHT

EMBERLY

Several minutes later, I return to the mansion, desperate to find that attorney's business card. I remember slipping it down the bodice of my dress before bullets rang through the ballroom. After that, Jim's colleague tricked me into leaving the building with him.

There's no sign of the cards in Roman's bedroom, so I return to the pool house to see if I left them there. When I don't find them, I try calling Mr. Lubelli, but my phone doesn't have any credit.

After wasting precious time working out how to add money to my prepaid SIM card. Once it's charged, I call the MoCa art gallery. The receptionist takes her time putting me through to Mr. Lubelli, who greets me with his usual warm enthusiasm.

"Emberly, my dear," he says. "Don't tell me you've created another masterpiece already?"

"Actually..." I clear my throat. "The night we met, the blonde woman you were with asked if I could paint her portrait—"

"Martina?" he asks.

I hesitate. "She was an attorney. I lost her card, and I was wondering if you could pass on her number."

"Leave it with me." Mr. Lubelli pauses for a few seconds, then my phone buzzes. "Did you get it?"

I glance at my screen. Martina's name and number appear on the display. "Got it. Thank you."

"Good luck," he says before hanging up.

What?

I shake off my confusion, telling myself not to look too deeply into Mr. Lubelli's parting words, and dial her number.

She answers in one ring. "Di Marco Law Group, Martina Mancini speaking?"

"Hi, you probably don't remember me." My words come out in a rush. "My name is Emberly Kay. We met at Roman Montesano's—"

"Miss Kay," she says, her voice so sharp that I flinch. "Where are you?"

I glance around the studio, wondering why she sounds so panicked. "Somewhere safe. Why?"

"Are you alright? We've been trying to reach you for weeks."

My heart skips several beats, and my paranoia rears back to the surface. If she's one of the lawyers Mr. Callahan said were trying to find me, then why didn't she say something at the party?

Maybe she planned on cornering me when Mr. Lubelli was out of earshot, but the event exploded into pandemonium.

"I'm fine, thanks," I reply, my voice guarded. "What did you want with me?"

She exhales a long breath. "It's related to the recent death of your father."

"Who?"

"Frederic Capello," she replies.

The word hits like a punch to the heart, and I drop the phone.

This is bullshit.

There's no way in hell my father is the man who framed Roman for murder. I stare at my latest canvas, my heart pounding hard enough to splatter blood all over my unfinished painting. It contains wildflowers I found on a patch of land beyond the electrified fence.

My mind dredges up Mr. Callahan's parting words:

Why the fuck are you shacking up with the man your father framed for murder?

No.

I can't be related to a mafia boss. Mom would have said something...

"She did," I whisper. "Every fucking day."

I bow my head, recalling how Mom used to scream at me whenever I got into a fight at school that I was just like my father, who thought rules never applied to him. If I ate too much at dinner, I would be a crook, just like him.

My phone rings, snapping me out of my thoughts. I glance at the display, which says Martina Mancini, Di Marco Law Group. I ignore the call, letting it go to voicemail.

A few days before I met Roman, all the newspapers reported the death of the family who owned the Capello Casino. In a single night, a lone gunman murdered Frederic Capello, his wife, his twin sons, and a whole host of relatives who had stayed over to celebrate his sixtieth birthday.

With trembling fingers, I search the internet for photos.

Frederic Capello is a dark-haired man with tanned skin, heavy features, and a strong jawline. I shake my head, seeing zero family resemblance. Millions of people have green eyes. It's nothing unique.

I scroll through Google Images for pictures of his sons and pause at one that makes my stomach flip.

Gregor Capello has the same long curls as mine, with eyes the exact shade of green. He's one of the twin sons who died in the massacre, but that doesn't mean a thing.

Lots of people have curly dark hair and green eyes, right?

My breath shallows.

It can't be true.

But Mom spent her entire life paranoid that someone was tracking us. It's the reason why we never stayed in the same home for longer than a year. She was terrified that someone would take me away from her.

A recent memory hits me like a slap.

Dominic.

The man Roman left to guard me knew Mom's name and said he knew my father. He said the old man never stopped searching for me and that his uncle helped to keep us hidden. At the time, I dismissed his words as bullshit, but what if he'd been telling the truth?

Before Dominic tried to kill me, he told me I was marked for death the moment my father died. Then there was something else.

Sam sends his regards.

I turn my attention to the phone and scroll through the pictures to find an image similar to Gregor Capello's. His hair is shorter, and his features are harsher, but there's no mistaking the family resemblance.

It's Samson Capello.

What if Samson was Sam?

What if Samson survived the massacre and wanted to get rid of anyone who stood to inherit his father's millions?

The phone rings once more. This time, I answer.

"Hello?" I croak.

"Emberly, it's Martina Mancini from the Di Marco Law group. Please, don't hang up," she says.

"What do you want?" I ask.

"Can you meet me today?"

I swallow. "No."

"How about tomorrow?"

"About what?"

"It's about your inheritance."

My stomach twists and churns. Roman told me all about the man who betrayed his father, stole from the Montesano family and framed him for murder. After everything Roman did to help me, I can't possibly claim this blood money.

"I don't want it," I rasp.

She pauses for several moments before saying, "Will you at least meet me for coffee? I'd like to fill you in on a few details."

"Where?"

"My firm's address is—"

"No," I say. "Let's meet tomorrow at a coffee shop. Do you know the Stargazer on 5th and Main?"

"Great. I'll see you there tomorrow at ten."

She hangs up before I can change my mind, leaving me feeling shivery and nauseous. I pick up my pallet and a tube of paint, then squeeze a dollop of cadmium red. My gaze hones in on the wildflowers. I need to focus on something other than mafia, massacres, or mob money.

Hours later, I'm still painting when Roman enters the studio. I straighten, my throat tightening with guilt, unable to look him in the face.

He brushes back my hair and plants a kiss on my neck, infusing my skin with warmth. "Sorry about this morning. I had to take care of some things for the family."

"It's fine." I force a smile.

Roman massages my bare shoulders, but his touch is stilted. "Why are you still wearing last night's dress?"

"What?" I glance down, finding tiny splatters of paint over the beautiful gown, and my eyes fill with tears. "Oh, Roman. I'm so sorry. It's ruined."

He takes my chin in his hands and tilts my face, so our gazes meet, and my heart shatters at the intensity of his concern. I've never seen Roman look so sick with worry.

I close my eyes, and tears spill down my cheeks.

Roman pulls me into his chest. "It's just a dress, baby. Don't worry about it."

"No," I rasp. "Something happened today."

He stiffens, his heart pounding so hard that I feel its vibrations against my chest. "Gil told me about the corpse that fell out of its casket," he says with a shaky laugh. "Is that why you refused Sofia's risotto?"

"It's something I heard from Jim's dad."

Roman pulls back, his eyes narrowing, his lips flattening over his teeth. "What did that bastard's father say?"

"My father is Frederic Capello."

He freezes, and all the color leeches from his skin, leaving him sickly pale. It's the strangest expression, even though he's always so calm. It's always me who's controlled by my emotions and him who's the rock.

Right now, Roman looks like a dam about to break.

"Say that one more time," he says, his voice even.

Cold sweat breaks out across my skin, and I quake under his stare. "Jim's dad told me I'm the daughter of the man who framed you for murder."

"That bastard," Roman snarls, his gaze darting to the door. "I'll kill him."

"Wait." I grab his shoulders. "Did you hear what I said?"

He turns back to me, his eyes softening. "I heard you, baby, but you're not your father. You're the woman I love."

My mouth falls slack. I'm so confused. Why is his anger directed toward a drunken old man? How can Roman forgive me for something so heinous? Before I can push for answers, he pulls me into a kiss.

His lips are inviting and warm, just as they were yesterday at the casino. The casino he wrestled back from my monstrous biological father. How could he kiss me like this after finding out my heritage?

Maybe he's in shock. Maybe this kiss is so intense because Roman knows it's our last. Cracks spread across my heart, each fissure oozing liquid agony. I melt into the embrace, my fingers tangling in his hair. If this is the end, then I want to make it memorable.

Roman lifts me off my feet and carries me into the back bedroom. "Nothing could ever come between us," he murmurs against my lips. "I love you too much."

No matter what he says, I can't believe it. As he lays me onto the bed and trails kisses down my cleavage, I stare at the ceiling, my mind whirring with questions.

Is Roman in denial? How could his love for someone he's known for less than a month outweigh the depth of my father's betrayal?

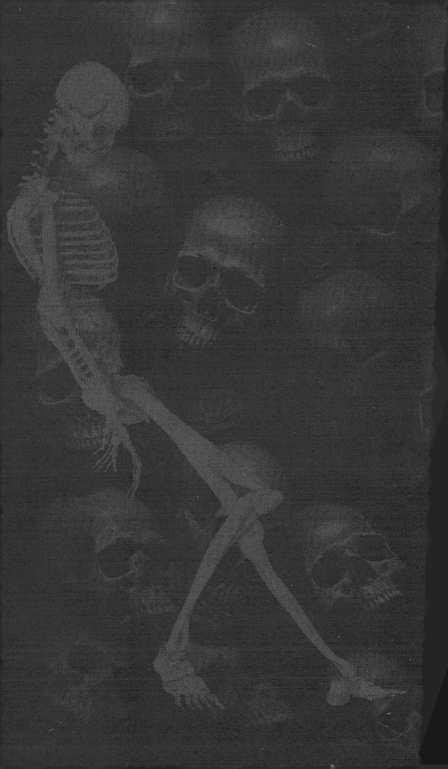

FIFTY-NINE

ROMAN

Fuck.

Fuck.

FUCK!

It took me hours to get Emberly to stop asking questions about Capello. Hours of kissing and touching and making her moan my name until she was nothing but a puddle of bliss.

Now that she's asleep, I can no longer hold back the guilt. It burns through my resolve, leaving only embers of regret. I should have told her the truth from the moment I saved her from Dominic.

That would have been the perfect time. She had been grateful that I saved her life. I was her hero. I could have explained that her half-brother wanted her dead to make sure she didn't inherit the Capello fortune.

The morning sun streams through the windows, warming her skin with its golden light. I can't even savor the tranquility of the moment or bask in her beauty, when my heart is sinking with dread.

Emberly and I might never have a chance if I tell her the truth about the extent of my lies. What if she leaves? I can't bear the thought of losing her.

My gaze drops to her breasts, which I'm sure are bigger than they were when we first met. If she's carrying my child, that might be the distraction I need while I figure out how to make things right.

Until then, I'll keep my mouth shut. I'll do whatever it takes to keep Emberly, even if it means never telling her the truth.

After kissing Emberly on the lips, I return to my office, where Nick Terranova hands me the keys to the safety deposit boxes. The man's grin is wider than a crocodile's because he's helped us achieve the impossible.

"Miss Kay also inherited the mansion in Queen's Gardens and its contents, all vehicles, personal effects, as well as Mrs. Capello's jewelry."

I sit back in the leather seat and nod.

"Would you like me to draw up some contracts to transfer those assets to you?" Nick asks, his eyes sparkling.

"No." I wave him off. "Those belong to Emberly."

Nick's brows pull into a frown. "Not even the proceeds of Mr. Capello's life insurance policy?"

My jaw tightens. "I only wanted what was rightfully ours. Capello was a rich man before he ripped us off. I don't want his money."

Our lawyer inclines his head. He's tactful enough not to bring up my original plan to murder Emberly. "Understood. It was a pleasure doing business with you."

"How are things going with getting your license back?" I ask.

He flashes me a smile. "The appeal was a success."

"Makes a fucking difference when everyone blocking it

is dead," I reply, thinking about my own failed appeals over the years.

One of the reasons I like Nick Terranova is that our lives took similar paths. While Capello screwed us over, his lawyer, Joe Di Marco, stole Nick's share of their law firm and got him disbarred. We're both on similar paths of vengeance, except I doubt that Nick would be able to seduce Di Marco's daughter for her inheritance.

"And the Di Marco Group?" I ask.

"Joe is dead. His wife left town. His daughter, Ginevra, is a nervous wreck. The woman Joe was screwing is trying to take advantage of the vacuum of power, and it looks like she's put a hit on the daughter. I'll sit back and let them kill each other before swooping in to collect what's mine."

I chuckle. It looks like Ginevra Di Marco is finally getting what she deserves. She was engaged to Benito years ago, before our family went to shit. Without explanation, she dumped my brother to hook up with Samson Capello.

We all overlooked that first sign of the Capello and Di Marco alliance. Much to our detriment.

"What's the name of Di Marco's mistress?" I ask.

Nick waggles his brows. "Martina Mancini. I heard she's as hot as she is ruthless."

I shake my head. "Sounds like she'll destroy Ginevra."

The patio door opens, and Emberly walks in, wearing a cream-colored sundress that hugs her curves. Nick's eyes follow her as she approaches, and he rises off his feet like the gentleman he isn't.

I also stand, drinking in her radiance.

"Roman," she says. "I'm going out for coffee to discuss a new commission."

Joy bubbles up from my chest at seeing her distracted from last night's conversation. As I round the desk with the urge to pull her into a hug, I make a mental note to scrounge up an entire waitlist of customers to keep Emberly's mind off Capello.

"Getting more work already, baby?" I ask.

She flashes me a sunny smile. "Maybe. I brought my digital portfolio. Do you mind if I show them the pictures I painted of you?"

I wrap an arm around her shoulders and plant a kiss on her soft lips. "Of course not. Knock them dead with your talent."

Emberly kisses back and exits out through the patio door, where Tony follows behind her. As she walks around the house, the two of us exchange nods. Tony will grab someone else to accompany them to Beaumont City and keep an eye on Emberly while she speaks to her new client.

————

Less than three hours later, I'm enjoying a glass of chianti on the patio with Gil. The afternoon sun bathes the lawn in a warm glow, and a gentle breeze carries the mingled scents of juniper and flowers in bloom.

I've clawed back everything Capello stole and have gained the love of his daughter. If I'm lucky, she'll give me something more precious than money—a child to bind us for life. I want to congratulate myself for launching her art career. Without giving her an opportunity to shine, I might never have noticed she was my perfect match.

Emberly rounds the corner with Tony. If I thought she looked radiant before, I was mistaken. She's fucking glowing. Incandescent. I have never seen her look so alive. My love, my wife, the potential mother of my children, has never looked so powerful or so in control.

She's beaming, and I can tell she's secured a commission

with her new client. I place my glass on the table and stand up with my arms outstretched.

"How did it go, baby?" I pull her into a hug.

She wraps her arms around my neck and presses her body into mine. My cock swells at the fullness of her tits, and I'm already imagining her carrying the next generation of Montesanos in her belly.

"It was a success. She loved your portraits." She reaches down my back and cups my ass. "And she's given me an idea for my next painting!"

"What is it?" I ask.

She draws back, her eyes shining. "Have you heard of Gulliver's Travels?"

I cock my head to the side. "The man who went to the land of tiny people?"

"There's a scene where Gulliver gets tied down to the ground by the Lilliputians," she says with a nod. "I'm going to combine images of a perfect male specimen bound by all the plants I've been painting around the estate. It's going to be a masterpiece."

My heart swells with pride. "What a great idea. I'm sure it's going to be stunning."

She nods. "I have enough funds to hire one of the most beautiful male models in New Alderney—"

"No."

Emberly frowns. "What do you mean?"

"You don't need a model." I raise my chin and puff out my chest. "You have me."

She licks her lips, her palms trailing down my pecs. "Are you sure? Some of the poses might be a little edgy..."

My breath catches. The first time I posed for her, she watched me jack off and refused my invitation to join me, even though she looked sorely tempted. I'm not missing the chance for Emberly to unleash all her raw passion and sexuality on me. This time, she won't even try to hold back.

"When do we start?" I ask.

"There's a special studio on the edge of town." She gazes up at me through her lashes. "Can I direct you?"

If it's as magical as Simon's Pond, I can't wait.

In the next ten minutes, Emberly packs up her portable art kit, and I direct her around the side of the house and into the garage, where I've parked the 1965 silver Mercedes Cabriolet.

As I place her things in the back seat, she gazes at the convertible with a frown. "It's not bulletproof."

"That shit with the police is over." I gather her in my arms and place a kiss on the tip of her nose. "Let's turn this into another date. I can take you for dinner after. Anywhere you want."

The smile she gives me is dazzling. "Let's do it."

I rush around to the passenger side and open the door.

"You look dazzling, baby," I murmur as she slips into the seat.

"Ugh. I don't feel it," she mutters.

My heart skips a beat.

Morning sickness?

"Do you need anything for the journey?" I ask, my brows pulling together. "Water, crackers, ginger tea?"

She shakes her head. "I had a tuna melt at the coffee shop. Let's get going."

I drive her through the garage, out of the estate and down the winding road. The afternoon sun sets the skies ablaze and bathes Emberly in its warm light. She closes her eyes and smiles, letting the wind blow through her curls. She has never looked so radiant.

"Nice car," she murmurs.

"My dad acquired it at the casino," I reply with a laugh.

"What does that mean?"

"One of the customers couldn't pay their debts and offered it up as a form of payment."

"That must have been some debt," she mutters.

I chuckle. "It was a rust bucket, but Dad saw its potential. We spent months working on it together." Nostalgia thaws my heart, and I sigh. "It's one of the fondest memories I had of him before he died."

Emberly turns to me, her gaze warming the side of my face. "What was he like?"

I shake my head. "After he died and I was locked up, I used to think he was weak. Dad put too much trust in his friends and wanted us to have college educations instead of going straight into the family business. He should have kept us close instead of relying on outsiders."

"It sounds like he wanted you to have a better future."

My throat thickens with regret. "Things might have worked out differently if he'd brought us into the business much earlier."

"What do you think of him now?"

"Flawed. Unfocussed," I say, my voice tightening. "He placed his feelings before the family legacy."

"And you never want to be like that?" she asks.

"He was a hedonist," I reply. "That made him a fun dad, a great host, and the life of the party, but where did that get him?"

She doesn't reply, so I continue. "He cared more about pleasing himself than securing the family's future. That attitude almost broke us apart."

Emberly reaches over to squeeze my hand. "It's not too late to make things right."

She's too much of an optimist. No amount of money can compensate for the five years I spent on death row or for the upheaval to my brothers' lives. We fall silent as we reach the bottom of Alderney Hill, and Emberly directs me through the back streets into an upscale neighborhood of townhouses.

"Are you sure this is the place?" I ask.

She leans across the front seat and murmurs into my ear. "Don't worry. I don't plan on getting you naked where anyone else can see."

"It's a studio?" I ask.

"A kink hotel. One of my friends makes erotic paintings, and she gets artist's rates."

Heat rushes through my veins and settles in my cock, and my lips lift into a salacious smile. The sex between us is mind blowing and only getting better. I follow more of her directions until we reach a three-story house on the outskirts of the community.

"I can't wait to see this kink hotel."

Emberly squeezes my thigh. "I can't wait to get you alone."

We exit the car, and she leads me into the house's front door and enters a number on a keypad. The lock clicks, and we step into a dimly lit hallway that smells of incense.

Erotic artwork adorns the black walls, some of them making my breath hitch. Every image depicts women in positions of strength, with male figures as submissive. It's like a secret world of female empowerment, and I'm completely enthralled.

I can't help but stare at a mural of writhing figures as Emberly leads me down the stairs to a basement room secured by another digital lock.

Once inside, Emberly flicks on the lights, revealing a playroom of red leather furniture that I can tell has been designed by a woman. The decor is more like the Dolce Vita boutique than Cesare's chamber of carnage. It's the perfect environment for Emberly to unleash her desires.

I set the art supplies down on a side table and ask, "Where do you want me?"

Emberly reaches into her bag and pulls out some wet towelettes. "Take off your clothes, and I'll sterilize the bondage table."

The command in her tone sends sensation shooting straight to my erection. Who would have thought I would enjoy this side of Emberly?

I peel off my shirt and ease my pants down to the floor, my heart pounding with anticipation. Emberly wipes down a leather bed shaped like an X, making sure to clean the cuffs hanging from each of its sides.

She stands back and grins. "Get on the table and let's make some art."

My erection strains against my boxers and dampens the silk fabric with pre cum. I climb onto the bed, and Emberly fastens the cuffs around my wrists. She runs her hands along my biceps, tracing the muscles with her fingertips before sliding her tongue down the dip between my pecs.

A low, guttural groan escapes my lips as she trails her fingers over the ridges of my abs, her touch sending shivers down to my balls. Her fingers graze the waistband of my boxers, teasing and tantalizing, before she pulls back with a smirk.

My body is aflame with desire. The anticipation is almost unbearable as I wait for her next move. She holds me in suspense, waiting inches away from where I ache for her most.

"Lift your hips," she says, her voice husky.

"Fuck," I groan, my breath shallowing.

I do as I'm told, letting her slide off my boxers. Cool air swirls around my erection, but it's nothing compared to the heat of her gaze on my shaft. Emberly licks her lips, and I swear to everything that's holy that I feel the swipe of her tongue on my cock.

She shakes her head, her gaze wistful. "You're so fucking beautiful. Absolutely exquisite."

Her words send a shiver down my spine, and it settles in my balls. Emberly has never sounded so aggressive. She moves on to secure my ankles, making sure to tickle the soles of each foot. A current races up my legs, making me jerk within my bindings, but they're secured tight.

Laughing, I squirm on the leather. "What are you doing, baby?"

Emberly doesn't reply. Instead, she turns toward her bag to extract something and looks me dead in the eye.

"I know everything," she says, holding up a meat tenderizer the size of a mallet.

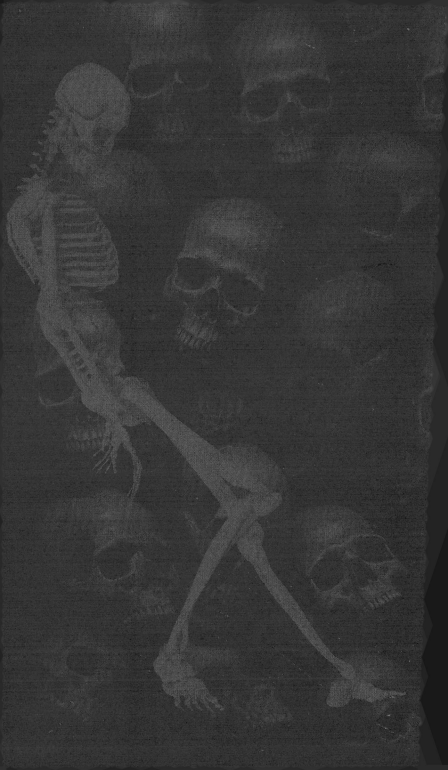

SIXTY

EMBERLY

For once in my fucking life, it feels great not to be the butt of the joke or the unwitting pawn. I'm no longer the damsel in distress.

Everyone I ever lived with wielded power over me and kept me in the dark, starting with Mom. She did it because my biological father was a violent, backstabbing psychopath who wanted to steal back his daughter. The others did it to fulfill their sick goals.

I'd been so used to being controlled that I didn't even notice Jim was a manipulative, malignant narcissist until I became his prisoner. The drip, drip, drip of abuse was so subtle, I could only notice it with hindsight.

Mom and Jim locked the doors, hurt me with insults, isolation, and control, but I saw the monsters inside them and protected my heart. Roman made me feel like I was beautiful, talented, and worthy of love, only for me to realize he was just a more skillful puppet master. Roman Montesano is the worst of my abusers.

He stares up at me through wide eyes, his arms jerking

against their restraints. "Emberly," he says, his voice strained. "What are you talking about?"

"I've been throwing up all morning since discovering the truth." I clutch the tenderizer to my chest.

Swallowing hard, his gaze drops to my weapon's aluminum spikes. "You're going to use that on me, baby?"

"I will if you keep treating me like an idiot."

His eyes meet mine again, only this time, he's breathing hard and fast, even though his face is a mask of calm. "Emberly, what is this about?"

Baring my teeth, I bring the tenderizer down on the table's metal frame, sending a shockwave through the surface that makes him flinch. "Next time you play ignorant, this is going straight to your balls."

He shudders. "Don't do this. Untie me, and we'll talk. I'll explain everything."

"No need," I snarl. "I already know."

Roman squeezes his eyes shut. "Emberly—"

I slam the blunt end into his balls, making his arms and legs jerk within the restraints, and every muscle on that perfect body to tighten. He groans, his mask cracking and finally showing some pain.

Hot satisfaction sears my veins, inflating my spirits with a surge of victory. This is Roman Montesano's most genuine emotion.

"No more bullshit," I hiss. "No more deflection. The next time you open your mouth with a lie, I'll use the tenderizer and I won't stop until there's nothing left for the doctors to repair."

His eyes snap open, and his Adam's apple bobs up and down.

"Is that understood?" I snarl.

He nods.

"I went to see an associate from the Di Marco Law Group today. Do you know what she told me?"

Roman's eyes widen, and he clamps his mouth shut.

"I'm the daughter of Frederic Capello, but you already knew that, didn't you?"

He gives me a stiff nod.

I point the tenderizer at his face. "Correction. You knew it all along. Before we even met."

"Yes," he rasps.

"According to the attorney, I'd already claimed my inheritance via registered post and even provided a blood sample. Do you know how that happened?"

Roman grits his teeth. "We set up an email address for you and a post office box only we could access. We took the blood just after you threatened to jump off the balcony."

"Right. Back when I *knew* I was your prisoner. Then you convinced me you weren't a trafficker."

He grimaces. "You've got to understand—"

"Stop." I raise the tenderizer, and his jaws click shut.

"My biological father ruined your lives." I try to keep my voice from trembling, but it breaks. "A man whose name I didn't even know. The man who kept my mother and me living in a life of constant fear. You knew I was ignorant of my roots, didn't you?"

He glances toward the door.

"Look at me!" I smash the tenderizer on his thigh, making him growl.

Roman's gaze snaps back to mine. "Yes."

"I understand why you murdered him and his entire family. I even understand why you transferred the wealth I inherited from him over to Montesano Enterprises. What I want to know is how?"

His nostrils flare. "Untie me and I'll explain."

"Explain, or I'll tenderize your cock," I snap.

Roman's eyes bulge. He parts his lips to speak and sighs. "Your art."

My eyes sting. I'd already guessed the answer, but I need to hear it from him. I need to know exactly how after getting swindled by Lafayette, I managed to fall for another scam.

"What about it?" I ask.

"Inside every Art Purchase Agreement you signed was a contract that transferred the ownership of each asset to me for twenty-five grand."

"You made me think I had talent," I whisper, my voice trembling with fury.

"You do—"

"Shut up!" I swing the tenderizer, not giving a shit where it lands.

Roman roars in agony.

Betrayal burns into my being, blistering and blazing and bitter. I clench my teeth as he struggles against his binds.

"Why did you go to such lengths to deceive me?" My eyes blur with hot tears. "Why didn't you just put a gun to my head? I would have signed everything over, but you made me think—"

Emotion grips me by the throat, and I double over. The heavy tool drops to the floor with a loud clang.

"Emberly," Roman screams.

"Just fuck off," I cry, my knees hitting the concrete.

"Baby, talk to me," he says, his voice hitching. "Are you alright?"

"Why the fuck do you care?"

"I'm sorry. It was the only way to sign the contracts without using coercion. Imprisoning you didn't work. You would rather die than be locked up. When I saw you threatening to jump, I changed tactics."

"So, you pretended to be interested in my art, then set

up all those fake assassinations?" I ask, my head resting on my thighs.

"No," he rasps. "None of that was me. Everyone who came after you was sent by someone else."

My heart thuds a sluggish beat, and my breaths turn shallow. Roman Montesano's most maddening trait is the outlandish lies he tells that sound like the truth. Every time I ever raised a suspicion, he had a clever answer. It's like trying to spar with the devil when you're blindfolded, hand-cuffed, and gagged.

"Who was Sam?" I ask.

"Samson Capello." He hesitates. "Your half-brother."

Rising to my knees, I hold on to the edge of the table and pull myself up to standing. Martina Mancini explained that the law firm reached out to me after the massacre, thinking the entire family was dead. Days later, they discovered Samson had survived. Samson discovered I was trying to claim his inheritance while under Montesano control. That's why he paid Dominic to snuff out my life.

Roman had a head start over the law firm. Only he and his allies knew Frederic Capello and his entire bloodline would die. That's how the Montesano family found me before the Di Marco group even considered me a candidate for the inheritance.

"What happened with Samson?" I ask.

"My hitman made a mistake." Roman exhales a shud-dering breath. "We waited until Capello's sixtieth birthday, when the entire family was in one location, but Samson stayed the night with his fiancée and let a cousin use his room."

"Hence, *Sam sends his regards*," I spit.

Roman flinches.

"That was the last thing Dominic said he when tried to kill me. Why did you say Dominic was sent by Jim?"

"So you would stay with me," he rasps.

"What happened to my half-brother, then?"

"We caught up with him. I delivered his head to the Di Marco Law Group," Roman says.

"And that's when you got control of my inheritance."

He nods.

"Use your fucking words," I snap.

"Yes," he says through clenched teeth.

"You used my aspirations as an artist as the carrot and the threat of Jim as a stick. You made me think Jim was desperate to get his hands on me."

"He was trying to get you," Roman hisses. "He knew about your inheritance, too."

Nodding, I straighten and glare down into his handsome features as they break out in a sweat. Martina explained that her firm tracked me down to Jim's house and left me a letter. That's the reason Jim's father ranted about me striking it rich.

"You don't believe me," Roman says.

My jaw clenches, and my chest rises and falls with rapid breaths. He's doing it again. Using the truth to obscure the lies. Making me waver, making me doubt.

"That footage of Callahan at the gates was real," he adds. "That cop who disguised himself as a waiter to drag you off the premises? Real. The bastard even paid your little blonde friend to convince you to walk into a trap."

I squeeze my eyes shut, not knowing or caring if he's bullshitting about Annalisa. "But why did you make me think you loved me?"

"Emberly, I do love—"

I silence him with a slap across the face.

Roman grimaces. "The more time I spent with you, the more I liked you."

"That's a lie." I shake my head. "You loved money. You

loved revenge. You loved the idea of fucking over the daughter of your enemy. What was your endgame, Roman? Were you going to take me into a room like this and tell me it was all a scam?"

"No." His voice breaks.

"But you admit to locking me in that tower bedroom."

"Yes."

"That's where I would have stayed until I outlived my usefulness."

His nostrils flare.

"Answer me," I snap when he doesn't respond.

"That's before I knew you. Before I fell in love—"

"Shut up!" I flash my teeth. "You and Cesare would have had me on my knees and laughed at my tears while you explained that I was a pawn in your twisted game of vengeance. Then you'd put a bullet through my head and send me to my biological father in hell."

"Never, Emberly."

"Lies." I walk to my bag, pull out a craft knife, and return to his side.

Roman closes his eyes and sighs. "You want to kill me, baby?"

"Maybe I do." I position the blade at his throat. "Maybe that's the only way to force you to tell the truth."

"When you were just a photo and a name, I wanted to kill you," he says. "But I changed my mind."

"Eyes on me," I order, using his own words against him. "Look at me when I'm threatening your life."

His eyes snap open.

"When?" I dig the sharp point into his skin.

"You're spiraling. We're going around in circles."

"Only because you keep feeding me lies. When did you decide to spare my life?"

"When I talked you off that ledge and carried you into

the room." He swallows. "You were vulnerable. Human. Scared of going through what Capello made me endure."

The lies hit me like a punch to the throat, and I laugh, the sound bitter. "Where did you learn to sound so honest? Admit it. You kept me alive because I was your golden goose."

"No," he rasps.

"Fuck you, Roman. And fuck your bullshit."

I carve an L on his chest in the space between his pectoral muscles, drawing a thin stream of blood. "Drop the mask."

"There is no mask," he says through clenched teeth.

The next letter I carve is an I. "Tell me how you fucked with my mind."

Roman flares his nostrils. "The only direct lie I told you was that Dominic was sent by your ex. Everything else was based on the truth."

"Stop playing word games." I carve an A. "Tell me how you tricked me into loving you."

"If you love me, then it's because I fucking love you," he yells.

"Liar!" I carve the R. There's so much blood on his chest that it pools down to his neck and fills the room with the scent of copper.

Nausea washes over my senses, making my vision blur with tears. My stomach churns, and my mouth fills with saliva. I twist to the side and dry heave before finally bending over to vomit.

Roman yells my name, but his voice is muffled by my retching. I gag, cough, and spit out the sour bile. When I'm done, I stagger around the room and gather his clothes.

"Baby, you're sick. Please, let me help you."

Huffing a laugh, I stuff his clothes in a bag, along with his wallet, phone, and shoes. "Yeah, I'm sick alright. Sick for ever listening to you. Sick for thinking you might admit the truth and try to make amends."

"Alright." His voice shakes. "I'll tell you—"

"Too. Fucking. Late."

After grabbing the art supplies, I slip the car keys in my pocket, open the door, and toss the two bags out into the hallway.

Without sparing another glance at Roman's bound and naked form, I switch off the light and plunge him into the darkness.

"The table is welded to the floor. You can struggle all you want, and it won't topple over," I say.

"Emberly," he growls. "If you leave me here—"

"By the time you break free, I'll be gone. Don't think about coming after me. You can keep the cash, the casino, the loan company, the stocks, the real estate, and the safety deposit boxes. They were never mine."

"Emberly—"

"I don't even want the mansion where those people died or any of their shit. Take it. It's all yours."

I extract the black card he gave me, pull his phone from my bag, and navigate to the website of the women's shelter that helped me when I escaped Jim. With fingers that won't stop trembling, I donate a million dollars and check the box to make it a recurring gift.

"Goodbye, Roman. I can't say it was ever a pleasure."

As the security door clicks shut and the lock resets, I pick up my bags and stumble up the stairs. My breath comes in heavy pants, partly out of nausea, but mostly out of grief.

Roman was too good a liar to allow our relationship to sour. He would have kept me madly in love, even as he pulled the trigger and exacted the final phase of his revenge.

It's only natural that my emotions will linger. Life

without him will be dreary and dark, but I'd rather face the harsh truth than live in a blissful lie.

It had to be done. Martina from the law firm, warned that Roman planned to kill me before I could revoke the contracts for fraud. She advised against confronting him and tried to scare sense into me with pictures of Samson's severed head.

But I needed closure.

When she couldn't convince me not to risk my life, she made a video call to the only man powerful enough to protect me from Roman and his men.

I exit the house, throw everything into the back seat, and drive to the highway. There, I follow the signs to New Jersey to meet my third cousin once removed, Tommy Galliano.

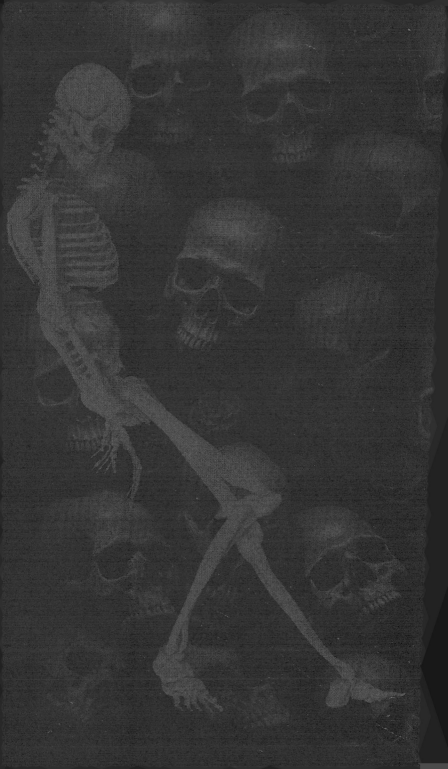

SIXTY-ONE

SIX MONTHS LATER
ROMAN

It's three thirty-five in the afternoon, and the usual knot in my stomach forms every time I sit at the parking spot, watching parents and kids streaming out through the gates of Saint Catherine Elementary in Carmel, New Jersey.

Drumming my fingers on the steering wheel, I check the clock on the dashboard for the eighth time since the clock struck half-past three. She usually leaves around this time, and I wonder why she's running late.

My gaze drops to the gold band on my ring finger, and I clutch the chain containing its smaller counterpart. I would have received a text already if something had happened to Emberly, but the knot in my stomach refuses to loosen.

Finally, she emerges from the single-story building, wearing a long jacket that barely conceals her swollen belly. Relief eases my tension, and I release Emberly's ring.

She says goodbye to the people she passes and continues out through the gates and crosses the road to stroll down

Bologna Street. I sit back, watching her make the short walk to her apartment and wait for her to round the corner before I start the engine.

I drive the long route down Groove Avenue, take a left into Vigri street and park in a spot where I can see her building's front entrance.

In perfect timing, she emerges from around the corner and continues home, completely unaware of my presence. Every morning, I watch her walk to work and I return to see her home each afternoon. Emberly has become my obsession, my biggest regret. I could have been happy with her if only I'd told the truth.

I stayed on that table for three days before Gil drilled a hole through the door and set me free. They knew something was wrong after twelve hours, when Benito tracked the Mercedes to a scrap yard, where it was being crushed into a cube of metal.

The car Dad and I spent years restoring. Our last fond memories together. Gone.

Emberly chose the worst combination of revenge: physical restraints that took me an hour to escape, and imprisonment, all while being frantic with worry that she might drive into a ditch or turn her fury onto herself.

Her revenge pales in comparison to the depths of my betrayal.

I almost lost her forever.

She was clever and didn't touch a penny of the money in her account she'd earned from painting and only used the black card I gave her to donate to a charity. For the first frantic days of her disappearance, she was impossible to track.

Remembering how Emberly escaped her last abusive relationship, I hired every detective I could find to scour youth hostels in a 200-mile radius before one of them found a housekeeper living onsite that fit her description.

Somehow, she acquired a fake ID and now calls herself Kate Edwards and she lives in the worst possible location: New Jersey.

The detective confirmed that she was suffering from morning sickness. I had to pull a lot of strings to lure her to a township close enough to New Alderney so I could drive to her without alerting Tommy Galliano that I was encroaching on his territory. That involved finding her the kind of work I knew she would find irresistible and a ground-floor apartment in a safe area that wasn't too suspiciously affordable.

Emberly enters the building, and I turn my attention to my phone, where I power up the surveillance app.

I've stationed men in the building across the road and have paid others to watch out for her along the usual route she takes home, but keeping a close eye on her myself is the only thing that eases my mind.

She kicks off her shoes, hangs up her coat, and walks into the combined living room and kitchen to turn on the kettle.

I zoom in on her face to find dark circles beneath her eyes, another sign that she's having trouble sleeping. Emberly cries in bed most nights, and sometimes wakes between one or three in the morning from nightmares.

The sound of her pain sears like a brand, and I want to reach through the app and give her comfort. Sometimes, I drive through the night and stand outside her window with my hand pressed on the glass, trying to offer my silent support.

When I told Emberly I loved her, it was a lie. Love can't describe the depth of my longing, the ache of my obsession. If I had to choose between Emberly or breathing, I would rip out my lungs and burn them for her as an offering.

"Roman," she whispers.

I bolt upright, my heart wanting to leap through the windshield.

"Why?" She shakes her head and walks away from the boiling water.

"Make your tea, baby," I murmur.

When Emberly walks out of the kitchen, I switch cameras to find her standing in the doorway to the box room, which she converted into a studio.

A medium-sized canvas sits on an easel, with brushes and paints set up on a side table. The weekend she moved into the apartment, I arranged for a neighbor to hold a garage sale containing second-hand items she might find useful. I made sure to include supplies they'd supposedly purchased for a teen who changed their mind about wanting to pursue art.

Emberly set up her studio months ago, yet she seems afraid of failure. Every evening after work, she stands in the doorway, staring at the blank canvas. She's never gotten close enough to touch it, let alone pick up a brush.

"Sit down," I say to the screen.

She closes her eyes and inhales a deep breath, as though psyching herself up to step inside.

Once again, guilt punches through my rib cage and grips at my heart. Not even Jim Callahan's abuse put Emberly off painting. A few weeks in my company destroyed her will to produce art.

"Go inside," I say.

She grips the doorframe with both hands and flares her nostrils. My heart skips a beat. Will she do it today?

Emberly takes one step into her studio, followed by another. Holding my breath, I send her encouragement through the screen.

Her gaze wanders around the room, looking everywhere but the empty canvas, and she picks up a pencil.

"That's right, baby," I murmur. "Now, please, sit down."

"Fucking hell. I can't do it."

"You can, sweetheart," I say. "Don't let anyone take away your gift."

Emberly sits on the stool and holds the pencil over the canvas, her hand trembling. I switch to another camera that gives me a view of her from behind.

She freezes.

I gulp, unable to take the suspense. It's been six months since she painted. Six months since she did anything but teach children to make art. My fingers itch to press down on the microphone button and tell her everything will be okay.

But I can't.

She drops the pencil and falls forward and claps her hands over her eyes. Her shoulders tremble with sobs that tear into my gut like claws. Hunching over the screen, I feel her pain so viscerally that I groan.

My head rests against the steering wheel, guilt wrapping around my neck like a noose. Of all the things I could have stolen from her, why did I have to take her soul?

A crash sounds through the speakers, making me jerk backward with a start. When I return my attention to the screen, she's tearing the studio apart.

"Shit, Emberly," I mutter under my breath. "What are you doing? Just stop."

As she kicks over the table containing her supplies, I send a text to the apartment's superintendent, ordering him to check on her.

"You're pregnant, baby. You can't let yourself get hurt."

Emberly picks up the canvas and smashes it against the wall, just as her doorbell rings. She pauses, looks around her studio, seeming to have broken out of her rage, and turns around to answer the door.

I watch over her from my car until it gets dark. Only when she's turned off the lights for the night, do I drive home.

———

The next morning, I wake up much later than usual. The app usually broadcasts Emberly in the evening so I can fall asleep, but her sobbing woke me around two-thirty in the middle of the night. She cried for over ninety minutes, and I stayed awake, my heart shattering in tempo with her sobs.

I don't know if the tears were because of her failure to paint, the hormones, my betrayal, or a combination of all three, but I spent the next several hours staring at her in the dark until my eyes couldn't stay open.

By the time I finally drag myself out of bed and walk to the pool house, the team of builders I hired for the extension are already gone. Only Gil and the foreman, Carl, stand by the edge of the patio sipping coffee.

Gil frowns at my disheveled appearance, but doesn't comment. The foreman is far too cautious to mention that I'm four hours late.

"Everything's ready for your final inspection, Mr. Montesano," Carl says.

I nod at them both before heading inside, where someone has covered Emberly's canvases with sheets. The area at the back is now twice its former size, with a more spacious dressing room, a bathroom large enough for two, and an adjoining nursery.

Emberly isn't thriving alone, and her situation will only get worse as the pregnancy progresses. I've given her space to process her heartbreak, but she needs to return to where it's safe to give birth.

I tell myself the renovations aren't connected to the grief weighing down my heart like an iron ball. They have nothing to do with the mounting dread at how she will react to seeing the man who shattered her soul.

My shoulders sag with the memory of the day I carried Emberly into the pool house, kicking and screaming. But now, all I see is a broken woman, shattered by love and loss. I would give anything to return to the days when she was smashing up the place and raising hell.

"Is everything to your satisfaction, sir?" Carl asks.

The phone rings before I can answer. It's an unknown number. My heart skips a beat. It could be Emberly.

"Hello?" I say, my voice calm.

"Mr. Montesano, this is American Express. We're calling because there's been another million-dollar transaction to the Beaumont City Women's Aid. Do you want to authorize this charge?"

My breath catches the way it always does whenever she uses her black card, even though I know it's just a recurring charge she set up the day she left.

"Yes," I say. "My wife can use the card as she pleases."

The woman on the other side of the line hesitates. "Sir, this is the seventh charge of this amount."

I gulp. It's been exactly six months and one day since she left.

"Mr. Montesano?" she says.

"My wife can do whatever the hell she wants with our money," I snarl and hang up.

The woman I love is miserable, alone, and unable to paint, and it's all my fault. She's had half a year to heal, yet her physical and mental state is deteriorating. Turning on my heel, I stalk out of the extension and back through the studio.

"Pack up all the completed paintings and send them to the MoCa Art Gallery," I say.

"Boss?" Gil says from the other room. "Where are you going?"

"To get my goddam wife," I snap.

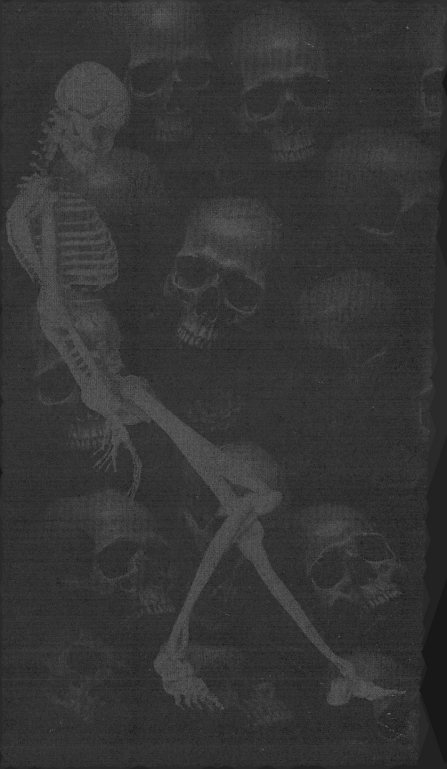

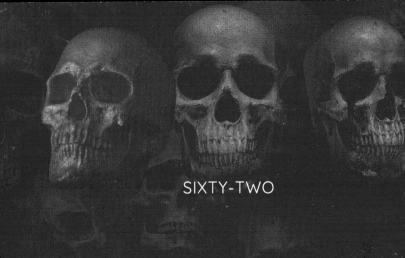

SIXTY-TWO

EMBERLY

Life could be worse.

Every Saturday, I trudge to my *Mindful Birth* class, knowing I'm the only mother-to-be who lacks support.

Carmel is a pleasant little pocket of New Jersey that's conveniently far enough from my cousin, so he doesn't come to visit. I've spoken to him several times on video chat, and I'm thankful our association was brief. His burning hatred for the Montesano family makes my skin crawl, as does his unusual fascination with Cesare.

He arranged my fake ID with the law firm and offered me a room in his four-story mansion that adjoined his master suite. I declined his attempt to keep me close, opting to take a live-in job at a hostel.

I only worked there for a few weeks before I overheard my manager talking about a private school that was looking for an assistant to help with classes. I looked up the opportunity online, sent off an application, and days later, I got an interview and a generous offer.

One of the wealthy mothers owns an apartment building

within a ten-minute walk from the school. She offered me a discounted rent in exchange for giving her daughter weekly drawing lessons. It was too good to refuse.

I should be happy, shouldn't I?

I have a stable job which includes medical, a comfortable home, and savings.

But I'm empty, even though I'm growing a new life.

Despite never wanting to become like Mom, I've inherited her predicament. I'm pregnant by a mafia boss and unable to shake off the feeling of being watched.

A cool breeze blows through my curls as I approach Carmel's community hall, which does nothing to soothe my churning stomach. Holding my features in a mask of calm, I ascend the steps and enter through the double doors.

Expectant mothers and their husbands bustle in the lobby, chatting about the class. A few turn around and glance my way, their features softening with pity.

I ignore them and stare at the notice board.

"Kate," someone says from within the crowd.

It takes a heartbeat for me to remember that I'm Kate Edwards, and I turn to face the voice. It's Lily, the instructor, who waves at me from the door, wearing a smile as bright as her blonde hair.

"There you are," she says. "Come to the front with me."

Lily disappears behind the door, and the crowd parts to let me through. I'm not the only single mother in the class. Those without romantic partners all have siblings, friends, or even parents, but I stand out because I'm alone.

The weight of everyone's stares bears down on me as I walk to the door, but I keep my head high. I reach the front of the room, where Lily waits on a large yoga mat, surrounded by blocks, bolsters, and blankets.

She pats the spot beside her with an encouraging nod. I sit, trying not to feel self-conscious in the spotlight.

The class is a combination of meditation, stretches, breathing exercises, and comfortable birthing positions. All eyes are on me, since I'm the teacher's demo partner. To keep my mind off all the attention, I allow my mind to wander.

How the hell did I manage to get pregnant when I always insisted on using condoms? Most of the time, it was me who rolled them onto his dick. Surely he would have said something if one of them broke?

The nausea from knocking Jim's corpse out of its coffin escalated into daily vomiting. At first, I dismissed what I was feeling as a macabre form of PTSD, but when my breasts became tender, I took a pregnancy test.

"Kate?" Lily's voice cuts through my musings.

"Yes?" I zone back into the class where all the husbands and other birthing partners are packing up their things.

"You did well today," she offers me a hand.

"Thanks." I let her help me to my feet.

Leaning in, she murmurs, "Have you thought about allowing me to support you in the delivery room? It's no trouble."

I part my lips, ready to refuse her offer, when a red-haired woman who always seems to hover close cuts in. "Lily! I didn't know you were a doula. How much do you charge?"

"I'm not," the teacher says.

"Could you help me with my labor?" another woman asks.

A crowd forms around us with all the other mothers-to-be asking Lily for her rates. I step back, not wanting to get trampled in the stampede. Lily shoots me an apologetic glance and I offer her a smile and a shake of my head. She was only trying to help me because I'm alone. Now she's inundated.

I gather my things and rush to the door, only for the redhead from earlier to step into my path. "Before you came along, we all had turns demonstrating with Lily. Do you think you could stop hogging her attention?"

"What?" I ask.

Her husband grabs her by the shoulders. "Don't mind Wendy," he says with a wink. "She's hormonal. We all love having you in the class, Kate. You and Lily look great together."

"Are you serious?" I ask.

The husband smirks. "Just a joke. Don't take offense."

I turn to Wendy to see if she plans on saying something, but she shoots me a venomous look, as though I'm responsible for her husband's wandering eyes.

"Do you prey on women at their most vulnerable or are you an equal opportunity creep?" I ask.

"Watch yourself," Wendy snaps.

Fuck this. I shove past the annoying pair and march home, my steps powered by fury.

What is it about men that makes them think they have the license to disrespect women? No matter how they try to disguise it, they're all the fucking same.

Predators.

As I round the corner and continue down the long stretch of road that leads to my apartment building, our superintendent, Mr. Wilder, spots me from a distance. The old man raises himself on his tiptoes and waves.

My stomach plummets. Carmel is a beautiful place, but nobody seems to want to mind their own business. I almost miss the anonymity of Beaumont City, even if it was riddled with the mafia.

I drag my feet as I approach the front door, where Mr. Wilder waits by a large box. Ever since I moved in, someone has been delivering organic groceries to my apartment, addressing it to Kate Edwards.

There are always enough large kits for seven days, giving me plenty left over. I've tried calling up the company to cancel, but they only allow me to switch up the menu options. The only person who knows me by this name and can afford such exorbitant prices is my cousin, Tommy. Maybe this is his way of saying he's watching over me.

"Hey there, Kate." Mr. Wilder booms, with a smile as gappy as his comb over. "Let me carry in your box."

I paste on a smile. "Thanks."

He opens the door to the building and lets me walk ahead to my apartment. This time, I let him in because I cleared up the other night's mess.

I haven't been able to paint since Tommy and Martina from the Di Marco Law Group helped me unravel that scam. No matter how much I try to forget about the man whose name I refuse to say, the child I'm carrying serves as a constant reminder.

The superintendent walks in after me and sets the box on the kitchen counter.

"Thanks, Mr. Wilder."

"Call me Arthur." He rocks forward with his thumbs tucked into the sleeves of his overalls.

I'll continue to keep my distance and address him formally. That's how Mom survived all those years and kept me away from my biological dad. That's how she kept us alive.

"Anything else I can do for you?" His gaze wanders around the room, looking like he's trying to commit everything out of place to memory.

"No, I'm good. Thank you though," I say, eager for him to leave.

With an absent nod, he heads toward the door. Just as he reaches for the handle, he pauses to give me a crooked smile. "You know, if you ever need anyone to talk to, I'm always here."

The nice thing to do is smile back and offer a word of thanks, but that's not how Mom kept us safe. She taught me to keep my guard up and to trust no one. No chit-chat, no smiling, no allowing them to linger. I nod, not wanting to be rude, but needing to end any further conversation.

As soon as he exits, I rush to the door, turn the lock, and walk to the kitchen counter to unpack the meal kits. When I looked up its price online, I nearly fainted. My subscription contains three meals a day, including smoothies and desserts.

I never have to buy food, my rent includes utilities, and the people I work with are more concerned with providing a quality experience for their students than with asking questions. My situation is perfect, so why am I always miserable?

A knock sounds on the door, and I roll my eyes. Why does Mr. Wilder always have a sixth sense for when I'm at my loneliest?

With a huff, I walk to the door and open it, expecting to see the old man standing at the other side with his hands clasped, but it's not Mr. Wilder.

It's Roman.

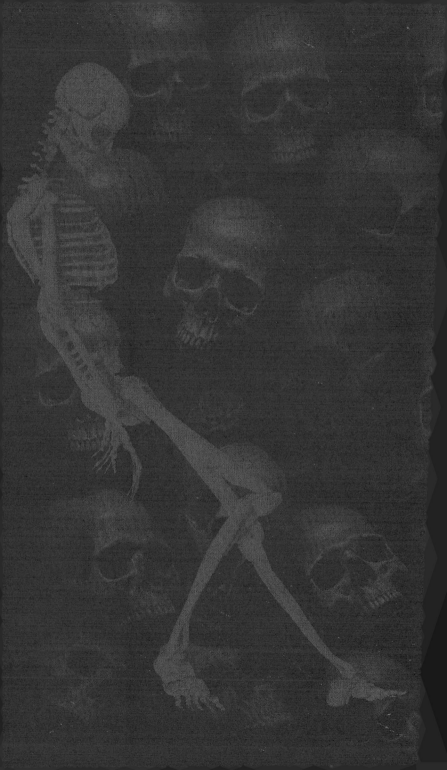

SIXTY-THREE

ROMAN

Emberly staggers backward, but I catch her before she hits the floor. Her soft curls tickle the side of my face, and my nostrils fill with her cinnamon and vanilla scent.

Being close to her feels better than the first sip of cool water on a hot summer's day. More intoxicating than the first taste of a cigar in five years, and more liberating than my first steps off death row.

My heart has been in a cage the six months I gave her space to breathe. Now, I'm free to bask in her presence. Our surroundings fade and my world concentrates on Emberly.

Her green eyes widen, darting around as though not believing the sight of my presence. Her bottom lip trembles, and her chest rises and falls with panicked breaths.

"How did you find me?" Her voice is urgent, tight, and bordering on alarm.

My heart sinks. Does she think I'm here for revenge? I walk her to the sofa and help her sit.

"Let go of me." She snatches her hand out of my grip.

When I drove here, I expected a cold reception, maybe even tears. Emberly is still hurt at my deception, yet this rejection lands like a slap.

"Emberly—"

"No."

She rises off the sofa and glares up at me, her features hardening, her hands balling into fists. "Answer my question. How the hell did you track me here?"

"I've been watching over you since before you moved to Carmel."

"Why?" she snaps.

"I was trying to give you space."

"If you're here for the rest of my inheritance, I haven't got it."

I flinch. "God, Emberly, it's not like that."

"Then what do you want?" She shakes her head. "Never mind, just get out."

I don't move.

"Get out of my apartment." She shoves me in the chest with enough force to strain herself and then winces.

My stomach plummets and my throat tightens in a fist of worry. I choke out the words, "Are you alright?"

Emberly lowers herself onto the sofa and grimaces. "I will be if you fuck off."

I kneel at her feet. "Baby, I can't leave you in pain. Let me call you a doctor. Tell me what you need."

The weight of her emotions presses down on her shoulders, and she slumps forward in her chair, defeated. Avoiding my gaze, she turns her head towards the window, her eyes fixed anywhere except on me. "Why did you wait until now to haunt me when I can't kick you out of my apartment?"

"I hurt you, and I can never take that back," I say, my

voice softening. "But I couldn't wait any longer. I came to tell you the truth."

Emberly snorts. "You had multiple chances to speak, but you chose to lie."

"And I regret it every day because I lost the one thing more precious than my family's stolen legacy."

"What's that?" she says with a sneer.

"You."

She rolls her eyes. "Go back to New Alderney. Nobody here wants your bullshit."

My gaze wants to drop to her swollen belly, but I keep it on her face. The last thing I want Emberly to think is that I've slithered out of the woodwork because of our baby.

"Ask me anything. Anything at all," I rasp. "I swear to god I'll tell you the truth."

Her nostrils flare, and her lips twist with contempt. "Fine. Who bought that painting Mr. Lubelli sold in the auction?"

I flinch. "Emberly?"

She turns to meet my eyes, her gaze venomous. "Who bid for my painting?"

My lips part, and I'm about to tell her I don't know, but I clench my teeth. "I paid Lubelli to make a show of selling it. The bidders were shills."

Emberly closes her eyes. "And all his other purchases?"

"Those were mine."

"Right." She blows out a long breath. "You once mentioned knowing a man who sold counterfeit art on the black market. Was that him?"

"Yeah."

"Figures," she mutters. "You two must have been laughing your asses off, making me think my art was worth something."

"It wasn't like that, baby."

"Don't call me that," she snaps.

"Emberly, I love your paintings."

"Oh, yeah?" She asks with a laugh. "And what do you know about modern art? Everything in your mansion is from centuries ago, if they aren't fakes."

My jaw clenches, and I swallow hard. She's right on all points, but I'm not going to debate the family's art collection when there's so much more at stake.

"I'm apologizing. Truly, sincerely, and without reservation. For everything. For lying. For hurting you. For being the kind of selfish prick too blinded by revenge to notice you're the goddess I needed to worship."

"Don't waste your time," she says.

"I love everything about you, and that includes your art." She scoffs.

"I love your view of the world. I love how you explored the grounds and found beautiful things I never noticed. The day you took me to Simon's Pond was the most relaxing I'd had since I was a kid. And that painting you created made me feel like Apollo—"

"Roman, stop," she says, sounding weary. "I understand why you did it."

My throat thickens. "What do you mean?"

"I even get why you held me in such contempt—"

"Never," I rasp. "It wasn't like that."

"I read the forums. They're saying Frederic Capello might have even engineered your dad's death. You spent five years locked up because of him. Anyone would be murderous."

My heart pounds so hard that it aches.

She shifts in her seat. "My biological father took so much from your family, and I was standing in the way of getting it back. I've had six months to come to terms with it, and I can't even say that I hate you."

"Emberly?"

"Thank you for coming here to apologize," she says, her words a monotone. "I appreciate the closure."

My brows pull together. This isn't my Emberly. Where's the rage? Where's the fire? She's flat. Cold. Dead. "What does that mean?"

"That I want you to leave. If you want your money back for the paintings, or the rest of what I inherited from Frederic Capello, get in touch with Martina at the Di Marco Law Group, and she'll send over the paperwork."

"I don't want your money."

With a groan, she rises off the sofa and heads for the door. Seeing her so distant is a kick in the balls. It's like I've broken her heart beyond hope. I hold her by the shoulder.

"Please, let's talk."

"There's nothing left to say." She shrugs me off. "You got what you wanted. In return, you gave me false hope that I was talented and worthy of love."

My eyes widen. "No—"

"Yes." She reaches the door. "You were using me to get back at my father and you've succeeded. Unless you're here to put a bullet through my heart, we're even."

My jaw drops. She's serious. Even though she cries herself to sleep and calls out my name at night, she still wants me to leave.

"But what about the baby?" I ask.

She glances down at her bump. "I was pregnant by the time we met. Didn't you ever wonder why Jim pursued me so relentlessly?"

I shake my head. "He wanted your inheritance. You're just saying that to hurt me."

Shrugging, she looks me straight in the eye. "If it was your baby, I would have had an abortion. I wouldn't let any part of you continue living in my body. The only reason I'm keeping this child is because his father is dead."

Shock steals my breath, and I reel forward. My detective didn't find any computerized medical records for her, so I know nothing about the rate of her pregnancy. Just as I'm trying to process Emberly's revelation, she walks out, leaving me alone in her apartment, staring at the closed door.

———

I wait all day for Emberly to return, hoping she isn't skipping out of town to find somewhere else to hide. If she's still in contact with the Di Marco Law Group, they might even help her relocate.

When it gets dark, I send a text to the men I've stationed in the apartment opposite to message me the moment Emberly returns. Then I walk to my car and drive back to New Alderney.

A numb fog clouds my senses on the journey home, and I replay our conversation again and again and again until I've analyzed every hurtful word.

Emberly gave me no room to maneuver. She wouldn't believe that while I was scamming her, my feelings for her had grown into love. She was even sympathetic to my reasons and offered me the rest of Frederic Capello's wealth.

I thought the baby would be my way back into her life, yet she cut me down. It even makes a sick sort of sense that she left Callahan the moment she discovered she was pregnant.

Fuck.

I can't even complain, considering I was the one who turned a simple kiss into a month-long abduction.

My phone rings, interrupting my thoughts. I pick up, hoping it's one of the men watching over Emberly.

"Roman?" says a familiar male voice. "It's Ernest. When shall I expect you at the gallery?"

"What?" I frown.

"Gil brought in Miss Kay's entire portfolio. I believe you wanted to talk about her art, so I've set it up in one of the viewing rooms?"

"I'm on my way."

Twenty minutes later, one of the MoCa assistants guides me into a private chamber in the back of the gallery. Lubelli rises from a chair in the corner, holding a glass of whiskey.

"Miss Kay didn't show me these five." He gestures at some oversized canvases filled with abstract shapes and patterns. "Did she complete them recently?"

Pain grips my insides at the memory of Emberly in the back of my vehicle, kicking the shit out of that sniveling Lafayette.

"I acquired them from another gallery."

Lubelli hums his approval. "She's very versatile. Would you like me to stage an auction for them individually or as a quintet?"

"Neither."

He takes a sip from his glass. "What would you like me to do with them?"

"What's your assessment of her talent?"

His brows shoot up to his hairline. "My assessment?"

I meet his gaze with an unwavering glare. He tears his eyes away from mine and glances back to the paintings.

"The talent is there. Her work is unique and captivating. As I said before, her range is wide but always with a unique perspective that stands out from other artists at her level."

"So, you could sell her paintings?"

Lubelli blows out a long breath. "Today's market is based on name recognition, not skill. Miss Kay is an unknown, but with proper marketing and exposure, her pieces could sell."

"Do it."

"But she doesn't have a social media presence."

I close in on the smaller man. "Make something happen."

"It'll be expensive," he says. "Unless she's willing to invest hours into this project, she'll need a publicist, a social media manager—"

"I'll cover the costs."

"And videos and photos of her works in progress," Lubelli continues as if I haven't even spoken.

"I have hours of footage from her studio," I say, thinking about the surveillance.

Lubelli finally nods. "Then I'll make it happen."

As I turn toward the exit, he clears his throat. "I still stand by what I said about these pieces."

I turn around to find him gesturing at the painting of me at Simon's Pond and a few other close ups of my physique. "What about them?"

"It would be a pity to sell such masterpieces," he says with a wistful smile. "The love she has for you jumps off the canvas. It's rare for an artist to infuse a painting with so much raw emotion."

A knot forms in my stomach at the mention of Emberly's love for me. I stare at the colorful paintings, each beat of my pulse tightening the tension around my heart.

Emberly loved me until she discovered my deceit. Emotions like that don't just fade into cold indifference, and a woman who feels nothing for the man who betrayed her doesn't cry herself to sleep.

"Don't sell those paintings. Have them delivered to my home, but the rest of her work needs to be on social media and available for sale."

A plan forms in my mind as I leave the gallery. I don't give a fuck whose child she's carrying. It was never about the baby.

Emberly Kay is mine, and I'll do whatever it takes to win her back.

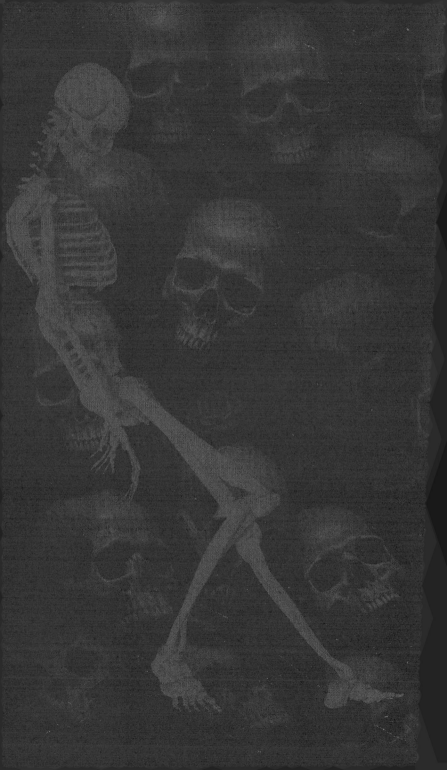

SIXTY-FOUR

EMBERLY

I spent the rest of my weekend at the Carmel Inn, feeling as though I'd ripped out my own heart. Seeing Roman at my door hadn't just been a shock. All the love and hurt and hatred I kept in a tight little ball reared to the surface, accompanied by something more insidious.

Mom always made me feel like a bogeyman was coming to take me away. Seeing Roman was like finally getting caught, only by a different monster. In the time we were apart, I'd built him up into a Machiavellian murder who wielded equal parts sadism and charm.

I thought Roman would drag me out of my apartment and demand his son. I feared being dragged back to New Alderney and being forced to spend the rest of my pregnancy locked in that tower. Roman's machinations are far more subtle. He knows that caging my body won't work, so I gave him a reason not to cage my heart.

When he implied I was more precious to him than everything he'd already taken, I knew for certain this was the beginning of another scam. He could take my biological father's vehicles, house, and personal effects, but he couldn't take my baby.

It's because of Roman that I'm no longer interested in creating art. He fooled me once, and I sure as fuck won't allow him to take the only thing left in my life that matters.

It took me a few minutes of distracting him with talk about the paintings until I could think of a way to make him go away. Since Roman used the threat of Jim as a way to keep me from wanting to leave him, it seemed fitting that I should tell him that Jim was the one who got me pregnant.

On Monday, I return to the apartment, relieved to find no trace of Roman. I spent the rest of the week on edge, heavy with dread and thinking every slammed door is his return. If I see him again, I might have to hide with my cousin, Tommy.

It's Saturday, which means another Mindful Birthing class, but I no longer cringe at the prospect of going alone. The alternative is far worse. I arrive outside the community hall in time to avoid conversations with the other mothers, but a smoking figure standing outside the doors blocks my path.

It's Wendy's husband, the creep who said he enjoyed watching me with the instructor.

"Kate," he says. "You're late."

My stomach roils. If I weren't six months pregnant, I'd knee him in the balls. Instead, I sweep past him like he's invisible.

He blows a cloud of smoke in my direction and winks. "Looking forward to today's class."

A shudder runs down my spine. I pause at the doorway and shoot him my filthiest glare. "I'll pass on what you said to Lily. Every woman in the class and their birthing partners need to know they're in the company of a predator."

His smirk drops, and I dart into the foyer and through the doors leading to the classroom. Lily stands in the front, her face lighting up when our gazes meet. As I'm about to make my way toward her, Wendy brushes past me and stands beside the teacher.

My breath shallows. Don't tell me the haughty redhead wants me to partner up with her husband?

Lily beams. "Welcome, Kate." She points at a spot in the middle. "Your partner already got you set up."

A large figure rises on my right. I turn toward him, expecting to find the smirking asshole sneaking up from behind, but it's Roman.

He's barefooted, wearing a white t-shirt and gray sweatpants, surrounded by a bolster, an exercise ball, blocks, and blankets. Sunlight streams in from the window, lighting him from behind, making him look as handsome and as majestic as the day I painted him in Simon's Pond.

The smile he gives me looks so genuine that the butterflies in my stomach flutter. It's probably the baby sensing his father, but I can't deny a part of me is relieved to have a buffer from all the prying eyes.

"Katie," he says, his voice melodic and deep. "Let me help."

"It's Kate," is all I can muster. Since everyone in the class is watching our drama unfold, I close the distance between us and let him help me onto the mat.

"What are you doing here?" I whisper.

"I'm here to support you," he murmurs into my ear. "And I don't care that the baby isn't mine."

My heart races as Roman follows Lily's instructions and sits behind me with my back resting on his chest. I relax against his larger body as he holds my belly from behind.

His hands are comforting and warm, making the baby

stir. I close my eyes during the introductory breathing exercises, trying to fight off the feeling of being protected.

"I missed you so much, baby," he says, his voice low. "Things between us started with a lie, but the love I feel for you is real."

He continues to pour honey into my ears, making my throat thicken with emotion. His hands glide over my belly in sync with my relaxing breaths, sending tingles across my skin.

"I'm so sorry. My mind was full of vengeance when I left prison, and by the time I realized you were nothing like your father, it was too late."

"Shut up. I'm trying to concentrate," I whisper.

His lips brush against my brow. "I'm not a good man or even a nice one, but you own my heart. I would lie, steal, and kill to protect you and your baby."

Tears prick at my eyes. "What are you trying to say?"

"Listen, I may not be ecstatic that your kid is half a cop, but the least I can do is provide for them, considering I got rid of their dad."

My noisy gasp is swallowed up by the relaxing music. I turn around and lock gazes with Roman.

He really killed Jim?

As though reading my silent question, he nods.

Lily moves onto stretches, while the birth partners support our backs and hold our limbs in position. Roman concentrates on the instructor's directions as though committing all the movements to memory.

I have to admit that it's nice to practice with a partner who's built like the Terminator. Whenever I demonstrated with Lily, I was always terrified of flattening her with my larger height and weight.

Lily directs us to variations of squatting poses, helped by the birth partners. We combine these with more vigorous breathing exercises to use during labor. Every time I look at Roman or catch his eye in the mirror, his expression varies from adoration to pride to concern.

I'd almost forgotten he could be so sweet.

As Lily guides us into the meditation and relaxation poses, I'm consumed by an overwhelming sense of safety and belonging. As Roman's hands linger over my belly, I remember all the different ways he came to my rescue.

He didn't just protect me from Dominic and Jim, he also delivered Lafayette to me hogtied, so I could kick the shit out of him. The same night, he made the restaurant manager who snubbed me grovel on his knees. He even spoke up for me when Annalisa criticized my choice of attire during the family dinner.

Oh, shit.

I can't let Roman worm his way back under my skin.

I can't let myself fall for his lies.

When the class ends, the birthing partners and expectant mothers pack up their equipment. I scramble to my feet and walk out through the doors, leaving him behind.

As I burst through the exit and onto the streets, a rough hand grabs my arm. "Isn't that man a mafia ex-con?" Wendy's vile husband asks, his smoky breath making my nostrils twitch. "If I'd known you went for the bad boys, I would have made my move sooner."

"Don't touch me." I yank my arm free.

"That type never sticks around," he says with a leer. "Either they're in and out of prison or making up for lost time fucking other women."

The double doors slam open before I can even retort, and Roman charges out, his fists flying. He grabs the creep by the throat and slams him so hard against the wall that his head bounces.

"Don't you ever touch my wife!"

Wife?

My jaw drops.

Roman can't tell the truth, even in the heat of the moment. The man is a compulsive liar.

I turn on my heel and walk away.

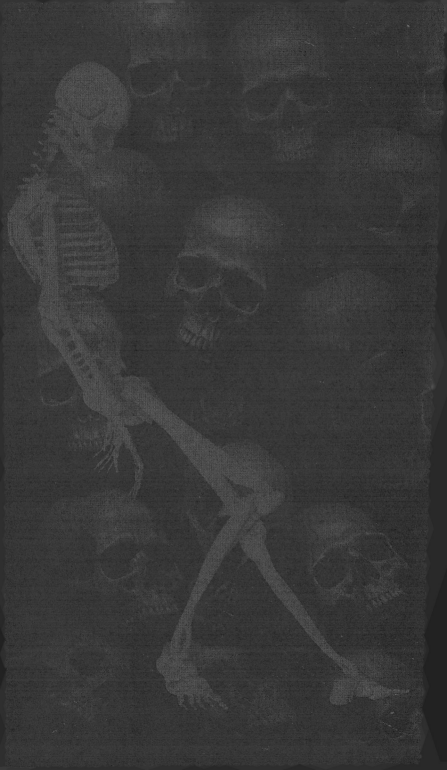

SIXTY-FIVE

ROMAN

I pour every ounce of my internal rage into throttling the asshole who touched Emberly. His eyes bulge, and spittle gathers in the corners of his mouth. I tighten my grip around his scrawny throat, turning his face from red to purple.

"You touched what was mine," I snarl.

"We were just talking," he rasps.

"Don't even look at my wife," I snarl. "Don't even think about my wife. Don't come within a mile of my wife. If I see you in Carmel again, I'll break your fucking back."

He nods. "I won't. Please, let me go."

Noise from within the community center alerts me that Emberly's friends are approaching. I release his throat, allowing him to stagger toward a blue sedan. The door opens, letting out the first few pregnant mothers and their husbands. By the time I turn around to check on Emberly, she's already halfway down the road.

My stomach sinks. Choking the shit out of a man in broad daylight probably isn't earning me brownie points.

"Shit."

I jog after her, but she doesn't look around or even flinch at the pounding of my feet on the sidewalk. Instead, she stares straight ahead and keeps her head high. This aloof version of Emberly is more challenging than the hellcat who used to fly into destructive tantrums.

"Why did you walk away?" I place a hand on her arm.

She doesn't even shrug me off. "Go back and collect all your equipment. Those bolsters are pricey."

"Fuck the bolsters. Tell me what's wrong."

"You're so much like Jim Callahan it isn't even funny," Emberly mutters. "I can't believe I didn't see that until now."

The words hit like a meat tenderizer to the balls, making my steps falter. My hand drops off her arm and I glare at her retreating back.

"A drug-addicted, corrupt cop who can't keep a woman unless she's imprisoned?" I ask.

She shoots me a glare over her shoulder and quickens her pace.

My jaw tightens. Was that expression on her features fury or fear and did she just put me in the same sentence as a sick coward who threatened to rape women in police cells only to silence them with overdoses?

No, she fucking didn't.

I walk behind her, my nostrils flaring. "You're seriously comparing me with that bastard?"

"There's more than one type of abuse." She rounds the corner.

"I never hurt you."

"Only in the worst possible way," she says.

Picking up my pace, I glare down at her pretty profile. "What does that mean?"

Her face tightens, and she draws in a long breath as though powering up for a tirade. "You think you're a good guy because you didn't pound into me with your fists? Or maybe because you didn't hurl the usual insults men use against women?"

I swallow hard and brace myself for what she'll say next.

"You're more sophisticated than the average brute. Your brand of abuse is psychological." She taps her brow.

"Because I lied to you about the paintings?" I ask.

She whirls around, her eyes flashing. "Every day I was with you, I was terrified Jim would find his way through the gates to carry out his threats."

I'm about to protest, but she continues. "You fed into that fear and built yourself up to be the big protector. Whether or not it was true, you chalked up any negative thing that happened in that house to Jim."

"Believe it or not, Callahan *was* trying to get to you."

She continues walking. "Gaslighting is one of the worst forms of psychological abuse. I don't doubt that I needed your protection, but you kept me agoraphobic and off-balance with all that talk about Jim and his friends."

"Emberly," I growl, unable to produce any words in my defense because she's right.

"When did Jim die?"

"What?" I swallow. "He had to die because he hurt you."

"You're deflecting." She shakes her head. "Again."

"I killed him just after we went to Simon's Pond. Is that what you want to know?" I ask.

"So, he was dead for two weeks before I found out from a news report." Her words are flat, but there's no missing the accusation.

I set up a stage where I made her believe Callahan and his corrupt cops would go to any lengths to get their hands on her, including staging my assassination. Hell, I even told her that the measures we took against the Moirai Group were an attempt to protect her from the crazy cop.

But I didn't stop at the gaslighting. The day she opened up about her relationship with Callahan and described how he manipulated her into becoming his prisoner, she painted a psychological profile of me that was so accurate that I couldn't rest until I destroyed the slimy bastard.

Instead of becoming a better man, I doubled down.

"I fucked up, baby," I murmur. "Back then, I would have done anything to keep you."

"And now?" she asks, finally looking me in the eye.

The agony etching her beautiful features grips me by the throat. I want to reach out to touch her and wipe away the pain I caused, but I'm paralyzed by guilt.

"Now, I love you from afar."

"What else did you do to keep me?" she asks, her voice soft.

"What do you mean?"

Emberly parts her lips to speak before shaking her head. "Never mind."

She continues walking down the street.

Up ahead, a truck stops outside her building. The delivery driver hops out, jogs to the back of his vehicle, and opens its doors. He hauls out a large package and carries it to the front door.

I glance down at my watch.

He's right on time.

The man rings the bell and waits about a minute before ringing again. When there's no answer, he leans the box by the door and hurries back to his truck.

I predicted Emberly would tolerate my presence until she reached her front door, after which she would tell me to get lost. The presence of a package she can't lift in her condition is my way into her apartment.

As we reach the entrance, she pulls out her keys, but the door opens and the superintendent steps out with a goofy grin. I grind my teeth as he examines the label on the package.

"Hey there, Kate," he says. "Let me help you with your delivery."

She glances its way. "That's not mine."

He chuckles. "Kate Edwards, apartment two, Vigri Mansions?"

"But I didn't order anything," she says.

I pick the box off the ground and brush past the old bastard. "Hold the door open while I help Miss Edwards."

The superintendent steps back, his eyes narrowing. He's probably wondering if I'm the man who pays him to keep an eye on the tenant in number two. I shoot him a glare, warning him to keep his mouth shut.

Emberly walks ahead of me into the building's small hallway and unlocks her door. The superintendent lumbers at my heels like a stray dog, and my hackles rise. I didn't tell him to hang around like he's begging for treats.

I carry the box into her apartment and slam the door in his face.

Emberly places a hand on her chest and exhales. "That guy gives me the creeps," she whispers. "Always lurking around and in my business."

"I'll tell him to back off."

She shakes her head. "He's just trying to be helpful."

"You sure?"

She smiles. "He doesn't need the Roman Montesano special."

My lip lifts, and I make a mental note to text the superintendent when I get to the car and warn him to keep his distance. Emberly only needs one nuisance in her life, and that will be me.

"Where do you want the crib?" I ask.

She closes the distance between us and tilts her head to

read the logo on the box. "The woman whose daughter I teach recommended this brand. I looked it up online, but it was too expensive."

"Maybe you have an admirer," I say. "Take a seat, and I'll set it up."

"What do you know about flat-pack furniture?" she asks.

"It's not rocket science," I reply with a smirk. "Do you want a cup of tea and something to eat before I get started?"

She walks to the sofa and sits, letting out a soft groan. My conscience twangs. Is it gaslighting if a man buys a bulky piece of furniture for a woman that's too heavy for her to assemble alone?

"You're not going to make me a drink and a snack?" she asks.

I flash her a smile. "Watch me."

Step one: infiltrate Emberly's apartment. Done.

Step two: get her to agree to have dinner with me. Done.

Step three: give her a full body massage with a happy ending. Not yet, but I'm optimistic.

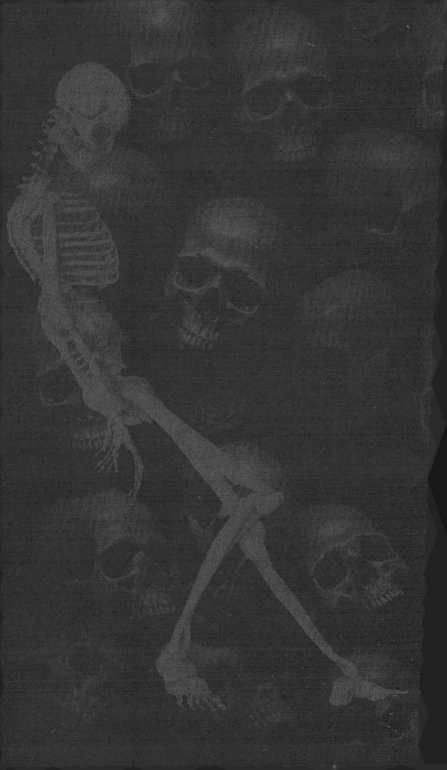

SIXTY-SIX

EMBERLY

Roman Montesano is the devil. The devil wearing gray sweatpants and a white top that accentuates every beautiful muscle.

I know he's a lying, manipulative bastard. He knows he's a lying, manipulative bastard. He knows I know he's a lying, manipulative bastard, yet he's slithered through my defenses.

Now, he's taking advantage of my vulnerable state. I'm lonely, heartbroken, touch-starved, and on the verge of becoming my mother, and he slides back into my life like the answer to my prayers.

Roman fills the kettle, opens the right cupboards to extract my honey, tea bags, and mug. While the kettle boils, he pads over to the refrigerator and extracts a glass container.

"Nice," he says. "Did you know that plastics leach chemicals into food?"

"I wouldn't know about that," I mutter. "The company that delivers my food provided these as a welcoming gift."

As he adds the perfect amount of honey into my mug, the corner of his mouth lifts into a smile.

I'm too exhausted from our argument to analyze his words or ask myself why he's spouting these facts. Or why he seems to know where to find the items he needs to make tea.

He appears in front of me with a mug. "Are you alright, baby?"

"What do you want from me?" I ask with a sigh. "There's nothing more for you to take. Why can't you just leave me alone?"

He lowers himself onto the sofa beside me and sets down the mug. "You already know the answer."

"There's no way you can love someone whose father destroyed your family. How could you not look at me and see Frederic Capello?"

"Emberly."

I squeeze my eyes shut.

"Look at me," he says.

I shake my head.

Roman leans so close that he's sharing his body heat. I reach out a hand and shove him back, but he grabs my wrist.

"What?" I look him in the eye.

"Did you know I grew up around Samson and Gregor Capello?" he asks. "They were the same age as Benito. I was too busy hanging out with my cousin, Leroi, to pay them much attention, but you could easily be their little sister."

I try not to bristle at the comparison to the Capello twins, but even I saw the family resemblance when I'd looked them up online.

"What are you saying?" I ask.

"I won't deny you're his daughter, but I do see you as your own person. You're nothing like that bastard and his psycho sons. Your mother spent your entire childhood keeping you away from them, and it shows."

"Meaning?"

He cups my cheek. "You're strong, brave, compassionate."

I roll my eyes.

"You are. How many women would see my arrangement with Officer McMurphy in prison as exploitation?"

"Well, she took advantage," I say with a sniff.

His eyes soften. "There you are, still looking out for my welfare."

My jaw clenches. He's doing it again. Bringing up something incendiary to shift my focus. Now I'm feeling protective.

"Just…" I shake my head. "Just get me a snack."

Roman kisses my forehead before handing me my tea, which is now the perfect temperature for drinking as well as the perfect level of sweetness. I lean back on the sofa and sigh.

Moments later, he places a plate of banana brownies on the coffee table. They're leftovers from the organic food box that he must have found in the glass container.

After taking two cans from the cupboards, he returns to the refrigerator and extracts a pile of vegetables. "Minestrone soup okay with you?"

My brows rise. That wasn't this week's food delivery. "You can make that?"

He turns the heat under a large saucepan. "I've been taking lessons from Sofia."

"Since when?" I ask.

"Since my social calendar became bleak."

He doesn't need to voice the last part of the sentence. Instead, he chops the vegetables with chef-like precision and adds them to the pan.

My lips tighten. I'm sure he wants me to think he's been pining for me since I left. The truth to his statement is more nuanced. In the month after he was released from prison, I was his biggest project. The heiress to his family's stolen fortune.

I should stay quiet, enjoy my brownie, and watch him make the fucking soup, but I find myself asking, "You own a nightclub, a casino, two hotels and you have nowhere to go in the evenings?"

He pauses, mid-stir. "I ruined the only social life I ever needed, and I'll do anything to get it back."

A lump forms in my throat, and I wash it down with a mouthful of tea. Roman doesn't get to come here, looking so handsome and vulnerable and apologetic. This is just another of his ploys to bring me under his control.

He tips the canned beans and tomatoes into the soup, adds a few more ingredients, and stirs. My eyes narrow. Does he really mean to make me believe he's spent the past six months with his housekeeper, learning how to cook?

He turns down the heat, leaving the soup to simmer. After wiping his hands, he walks to the other side of the living room and opens the box.

As he extracts the flat-packed pieces of wood, I sit up and frown. "The wood is unfinished."

Roman's eyes meet mine. "That way, you can paint it however you want. Do you remember all those mushrooms you found among the juniper trees?"

My eyes sting at the reminder of the joy I felt committing the plants and fungi around his estate to canvas. "What makes you think I can still paint?"

His face falls.

"I haven't touched a brush since realizing my dream art career was built on deceit."

"The sales were fake, but your talent is real."

"There's no need to keep up the pretense," I say with a sigh. "I'm happy nurturing the next generation of artists."

"Sorry isn't enough."

"What for?"

He bows his head. "I should have been building you up, but I was so blinded by revenge that I destroyed your confidence."

"Are you just saying what I want to hear?" I ask, my voice thickening.

"No," he rasps. "I knew I was digging a hole for myself with my lies, but being with you was so addictive I just couldn't stop."

I should stop speaking, look away, and wait for him to leave. As soon as he's gone, I can pack up some essentials and disappear. It's a sensible plan, yet I find myself saying, "Don't forget you had to keep digging to keep me signing those contracts."

Roman lays out the instructions, picks up two wooden pieces and clicks them into place. Silence stretches out, broken only by the bubbling of the minestrone soup. After completing the crib's base, he raises his head to meet my gaze.

The agony etched into his eyes makes me flinch.

"I have never loved anyone the way I love you. Never wanted anything so desperately that I'd risk everything to get it. I want to make up for the pain I caused, but everything I say or do seems to make it worse."

"You paid for the food boxes, didn't you?"

Nodding, he picks up a wooden slat. "I had to make sure you were eating right."

I run a hand through my curls. "How did you even know where to deliver it?"

Roman's features tighten. He slips the slat into place, his eyes focused on the crib.

I wait for him to answer, but he picks up another slat.

"Did you arrange the apartment?" I ask.

He remains silent.

"What about the perfect job with free medical care?"

He slips the second slat into place and then a third.

"Roman," I snap. "Was that you?"

"I couldn't let you continue sleeping in that flea-ridden hostel with no locks on the door," he says. "Do you know why nobody in the prison ever wants the top bunk?"

"So, you arranged my job, my apartment, my food. What else?"

He stares at me, his lips pressed in a thin line. There's more, but he doesn't want to admit to further manipulation. I think back on every stroke of good fortune I had since leaving the hostel and remember the garage sale.

"Did you arrange for that couple down the road to sell their brand-new art supplies?"

His gaze wanders to the side.

"Roman," I say. "Use your words."

"Yes," he mumbles.

I shake my head and sigh. "Some might call that unselfish, but I know you well enough to understand your ulterior motive."

His jaw tightens, but he doesn't speak.

"You wanted me to be safe and happy because you thought I was carrying your baby."

"No—"

"That's okay. I'm not criticizing you for that, but I want you to cancel the food delivery."

He rears back. "Why?"

I run a hand over my belly. "You're not the father."

Roman picks up another piece of wood from the pile and examines it for several heartbeats. Then he sets it down, picks up another piece, and slots it into the base.

My breath shallows as I wait for him to respond. I have no idea about the depth of his manipulations. If he's in contact with my doctor and asks for my due date, he'll know that the baby is his.

Finally, after screwing the wood in place, he raises his head.

"No," he says.

"No to what?"

"Giving you the things you need is my way of showing love, as is taking care of the child."

"Why?"

"I love you completely. Every single part of you, including your baby. If you want to hate me, fine. But I can never let you go."

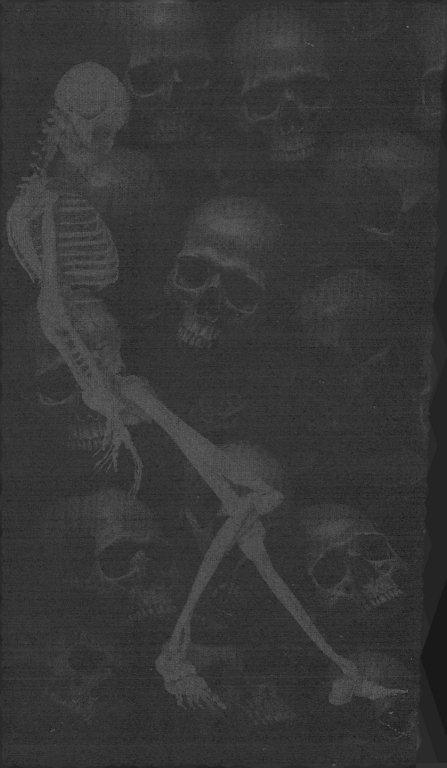

SIXTY-SEVEN

ROMAN

I meant every word of what I said. Emberly means so much to me that I even love her child. When she gazes at me through glistening eyes, I know I've finally reached her heart.

She places a hand on the armrest and tries to rise. "Roman, there's something I need to tell you—" Her face contorts with pain. "Ouch!"

My stomach drops. I spring to my feet, rush to her side, and wrap an arm around her shoulders. "What's wrong? Is it the baby?"

"Just a..." She grits her teeth. "Fucking twinge."

"Should I call a doctor?"

She shakes her head. "It'll pass."

My pulse races, and every fiber of my being wants to carry her back to New Alderney, where she can get the best care under my supervision. "Are you sure?"

"Yeah, just give me a minute," she says, her voice strained.

I loosen my grip on her shoulders but don't let go. All I

want is to point a gun at someone's head and make her pain disappear. Since that's not an option, I rub circles on her back, but even that gesture feels trite.

Emberly's head flops forward, and she exhales a sigh, the soft sound stirring up memories of her panting and moaning at my command. I push those thoughts aside and focus on easing her discomfort.

"That feels so good," she says, her voice breathy. "But then you always knew what to do with your hands."

Heat rushes to my cock, but I force myself to stay calm. Emberly is relieved, not ready for anything else.

"Glad to help," I say, my voice even.

"Aaah," she sighs.

My jaw tightens and my nostrils flare. When I was on death row, if anyone had asked me what I looked forward to after exacting my revenge and reconnecting with my family, it would have been an endless stream of pussy.

I would never have imagined it being six months of jacking off to the memory of a woman I'm loving from afar.

Half a year of celibacy is fucking with my mind. My brain is misinterpreting her every move as an invitation to fuck. I need to get a grip on propriety.

"Let me check on the minestrone." I pull back my hand.

"Don't stop," she moans.

I squeeze my eyes shut.

Fuck.

"I need to turn down the heat," I mutter.

"Hurry back," she says, and my cock swears she wants a deeper tissue massage.

I straighten, already feeling lightheaded because all sensation has gathered south. The horny bastard between my legs is at full mast, wanting to return to its favorite place in the world.

No matter how much I remind it that Emberly doesn't want that bullshit, it still manages to lengthen and thicken.

Dickhead.

I march to the stove and take the lid off the pot. A cloud of steam wafts over my face, reminding me I'm here to give comfort, not to satisfy my urges. After stirring the pot, I turn down the heat, take a few deep breaths, and count to five to gather my thoughts.

My cock doesn't want anyone else but Emberly, and neither does my heart. The ring around my finger is a constant reminder that there is no other woman for me but Emberly, yet the ring I wear on the chain around my neck presses down on my sternum like a brand.

To get her back, I need to at least act like a gentleman, even if every other part of me wants her on her hands and knees with me pounding into her slippery heat.

That's not happening.

When I turn back, Emberly waits for me on the sofa, her green eyes darkening with desire. She breathes fast through parted lips and her breasts strain against the fabric of her T-shirt.

My heart stops.

I clear my throat and try to clear my mind, but all I can think of is how badly I want to kiss her. How desperately I need to feel her body against mine.

"Hungry, baby?" My voice lowers a few octaves.

"Come back to me," she whispers.

I cross the room, my heart thrashing within its cage. Emberly doesn't want me. She just wants some comfort. I really shouldn't take advantage.

"Where does it hurt?" I rasp.

She rolls her shoulders and points at a spot at the base of her neck. "Here."

"Let's get you comfortable first," I murmur.

Emberly sits back, watching me arrange cushions and blankets on the floor. When I'm done, I help her settle between my spread legs, and she leans her back against my chest.

I push her curls aside, revealing her delicate neck. My mouth inches toward her exposed skin, wanting a taste, but I resist.

Instead, I massage her neck and shoulders with the tips of my fingers and my thumbs, relishing in her cinnamon-and-vanilla scent, and in the familiar feel of her flesh. Every muscle is knotted, and her breath is fast and shallow.

"You're tense," I murmur.

Emberly shivers, but doesn't speak. I move my thumbs in slow, circular motions, kneading away at the hardened tissue. She arches and gasps, her hips moving backward and grinding against my cock.

As I work away the tension on her upper back, Emberly finally relaxes against my chest and her breaths slow.

"Where else does it hurt?" I ask. "Show me."

"My bump."

I slide my hands down her sides and trace the curve of her belly. "Where?"

"Lower," she says, her voice breathy.

My hands move downward, so I'm supporting the weight of her bump beneath my fingers. Emberly rests her head against my shoulder, melding her body with mine.

I massage with gentle, slow strokes, enjoying the way she sighs.

"That feels so nice," she murmurs. "But I want more."

"Show me where you want it." My lips graze her temples.

Emberly wraps her fingers around my wrist and pulls my hand between her legs.

My cock surges, and my heart skips several beats. "You want me to stroke your pussy?"

Her breath quickens. "Yes."

Fuck.

I could twist this situation to lure her into my car. I could talk her into returning home with me, but I'm no longer that manipulative bastard. Besides, who am I to refuse the woman I love when she's in desperate need?

Emberly pulls the waistband of her leggings with her other hand and guides my fingers to her cotton panties.

"Touch me," she whispers, her voice tight.

I slip my fingers beneath the fabric, through her nest of soft curls, and meet her swollen clit. Her hips jerk, and she gasps.

"You like that?" I rasp.

"Yes," she replies, her voice barely a whisper.

I slide my fingers down her slick folds, all the while brushing my thumb over her clit. Emberly throws her head back, clamps her eyes shut and pants hard through her parted lips.

"You're so wet," I groan. "Is that all for me?"

She gasps and nods.

"Use your words if you don't want me to stop."

"Yes," she hisses. "I need this so badly."

I slide my fingers into her tight heat, my cock aching as her muscles clamp hard around the digits. My libido soars into overdrive, wanting her to take control of the situation and fuck. I clench my teeth, forcing down a surge of arousal.

This is about her needs. Not mine.

Despite my resolve, I run my lips over her neck, lavishing the soft skin with nips and kisses. Emberly's hips rise to meet my thrusts, her breathing becoming even more ragged.

"Pregnancy suits you," I growl. "I've never seen you look

so beautiful."

She shakes her head. "I don't."

I suck a spot on her neck. "You should see yourself through my eyes, baby. You're radiant."

She moans.

"And these tits." I cup a breast and roll her thick nipple between my thumb and finger. "I could play with them for days."

Emberly whimpers, and I increase the pace of my fingers, making sure to lavish attention on her needy clit. She grinds against my hand, meeting my movements with a hunger that takes me to the edge.

"Oh god."

"Try again, love," I murmur.

"Roman!" she shrieks.

"That's it, baby," I murmur against her flesh. "Let go."

Emberly cries out, her body shuddering at my command. Her pussy clenches and releases around my fingers with a force that nearly makes me come in my pants. I keep up the rhythm of my digits throughout her climax, continuing to pleasure her until the spasms subside.

"Oh, fuck," she murmurs. "That was amazing. Thank you."

I place a kiss on her temple. "It was my pleasure. If there's anything else you want, just say the word."

She sighs. "Roman, we need to talk."

My stomach tightens with dread. Now that I've given her what she wants, she'll ask me to leave. The next time I come to visit, she'll be gone. Bracing myself for the inevitable is excruciating. I have a feeling that whatever she says next will change everything.

Buying time, I place a kiss on her forehead.

"Eat first," I murmur. "Then you can tell me what's on your mind."

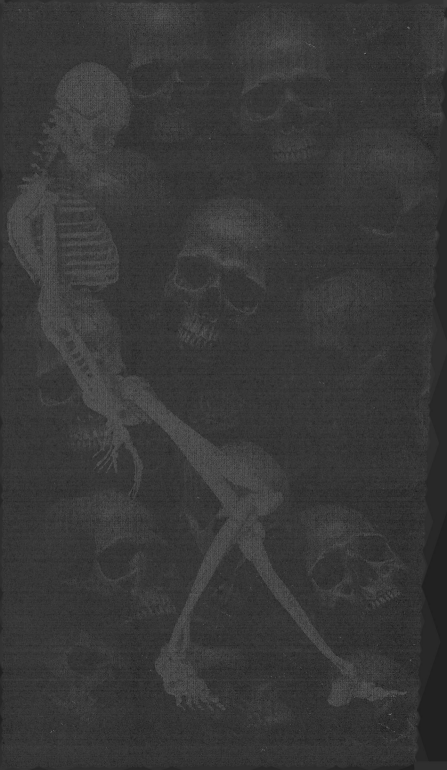

SIXTY-EIGHT

EMBERLY

Wow.

I flop back against Roman's chest and pant through the aftershocks of my orgasm.

That was exactly what I needed, but now I feel like a rotten bitch. I only told Roman the baby wasn't his because I was sick of his lies and wanted him to leave. Even so, he still wants to take care of us both.

I can't keep up with the pretense, and I also don't see the point of running. Maybe we can come to an arrangement?

He pulls his wet fingers out of my pussy and places them in his mouth. "Mmmm." The depth in his voice makes my spine shiver. "You taste even better than I remembered."

Heat rises to my cheeks, and I shift against his hard body. "Roman?"

"It can wait." He rises off the floor, helps me back on the sofa, and props up my spine with enough cushions to form a small fortress.

My shoulders sag as he walks to the kitchen, finds the bowls and spoons, then serves out the minestrone soup.

After grating a generous amount of parmesan over my serving, he drizzles it with olive oil and places it on a tray with a glass of iced water.

As he approaches and sets the tray down on the coffee table, I mentally rehearse my confession. My tongue darts out to lick my dry lips. "Roman—"

"Eat first," he says.

With a sigh, I pick up the bowl and take a spoonful. Roman stands over me, staring so intently that my breaths slow. He looks like I'm the judge about to deliver my verdict.

The soup is as rich and thick and delicious as it smells, with the perfect blend of tomatoes, garlic, and herbs.

"What do you think?" he asks, his voice halting.

"I can't believe you can cook so well," I say. "It's perfect."

He crouches beside me and smiles, the corners of his eyes crinkling. "Then all the time I spent making Sofia teach me to prepare your favorite dishes was worthwhile."

I take another bite and laugh. "What on earth made you want to learn?"

"You're moving into the final trimester and need extra help. I want to be able to tend to your needs any time of the night."

I stiffen. "What does that mean?"

"You get cravings, right?"

"Of course." I take another mouthful of the soup.

"And the school is giving you maternity leave?"

"So?"

"You're going to need help. I remodeled the pool house's kitchen to give me more space to cook, so I can whip up something healthy and fresh."

"But I'm not going back to you." I set down my spoon.

Roman frowns. "I know, which is why I'm offering you the pool house."

"No…" I say, trying to keep my voice even. "This is my home."

"What kind of man would leave his wife and child alone at her weakest? Even if Jim is dead, you're still a target."

I flinch.

Wife?

Once is a slip of the tongue I can dismiss as testosterone-fueled posturing. Twice is a proposal. Or maybe even an order.

"Roman." I twist around in my seat and look him straight in the eye. "We're not getting married."

He glances away.

"What?" I snap.

He remains silent.

"Roman, please."

"We're already man and wife."

"Bullshit."

He gazes down at me with an intensity that makes my skin break out in goosebumps.

"What does that look mean?"

"We're legally married."

"When?"

"Remember our date at the casino?"

My nostrils flare. "A half-finished taster menu and a few glasses of wine does not equal a marriage, even if it ends in bondage and anal sex."

"It happened when we checked into the hotel," he says.

I close my eyes, trying to remember what happened that night. Things got intense during the meal and Roman called for the hotel manager to make us sign the registration form…

WAIT.

My heart drops into my stomach, and all I can taste is acid. This is Roman Montesano, the man who can rob a woman blind while dazzling her with false love. The crook who will purchase a painting for twenty-five thousand dollars to get back a casino. He's capable of anything, including turning a stay in a hotel into a wedding.

Blood roars between my ears, and my veins flood with cold adrenaline. My nervous system kicks into top gear and prepares my muscles to fight.

"Are you saying you tricked me into signing yet another unfavorable contract?" I ask, my voice shaking, my fingers clenching around the soup bowl.

The backs of my eyes sting with betrayal, and the pain travels down my sinuses, into my lungs, and infuses my heart with poison.

He did it again.

Roman slipped beneath my defenses, bypassed my paranoia, and skirted around my common sense. He got me thinking he was a man too blinded by righteous anger to realize that he was hurting the woman he loved.

I was thinking of running away until that little speech about loving another man's baby. Then I allowed him to get too close. Just when I thought he was truly sorry and had confessed every underhanded machination, he reveals that he also tricked me into marriage.

"What else?" I ask, my voice hoarse.

"What do you mean?"

"You engineered our meeting, imprisoned me in your mafia fortress, swindled me into signing over an inheritance from a father I never knew, tricked me into marriage... This is your last chance to confess anything else you did."

"Emberly." He sighs as though I'm the one being unreasonable.

"If I find out you've done anything else—"

"Alright," he says. "We made VIP fliers to get you into the Phoenix."

I nod. "Anything else?"

Roman hesitates. "It didn't work."

"What didn't work?" I ask through clenched teeth.

"I tampered with the birth control because I wanted you pregnant. That time in the Dolce Vita, I poked holes in the condoms."

My arms tremble. I stare into my bowl of soup, my vision blurring with tears. Marrying me was inexcusable, but getting me pregnant is unforgivable. He fucked with my body, my hormones, my health, and exposed me to all the risks that come with unprotected sex.

I want to leap off the sofa and kick the shit out of him, but I'd only hurt myself and the baby.

"How could I have been so. Fucking. Stupid?" I growl.

"You weren't," he replies, his voice low. He reaches out to pull me into a hug. "You made me work hard to gain your trust. It wasn't easy. Not even the devil could have guessed the lengths I was willing to go. But I've changed. I'm sorry. I will never lie to you again—"

I hurl the hot minestrone.

"Fuck!" Roman jumps back, red soup dripping down his face and onto his white shirt.

"Never touch me again," I scream.

His hand twitches toward me, and I grab the water bottle and wield it like a club.

"Get out," I say through clenched teeth.

His gaze drops to the bottle, and he raises both palms. He swallows. "Don't do anything stupid. Think of the baby."

"Don't flatter yourself." I struggle to my feet, still brandishing my makeshift weapon. "Get out."

Roman steps back. "This isn't the end of it, Emberly."

"You haven't changed. You're still the same manipulative bastard who thinks I'm your property. If I never see you again, it'll be too soon."

He stands by the door, staring at me like he's trying to figure out another way through my defenses.

"Out!" I scream at the top of my voice.

A heavy fist pounds on the door. "Kate?" Mr. Wilder shouts, his voice tense. "Is everything alright?"

Roman's nostrils flare, but I keep my mouth shut. This is one time I appreciate the presence of that nosey old man.

Mr. Wilder's knocking continues. "If you don't reply, I'll call the police."

"Leave." I flick my head toward the exit.

"This isn't over." Roman walks to the door and flings it open.

The old man shuffles backward, his eyes wide. I hold my breath, hoping Roman doesn't lash out at the innocent superintendent, but he only grabs the handle and closes the door.

"Please, go away," I whisper, my breathing ragged.

Two sets of footsteps echo down the hallway until the external door creaks open and then shuts with a heavy thud.

I double over, clutch my temples, and force out a breath. My next inhale is so shallow that my vision dances with spots.

Sweat breaks out across my brow and trickles down my back. I knew Roman was fixated, but the forced marriage? The forced pregnancy? This is insane.

What should I do? If I run, he'll catch up with me. If I stay, he'll figure out a way to bring me back under his control.

The man is relentless. What if he escalates and decides to take me by force?

"Mom," I whisper. "I should never have called you paranoid."

The baby chooses this moment to kick, making me groan. He's right. I can't stay here like a sitting duck. I can't let this child grow up with a father who lies, manipulates, and gaslights.

A gentle knock captures my attention. I walk to the door, wondering what I can say to convince Mr. Wilder to drive me to the airport. My next escape plan needs to be more creative. Roman must never know where I've gone.

I open the door, expecting to see a gray-haired old man in a pair of dungarees. Instead, it's a man with whitened teeth, leathery skin, and slicked-back hair.

"Emberly." Tommy Galliano sweeps into the apartment. "How is my favorite cousin?"

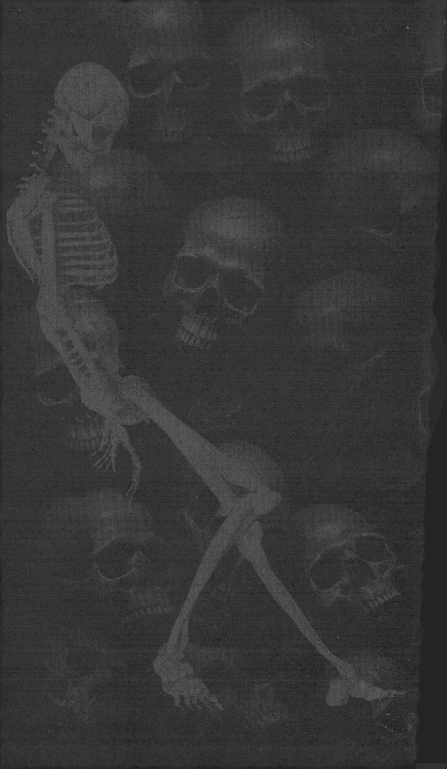

SIXTY-NINE

ROMAN

I walk through the hallway of Emberly's building, my face dripping with hot minestrone. The superintendent stays at my heels like a fucking guard dog. I lick my lips, capturing the tang of tomato, oregano, and parmesan.

Apart from that brief taste of soup, my mouth remains shut. The old bastard I'm paying to keep an eye on my wife needs to stop interfering. Wilder follows me out into the evening, and we walk in lockstep to my car. As I reach the door, I turn to meet his questioning gaze.

"Back off if you want my money to keep flowing," I snarl.

He straightens. "You're the husband?"

I pull off my shirt and wipe the cooling soup off my face. "Yeah."

His thick brows form a deep V. He's either looking at the ring dangling off my gold chain or he's noticed the word *LIAR* carved on my chest. He shakes his head and focuses back on my face.

"Ah... Sorry, but voices carry in the building. I was just keeping an eye on Kate—"

"Well, now you know." I open the door and slip into the driver's seat. "Keep me updated. If she gets into a car, I want its registration. If she deviates from her usual routine, I want details."

"Yes, sir." He nods.

I drive down the road, leaving him staring at my taillights. Emberly won't run. She's too encumbered by her pregnancy, too comfortable with her job, her apartment, and her medical plan.

Besides, it will take at least another day to create a new fake ID.

I wasn't lying about New Jersey being too dangerous. New Alderney also isn't safe, but that's where I can give her the most protection. Capello sympathizers still walk in the shadows and Tommy Galliano still evades my assassins. Any one of my enemies could use Emberly to get to me.

If she were any other woman, I would bring her back against her will. I call Nick Terranova at the stoplight, hoping the legal maverick who helped with the dodgy contracts can help me find a way to keep Emberly.

He picks up on the third ring. "Roman, what do you need?"

"It's my wife," I say. "She refuses to return to have the baby in New Alderney. Is there a way I can stop her from leaving?"

"Does she know you're married yet?" Nick asks.

"She just found out today," I mutter.

"And she told you where to stick your marriage?"

The lights turn green, and I pull out. "Something like that," I reply with a grimace.

Nick hums. "She's got you by the balls."

"Explain."

"Even if you filed a petition for an injunction or a temporary restraining order to stop her from leaving with your kid, Emberly could fight it in court on a number of grounds."

Nick rattles off a list of heinous shit I did to Emberly. I tune out partially because it's in legalese but mostly out of self-loathing.

No sane woman would give me a second chance, especially one with an innocent baby to protect. I won't give up, not just because I love her too much, but because I'm desperate to keep her safe.

"Bottom line," Nick concludes, "Unless you can convince Emberly that you've changed, there's no legal way to get her back."

"No illegal way that won't end in disaster, either." I snarl, remembering the incident on the balcony. "What about the baby? She claims it's not mine, but I'm her husband. Does that mean I get visitation rights?"

"Technically, but we're running into the same trouble as before. Her stack of complaints about you could send all five of us, including Ernest Lubelli, behind bars."

"Shit."

"My advice as a lawyer, a friend, and a potential co-defendant is to use that Montesano charm. It worked for you the first time."

The call waiting beeps, and Gil's name flashes on the screen.

"Got to go." I hang up and answer the second call. "Gil."

"There's trouble at the new meth lab," he rumbles.

"On my way."

I hit the accelerator and demand details. Gil says Tommy Galliano sent a pair of armed men to take it over, not knowing that four of the people working under our lead chemist are my foot soldiers.

Six months after freeing Isabella Cortese, half her team

quit the meth business for good, and I wanted replacements who could fight back.

I put my troubles with Emberly on the back burner and focus on the threat of Tommy Galliano. That greasy bastard has been quiet since we dealt with the Moirai Group. Someone murdered his younger brother and set fire to one of his homes. Looks like he's over the grief, because now he's back encroaching on my turf.

Business is stronger than ever, and our ranks have swelled in the past six months. It's time to deal with Galliano before he finishes the job Capello started.

Less than twenty minutes later, I reach the underground lab, and the fight is already over. Isabella and her team are shaken, but they've managed to protect the equipment and subdue the intruders.

The older woman gives me a crooked smile. "Looks like we took care of ourselves."

"Good work." I wrap an arm around her shoulder and pull her into a hug. "I'll assign more men to patrol the area."

She pulls back and points at a door at the other end of the chamber. "Gil's already in the restroom with them."

I stride past a line of vats and into the restroom to find Gil standing over a pair of round-faced men bound with zip ties and industrial-grade plastic wrap.

My brows rise. "What the fuck is this?"

"It's all the scientists had at hand to restrain Galliano's goons," Gil says with a shrug.

I kneel in front of them. "Here's the situation. Your boss sent you on a suicide mission."

One of them opens his mouth to speak, but I raise a finger. "He had to know I wouldn't leave the second lab unguarded, yet he sent you here anyway, proving he doesn't value your lives."

Neither of them can meet my eyes.

"What?" I ask.

"He told us to choose between attacking your lab or the lives of our mom and sister."

A chill ripples across my skin, and my insides tighten with dread. There must be something I'm missing. I glance at Gil, who shakes his head, looking just as surprised as I am about this ultimatum.

I focus my attention on the bound men, seeing some family resemblance. Even though one is balding and the other has a full set of hair, they share the same jowly cheeks and snub noses.

"Now, why would Galliano want us to perform your execution?"

The thinner of the pair speaks first.

"We fucked up on a job—"

"No," I snarl, my gaze boring into his. "Why did he send you to this lab?"

He bows his head. "Tommy said we weren't to speak about it until you arrived."

"I'm here now," I say through gritted teeth. "Start talking."

"He says to call your team in Carmel, NJ."

The words hit like a jolt of electricity to the heart.

"I'm on it." Gil pulls out his phone and dials.

"What else?" Straightening, I reach for my phone, not bothering to wait for the man to continue because I've already figured out the method to Galliano's madness.

My fingers tremble as I fire up the surveillance app and scroll to the saved clips. The last one is from twenty-two minutes ago.

I scrub through footage of Emberly doubling over, clutching her temples, looking like she's hyperventilating. Then she straightens and staggers to the door.

Alarm takes hold of my heart in a punishing grip. I want

to tell her not to answer, but it's already too late. She opens the door, and a tall figure steps inside.

He sweeps past Emberly, stares straight into the camera, and waves.

It's Tommy Fucking Galliano.

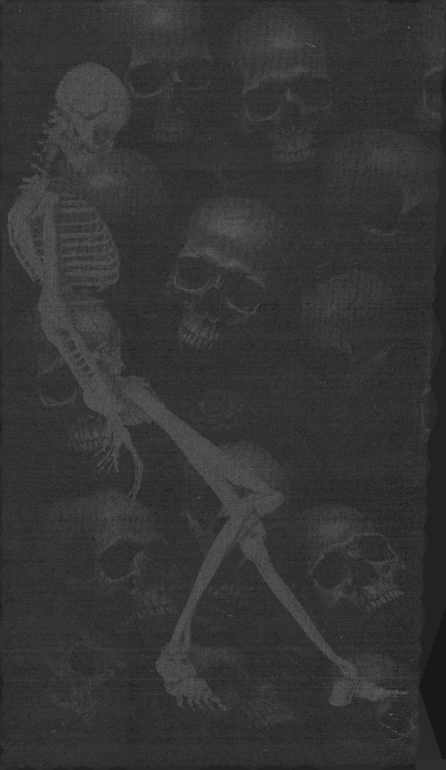

SEVENTY

EMBERLY

My breath stills, and the minestrone lingering on my taste buds turns sour. I'd always suspected that Tommy would keep tabs on my location, but seeing him at my doorway instills me with chills.

He walks past me as though I'm invisible, stands in the middle of the living room, and waves up at a spot in the corner.

"What are you doing here?" I ask.

He whirls around. "You're crying."

I gulp. Something in his demeanor tells me that confiding in him would be dangerous. Especially about the man who murdered an entire branch of his family. Tommy is determined to save me from Roman.

"It's nothing," I say. "Just hormones."

He cocks his head, his green eyes sparkling. "Just hormones."

His perfect mimicry of my intonation makes me bristle, but I clench my teeth. Tommy was perfectly normal via video conferencing or on the phone. When I discovered Roman had stolen my inheritance, the lawyer called Tommy, saying he was my biological father's close cousin.

In person, there's an edge to him that makes my skin itch. His movements are stilted as though his flesh is too tight for his bones, and then there are the turtlenecks and cravats and the tight-fitting fabric that covers every inch of his body. What kind of man always wears white gloves?

Tommy had been pleased to meet me and had spoken of Frederic Capello's relentless search for his stolen daughter. He offered me safe passage to New Jersey, where he said Roman would never venture.

Now, I'm wondering why he's come to visit moments after Roman just left. His presence here is too much of a coincidence.

"It's not hormones." Tommy advances on me, his eyes narrowing. "Montesano is trying to worm his way back into your life so he can steal the baby."

Swallowing, I back against the wall, still holding the door open.

"Your usefulness to him will end the moment you birth your son. Then he will hand you over to Cesare for torture and execution."

My pulse quickens, my breath shallows, and spots appear on the edges of my vision. Roman wanted to save my life, not end it. If he wanted me dead, he had more chances than I can count.

He flashes a mouthful of brilliant white teeth. "You don't believe me."

"Roman might be a liar, but he never physically hurt me," I murmur. "Besides, the baby isn't even his."

Tommy's arm springs out, and his gloved hand closes around my throat. I gasp, my eyes widening, but the air is already cut off. Struggling against his hold, I grab his fingers, trying to pry them off my neck, but his grip is too tight.

"I know everything about you, Emberly Kay," he sneers through artificial teeth. "Everything, including your due date. Your OB-GYN is in my pocket and reports directly to me. I've instructed her not to keep digital records of your pregnancy to force Montesano to continue crossing into my territory to check on your well-being."

My heart thrashes against my ribcage like a trapped bird, and the edges of my vision turn black. "Why?"

"Because I know you are Mrs. Roman Montesano."

"Let go of me."

His grip tightens. "You ungrateful bitch. I'm the one who's been running around, making your life easy. Who do you think arranged your well-paid job and this nice little apartment?"

Not Tommy. Tommy isn't the type of man to sneak around behind anyone's back and organize anything that doesn't directly benefit himself. His madness simmers beneath a veneer too thin to conceal his inner psychopath.

"I can't breathe."

"Answer my question," he snarls.

"You," I rasp. "You're the one who gave me the help."

He releases his grip, and I fall forward with my hands on my knees, trying to catch my breath.

"Good girl." He threads his fingers through my curls. "You should be on your knees, thanking me for saving you from Roman Montesano and his psycho brothers."

Tommy is the only one I need saving from, but defying him will endanger me and the baby. He's nothing like Roman, who is always calm when I'm frantic. Lashing out will only make Tommy escalate, so I need to play this cool.

"Why are you here?" I ask.

He pulls on my hair, sending lightning bolts of pain across my scalp. Wincing, I straighten to meet his gaze.

"Tommy, you're hurting me," I say.

He releases his grip and rests his hands by his sides. The viciousness on his features melts into a mask of concern.

"Emberly, are you okay?" he asks.

My jaw tightens. I stare up into eyes the same shade of mine but surrounded by whites riddled with tiny red vessels.

This man has to be on some kind of drug.

"I came as soon as I found out Roman Montesano had tracked you to your apartment," he says, his voice laced with worry. "He's going to kill you as soon as you give birth."

Fuck. This bastard just reset.

"Oh." I round my eyes and place a hand on my chest.

Tommy nods, looking serious. "I saved you once from Montesano, but he's returned to finish the job he started. Now, it's time to restore everything that bastard stole from you and make your son the don of New Alderney."

"What?" I step back. "But I already told you I don't want—"

He presses a gun into my belly. "Who said you had a choice?"

"Tommy," I say with a sob. "How can my baby become a don if you shoot him before he's born?"

Blinking, he frowns and pulls back the gun. "Right."

"Could you please give me a minute?" I ask.

He steps back, his gaze darting from my face to my belly to a point on the wall over my shoulder.

"Sorry." He puts away the gun.

I freeze, my heart hammering like it's trying to break through my chest. Tommy is clearly going through some kind of episode, and I need to wait for it to pass. Bolting might trigger even more aggression, so I take a deep breath and try to think of a way out.

"Are you okay?" I ask him.

He nods, his gaze still searching around me for goodness knows what.

"Montesano has been tracking you for months," he says. "We couldn't tell if it was because he wanted you or the baby."

"Okay..."

"What was the point of him parking outside your house and watching over you like a love-sick puppy?" he asks, his voice distant.

My eyes widen, and a breath catches in my throat. I can barely believe what Tommy is saying. Most nights, I cried myself to sleep, thinking Roman only viewed me as a pawn.

Hope sparks in my chest. If Roman has been watching over me all this time, maybe he's somewhere close?

"I had no idea," I murmur.

"He could have snuck in and banged you senseless, but he didn't," Tommy says, as though not hearing my question.

My stomach roils. Roman didn't do anything like that because he isn't sick.

"I planned on snatching the kid from the delivery room, but there's no point."

"What?"

Tommy's gaze fixes on mine. "Why do you think he resurfaced now? Because he wants you." He giggles. "I thought he was concerned about his baby, but it's you. Roman Montesano is head over heels in love."

I glance into the hallway, wondering if there's any chance I can run.

Tommy wags a finger. "My men are outside, murdering the guards Roman stationed in the apartment opposite to watch over you. What a waste of resources."

My heart drops.

I had no idea Roman went so far to make sure I was safe.

I had no clue he truly cared.

Tommy closes the distance between us, his larger body pressing mine against the wall. "Come with me, Cousin Emberly. You're about to serve me as bait."

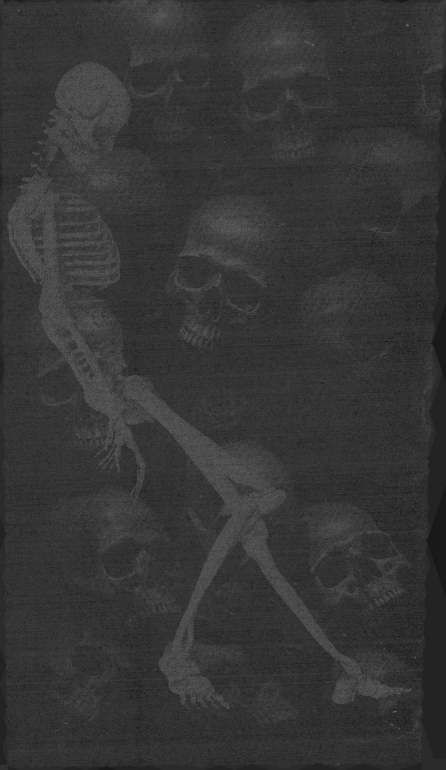

SEVENTY-ONE

ROMAN

I watch the events on the screen from over twenty minutes ago, my gut simmering with impotent rage. Fury boils in my veins, threatening to rip me into pieces. Galliano encroached on my territory, stole my meth lab, and now he has taken my wife.

This is one line he will not get away with crossing.

"Boss?"

Gil's voice hovers on the edge of my consciousness, but I can't hear what he's saying through the deafening thud of my pulse.

I want to tear through that scaly old bastard, rend him into tiny pieces, and incinerate what's left until all that remains is ash.

He touched Emberly. Choked my sweet, pregnant wife when she was at her most helpless. Now, he will die.

"Call him," I growl.

The number we have for Tommy is no longer in service. One of the men on the floor offers the use of his phone.

Dread coils in my gut like a cobra at the mere thought of

Emberly in the clutches of that maniac. He's the same man who lured our mother from the safety of the family home, only to have her butchered under the knife of a plastic surgeon.

My vision blackens, and worry mingles with fear for my wife. Emberly wouldn't know how to deal with a man as explosive as Galliano. He feeds off chaos and doesn't know when to stop. If he hurts her, I'll—

"Boss." Gil steps into my line of sight, holding the handset. "It's him."

Inhaling a deep breath, I force back all my fury, all my anxiety, all my fear. I can't show a trace of vulnerability or emotion. Not when I'm about to negotiate with the mad dog who has Emberly and her unborn child.

I take the phone and use my coldest, steadiest voice. "Galliano."

"Roman, my boy," he says. "So wonderful you're finally taking my calls."

"Cut the crap. What do you want?"

"Is this any way to speak to your cousin-in-law?" he drawls.

I flinch. Did Emberly tell him we were married or is that something he researched for himself? "Last time we talked, you were my stepfather."

He chuckles. "My favorite cousin and I have recently become very close, if you catch my drift."

He wouldn't fucking dare. If he hurt her, I wouldn't stop at burning down New Jersey. After razing his empire to ashes, I would feed that man his own entrails before putting him out of his misery.

"What do you want?" I ask again.

"A swap," he says. "You have one hour to get to the slaughterhouse at 12th and Spruce, where you will offer me your life in exchange for Emberly's and your son's."

I laugh, the sound bitter. "And walk into an ambush? How do I even know she's even alive?"

"Since you enjoy surveillance so much, the phone I gave Mike has a camera app with a live feed to her room. I will release her as soon as you're in my custody."

"Bullshit."

He snorts. "Come alone or she dies. For every minute you're late, Emberly will lose a finger."

The phone goes dead.

"Fuck!"

"Boss?" Gil says.

The phone's screen contains only four apps with icons I recognize. I click on the fifth, and the screen fills with a feed of Emberly running through an ostentatious bedroom.

"He's got Emberly." I show him the live feed.

Gil frowns. "Is there a microphone function?"

I click around the screen. "It's just a camera."

"What are you going to do?" he asks.

My gaze drops to the time on the phone. "We have an hour to find out where he's keeping Emberly, otherwise I'll have to swap my life for hers."

"But it's a trap," a familiar voice says through a speaker.

"Sorry, boss." Gil holds up his handset. "I group-called Cesare and Benito."

"Good." I run my fingers through my hair. "Galliano will want us to charge into New Jersey to rescue Emberly, so he can pick us off."

"That's what I'm thinking," Benito says from the other line.

"We can't let Roman hand himself over to that prick," Cesare says.

"If it comes down to it, I will sacrifice myself for my wife and unborn child," I say. "But I'm not going down without a fight."

As Gil and my brothers murmur their agreement, I turn to the two men on the floor. "If you want to get out of this alive, you're going to have to start speaking. Tell me everything you know about your boss, starting with his safe houses."

They exchange glances.

I pull out my gun.

"Wait," the larger of them blurts. "Tommy's a trickster, and he's also extremely cautious."

"Meaning?"

"He won't risk moving your woman into his home in case she's wearing something you can track."

The other one nods. "He once put a chip in some woman's neck so he could see where she went. Tommy might think you'd do the same."

"Then he's keeping Emberly in one of his buildings?" Benito asks from the other line.

"But if he's a trickster, won't he put her somewhere less obvious?" Cesare asks.

I take a screenshot of the room and send it to Gil. "Forward that picture to everyone and get them to ask around. Someone must recognize this interior."

"What are you going to do?" Gil says.

"Make sure I'm not a minute late to meet Galliano at that slaughterhouse."

I walk to the doorway, my heart thudding with dread. The meth lab is in full production, with chemicals boiling in their vats. Cooks wearing hazmat suits flit from station to station, their faces hidden behind masks.

Now that Galiano has slithered out from his hiding spot, I can call that firm of assassins I had on retainer and offer up a potential location.

I walk to the smallest of the cooks and place a hand on her shoulder.

"Got a minute?" I ask.

With a nod, she makes her way to the exit.

As I walk beside Isabella, I send a silent prayer to the gods of chemistry that she and her team can help me with my plan.

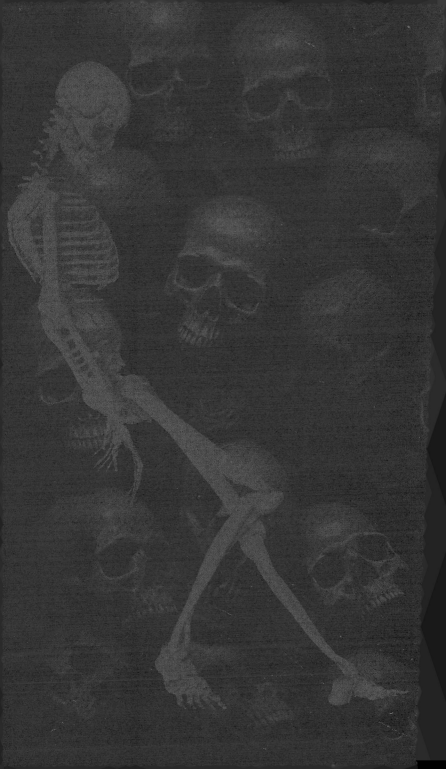

SEVENTY-TWO

EMBERLY

As Tommy bundles me out of my apartment, regret washes through my veins. Roman told me New Jersey was dangerous, but I didn't listen. I thought it was another one of his lies. He offered me a safe place to stay, where I would be protected, and I threw minestrone soup in his face.

I knew there was something off about my cousin, but never thought he would use me as a pawn in his vendetta against Roman.

His gloved hand grips the back of my neck like a vise, and he marches me through the building's hallway toward the exit. "Be a good girl and don't make a scene, or I'll carve that brat out of your corpse."

A shudder runs down my spine.

Mom always told me never to allow an abductor to move me to a second location, but that advice only works with scumbags who are afraid of getting caught.

Tommy would murder any witnesses before they even thought about calling the police.

The building's front door swings open, and Mr. Wilder steps inside. His large frame fills the doorway, and he stares from me to Tommy.

"You okay, Kate?" he asks, his chest rising and falling with deep breaths.

I grimace.

"Out of the way," Tommy snaps. "I didn't pay you to interfere in my cousin's business."

My jaw drops. Mr. Wilder was Tommy's spy?

The old man frowns. "Why are you manhandling Kate? You told me she was hiding from a psychopath."

Tommy pulls out his gun and points it at Mr. Wilder's face. "If I hear another word from you—"

Mr. Wilder's palms rise in surrender, and he ambles toward the door on the left. "Alright, alright. I'm going."

"Good man." Tommy's grip around the back of my neck tightens, and he marches me toward the exit. As we reach the door, he leans close and snarls, "Open it."

My heart sinks. It's really happening. Roman is probably halfway back to New Alderney, and if what Tommy says is correct, the men he stationed close by are already dead.

As I pull the door open, Tommy whirls around and fires several shots at Mr. Wilder.

Adrenaline kicks me in the heart. I scream, my ears ringing, and dart into the street. Surely someone must be looking out of the window for the source of the sound?

At this time in the late afternoon, most residents of my street are either away for the weekend or inside watching TV. I don't have a plan, but I tear toward the road. Maybe I can flag down a car.

A burly figure appears from my right and grabs me off my feet.

I scream, "Let go of me—"

He clamps a huge hand over my mouth. Before I can even struggle, he's bundling me through the open doors of a van and throws me inside.

I land on my hands and knees, just as the door slams shut and encases me in the dark. Terror grips me by the throat, cutting off my air. My heart pounds so hard and fast that it feels like it might burst.

My mind dredges up every nightmare scenario Mom used to frighten me into compliance. Men coming to take me away and subject me to gags, ropes, starvation, and locked rooms. It's only a matter of time before Tommy takes me to a dingy hideout, and I'll never see Roman again.

I pound against the van's metal doors. "Help! Please, somebody help."

The vehicle lurches forward, and I'm hurled onto my side. Pain lances through my shoulder, making me gasp. I struggle to pull myself up, but the van takes a sharp turn that throws me onto my front.

Light streams in from a hatch above my head, and I look up to see the driver's silhouette. Tommy's face looms into view, flashing those sinister white teeth.

"You can either shut the fuck up, or I can shoot you in the shoulder. The way this asshole is driving, I might miss and hit something vital."

My stomach plummets.

The driver snickers.

"What's it going to be?" he asks.

My survival instincts take control, and I freeze. Tommy is using me to lure Roman or as some kind of bargaining chip. This doesn't necessarily mean he needs me alive.

"I'll stay quiet," I rasp.

"Smart move." He slides the hatch shut.

The van makes a few turns before rumbling down the

highway. I wrap my arms around my belly, sending comfort to my baby. For his sake, I need to stay calm, stay alert, and watch closely for an opening.

As soon as their backs are turned, I will escape.

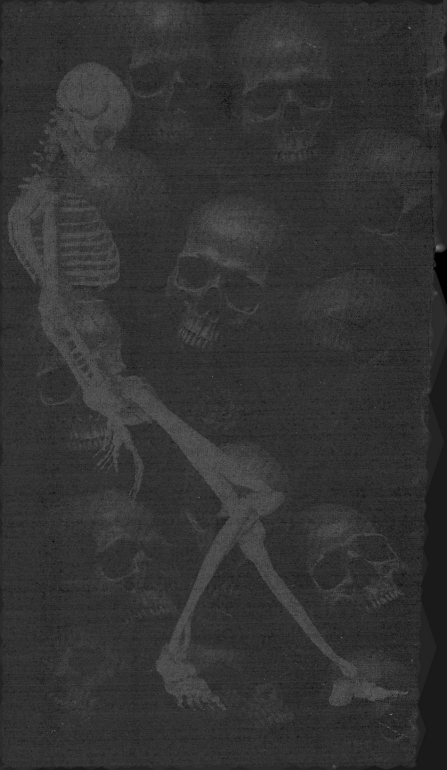

SEVENTY-THREE

EMBERLY

Every meditation technique I learned from my birthing class helps slow down my heartbeat until I can finally think through the panic. My eyes are closed, and I sit with my back against the wall for support.

There's no mistaking that Tommy is a mad dog with a vendetta. He either despises the Montesano family as much as my bio father did or is desperate to claw back Roman's assets. And I'm both a meal ticket, a pawn, and a weak link.

Shit.

I'm pregnant with the child of a mafia boss and living miles away from his stronghold. No wonder Roman had to drive over to watch over me and insisted that I returned to New Alderney. I was an easy target.

Mom was right. No matter how far I try to run from my past, I will always be a burden. My mind runs through all the ways she taught me to survive an abduction, and the backs of my eyes sting with tears. I held Mom up as a cautionary tale and swore I wouldn't fall prey to paranoia when all the time, she was right.

"Focus." I curl my hands into fists. "This isn't helping."

Several minutes later, the van slows before coming to a stop. I sit up, my heart bursting into action.

"Stay calm, don't fight, stay calm," I whisper over and over until the words blur.

The doors burst open, bringing in a burst of light. My body flinches forward before I catch myself. Resisting my instincts to bolt, I stay seated and blink away the brightness.

"There she is," Tommy says with a dry chuckle. "My pretty little cousin."

He reaches in and offers me his hand. It takes every effort not to slap it away.

"Thanks," I say through clenched teeth and let him haul me to my feet.

Tommy helps me step down into a large driveway surrounded by manicured gardens. Beyond the lawn stands tall hedges that block out the view of the outside world. We could be anywhere, and I wouldn't know, since I can't see a single landmark.

I turn around and stare up at a sprawling mansion of brown bricks with tall white windows. It's twice the size of where Tommy lives in New Jersey, twice as ostentatious, yet it looks vaguely familiar.

"What is this place?" I whisper.

Tommy wraps an arm around my waist. "Your home."

"What?" My voice trembles.

"Cousin Freddy left this place to you in his will."

I try not to shudder as he marches me up the steps, leading to a set of double doors. Now I remember where I first saw this place. It was all over the news when the entire Capello family was murdered the night of my bio father's sixtieth birthday.

"This is where they all died," I whisper.

He snickers. "Don't tell me you're afraid of ghosts."

"I'm more afraid of you," I murmur.

Tommy throws his head back and laughs. The huge man who threw me in the truck also chortles. They all think my terror is a joke.

Fuck these assholes.

Tommy kicks the front door. "Hey, it's me."

Another man, as large as the one behind us, opens it. The gun in his hand lowers as soon as he spots his boss.

We enter a marbled interior that reminds me of the Montesano mansion but gaudier. Its chandelier is so enormous that I could reach some of its crystals. Marble tiles cover the floors, but the uniformed patterns suggest that they're fake.

A huge portrait hangs on the mezzanine of a round-faced man dressed like Al Capone, complete with a fat cigar. He stares down at me through vibrant green eyes tinged with malice.

Tommy marches me up a grand staircase and says, "You see it too?"

"What?"

"Cousin Freddy was jealous as fuck of Enzo Montesano. Enzo had a better house, better wife, better sons, better reputation. Freddy wanted to take everything from that clit-sucker."

I turn to meet Tommy's green eyes.

"Hey, don't look at me. It's not like I told your old man to stab Enzo in the back."

My lips tighten. I'm pretty sure that's a confession.

We walk in silence to a bedroom at the end of the upstairs hallway, which is also dominated by a chandelier. Daylight streams in through gaps in velvet curtains that obscure tall windows that overlook the gardens. I glance at a canopy bed covered in the same style of drapes, wondering if those might form a suitable noose.

Tommy leans into my side and murmurs, "Tacky, ain't it?"

"What happens now?" I ask.

"We'll remodel." He squeezes my shoulder, making my heart shudder. "Anything you want."

"Pardon?"

He flashes me a predatory grin. "After all, this is your home."

This may as well be my tomb. Tommy Galliano will make sure I don't leave this house alive.

"Is Roman coming here? You said I would be bait."

Tommy bows his head, his shoulders shaking with a chilling laugh that increases in volume until it fills the entire room. He rocks back, his eyes finally meeting mine, and his laughter fades to a sinister grin.

Electricity runs across my skin, and the fine hairs on the back of my neck stand on end. Is he acting weird on purpose to throw me off balance?

When I step away, he snatches my arm.

"I'm going to send Montesano to a meeting point close to your old apartment. Once he's dead, I'll send the order to my men to kill his brothers, attack his businesses, and take back my meth lab."

The full horror of his plan hits me in the windpipe, and my breath catches. "That's..."

"I know." He winks. "In a few hours, you'll be a widow and by this weekend, you'll become Mrs. Tomaso Galliano."

"Why?" I rasp, trying to shrink from his grip.

"So I can take control of the Montesano heir," he replies, as though the answer is obvious.

I reel backward, my mind spinning. I need to think of something to stop this assassination. I can't let him leave.

"Roman won't come," I lie. "The only reason he wanted me back is for revenge."

Tommy stares at me with an intensity that cuts through my defenses. I'm rooted to the spot, powerless to tear my gaze off his inhuman face.

Up close, I realize what I found so uncanny. That layer of pigment on his skin isn't fake tan, but foundation. It's even on his lips. I try not to think about what's underneath all that makeup, but now I'm imagining the worst.

"That's what I thought at first," he says. "I pictured him locking you in a room, fucking and beating you senseless while you pleaded for mercy."

My throat tightens, and I gulp.

"If Freddy had fucked me over like that, I'd put a collar around your neck and drag you around like an animal on a leash. At night, I would chain you to my toilet. The only thing you'd eat is my piss and shit and cum."

I tremble, my veins filling with ice.

"But Roman loves you desperately," he murmurs, his voice tender. "And he'll walk into an ambush if it means I might spare your life. When he does, I will bring you his heart."

A sob catches in my throat. I want to beg Tommy not to leave, but I can't think of a single thing that might stop him from murdering Roman and taking control of my son.

I lower my lashes, but Tommy grips my chin, forcing our gazes to meet.

"Wish me luck." The pressure of his fingertips tightens, and he leans so close that I back toward the wall.

Tommy looms over me like a wolf about to devour its prey. He's two decades older than Roman and with a wiry build, yet he's ten times as menacing. He leans so close that his body heat makes me sweat.

My breath hitches. "Wait—"

His mouth crashes against mine with a ferocity that makes my stomach lurch. I struggle within his grip and shove at his chest, but he's too strong. Tears prick my eyes as his tongue parts the seam of my lips, but I clamp my teeth shut.

The forced kiss continues until my lungs burn and I'm forced to inhale. My nostrils fill with the mingled scents of chemicals and cigarettes and blood. Nausea takes control of my system, and I retch.

Tommy grinds his erection into my belly and moans. As he grabs my breast, his phone rings.

Finally, he pulls away, his eyes shining with madness. "You're going to look so pretty, crawling on your hands and knees with that belly dragging on the ground. I can't wait to cover you with my shit and piss."

Nausea slaps me in the gut and my skin crawls with revulsion. I gather every ounce of strength from enduring months of Jim's abuse and hold my features into a mask of calm.

"Aren't you going to answer that?" I nod toward the bulge in his shirt.

He pulls out the handset, taps a button and grins. "Roman, my boy. So wonderful you're finally taking my calls."

I listen to the one-sided conversation with a hand over my mouth.

Roman just agreed to sacrifice his life for mine, but Tommy has no intention of letting me go.

There's no way for me to warn Roman he's about to walk into a trap.

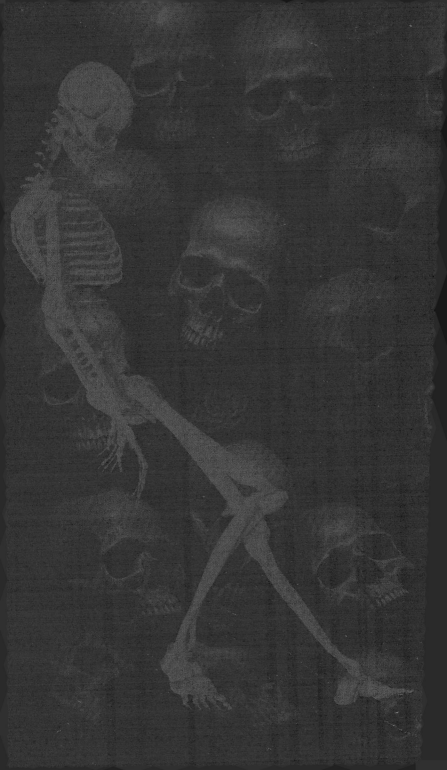

SEVENTY-FOUR

ROMAN

I'm ten minutes early to the rendezvous. Isabella Cortese insisted on accompanying me, saying the items I requested are volatile and require special care. After setting up our surprise for Tommy Galliano, she left.

Thoughts of Emberly being tormented by that psychopath supersede my curiosity about Isabella's motivations. I won't complain if she wants to kill the man who forced her to cook meth for nearly five years. From what I understand, Galliano despises educated women.

After our mother left, I reached out across the prison grapevine to gather every scrap of information I could find about Galliano. The rumors about the way he treated women were too outlandish to be believed.

There was no way our mother could leave the comfort and safety of the Montesano family to shack up with a monster like that. We all tried to reach out to her, but her responses were cold.

Now that he has Emberly, I can't stop picturing her

being locked away, her mind splintering under the trauma of being imprisoned.

My phone buzzes with a text from Tony, confirming that the men I stationed in the apartment opposite Emberly's are dead.

My jaw tightens. How the fuck did Galliano learn the extent of my surveillance? I set up the guards and cameras before Emberly even signed her lease.

Another message arrives to inform me that a convoy of vehicles are heading toward the meth lab. The five men I stationed there are already taking strategic positions to defend the cooks with long-range rifles.

My gaze flicks to the clock.

Five minutes to go.

This is a trap.

I know it. Galliano knows it, and so does everyone with two functioning brain cells, but I don't have a choice.

That bastard has taken the one thing I value above all else, revenge and even the family legacy: Emberly.

I would die for her. Kill for her. Lay entire states to waste for her. Which is why I wear a layer of explosives beneath my jacket powerful enough to reduce an entire city block to rubble.

My phone buzzes as I reach for the door handle. It's probably another report of Galliano's troops attacking one of my operations, but I take a glance at the screen.

It's a message from Emberly's superintendent.

Kate is gone.

I'm about to slip the handset into my pocket when another message appears.

Her cousin shot at me and took her.

My eyes narrow. How did the old man know they were related? I picture him trying to interfere with the abduction, but I can't imagine Galliano pausing to make introductions.

Holding onto the phone, I walk to the slaughterhouse and wait for the superintendent to get to the point.

I followed them into New Alderney.

My steps falter, and I gape at the screen. Galliano took Emberly where?

Lost them when I crashed the car into a ditch.

My gaze snaps to the clock. Two minutes to go. I send a message to Benito, Cesare, and Gil to order everyone back to New Alderney and to keep circulating the video clip of Emberly to see if anyone else recognizes the room.

I could leave, knowing that Emberly isn't close, but I would lose my chance to lure that scaly bastard out from hiding. She and her baby will never be safe as long as he's alive.

After slipping my phone back into my pocket, I walk through the slaughterhouse's open doors. The rancid tang of death and decay coats my sinuses as I step into a chamber illuminated by flickering strip lights.

Up ahead, rows and rows of gutted carcasses hang from steel joists. I glance around, searching for signs of life. Even though I've arrived on time, Galliano is still playing games.

His chuckle echoes across the walls, setting my teeth on edge. I knew that psycho bastard wouldn't miss the chance to watch me die.

This is a suicide mission, but Emberly and the baby will never know a moment's peace as long as Galliano still lives.

"Roman." His voice pipes in through a speaker. "How nice of you to finally cross state lines with an invitation."

Translation: he knows I've been entering New Jersey to watch over Emberly.

My phone buzzes with two more messages, but I can't afford to divert my attention. Instead, I turn to the source of the sound.

"You going to show yourself or keep taunting from the sidelines?" I snap.

A door creaks open and footsteps echo through the chamber. Galliano steps out of the shadows, flanked by a quartet of men in black.

He wears his usual leather blazer and black turtleneck with matching pants and green cowboy boots that click with every step. My hackles rise at the smirk plastered over his leathery face.

I thought I hated Frederic Capello, but the disdain I have for this asshole burns hotter than four funeral pyres.

"Release Emberly," I say, already knowing that he won't.

Galliano flashes his veneers. "You fucked up my plans when you took Freddy's spawn. I waited patiently for you to kill her so I could get my inheritance, but you had to be greedy."

"Stop whining about my assets," I snarl. "Get to the point."

He bristles, his gaze darting from side to side. Sweat glistens on his brow, and his breaths are labored.

My brows pinch. Is this motherfucker high?

"Keep talking like that and I'll put a bullet through your skull," Galliano says.

"Do it." I slide off my jacket, revealing my waistcoat of explosives. "The moment I hit the ground, this slaughterhouse and everything within a three-hundred-foot radius will be reduced to ash."

Tommy twitches, his gaze darting from side to side.

The men surrounding him stiffen.

I nod. Rumors have spread across town about how Cesare and I took out an entire firm of assassins. Some of Galliano's lackeys have the good sense to understand my threat isn't bullshit.

"You're bluffing." The waver in his voice suggests that he isn't sure of my intentions. "You ain't gonna do shit."

"You want to bet your life on that?" I pull out my gun and wave it toward the four men. "How about you?"

"Don't move," Tommy hisses at them.

They back away, their eyes widening.

"Looks like they remember what happened to the last people who fucked with the Montesanos." I raise my gun and aim at Galliano's head. "You're not paying them enough to risk getting blown to pieces."

His nostrils flare. "The first man who abandons me won't just die. I know where your women and children live. Don't betray me, and I won't put them to work in my brothels."

I laugh, the sound harsh. "This is why you men are loyal? Because he threatens your families?"

"Watch your mouth." Galliano raises his gun, but I'm faster. A bullet hits him in the chest, and he falls to the ground with a satisfying thud.

"Who's next?" I ask, keeping my aim in their direction.

His men swap glances, looking like they're debating whether to run or exchange fire.

Bullets fly from the shadows, hitting each man in the head. Blood and brain matter splatter against the hanging carcasses, and each man falls dead.

That hesitation cost those men their lives.

Galliano told me to come alone, but he didn't tell me not to surround the building with assassins. It looks like the firm we paid to track him are finally earning their retainer.

"Thank you," I say into the darkness.

I'm too focused on Galliano's fallen body to notice the assassins leave.

The slaughterhouse is quiet and still, save for the faint whir of an electric fan. Galliano lies flat on his back, his chest barely rising and falling, his fingers still curled around his pistol.

I shoot the hand holding the gun, making Galliano's fingers spasm around its trigger. A bullet lodges in his leg and he roars.

"Playing possum?" I walk a wide circle toward him, using the hanging carcasses as shields.

"Kill me, and Emberly dies," he grinds out through ragged breaths. "My man has instructions to slit her throat if I don't return to the hideout."

"Where is it?"

He cackles. "Come here, and I'll whisper its location."

Heat flushes through my veins, and my nostrils flare. Galliano knows he's lost. He's more likely to shoot at me with a second gun and detonate my explosives, so we both die in a blaze.

The air thickens with enough tension to make my ears ring. I need to disarm myself and get close to Galliano. Now. Keeping my distance, I fumble with the fastenings of my vest to loosen the explosives. Every second feels like an eternity as my fingers tremble over the delicate clasps.

Isabella said the compounds were volatile to friction, heat, and shock. One false move and I won't live to earn Emberly's forgiveness.

"Don't tell me the great Roman Montesano is afraid of an injured man?" he croaks.

The corner of my mouth lifts into a smirk. He'll have to do better than that if he wants me rattled. I breathe hard, forcing my fingers to slow down as I work the fastenings.

"You never asked about your mother," he says, "Or how she degraded herself every day to save your brothers."

My jaw clenches, and my fingers freeze over the explosives. I need to continue freeing myself and ignore his desperate rantings, but I say, "That's low, even for you."

He barks a laugh. "Cousin Freddy and I knew your little brothers would come after him, and he wanted them dead. Your mother made a deal."

Finally, I loosen the last clasp, ease the vest off my shoulders. My pulse quickens. This is the most precarious step of disarming the explosive. With painstaking slowness, I lower the vest on the concrete floor.

"The things that woman did to keep them safe," he says with a dry chuckle.

Blood roars through my ears as I approach Galliano with furious, measured steps. He rises onto his knees, using the carcasses as cover. One of his arms hangs limp at his side, his white glove dripping with blood. Just as I predicted, the other hand holds another gun.

"The woman used to eat my shit and drink my piss like it was champagne. Toward the end, she used to love rubbing—"

I pull the trigger and hit him square in the chest, but he only flinches.

Galliano shoots back, his bullet whizzing past my ear and lodging in a nearby carcass.

I take cover and grind my teeth. The bastard must be wearing a bulletproof vest. How did I let him into my mind? He fires again, this time at my foot. I break into a run.

Tommy cackles. "I know you've taken off your vest. You can't kill me, but I'm free to fill you with bullets and take Emberly as my wife."

Rage boils in my veins, powering my steps. This bastard knows I need him alive. "Don't think I won't shoot at the explosives and take us both down."

"You're too much of a coward, just like your siblings who hid within the walls of your mansion while my brother and I debased your mother—"

I shoot, my bullet catching him in the shoulder. His gun

arm drops, and I use the opening to shoot two shots into each knee.

Galliano drops to the floor with a howl.

I take another shot at his hand, and his gun falls to the floor with a clatter.

"You're going to tell me everything." I close the distance between us and lift his head by the hair. "And you'll start with where you're hiding Emberly."

He glares up at me, his eyes burning with hatred. "She'll die, just like you killed Cousin Freddy."

This time, I don't wince. My pocket is buzzing with messages. Either someone already identified where he's hiding Emberly or is close. Galliano is without hands that work, without men, and without hope. After he directs me to Emberly, I'll store him in the basement, where he will repeat what he said about our mother.

I drag his limp carcass across the slaughterhouse floor. "Tell me where she is or look forward to a long life full of pain and degradation."

"What are you doing?" he growls.

"Taking you somewhere with more space to work. When I've finished, you won't just be begging to spill Emberly's location, you'll be begging for death."

When I'm outside, the sun hangs low in the horizon, casting long shadows across the street. I'm about to slip a hand in my pocket to check on the phone, when Gil drives by in one of the bullet-proof vehicles and winds down the window.

"Did you get the text?" he asks.

"What?"

He opens the door and steps out. "Leroi recognized the room."

"Where is it?"

Gil lifts Galliano by the collar and drags him to the back seat. "Frederic Capello's old house."

Fuck. Galliano's lackey told me he was a trickster, but keeping Emberly captive at the site of her family's massacre is twisted.

"Let's go."

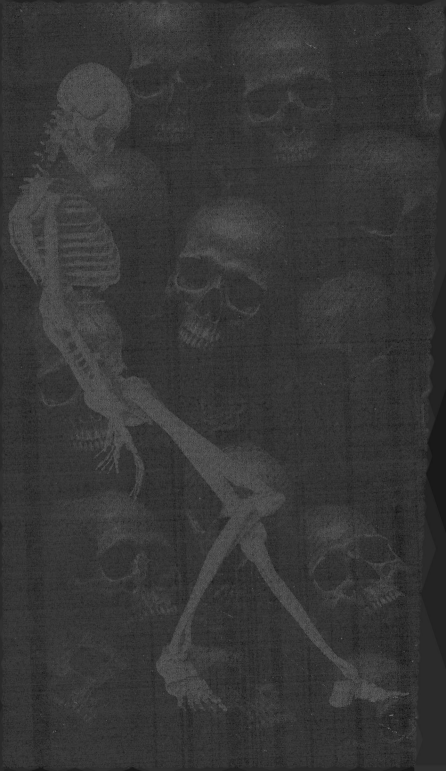

SEVENTY-FIVE

EMBERLY

Tommy walks out, leaving me sliding against the wall, my mind teetering on the knife-edge of hysteria.

As a key turns in the lock, several truths hit me in the chest.

Roman will die, closely followed by his brothers.

What's left of my life will be full of degradation and pain.

Tommy will kill the baby for his inheritance.

My chest tightens, and I struggle for air as my mind conjures up new phobias. Panic sets in, threatening to overwhelm my senses. If I can't conquer these paralyzing fears, Tommy will win, and we'll all lose our lives.

The mere thought of Tommy sends up a wave of revulsion. My mouth turns sour, and my stomach heaves. I stagger around the bed toward a door I hope leads to a bathroom and fling it open.

Stumbling through the tiled space toward the toilet, I clap a hand over my mouth. I make it a few steps before falling to my knees and throwing up bile. Tears stream from my eyes, and my breath comes in panicked pants.

If I don't calm down, I'll inhale my own vomit.

My vision blurs. I clutch the toilet seat, forcing myself to stay upright, but my stomach won't stop heaving. It's a mix of hormones and panic and fear.

I need to stop.

I need to take control.

I need to escape and warn Roman.

I need to make sure Tommy never touches my baby.

Minutes pass, and I'm trapped in a cycle of nausea and panic until my body runs out of steam. Eventually, the spasms subside, and I crawl to the sink and force myself up to standing. The room spins, threatening to pull me back to the floor. I cling to the counter, placing my weight on my arms, and turn on the cold tap.

"Come on, girl," I growl through clenched teeth. "You can do it."

I move my trembling fingers into the water and splash it on my face. The chill helps me focus and my breathing evens.

"What a mess."

If I studied what was reflected in the mirror, I would see a woman who allowed herself to break. Mom taught me to be independent and alert, yet I dropped my guard at the first sign of a man offering a helping hand.

Maybe I would have seen through Roman's bullshit if I had scrutinized every contract as thoroughly as I'd read the first. Then I would have asked what he was doing and worked out an agreement, but I was so dazzled by the promise of selling my art that I signed away my inheritance.

"Stop," I whisper.

Now's not the time to ruminate.

Time is running out.

I gather handfuls of water and rinse the sour taste from my mouth. After quenching my thirst, I turn off the tap and walk out of the bathroom.

My gaze darts around what looks to be a master suite, and I take in the thick curtains, heavy furniture, and the locked door before finally settling on a set of patio doors that lead to a balcony.

I'm no longer a four-year-old child trapped in a burning apartment, or the frightened woman held hostage by a violent cop. Those parts of me went away when I became a mother. According to Roman, I'm his wife, which means I'm about to lose my husband to a psycho.

Pacing the room, I psych myself up to climb the window. Who knew I'd find something worse than being imprisoned? I'm shivering at the thought of scaling down a building and endangering the baby.

Pregnancy has fucked up my physical confidence, my coordination, and my center of gravity. If I screw this up, we're both dead.

Why didn't Tommy abduct me two months ago, when I was limber and more agile?

I clutch my temples. "Stop spiraling."

What would Roman do in this situation? He wouldn't jump out of a window unless he'd exhausted every other option. He's too cool-headed, too calculating. Instead, he would scan the room for a way to communicate with backup, a tool to unlock the door, or a weapon.

If that didn't work, he might tie the sheets together and climb down to make an escape.

I walk around the room, searching closets, pulling open drawers, and looking through cupboards. There's nothing. Someone must have emptied out all the family's possessions after the massacre.

"Shit."

I suck in a deep breath, push those anxieties aside, and force myself to the patio door. I turn its handle. As expected, it's locked, but that's no obstacle to balcony escapes.

The first thing I need to do is find out if he's left me here alone. If there's a guard outside in the hallway, he'll hear me breaking the glass.

I walk to the other door and try the handle. When it doesn't open, I yell, "Excuse me?"

There's no answer, which isn't necessarily a sign that I'm free to proceed. After pressing my ear to the door and hearing no sound of movement, I lower myself onto my hands and knees to peek through the gap beneath the door.

The hallway is empty. On the plus side, at least I'm wearing shoes. The last time I needed to escape a locked room, I was naked and all I had to protect myself was a shard of glass and a few bedsheets.

Sending a silent word of thanks to whoever furnished this bedroom with thick curtains, I grab one side of the bed's velvet drapes and yank it down with all my strength.

The fabric tears with a loud rip, leaving me with about eight feet of material for a makeshift rope. I move onto the second, then the third, and the fourth until I can make one rope long enough to reach the ground or two shorter ones that will require a small jump.

"Let's go for two," I mutter.

If one fails, then the other will stop me from tumbling down to the ground and turning a hostage situation into a tragedy.

I tie the ends of two drapes together and create a double knot before doing the same with the second pair. After pulling the fastenings taut, my gaze wanders to the curtains on the wall. With a bit more time, I might be able to make the ropes longer, but I'm going to need them for covering the broken glass.

"Let's do this."

I tear down the curtains around the window, wrap them around the top of the bedside table, and ram my makeshift mallet into the bottom pane. The soft pressure makes a clean crack, and I repeat the process until I can remove large pieces of glass using the fabric to protect my hands.

Once I'm done, I fold over the curtains, lay them on the floor, and crawl out onto the balcony with my two ropes.

Sweat breaks out across my brow as my mind dredges up thoughts of Roman. Did he go to the meeting point with backup? Was there enough time for him to wear a bullet-proof vest?

A breeze drifts across my face, cooling my skin. Worrying about Roman won't improve his chances of survival. If I break my neck escaping Tommy, then he will have sacrificed himself for nothing.

Sacrifice.

My breath catches, and I choke back a sob. The thought of Roman being dead is too much to bear. Squeezing my eyes shut, I fill my lungs with air, just as Lily taught us in my birth class. With a sharp exhale, I force out my anxiety.

It's time to focus on getting out of here alive. For myself, the baby, and for Roman.

I secure the ropes to the balcony railing using double knots and yank hard to test their strength. When they hold firm, I grip the ledge of the balcony and swing one leg over the other side.

My back seizes with a twinge, and every muscle that tightened during the harrowing ride in the back of that van begins to protest.

"Fuck." I grit my teeth through the pain.

There's no time to rest. I wasted so much time hurling out my guts, and there's no telling when Tommy or one of his henchmen will return.

Gripping the balcony's metal railings, I lower myself down the side of the building. My body is so unwieldy that every inch of progress is a struggle. When my hands finally reach the balcony's concrete base, I take hold of the ropes and descend.

My heart beats so hard that its vibrations reach my fingertips, and every inch of skin is coated with sweat. The only thing keeping me from sliding down to my death is the fabric's friction.

The ropes strain against my weight, and each time I release one of them to get closer to the ground, it feels like I'm losing a lifeline. Adrenaline surges through my veins, and I swear I can hear footsteps. Intrusive thoughts urge me to speed up, check my progress, or jump down and land in a crouch, but I continue my slow descent.

"Hey!" booms a deep voice.

My head snaps up to the balcony, and I lock gazes with a man with Tommy's slick features and black hair. He grips the railings and glares down at me, his eyes wide with shock.

Dread kicks me in the gut, and I fumble with the rope. The baby chooses that moment to kick back. He's right. I can't stop just because I've gotten caught.

"What the fuck are you doing?" the man snarls.

This must be Tommy's son. Why else would he look so much like my captor? If they're anything alike, then the consequences for trying to escape will be dire.

Not wasting any energy to answer, I continue climbing down.

He disappears for a moment, making me wonder if he's untying the ropes. A bead of sweat dangles off my lashes and threatens to sting my eye. I blink it away and quicken my descent.

The man reappears, holding a gun. "Stop moving or I'll shoot."

My nostrils flare. Is everyone in this family insane?

"Did Tommy give you permission to kill the pregnant woman?" I yell at the top of my voice.

"Danillo! The bitch is trying to escape through the balcony." He crouches to the base of the railings and pulls at the ropes, and one of them loosens.

Terror seizes me by the throat, forcing out a scream. "Stop!"

The rope falls to the ground. I grab the second and pray the man isn't malicious or stupid enough to let me fall to my death.

"What the fuck?" screams a voice from below.

Shit. My heart slams against my ribcage and anxiety wraps around my throat. I'm surrounded.

"Don't. Look. Down," I growl at myself.

At the sound of yells and footsteps, temptation forces my gaze to the ground.

The drop is about a story and a half deep and four men race toward me holding guns. I whimper, my eyes snapping back to my hands, which won't stop shaking.

A gunfight erupts below, and I flinch with every shot, imagining myself being hit with each bullet.

My insides riot. I can't tell if it's the baby or an advanced state of panic. My palms become slick, and my fingers won't stop trembling. sweat pours in my eyes, making them sting.

I can't fucking see.

My ears won't stop ringing.

I'm losing control of my senses.

Tears pour freely down my cheeks, and I exhale a sob. I'm stuck between a shootout and an asshole trying to untie my last rope. Roman has probably already sacrificed himself in an ambush trying to save me and the baby, and Tommy is already on his way to turn me into his personal toilet.

I can't hold on for much longer. My biceps ache and my forearms feel like they're about to burst into flames.

At this rate, my only way out is falling to my death.

They say your life flashes before your eyes when you're about to die, but all I see is Roman and all the times he was there when I needed him the most.

Our first kiss at the nightclub when I was desperate to escape arrest and certain assault. The way he punched Dominic so he would release my throat. The way my kidnapper's head exploded into a cloud of blood and gore, only to reveal Roman with a gun.

My chest releases a hysterical laugh. He even rescued me from becoming a spectacle at the *Mindful Birth* class.

I wish Roman could save me now, but he's probably dead.

My fingers ache and spasm. They're so wet with sweat that I slip a few inches toward certain death.

The gunfight picks up in intensity, and my thoughts drift to Mom. If my biological father was anything like Tommy Galliano, then I understand why she never stopped running. She saved me from a life of corruption and degradation.

"Mom," I whisper into the sound of gunfire. "I know what you were trying to escape. Thank you for my life."

"Emberly," yells a familiar voice.

I crack open an eye.

Among the dark figures stands one wearing black, white, and gray. My vision is too blurred to make out his features, but my chest fills with hope.

"Roman?"

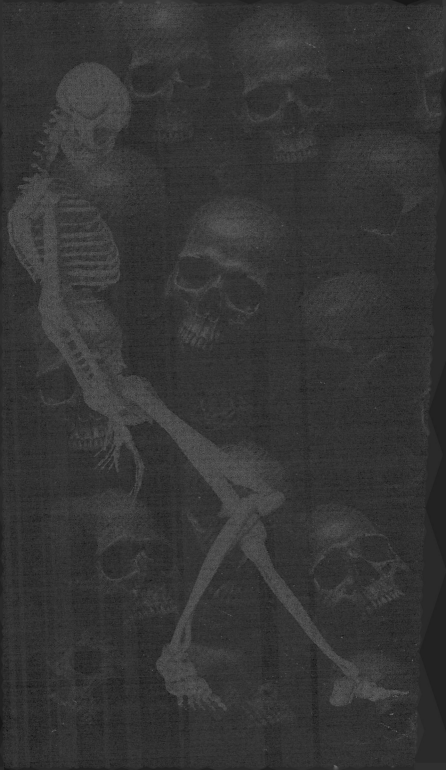

SEVENTY-SIX

ROMAN

Gil drives like a demon through the streets of Carmel, New Jersey, and tears through the highway like it's his own personal circle of hell. I send messages to every man at my disposal to storm Capello's old mansion in Queen's Gardens.

Galliano rolls around the back seat, moaning so loudly that I'm tempted to put him out of his misery. The only thing stopping me from filling him with bullets is the threat that his team might kill Emberly if he doesn't reappear. That, and my brothers. They deserve to know the truth about why our mother left.

My phone blows up with messages. Cousin Leroi is the first to arrive, and he's positioned his girlfriend on the roof of a nearby house with a long-range rifle. He's an expert on siege situations, so he's on the ground, directing the troops.

"What's happening, boss?" Gil takes a sharp turn that nearly tosses me out of my seat.

"Focus on the road," I growl.

With a grunt, he swerves into the shoulder lane and

floors the gas pedal. I jerk backward, catching a glimpse of the speedometer, which passes 120 mph. The trees on either side of the road blur into a mass of green and brown.

I send a message to Leroi.

Have you seen her?

There's a minute's delay before he texts back.

Not yet.

While waiting for another update, I slip on a bulletproof vest. Dread coils in my gut. I turn to Galliano.

"Tell me what happens if you don't text your son?"

He groans. "Get fucked."

"If anything happens to my wife, I won't just kill your sons. I'll keep you in a basement and feed you their body parts. Season up those assholes, so they taste better than your grandma's meatloaf."

Galliano's eyes widen. "You sick fuck."

"Tell me," I snarl.

"It was a fucking bluff!" he screeches.

My jaw clenches. "You had better be."

"Almost there," Gil says.

Leroi sends another message.

Seraphine spotted a heavily pregnant woman climbing off the edge of a balcony.

"Fuck," I roar.

"What's happening?" Gil asks.

"Remember her first morning at the house?"

"Don't tell me she's trying to jump?"

I message Leroi.

Where is she?

Four frantic heartbeats later, his text appears on my screen.

East wing of the house.

Leroi and I exchange a volley of texts, including messages from his bloodthirsty girlfriend, who's watching

Emberly through the scope of her rifle. When she announces that a man just appeared on the balcony and unfastened one of her ropes, I give the order to shoot.

The car bounces over a bump, making me jolt forward. Galliano fills the back seat with screams. I look up to find us charging through the gates of the Capello estate.

I grab Gil's shoulder. "She's around the far side."

Gil passes the mansion's double doors and swerves around its side before halting behind a line of trees. I fling open the door, leap out, and break into a sprint.

Emberly hangs fourteen-feet in the air, still dressed in her leggings and white maternity shirt. Both hands cling onto a pair of burgundy drapes fashioned into a rope, and another lies puddled on the ground.

Alarm shoots through my system like electricity, charging my steps. I pick up speed, sprinting through the shooters and leaping over fallen corpses. Bullets fly past. One of them hits me in the back with a burst of pain that I dismiss.

All I can think about is my wife dangling by a precarious rope.

"Emberly!" I roar.

She twitches, still clinging onto the curtain. "Roman?"

"It's me," I say, my voice thickening. I position myself directly beneath the hanging velvet. "I'm here."

Emberly says something that's muffled by the gunfire.

A man in a black suit appears from around the corner and rushes at me with a pistol. He fires two shots into my chest. Pain slices through my ribs, and I stagger backward from the impact. I fire back and hit him between the eyes.

The gunfire stops, but I'm so focused on Emberly that everyone around me fades into insignificance.

"Let go, baby," I yell.

She whimpers, reminding me of a cat that's climbed too far up a tree and is now too afraid to move.

Silence stretches across the garden, broken only by Emberly's ragged cries. My heart pounds hard, but my ears remain attuned to Emberly's voice.

"I'm too high up," she cries.

"Don't worry. I'll catch you when you fall."

"But I'm too heavy."

The makeshift rope sways, making my stomach plummet. Either it's about to come loose from the balcony railing or the knot she made to connect the two drapes is unraveling. If she clings on much longer, she'll fall against her will.

Gil appears at my side with Leroi, as do Cesare and Benito, all four of them ready to catch her, providing silent solidarity and support.

"Emberly," I say, trying to remain calm. "You're the strongest, bravest woman I know, and you've survived worse than this. Just trust me and let go."

"A-Alright," she says, but doesn't move.

Of course, she doesn't. Why would she trust the man who's told her nothing but lies?

"Let go of that drape," I command. "Now."

She finally releases the velvet and plummets with a scream. My heart thunders. My adrenaline surges. My stomach lurches as though it's me who's just made the jump. A heartbeat later, I catch her trembling body and crush her to my chest.

The agony ripping through my shattered rib cage fades with the euphoria of having her safe in my arms. I bury my face into her curls, inhaling her sweet scent, my heart soaring with gratitude.

"You caught me," she whispers.

"Emberly," I murmur into her hair. "I will never let you fall."

She gazes up at me, her green eyes shining with tears. My companions draw back, leaving us alone beneath the balcony.

"Did you see Tommy?" she asks, her voice breathy.

"He's filled with bullets in the back seat of my car," I say.

"Dead?"

I chuckle. "He wishes."

Her eyes flutter closed, and she exhales a long sigh. "He's a monster. You don't even want to know what he planned for me and the baby."

My jaw tightens. "Did he touch you?"

"I'm fine. It was mostly threats, but the man is unhinged." She pats my chest in the universal sign to let go.

I release her legs, letting her feet touch the lawn. Emberly glances up at the balcony and then down at me as though she can't believe she's still alive.

"Roman," she says, her voice breathy. "Thank you for coming. Tommy said you were going to sacrifice yourself—"

"Stop," I murmur.

Her eyes widen.

I swallow hard and lower one knee on the ground, followed by the other, and clasp my hands to my chest.

"Emberly, I'm sorry," I say, my voice hoarse, my chest tightening with regret.

I gaze up into her beautiful features, knowing I don't deserve her forgiveness, but I keep talking because being without her has been hell.

"Sorry for manipulating you before we even met and continuing to manipulate you after I realized you were nothing like Capello. I took advantage of your dreams, your fears, and your good heart to keep you under my control. What I did to you was unforgivable."

"Roman," she whispers.

"If you want to leave me, I'll let you go. I'll annul the marriage and continue donating to the woman's shelter."

Her lips part. "What?"

"Even if you don't want me, I will still love you from afar." My voice wavers. "But if you take me back, I will spend the rest of my life making it up to you."

She places a hand on my shoulder and squeezes.

My heart races. My gut tightens to brace myself for words of scorn or a slap.

"Tommy said you were going to sacrifice your life for me and the baby," she says, her eyes shining.

"That was the plan," I rasp.

"Why?"

"I spent five damn years locked up, convinced that all I needed was revenge and to take back what we lost. But it only left me feeling empty." My voice cracks, and my throat clogs with emotion.

She gazes down at me, her eyes widening.

"Living without you is like trying to breathe without air. Every good thing I ever felt is because of you. You're in my blood, in my bones, in my fucking soul. I can't even function without you, Emberly."

She makes a strangled sound in the back of her throat, but I continue.

"When Galliano gave me the chance to choose between me and you, I was ready to sacrifice my life. My death in exchange for redemption."

Her breathing quickens.

"I'll do whatever it takes to fix things between us. Fuck, baby, I can't believe I was so dumb, blinded by vengeance. I was an idiot for breaking your heart."

"You were," she says.

"And I'm sorry." I shake my head and gaze up at her through blurred eyes. "Words aren't enough. Losing you is like getting my chest ripped open and losing my heart."

I blink, loosening tears. Every fiber of my being aches with sincerity, but I've told so many lies that I'll never convince her of my truth.

"You're everything I ever wanted, baby. Hell, you're everything I didn't know I needed. I'm here on my knees, ribs all busted, with tears pouring down my cheeks, begging you for something, anything. Even a crumb. I'll crawl over broken glass just to get you back."

Seconds pass, and my throat closes up until my breath becomes shallow. I wait several agonizing moments for her to speak.

"I also have an apology to make to you," she murmurs.

My brows pull together. "What is it?"

She drops her gaze to her swollen belly. "It's the baby. He's yours."

"A boy?" I whisper. Galliano hinted at the gender, but it didn't register. I was too preoccupied with Emberly's safety. The real message behind her words hits me in the gut.

"And he's mine?"

"Yeah." she says, her eyes shining with tears.

"You're sure?"

She gives me another nod.

"Because it doesn't matter if he's Callahan's son. I'll love him all the same."

Emberly takes hold of my face with both hands. "Roman, he's your baby. My due date is in three months."

Love blooms in my chest, along with a wave of possession. I force back the urge to claim them both. My days of controlling the woman I love are over. If Emberly wants to walk away, I won't force her to stay.

"I've set up an account for you containing ten million dollars. It's yours. Lubelli is working on setting up an online business for you, so you can be independent. You'll always have your freedom. I will never make you feel trapped."

Silence stretches out as I gaze up into her tear-streaked face, which has never been more beautiful. Emotions war across her features, and I hold my breath, waiting for her to speak.

"I understand why you did it," she says, her voice wavering with pain. "He took so much from you and your family, but you broke my trust."

My heart stills, forming a deep ache that I'm desperate to dispel. I want to beg for her forgiveness, assure her that I've changed, and promise that everything will be different.

But I can't.

Part of being the better man Emberly needs is respecting her decisions and allowing her to make her own choices. Misery seeps into my bones at the thought of her walking away with my son, but I force down the urge to speak.

Emberly lowers her lashes, and more tears spill down her cheeks. "You didn't just lie, you fabricated an illusion based on my deepest fantasies. I had everything I ever wanted, only to discover it was all a manipulation. That's not something I can forgive."

"I know, baby," I rasp.

"Then you took away my choices by marrying me without my knowledge and getting me pregnant."

I swallow hard, my jaw tightening. It's all true. There is no excuse.

She licks her lips. "But one thing you said is true."

"What's that?"

"It's not safe out there. You have too many enemies. Now that I know the identity of my father, it looks like I'm also a target."

My breath hitches. "Emberly?"

"If it's alright with you, I'll move into the pool house."

My lips part, but I make no sound because I'm trying to process her words.

Is she taking me back?

No.

She's accepting my offer of protection. It's a start. Maybe returning home will encourage her to paint. Joy swells in my chest, threatening to burst. At least I'll be close by to help with her needs.

"Of course," I reply, my breath shallowing. This is more than I deserve. "And I still stand by the offer to take care of all your needs."

With a laugh, she offers me her hand. "You wish."

Actually, I do. If she wants soup in the middle of the night, I'll be there. A foot rub, call me Mr. Masseur. An orgasm, she can use any part of my body she wants to relieve her tension.

I bring her hand to my lips and kiss each of her knuckles before finally meeting her eyes. What I see there makes my heart soar. It's a glimmer of hope.

"Stay for as long as you want," I say. "And what about us?"

"You'll need to grovel a lot more than that," she says with a hint of a smile.

"I'll do whatever it takes," I say, my chest tightening with relief. "Anything to earn your forgiveness."

When a man steps out of death row for a murder he didn't commit, the first thing he should do is appreciate the people who stood by him during his darkest hours and embrace the chance of a better future.

Capello might have ruined my life, but he left me the most precious gift. The most beautiful, loving creature in the world, who's about to give me a son.

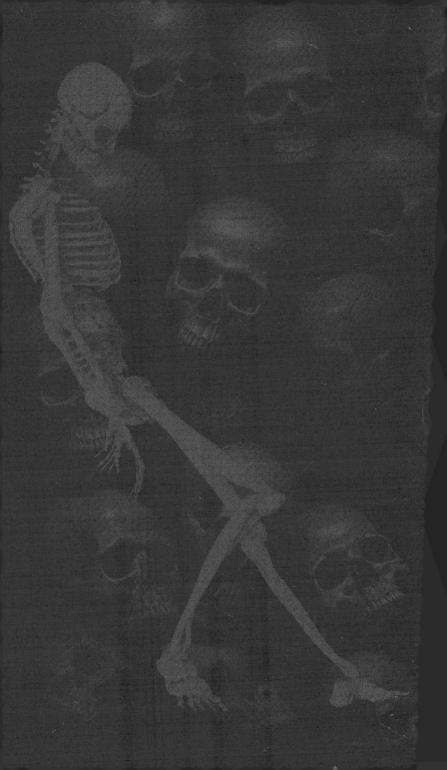

SEVENTY-SEVEN
EPILOGUE

THREE MONTHS LATER

EMBERLY

I wake up from my nap with a groan. The setting sun glistens on the pool's surface, reminding me that another day has passed, and the baby is still not showing any signs of coming. I lean back on the rocking chair and sigh.

At forty-one weeks, it feels like I'm carrying a tiny planet, complete with its own gravitational pull. Even though the OB-GYN assures us that this is normal, I'm anxious to meet my little boy.

The baby stirs and I wince. All I want to do is crawl into bed, never leaving until he decides to come, but Roman has turned taking care of me into his full-time job.

Every morning, he wakes me up with a cup of tea, then we take a walk together around the estate. When I don't want to eat breakfast with the rest of the family, he makes me something from scratch in the pool house's kitchen.

After eating, we take a swim together in the pool,

followed by assisted stretches. He's become my own pregnancy butler—always ready to offer a snack, a massage, or a hug.

But today is different. Today marks one week past my due date, and frustration builds inside me like a pressure cooker. My patience is about to snap, even though Roman continues his routine with unwavering determination.

The door behind me opens, and Roman emerges from the pool house. "Hey, baby. How are you feeling?"

"Nothing's still happening yet," I mutter.

Chuckling, he brings me a steaming cup of tea. "That's because our son is half a gorgon. He'll come when he's good and ready."

"Stubborn Montesano genes, more like," I reply with a smirk.

My nostrils twitch at the familiar scent. "Is that raspberry tea?"

"I picked the leaves myself." He sets down the cup on the side table.

Roman pulls up a chair and sits at my side. He's shirtless, save for a pair of gray sweatpants that accentuates the outline of his thick cock. I pull my gaze away from the appendage that got me into this mess and try to forget it's been an eternity since we were intimate. Instead, I focus on the figure tattooed between his pecs, which holds so much meaning for us both.

Shortly after I returned from being abducted, Mr. Lubelli came to see me in my studio and apologized for his part in the deception. I was still struggling with artist's block and wasn't interested in his excuses, but then he showed me my artwork on social media. There were hundreds of clips of me painting in the studio, and a lot of them had gone viral.

His assistants also set up an online store to sell prints of my paintings, generating thousands of dollars. Scrolling through the comments restored my confidence in my art. Inspiration struck after he left, and I picked up a pencil to make my first sketch.

It was a tattoo to transform the word LIAR that I carved into the center of Roman's chest into a full body portrait of Medusa. I sketched several others, including an angel, a cross, and symbols, but Roman said the Medusa reminded him so much of my temper. He even insisted that I change her face to match mine.

I take a sip of my sweetened raspberry leaf tea. "Thank you. Do you think we could skip the afternoon walk? Nothing seems to be working."

His gaze drops to my breasts. "Walking isn't the only way to induce labor."

Heat rushes to my cheeks, and I stare into my cup, trying to hold back a wave of desire. Roman and I haven't been intimate since before I was abducted. In fact, he's been the perfect gentleman.

Nearly losing me has made him more protective, and he hasn't made a single move. He still gives me massages but without the happy endings, and he always pulls away before things get too heated.

The lack of sex has deepened our friendship, and we have found so many things we like in common. Last month, we traveled to New York City to buy a Roger Thango painting, along with another mask.

The next day, we went to a car auction together to pick a vintage Mercedes to replace the one I destroyed. Roman wants to restore it with me and the baby when he's older. He's even introduced me to mafia movies, and he insisted that I teach him how to make art.

We spend hours together, both inside the studio and across the estate, painting whatever we see. Roman's enthusiasm has gotten rid of my artist's block, and I've created several beautiful pieces for the nursery.

It's sweet that he's stopped using his sexual prowess to bend me to his will, and I've gotten to know another side of Roman. Our friendship may have deepened, but the lack of sex is driving me insane.

My tongue darts out to lick my lips. "If you're not taking me for a walk, then what are you suggesting?"

He slides a hand over my belly, making my skin tingle. I shift on the bed, my breath quickening.

"Did you know that nipple stimulation can bring on contractions?" he asks, his eyes sparkling.

I gulp.

And the way he's staring at my nipples is making them tingle even more.

"Anything else?" I ask, my voice breathy with desire.

His eyes darken, and his gaze drops to my lips. "There's another method, but it's more intimate."

"Are you trying to get laid?" I ask, my lips quirking.

His smile widens, revealing his perfect teeth. "I don't need to fuck you to give you an orgasm."

My heart flip-flops at his directness. A part of me has been aching for his touch, but I don't want to disturb our truce.

We did couples therapy with a woman named Monica Saint who has a practice downtown and provides services to people in the underworld. She helped us unearth what went wrong in our relationship and brought us to a better understanding of each other's fears.

The time we've spent together has helped me understand Roman better, along with the past struggles and fears that motivated him to lie.

He told me about the dark days he spent in the judiciary process, having no way to prove his innocence. I learned about the depth of my father's betrayal and the powerlessness he felt as his family fell apart. Knowing the despair that plagued him during his time on death row brought me to tears.

In turn, I shared stories from my nomadic childhood, the incessant feeling of being hunted, and the constant terror I faced of succumbing to Mom's heightened paranoia. Those conversations put everything into perspective for Roman, making him commit to always telling me the truth.

He strokes my cheek with a featherlight touch that makes my eyes flutter closed. His seductive voice wraps around my senses like silk. "Let me help induce your labor, baby."

"What if it doesn't work?" I whisper.

"Then you'll get an orgasm that will lighten your mood."

I crack open an eye, meeting his heated gaze. "And what do you get in return?"

His warm hand stills on my cheek, and he leans in so closely that our faces are mere inches apart. He gazes at me with an intensity that makes my heart flutter, and his warm breath fans against my lips.

"I get satisfaction knowing I made you feel good," he murmurs, his voice filled with promise. "Do I have your permission?"

My back aches, my feet are swollen, and I feel like I'm carrying the weight of the world. If anyone deserves a moment of pleasure, it's me.

"Fine," I say, my pulse quickening with anticipation. "But you're only using your fingers and tongue."

His grin widens, revealing a set of perfectly white, straight teeth. "As you wish, baby."

"I can work with that." I meet his smile with a smirk.

His fingers trail down my neck and glide over my collarbone, igniting sparks across my skin. His lips follow suit, pressing soft kisses against my sensitive skin and causing my pulse to rise.

He reaches the lace cups of my dress. "May I?"

"Please," I whisper, my heart pounding.

He pulls down the stretchy fabric, freeing my breasts. His kisses continue downward until he sucks one nipple between his lips while his finger and thumb close in around the other.

My back arches in response, and I moan, my thighs tightening. Every nerve in my body comes alive as he rolls one nipple while lavishing the other with gentle licks and soft pulls.

Heat pools low in my belly and the pulse between my thighs pounds hard and fast. I lean back against the backrest, twisting my fingers in his dark hair as I give myself over to his touch.

"Roman," I say with in a long exhale, my body shivering. "That feels amazing."

He gazes up at me, his eyes twinkling. "Do you know how much I've wanted to make you feel good?"

Panting through my parted lips, I shake my head, not trusting myself to speak. He slides his free hand lower, tracing over the curve of my belly down to where my lace hem gathers at my thighs.

"Every day has been a battle of self-restraint," he says around my nipple, his voice thick with desire. "But I'm glad I had this time to understand what's in your heart. Things would have been so different if I'd taken the time to get to know you better."

I squeeze my eyes shut. "Roman, you've apologized enough."

"Never," he growls against my skin, his breath hot, his fingers sliding between my thighs. "Not until I've made things right."

A sigh slips from my lips. Roman was willing to sacrifice his life to save me and the baby. That's the kind of grand gesture that doesn't need words. Every day, he apologizes, and every day, he proves that he's grown from the man who was blinded by revenge.

He knows I forgave him months ago, even before he rescued me from Galliano's goons, and he's apologized enough. After three months of sharing our pasts and deepest thoughts and feelings, he's completely earned my trust.

"Permission to grovel at your feet?" he asks around my nipple.

"Again?" I ask.

"This time, I don't think you'll want me to stop."

Oh. *That* kind of groveling.

Shivers run down my spine, and the muscles of my pussy tighten in anticipation of his tongue. Roman once described me as a drug, but he was projecting. He's the one who's addictive.

It's been nearly nine months since he's given me oral pleasure. My craving for him borders on physical pain.

"Grovel away," I manage to rasp.

Releasing my nipple with a soft pop, he grins at me, his eyes sparkling with promise. My heart flutters, and every inch of my skin tingles.

"I don't get on my knees for anyone," he says, his voice dark and rich. "But for you, I'd descend into the depths of hell."

My breath quickens. Roman has a way of shifting reality, so nothing else matters but our connection. Heat flares across my skin, and I lose track of backaches, swollen feet, and due dates. All that matters at this moment is him.

He lowers himself onto his knees, just like he made that restaurant manager. Just like he did three months ago after running through a gunfight to save me from falling.

Roman's eyes never leave mine as he positions himself between my trembling legs and trails his hands up my thighs. I swallow hard, my gaze locked on his as he places a soft kiss on my knee.

"I've been dreaming of getting the chance to worship at your temple," he growls, his thumbs rubbing slow circles on my sensitive skin.

"Really?" I ask, my voice breathy.

"Every damn day."

He works his way up my legs, placing tender kisses along my inner thighs. Each press of his soft lips makes the pulse between my legs pound so hard that its vibrations reach my toes.

My clit swells to the point of agony as his fingers slide beneath my lace hem, making me squirm with need.

His breath is hot and wet against my skin, parting my thighs with every kiss. When he reaches my pussy, he pauses to groan.

"No panties?"

A giggle bursts from my chest. "What's the point, when I could drop a baby at any moment?"

He laughs, the sound rich and deep. For several heart-beats, he gazes up at me with so much reverence that I feel like a goddess.

"I've missed you," he murmurs, his voice choked. "Missed us."

The sincerity in his words makes my eyes prick with happy tears. I finally have the man I always needed. The man who doesn't just bear gifts but bares his soul. The man who gives me freedom and only holds my heart captive. The man who reveres me as his equal partner.

Before I can reply, he leans in, his tongue swirling around my swollen clit. Bolts of pleasure shoot through my core, robbing me of my breath.

I thread my fingers through his hair, pulling him closer as he continues lavishing me with slow slides of his tongue.

"Ah, just like that," I moan.

"You're so beautiful like this," he says from between my legs, his hand tracing the swell of my belly with a tenderness that makes me pant.

The hand not entwined in his hair grips the rocking chair. With each flick of his tongue, Roman pushes me closer and closer to the edge. My breath comes in rapid pants as I focus on the sensations.

"That feels amazing," I moan. My thighs tremble. My hips buck against his face. At this rate, I'm going to unravel. "Keep going. Don't stop."

"I could eat your pussy forever."

Tension builds in my core, a delicious sensation that has me gasping. Electricity charges the air, intensified by the heat of his mouth, the deftness of his strokes, the depth of his pleasured groans.

He reaches a hand up to my exposed breast and rolls my nipples, just as my eyes roll to the back of my head.

My toes curl. After all this time, he still knows how to make me feral.

Sweat breaks out across my brow, slides down my temple and into my flushed cheeks. I gasp for air, feeling every muscle in my body tense as he takes me to the brink of ecstasy.

The tension in my core coils tighter as he continues worshiping me with his talented digit and tongue.

Fingers interlacing with mine, he quickens his pace and says, "Come for me, baby."

My back arches against the rocking chair and I cry out with the force of my climax. Stars dance behind my closed eyelids, and his name rushes from my lips.

Somewhere on the edge of my consciousness, I hear

Roman groan through his own orgasm as he continues lavishing my clit through mine. He draws out the pleasure as I fall limp against my seat. Pleasant aftershocks ripple through my core, building in intensity until they become unbearable.

"Roman," I say through clenched teeth.

He draws back, his hooded eyes meeting mine with a dreamy smile. "I love you more than words can express, baby."

"Roman." My voice sharpens as the pleasure morphs into pain.

His smile falters. "Emberly, what's wrong?"

"Fucking hell. I'm having contractions!"

His eyes widen. "Are you sure?"

I laugh so hard that I can barely breathe. "The baby. We're about to meet our son."

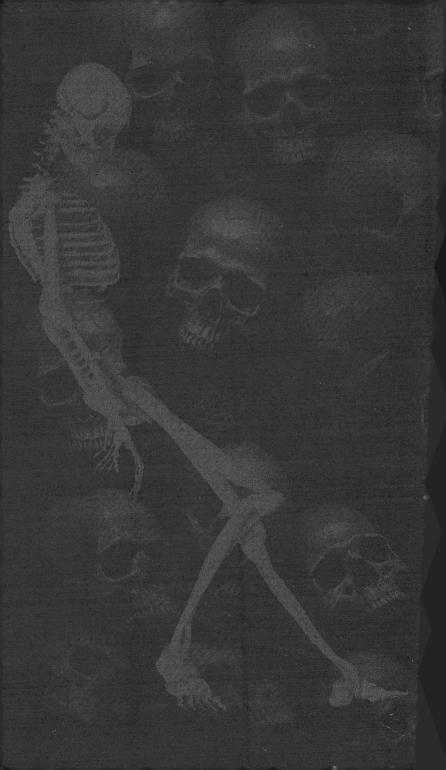

SEVENTY-EIGHT

EPILOGUE

TWO DAYS LATER

EMBERLY

I sit in the back of the limousine, snuggled up to Roman's side. Our baby sleeps in my arms, swaddled in a cashmere blanket. Strands of black hair peek out from beneath his little blue bonnet and my heart warms at the sight.

"Paulo awake yet?" Roman asks.

"Newborns are asleep more hours than they're awake," I say with a smile.

He plants a kiss on my temple. "How are you doing?" he asks, his voice low. "You had a rough time back there."

I tilt my head and let him kiss me on the lips. "The labor could have been worse, but I had the best birthing partner."

His gaze softens and the arm around my shoulder tightens. All those sessions Roman had with Lily and me, learning how to assist me during labor, and it paid off.

He held my hand, massaged my aches and agonies, and

coached me through the breathing when all I wanted to do was push. When the doctors were being a pain in the ass and underestimating my progress, Roman was the one who made them listen to my needs.

I'm so thankful that I got through childbirth without needing much medical intervention or even stitches. It was the most painful and beautiful experience of my existence, and I'm glad he was at my side.

"Thank you for my son," he murmurs.

"Thank you for looking out for me," I reply.

I've had time to think through my situation. Jim wanted to reclaim me because I'd inherited a fortune. He would have kept me as his cash cow until he gained control of my assets. I seriously doubt that he and his dad would have allowed me to live long enough to enjoy my money.

Tommy Galliano was the next in line to inherit my biological father's estate. If he had found me before Roman did, then he would have put a bullet through my head. In his own way, Roman saved me from two terrible fates. He may have arranged the death of all my blood relatives, but he's also given me a family.

My cousin is dead. Days after Roman rescued me from that balcony, he brought me to a basement in his mansion, where the brothers were keeping Tommy alive to make him suffer for the death of their mother.

Tommy revealed that my biological dad had planned on discarding Mom to one of his brothels when he discovered she was pregnant. My mom escaped after one of her doctor's appointments and never stopped running.

"What's the first thing you're going to paint?" Roman asks.

"My beautiful little muse." I gaze down to find him staring up at me through dark brown eyes the exact shade as my husband's.

"With all the beautiful pictures you made to decorate his room, I think he'll become a painter."

I turn to Roman. "Would you want him to be an artist?"

He chuckles. "I love you. I love what you do."

"Even though Paulo's going to inherit the Capello estate?"

Roman smiles.

"I'd be honored for my son to follow in your footsteps," he says.

The backs of my eyes sting with happy tears, reminding me of yet another way Roman has shown his love.

Bunches of flowers line the back seat. One of them was sent by the Beaumont City Women's Aid. I made Roman switch the monthly million-dollar donation to an annual one. I now sit on its board of directors. Thanks to him, we're opening shelters all over New Alderney.

A knock sounds on the tinted window. I glance up to find Gil grinning at us from the courtyard.

Roman nods at him to open the door, letting in a gust of juniper-scented air.

"Welcome home," Gil says.

Roman steps out first, then he turns around, takes my hand and helps us out. Applause fills the air, making me startle. The staff form a line at the double doors that stretch down the stone steps and into the courtyard.

My breath shallows. The first time I saw the staff gathered like that was the day Roman was released from prison. Back then, it had been overwhelming, even embarrassing, since I was naked, save for his jacket and in the middle of a one-night stand.

Now, I'm overcome with love.

Roman wraps an arm around my shoulder and tucks me into his side, lending me his strength. I glance around, meeting the warm gazes of Tony, Gil, Sofia, Benito, and

Cesare, who all welcome me like I'm a valued member of the family.

"Are you okay with saying hello to everyone before I take you back to the pool house?" Roman murmurs.

"No," I say.

He stills. "Are you alright?"

I meet his concerned gaze. "I want to return to the master suite."

His eyes widen. "What are you saying?"

"I want this marriage. I want us."

Roman goes down on one knee, and my heart skips several beats. He reaches into his shirt and pulls out a gold ring encrusted with diamonds.

And it's attached to a chain.

"I've carried this around for nine months," he says, his eyes shining. "Waiting for the right moment to ask. I should have done this properly the first time. If you don't like this ring, we can get something more suitable—"

"Yes," I say.

He laughs. "I haven't even asked."

I cup the side of his face. "My answer is yes. Now, stand up and let's greet our family."

Roman's smile is so bright that my heart skips a beat. "Have I told you that I love you?"

I smile back. "Every single day, and I love you, too."

He removes the ring from the chain and slips it onto my finger, only to elicit another round of applause. Just like everything else Roman has bought me, it's the perfect size.

"You know what's next?" He rises, his eyes twinkling.

"What?"

Roman scoops me off my feet and carries us both up the stairs and across the threshold.

"Welcome home, Emberly," he murmurs. "I'm going to

spend the rest of our lives showing you how much I love you."

Dear Reader,

Thank you so much for reading Snaring Emberly! I hope you enjoyed Roman and Emberly's story.

The next book in the series is about Cesare and Rosalind with longer glimpses of Leroi and Seraphine.

Sign up for a bonus epilogue featuring Daddy Roman here:

http://gigistyx.com/daddy

I hope to connect with you again soon!

Love,

Gigi

READ CESARE & ROSALIND'S STORY

ABOUT THE AUTHOR

Gigi lives with her husband and two cats in London. When she's not crafting twisted dark romances with feisty heroines and the morally grey villains who love them, she's cuddled up on the sofa with a cup of tea and a book.

Sign up for Gigi's updates at:
www.gigistyx.com/newsletter

ALSO BY GIGI STYX

Taming Seraphine

Snaring Emberly

Breaking Rosalind

F*ck Pals - a stalker romance

60734069R00427